continued . . .

Warlord

ANGELA KNIGHT

BERKLEY SENSATION, NEW YORK

THE BERKLEY PUBLISHING GROUP
Published by the Penguin Group
Penguin Group (USA) Inc.
375 Hudson Street, New York, New York 10014, USA
Penguin Group (Canada), 90 Eglinton Avenue East, Suite 700, Toronto, Ontario M4P 2Y3, Canada
(a division of Pearson Penguin Canada Inc.)
Penguin Books Ltd., 80 Strand, London WC2R 0RL, England
Penguin Group Ireland, 25 St. Stephen's Green, Dublin 2, Ireland (a division of Penguin Books Ltd.)
Penguin Group (Australia), 250 Camberwell Road, Camberwell, Victoria 3124, Australia
(a division of Pearson Australia Group Pty. Ltd.)
Penguin Books India Pvt. Ltd., 11 Community Centre, Panchsheel Park, New Delhi—110 017, India
Penguin Group (NZ), 67 Apollo Drive, Rosedale, North Shore 0745, Auckland, New Zealand
(a division of Pearson New Zealand Ltd.)
Penguin Books (South Africa) (Pty.) Ltd., 24 Sturdee Avenue, Rosebank, Johannesburg 2196,
South Africa

Penguin Books Ltd., Registered Offices: 80 Strand, London WC2R 0RL, England

This is a work of fiction. Names, characters, places, and incidents either are the product of the author's imagination or are used fictitiously, and any resemblance to actual persons, living or dead, business establishments, events, or locales is entirely coincidental. The publisher does not have any control over and does not assume any responsibility for author or third-party websites or their content.

WARLORD

PRINTING HISTORY
Jane's Warlord: Berkley Sensation mass market edition / June 2004
"Warfem" from *Kick Ass*: Berkley Sensation mass market edition / September 2006
Berkley Sensation trade paperback omnibus edition / September 2007

Berkley Sensation trade paperback ISBN: 978-0-425-21784-9

PRINTED IN THE UNITED STATES OF AMERICA

10   9   8   7   6   5   4   3   2   1

CONTENTS

Jane's Warlord
1

Warfem
285

The Warlord and the Fem
369

Baby, You've Changed
397

Jane's Warlord

This one's for Michael, who saved me.
You're the heart of every hero I write, babe.

One

They'd told him he wouldn't feel it when the energy beam ripped him apart. They'd lied. Baran Arvid experienced every burning nanosecond as the hot force blazed from cell to cell, searing him away. For an instant he felt himself falling into a cold, familiar peace. He'd died so often, it no longer came as a surprise.

Then the temporal beam reassembled him again, tormented muscles jerking, optic nerves overloaded by blinding purple starbursts. The dazzle-induced blindness triggered his every combat instinct into roaring protest, but Baran refused to panic. Instead, he locked his knees and concentrated on remaining on his feet while the afterimages faded from his vision.

Gritting his teeth, he ignored the spasming muscles, the nervous system reverberating with residual agony, the stomach fighting to turn itself inside out. He had no intention of showing weakness in front of that bastard from Temporal Enforcement.

"Well, we're still alive, so we didn't trigger a paradox," the bastard said. "Guess you two are supposed to be in the twenty-first century after all."

"Kiss my furry black ass, Enforcer," gasped the timber wolf, gagging violently. Apparently he was as sick as Baran. Freika, however, had the luxury of showing it.

"And you're speaking colloquial English already. Nice processing speed. I'm impressed," the Enforcer said. He'd refused to tell them his name. "How about you, Arvid? You look a little pale around the lips."

Baran blinked his tearing eyes until he could see again. Searching his new vocabulary, he found an appropriate phrase. "Fuck you."

"Very good. Suitably crude and American." The Enforcer laughed, his teeth flashing white, eyes metallic gold against the inky black of his skin. His hair fell in a mop of curly fire around an ebony face so stylized and perfect, he didn't look entirely human. Whoever had tinkered with his DNA had possessed a taste for the dramatic.

"Glad you approve." Baran turned to scan their surroundings for possible threats in a search that was so ingrained he was scarcely aware of making it.

He, the Enforcer, and the timber wolf stood in the shadow of strange Earth trees, a full moon riding bright and cold overhead. The air smelled of vegetation he didn't recognize, and unidentified life-forms buzzed and sang and scuttled all around them. Baran's aching muscles coiled even tighter. Being on alien planets always made him twitch. Too many unknown threats, too many ways you could be taken off-guard. And Temporal Enforcement's habitual mind games weren't helping at all. "You might have warned me the damn Jump would leave me sick and half-blind."

The dark scales of the Enforcer's temporal suit rippled with an iridescent sheen as he shrugged. "You couldn't have done anything about it anyway. Everybody gets Jumpsick their first time. Though I suppose it would be even worse without a T-suit."

"You might say that." Baran pulled up his sleeve to display the slabs of muscle still jerking in his forearm. He wore nothing more than the twenty-first-century garb they'd given him: shirt, pants, and a long rustling coat in some kind of hide. "I feel like somebody worked me over with the butt of a beamer rifle. Temporal armor would have been appreciated."

The Enforcer's smile was faintly taunting. "But then you'd have been able to Jump to whatever time you wanted. We can't have you wandering loose around the time plane causing paradoxes."

Freika lifted his head with a canine moan. "Like I'd want to go through *that* again anytime soon. I've had more fun being shot."

Though Baran could understand him perfectly, the words sounded oddly guttural compared to the wolf's normal liquid speech. Then again, it always took Baran a few hours to adjust to a new language after the comp had reprogrammed his brain to speak it. Even his thoughts felt off-kilter as he automatically used American slang instead of the Galactic Standard he normally spoke. "Your vocalizer working all right?"

Freika hesitated, pale blue eyes going blank as he listened to the mental voice of his computer implant. Then he shook his furry head. "Everything's fine. Guess English is supposed to sound like two cats fighting in a very small sack."

"You both speak as if you were born here," the Enforcer told them impatiently. "We don't give our operatives inferior language files. Or inferior anything else."

"That's reassuring," Baran said, pitching his voice to a tone of silken menace. He was sick of the agent's arrogance. "I'd hate to be . . . disappointed." Artistically, he added his best lethal smile, as though imagining just what he'd do to anybody with that much bad judgment.

The Enforcer's gaze flickered. Despite his weapons, despite his training, they all knew he was no match for Baran. He was, after all, only human.

Baran was a Warlord.

His genetically engineered body was a good five times stronger than any human's, and his bones were so dense they were practically unbreakable. As if that weren't enough, a neuroweb combat computer wove through his brain, giving him access to both a vast data bank and information from the sensor implants scattered throughout his body.

Thanks to his computer, anything Baran aimed at, he hit. And thanks to his strength, anything he hit went down hard. Add his well-deserved and very ugly reputation, and it wasn't surprising the TE agent swallowed visibly. "Oh, you'll be very pleased with our equipment."

"I'd better be. I'd hate to have to show you what I can do with mine."

The agent stiffened, finally realizing he was being played. "You do menace well, Warlord. I hope you can back it up with action, because the Jumpkiller is somewhere out here. And he definitely lives up to *his* reputation."

"So do we," Freika growled, sitting back on his haunches and wrapping his tail around his toes. "And we've pulled off enough combat missions to prove it."

"But we could finish this up faster if you'd tell us exactly what we're supposed to do." Baran glanced restlessly past the Enforcer to the primitive two-story wooden residence that stood just beyond the tree line. He knew the woman lived there, but that was about it. He hated going on missions blind, particularly when it was so bluntly obvious his superiors knew more than they were telling. "The more information we have, the better our chances."

The Enforcer gave him that dismissive glance again. "You know everything you need to know: your orders. Keep the Jumpkiller from gutting Jane Colby, preferably by killing him first."

"Look," Baran said impatiently, "you obviously have access to historical records from this time, or you wouldn't have known I needed to be transported here. And that means you have a pretty good idea what's going to happen over the next few days. I just want to know where, when, and how I'm supposed to kill the son of a bitch."

The agent curled a flawless lip. "How do you usually do your killing?"

"In a wide variety of ways." Which he was strongly tempted to demonstrate.

"Fine. Pick one."

"I don't go on missions blind, Enforcer."

"You do this time." Baran opened his mouth to protest, but the agent cut him off. "Warlord or no, Arvid, you're not Temporal Enforcement. You're not trained for time travel. The more information you have, the greater your likelihood of causing a paradox. So I'm not telling you a damn thing. Except this: get the Colby woman under control and wait for Druas to show up. When he does, finish it, and I'll take you home to your war."

Suppressing a violent impulse to plant his fist in the Enforcer's face, Baran folded his arms. "I'd be delighted. But considering he's got a T-suit and I don't, it's not going to be that easy. Even if I manage to corner him, all he's got to do is Jump somewhere else."

"And he will." Freika flicked an ear lazily. "He's not going to want to go against Baran if he can avoid it."

"We've already taken care of that." The agent bent and fished around in the pack that lay between his booted feet. He straightened, holding something small that he handed over to Baran. "Suit neutralizer," he explained as the Warlord examined the intricately filigreed ring. It was set with a red gem cut into complex facets that shattered the cold, pale moonlight into sparks. "When you get close enough, press the stone against the Jumpkiller's suit for several seconds. It'll short out the T-field generators, and he'll be trapped. Then you can take your time killing him."

Baran looked up. "Several seconds? How do I keep him from Jumping before the stone finishes the process?"

The Enforcer gave him a malicious smile. "I'm sure you'll figure something out."

Frowning, Baran slipped the ring on. The metal seemed to squirm as it automatically adjusted to the diameter of his finger. "Sounds like I'll need to stun him somehow. Got any weapons?"

"Are you insane?" The agent snorted. "Take anything with a tachyon power pack on a Jump, and you'd end up at the bottom of a crater."

"Believe it or not, I do have a knowledge of basic physics," Baran growled. "But they've been making weapons without Tach Packs for the past million years."

"Yes, they have. Which is why I suggest you look for one." He picked up the bag and handed it over with a grunt of effort. Baran accepted it, barely noticing the weight. "This has everything else you'll need: twenty-first-century clothing, currency, the usual equipment we pack for jobs like this. Colby should be leaving in the next few minutes, since the Jumpkiller has already claimed his first victim in this time. Move in, establish your base while she's gone, and take her into custody when she returns. I'll see you soon."

"How soon?"

He smiled in a toothy display every bit as feral as Baran's. "For me, in the next few minutes, since I'm Jumping there right now. For you . . . it'll be a little longer. Good hunting, Warlord."

Baran looked at him for a long moment. "Eventually," he observed in a silken voice, "we won't be on your turf anymore, Enforcer."

The agent's eyes widened at the implied threat. Then he recovered and snapped, "Step clear."

Baran and the wolf retreated a safe distance and turned their heads away. Neither had any desire to get caught in the backwash of a Jump.

Even through closed lids, Baran could see the white-hot glow of the temporal field blooming from the agent's T-suit. It intensified, growing brighter and brighter as residual energy danced in stinging waves over his skin. Thunder cracked, and a hot wind blew into his face, smelling of ozone.

When he opened his eyes, the Enforcer was gone.

"You know, you could probably have forced that little prick to tell us more," Freika said as the echo died. "He found you pretty unnerving." He grinned a canine grin. "But then, so many do."

Baran shrugged. "True, but I don't care to end up before a Temporal Court for assaulting an Enforcer. We'll just have to—" He broke off as exterior lights flashed on around the woman's home.

They turned warily. A wooden door opened, swinging outward rather than sliding into the wall as it should. Jane Colby walked out, moving in an intriguing, long-legged saunter that made Baran's eyes narrow with interest. Even across the distance that separated them, he saw her look in their direction and frown. She must have heard the sonic boom of the Enforcer's Jump. He tensed, wondering if she'd come investigate.

Then she shook her head and turned to get into a boxy, wheeled vehicle parked beside the house. It produced a startling roar and a cloud of petrochemicals that lingered even after it backed up, turned around, and rolled off on its thick tires.

"No wonder this planet's a polluted pit, with millions of those things everywhere," Freika commented, watching its running lights recede.

"They'll invent gravlev eventually," Baran said, hoisting his new pack. The long hide coat of his twenty-first-century garb swung around his calves as he started toward the house. "Come on, let's get to it."

When they reached the front door, he drew a slim metallic needle from the interior pocket of his coat. Crouching, he inserted it into the lock set in the door's round handle. The forcepick vibrated slightly between his fingers as it sent out a precisely shaped force field that filled the space intended for a key. The field rotated, tripping the primitive tumblers until the lock clicked open.

Patiently Baran used the same procedure on the second lock, the one the computer called a deadbolt. Once it, too, clicked, he turned the knob and pushed the door open.

Moving as one, he and the wolf vanished inside.

* ★ ★

Damn, she hated murders.

Jane Colby got out of her SUV and slammed the door, aiming a brooding stare at the swaying strip of yellow plastic strung across the yard. She sometimes felt she'd spent her entire life staring at crime scene tape, waiting to find out how someone had died.

Hunching deeper into her windbreaker against the April chill, she walked to the tape and studied the small home that stood some distance beyond it. Strobing blue light from the patrol cars parked along the street rolled across the house's neat brick face, casting unnatural shadows between the azalea bushes. Beyond backlit lace curtains, the silhouettes of sheriff's deputies milled around like guests at a morbid party.

In the distance a dog barked in a frenzy at the K-9 team that searched for the killer. Jane could hear the cops' radio chatter through the portable police scanner in the depths of her purse. Their voices sounded grimly subdued. She listened absently, hoping for that rising note of tension and adrenalin that would mean they'd found something.

The hissing rumble of an approaching car drew her around. Stepping back out of the roadway, Jane threw up a hand to shield her eyes against the blaze of its oncoming headlights.

God, she hoped it wasn't family. She'd lost count of the times she'd watched people race toward a scene, eyes wild and tears streaming as police ran to stop them before they saw something they shouldn't. Jane never failed to feel a twist of pity as she listened to the desperate, heartbreaking argument she'd heard over and over, *"But it's my . . . "* Wife, husband, father, mother, brother, sister, daughter, son. The relationship changed, but the horror and suffering was always the same, whether it was a car accident, a fire, a fatal fall. Or a murder.

But murders were the worst.

Jane pitied the victims for the terror and agony of their last moments, but she also knew their suffering was over. It was the survivors who really bothered her, because their pain was only beginning. She'd interviewed enough of them to know it never really ended, even years afterward.

But when the primer-flecked Trans Am simply slowed to a stop, she relaxed. Family always slammed on the brakes and jumped out running. The blond driver leaned across to roll down her passenger window and eye the patrol cars lining the street. "What's going on?"

Jane shrugged. "Evidently somebody's been killed."

The woman's interest took on an avid edge. "Yeah? What happened?"

"They haven't told me yet."

"You family?"

"No, I'm a reporter for the *Trib*."

The blonde's expression chilled, and Jane saw the silent judgment in her eyes. *Vulture.* "Guess I'll read about it in the paper, then."

"Guess you will."

The Trans Am pulled off in a gust of exhaust, its taillights receding into the darkness.

At least it hadn't been family. Jane knew she'd have to talk to them eventually, but she liked to give survivors at least a few hours to adjust to the shock. Back in Atlanta she'd often been forced to interview them before the bodies had even cooled. Sometimes you got more that way because their defenses were down, but she'd always felt it was dirty journalism. People deserved a chance to process the massive shock of a murder without someone working them over for a quote.

She'd even considered stopping the survivor interviews altogether now that she'd become the publisher of *The Tayanita Tribune* in the wake of her father's fatal stroke. *The Trib* only came out three times a week, so any big crime was often old news by the time it made the paper anyway.

The trouble was, without the emotional content from survivors, people read crime stories as a kind of horrific entertainment. Interviews gave families a chance to describe the person they'd loved, to transform him from another faceless victim to a person in the public mind. For Jane, that meant an opportunity to bring the tragedy of murder home to readers who had become numb to it.

Which was why she was standing alone on a country road at midnight when she didn't go to press for two more days.

As for the nagging awareness that a killer might be somewhere out here, too . . .

She wasn't going to think about that.

Baran and Freika searched Jane's house with speed, silence, and a ruthless efficiency that left nothing untouched—or visibly disturbed. Unfortunately, there was nothing to find. There was no trace of the Jumpkiller's presence, not even his scent. Kalig Druas had not been here.

Yet.

The search did, however, tell Baran it wouldn't be easy keeping him out once he did make his appearance. Every room had fragile glass windows that would take very little effort to break, assuming that the Xeran didn't simply Jump inside. If they left Jane alone for even a moment, Druas could easily slaughter her before they even knew he was there. Which meant Baran and Freika would have to stay with her at all times, whether she liked it or not. And she wouldn't.

Unfortunately, she had no more choice than they did. Baran himself had another monster to kill back in his own time, but Temporal Enforcement had made it clear this one had priority. Never mind that General Jutka's death would leave the Xeran forces in disarray and save the lives of thousands of Vardonese soldiers. TE wanted its mission taken care of first.

He'd argued he could make the Jump after he'd assassinated Jutka, but the Enforcer hadn't bought it. Once he saved Jane, the agent told him, TE would return Baran to the very moment he'd left his own time so he could kill whomever he chose. Since nobody ever argued successfully with Temporal Enforcement, that plan had trumped his.

The whole thing was irritating. Baran was a Warlord, not a time traveler. He didn't even work for Temporal Enforcement. But TE had found a three-hundred-year-old video recording of him during Druas's rampage in this time. They'd decided if a Warlord had been in the twenty-first century, it was because TE itself had put him there, presumably to stop the Jumpkiller. So they'd drafted Baran to make sure he got back here to do whatever he was supposed to do. Otherwise, they all risked creating a catastrophic paradox, and nobody wanted that.

He only wished he had a few more details about what was actually going to happen. Unfortunately, TE seemed to operate under the theory that once you got where you were supposed to be, you automatically did whatever you were supposed to do.

With a grunt of impatience, Baran continued his inspection of Jane's primitive kitchen. When he turned a round knob on her cooking unit, one of the flat metal spirals on top of it slowly began to heat. His computer implant sent him an image of a metal container sitting on the spiral, bubbling. Might be interesting to experiment. Once when the rations had run low, he'd cooked a treehopper over a captured Xer Tach Pack.

You could do all sorts of things with a Xeran power pack, if you were creative enough.

"Baran, it's under the bed," the wolf called from upstairs. "I see its eyes glowing."

"Leave it alone, Freika." He turned the coil off with a snap of his wrist.

"But I'm hungry!" A snarling feline yowl rose. "And do you hear the way it's talking to me?"

"Eating the target's cat would not create the first impression we want."

"Just one bite?"

"No. This is going to be difficult enough as it is without you snacking on her furry friends."

"How could anybody be friends with a *cat*?"

"Well, for one thing," Baran said, walking into the living area, "it's soft, it purrs, and unlike some I could name, it doesn't mouth off."

Despite the genetic engineering that gave Freika sentience—and the computer implant that made him a four-legged library—Baran's partner still had a timber wolf's personality and instincts. Though useful in combat, those characteristics could be maddening the rest of the time.

"A nibble?"

"*No.*" Deciding not to trust Freika's questionable self-control, Baran bounded up the stairs.

It seemed to be his week for saving Earth residents from predatory time travelers.

Beyond the crime scene tape, a storm door creaked open and closed with a metallic bang. Jane turned as the detective in charge of the case stumbled down the steps. Good, she could get the details of this thing and go home.

Before she could open her mouth, Tom Reynolds leaned over and heaved the contents of his stomach into the budding azalea bushes.

Jane winced. "That's so not a good sign," she called. "What's bad enough to make you toss your crullers, Tom?"

Reynolds jerked upright, a flustered expression on his round face as he hurriedly wiped his mouth. "Tell me you didn't take a picture of that, Colby."

She grinned and toyed suggestively with the digital camera that hung by a strap around her neck. "Would I do that to you?"

"Not if you ever want another exclusive." Reynolds started toward her, shooting a hunted look around the taped-off perimeter of the yard. "How about TV? Are those vultures from WDRT here?"

"Nope," Jane said. "I'm the only one circling at the moment. I figure it'll take DRT another twenty minutes to get here from Deanville."

"That's something, anyway." Tom pulled a wadded napkin out of a pocket and wiped his mouth, aware of Jane's sympathetic gaze. If he had to catch a reporter on this nightmare so soon, he could have done worse. She'd never misquoted him, and if he asked her to withhold something to avoid blowing a case, she did it.

And God knew she was easy on the eyes. Jane's long-legged walk was a pleasure to watch even at a crime scene, and he'd caught other cops telling her intriguing cleavage more than they should. Her face always made him think of magazine covers: high cheekbones, big brown eyes, and the kind of wide, sensual mouth a happily married man had no business fantasizing about. With all the dark hair tumbling in curls around her shoulders, she could have done shampoo commercials. Yet he'd never seen her use her looks. She didn't even seem aware of them.

The nasty taste in his mouth suddenly reminded Tom he must have the breath of a frat boy the morning after a kegger. He grimaced, shoving aside the memory of just why he'd lost control of his lunch. He really didn't want to throw up again, especially not on Jane's pretty boots.

Observant brown eyes softened as she looked at him. "I've got a bottle of water in the SUV. Want it?"

"Yeah." He sighed and admitted, "Taste in my mouth ain't helping my stomach any."

She nodded and walked to her red Explorer. Tom trailed behind to watch appreciatively as she opened the door and bent over, fishing around in the cooler she kept in the backseat. Jane's heart-shaped ass in those snug jeans would draw any man's eyes, married or not.

She turned and handed him a bottle dripping with ice and condensation. "Thanks," he said, twisting the cap off as he headed for the nearest ditch to take a swig and spit.

Jane watched him sympathetically. Reynolds wore the standard Southern detective uniform of chinos, blue sports coat, and blue oxford cloth shirt, slightly frayed at the collar because he had to watch every dime of his salary. His tie featured Wile E. Coyote and a ketchup stain. Short and balding, he had a face like a bulldog, with a little too much lip and weary blue eyes.

He was the best cop she'd ever known.

She shook her head. "Tom, I've seen you eat barbecue after working a house where a guy had been dead three weeks. In July. What's bad enough to make you abuse the azaleas?"

The detective didn't answer, his eyes shifting away from hers to scan the street. Since the nearest neighbors lived half a mile away, the only illumination came from the cars' blue lights. Judging from the tension in his shoulders, he didn't find the darkness reassuring. "Why are you here, Colby?" he asked finally. "You don't go to press again until Monday. Call me tomorrow and I'll fill you in."

"Can't work a murder over the phone, Tom. Besides, when have you known me to miss a crime scene?"

He sighed and hunched, his gaze now flicking warily across the trees that ringed the wooded lot. "This is not a good time to be conscientious, kiddo. I don't like you out here all by yourself."

Jane gaped at him. Despite their long friendship, it was an unprecedented comment for him to make on the job. Police normally treated reporters little better than the vultures he'd called the WDRT crew. The last time a policeman had expressed concern over Jane's safety, she'd been standing in the middle of I-85 watching a guy with a sniper rifle hold off thirty cops. The officer's actual words had been a snarled, "Get your ass back, lady."

"Okay, what the hell is going on? I've never seen you this spooked." She reached into her purse to dig out a notebook and pen.

Tom shrugged and spat another mouthful of water into the ditch. "We have an unidentified female victim."

She looked up from her notebook. "Who lives at this address? That should narrow things down."

"Maybe, but she doesn't exactly look like herself at the moment. We know she's a Caucasian blonde, but that's about it."

Jane grimaced. "That doesn't sound good."

The detective's eyes went bleak and flat. "Believe me, it's not." Something in his tone sent a wave of icy prickles washing over her skin.

Whatever had happened in that house, it wasn't a typical Tayanita County murder.

Two

Roaring case of the creeps or not, Jane reminded herself she had a job to do. She shook off her unease, cleared her throat, and asked, "Cause of death?"

"Haven't done an autopsy yet."

Sometimes she thought it would be easier mining diamonds with her fingernails than getting details out of a cop. "Tom, don't go technical on me. Gun, knife, fists, what?"

"That's for the coroner to decide." He took another swig of his water.

"Like that ever stopped you before. Look, here's a clue—if there's a small round hole on one side and a big ragged hole on the other, that means she was shot."

"Smartass. She wasn't shot."

"Okay, so what was she? Or do we play Twenty Questions until I guess right?"

"Why not? The rest of us are." Giving his shoulders an uneasy roll, Tom admitted, "Looks like some kind of knife. Sharp." His lips thinned. "Real sharp."

"Sharp as in box cutter, or sharp as in steak knife?" Box cutters were the preferred weapon in certain nasty quarters because the blade was short enough for legal carry in South Carolina. In domestics gone bad, though, spur-of-the-moment killers tended to grab whatever they found lying around the kitchen.

Wearily he pinched the bridge of his nose between his thumb and forefinger. "Butcher knife, maybe. Autopsy'll tell us more."

"So assuming your victim is the homeowner, how airtight is her significant other's alibi?" If a woman was murdered in the rest of the country, her husband, boyfriend, or ex- was usually the one who did it. In Tayanita County those odds were a virtual certainty.

"We're looking for him." His voice dropped into a harried growl. "And praying like hell he did it."

Jane straightened, reporter instincts immediately roaring into full cry. "This isn't your standard redneck soap opera, is it?" she asked slowly. "This isn't even I-caught-her-with-my-brother overkill. Twenty or thirty piddling stab wounds wouldn't make Tom Reynolds heave his Ho-Hos. What's inside that house?"

"The worst I've ever seen." He started scanning the street again, blue eyes brooding. "Tell you one thing, though. We'd damn well better catch this son of a bitch. Quick. He enjoyed himself a little too much."

"What makes you say that?"

"No comment."

She watched him a moment and tried again. "What'd he do to her, Tom?"

"Nothing anybody wants to read about over their Wheaties." He sighed. "Look, I'll have more for you by the time you go to press. Go home." His mouth tightened. "And lock your doors."

Sometimes asking stupid questions was part of the job. "You saying women in this town have a reason to be worried?"

Something in his expression made it all too easy to imagine what was inside that house. "Jane, *everybody* in this town has a reason to be worried."

★   ★   ★

Baran banished Freika from the bedroom and sent him down-stairs to keep watch. Jane's cat, thoroughly traumatized, did not stir from its hiding place even after the wolf was gone. When Baran crouched to look under the bed, the poor little beast hissed at him with such frazzled hostility he decided to leave it alone.

With a sigh, he rose to his feet, then paused when a flash of red caught his eye. A length of crimson silk lay spread across the bed's tumbled white coverings. Curious, he picked it up. The fabric seemed to wrap around his hand, soft and sensuous against his weapon-calloused skin. Shaking out its folds, he realized it was evidently in-tended to drape like a scarf over interesting feminine curves.

Negligee, his computer whispered in his mind, then added syn-onyms. *Nightgown, lingerie, sleepwear.*

Negligee. Even the word sounded sensuous. But as he appraised the gown's whisper-thin folds, Baran realized how small the woman who wore it must be. The top of her head would barely reach his shoulder.

He frowned. If Druas ever got his hands on her, she'd have no chance at all.

The thought made his fingers tighten on the silk. A delicate trace of musk drifted up from the fabric, teasing his senses. Baran inhaled more deeply, letting his hyper-keen senses process it. Perfume, some kind of chemicals his computer identified as being from the body cleanser she used, and beneath that, the woman's own unique scent. Intrigued, he lifted the gown to his face and breathed deeper. His nose was almost as sensitive as Freika's, and each inhalation carried a wealth of information.

Now one deep breath told him she was healthy, young, female—and intensely, deliciously aroused. Startled, he sniffed again. The rich smell of desire was unmistakable.

If he'd been able to slip a finger into her sex, she'd have felt like hot, slick cream. Just waiting for a man to . . . Baran swallowed.

What had aroused her? The only male scents he'd detected in the house were weeks old and confined to the living room. He was willing to wager she had no lover.

Though she obviously wanted one.

Pull up her image file, he ordered his comp. Obediently the implant created a picture in his mind.

Jane Colby wasn't the most exquisite woman Baran had ever seen; in his own time, genetic engineering had made perfect beauty commonplace. Yet there was an appealing warmth in the eyes that were simple human brown instead of the metallic shades fashionable back home.

She was also lushly female compared to the almost androgynous shape he was used to in civilian women. Her breasts rode high and rounded on her narrow rib cage above gently curving hips and legs that seemed to make up most of her height. She reminded him of the Warfems of his own kind, but without the tough, muscled build. The combination of curve and delicacy made her look both feminine and intensely sensual, as if she'd welcome passion instead of rejecting it.

Baran wondered what her soft pink mouth would taste like, how her breasts would fill his hands, if her skin would feel as silken as it looked. His cock hardened, going long and tight behind his fly. With a soft growl of hunger, he rolled his head against the gown in his hand, drinking in her smell, the slide of the slippery fabric against his face, the rasp of lace. He imagined thrusting into her for the first time, feeling all that wet arousal gripping him, milking him. . . .

It had been far too long since he'd had a woman. Days, weeks—he couldn't remember and didn't much care. All that interested him suddenly was this woman, this Jane Colby, with her pretty eyes and small, lush body.

He breathed in her scent again as his hunger spiraled, tightening in demanding coils around his balls. The same genetic engineering that enhanced his strength made his lust even more intense than a normal man's. Now that hot-burning need sent carnal images spinning through his mind—Jane, naked, on her back, on her knees, spread and ready for him, plump sexual lips slick with thick female cream. . . .

A rumble of hunger vibrating his chest, Baran opened his eyes and glared down at the bundle of red silk in his fist. He ached to open his fly and wrap the cool, slick fabric around his cock.

Better not. Jerking off in her negligee would send a worse message than eating the cat.

He took a deep breath. Blew it out. Fought for the discipline, the control, he'd learned with such difficulty, at such cost. He knew he couldn't afford this kind of lust on a mission, any more than he could afford blind rage. Violent emotion could get a man killed. The Xerans had taught him that when they'd murdered Liisa.

Hoping to distract his inconvenient libido, Baran glanced around Jane's quarters. His eyes fell on a thick sheaf of bound papers lying facedown and open across the sheets. *A paperback book,* the computer whispered, flashing him images of massive drums spinning words onto long ribbons of white paper. Restlessly he picked up the little book. The English language download he'd absorbed the day before allowed him to read the text.

She writhed, tugging at the silken ties that bound her to the bed as he delicately tasted the tender folds between her thighs. Any thought of resistance disappeared with each wet stroke of his tongue. She found herself begging for him and felt an instant's shame. Then she looked down and forgot everything else as he lifted his head and smiled, lazy and taunting, before he . . .

Baran blinked as his erection kicked behind the primitive metal closure of his slacks. *So that's why her gown smells like sex.* Unconsciously, his fist tightened around the fragrant bundle of silk. Her scent drifted up to his nose again, teasing. He licked his dry lips.

Helplessly drawn, Baran's gaze dropped to the bed. A new image appeared in his mind—himself, face buried between her thighs, breathing her scent, tasting her as she lay spread and bound.

No.

Why not? whispered a dark, suggestive mental voice. She dreamed of a lover. If he seduced her, wouldn't she be more inclined to co-operate, allow him stay at her side as her guardian as well as her bed-mate?

And while he was there, he could have her however he wanted, however *she* wanted.

That restless thought blew apart his nascent effort at self-control. Goaded, he reached for his fly to free his aching cock.

No. He dropped his hand and balled it into a fist. He had to keep his mind on the mission. He couldn't afford to let her have even this much power over him. *You know better, Arvid*, he told himself savagely. *The minute you let a civ get control, you're headed for disaster.*

Another woman had taught him that lesson all too well twenty years ago.

Following an order he wasn't even aware of giving, his computer plunged him into memories so vivid, they might as well have been real.

Liisa was screaming. She never screamed. He tried to straighten, but the virus they'd used had infiltrated his computer and turned the implant against him. Now it held him paralyzed, bent, as helpless as if they'd locked him in chains.

Somewhere something hard struck human flesh. A male voice—Lieutenant Ullock?—grunted in that distinctive way Baran had learned to associate with a deathblow.

"Baran!" Liisa screamed.

He fought to go to her, fought as his heart thundered uselessly, fought until the blood pounded in his skull.

The only movement he managed was the slow roll of a tear down his cheek.

Shit. Baran shook his head hard as the twenty-year-old memory released its grip. The computer-induced flashback had done what it was intended to do: harden the resolve that was already pretty damn hard anyway.

No civ would ever have the chance to betray him like that again. Jane Colby would do exactly as she was told, exactly when he told her to do it. If that meant he had to tie her up and fuck her brains out to gain her cooperation, fine. But even then he'd maintain a safe emotional distance.

Which didn't mean he couldn't enjoy himself.

The thought slid through his mind, carried on the black mood the memory of his team's death always inspired. Glancing down at the silky negligee still clenched in his fist, Baran felt a cold, dangerous smile stretch his lips. Maybe he'd have her put the gown on before he . . .

"Hey, Baran!" Freika called, snapping him from his erotic preoccupation. Claws clicked on the flooring as the wolf raced toward the stairs. "I see a vehicle's lights approaching. I think it's the woman."

"Stay downstairs and hide." Baran dropped the gown back on the bed. "I want to talk to her first." Freika could be terrifying to the uninitiated, and this conversation was going to be tricky enough as it was.

The click of claws stopped, then started again as the wolf trotted off, presumably to find some hiding place large enough for his hundred-kilo body. *Good luck,* Freika transmitted to him through their communication implants. *Somehow I think you're going to need it.*

Jane pulled into the paved parking space in front of her beige-and-white two-story contemporary. Turning off the SUV's engine, she stared uneasily into the thick woods surrounding the house. How many places to hide could a killer find among all those trees?

She could almost hear her father's ghostly sneer: *Don't be such a little coward, Jane.*

Squaring her shoulders, she got out and strode to the front door. Intensely aware of her own vulnerability as she unlocked it, she barely managed to control the nervous rattle of her keys.

Once the door was locked behind her again, Jane blew out a breath and walked across the foyer's parquet floor into the main part of the house. She'd left all the lights on when she'd gone out on the call; working murders always gave her a roaring case of the creeps. William Colby, of course, had considered that quirk further proof his only child lacked the Colby steel.

She set her jaw. *Old news, Jane.* For years she'd believed she had outgrown her obsession with her father. She'd done a damn good job in Atlanta, winning the respect of her peers and writing stories she was proud of. She'd even begun to believe in her own talents despite years of his verbal abuse.

But since returning home, it seemed Jane saw her father's disapproving frown everywhere she looked. Like the Cheshire cat's grin, it lingered.

Dammit, Jane, cut that out. Blowing out a breath, she made herself scan the living room she'd spent so much money to decorate. The rich cream leather couch and armchairs had not been cheap, and neither had the antique coffee table or the flat-screen high-definition television. Her journalism awards hung between original works of art she'd bought in Atlanta—here a watercolor of an old Southern mansion drowsing in the sun, there a pastel of a child in a straw hat, the sharp, vivid blue of her eyes skillfully captured in fine detail. The wall lamps had stained-glass shades, and the pale rose carpet was thick and plush under her feet. All of it was a silent statement of Jane's capability and success.

Take that, Daddy.

Okay, that really was pathetic. Dragging both hands through her hair, she sighed in disgust. *Face it, girl, you can't win a war with a dead man. Hell, the only battle that counted was lost when you were ten. Deal with it.*

Definitely time for bed. She always got maudlin when she was tired.

"Caller said his neighbor's beating his wife in the front yard," her scanner announced from her purse as she crossed the living room on her way to the stairs, feet sinking into the pile. "Said he's Code

Five with a baseball bat. The female half is on the ground. One-oh-two Bridgemont Street. Better step it up, guys."

Typical Tayanita scanner traffic. Not the kind of incident Jane covered unless there was major trauma involved. Besides, she was so damn tired she wasn't going out again unless they caught the killer or he murdered somebody else.

The scanner fell silent. Jane could hear the refrigerator hum in the kitchen. Damn, the house was lonely. Maybe she should get a dog, assuming she could find one Octopussy could tolerate. Her seal-point Siamese was definitely not a canine fan.

A man might be a better idea. These days the closest she got to male companionship were the romance novels that were her secret vice.

Jane had always been too obsessed with her job to devote any real attention to finding a lover. And now that she was back in tiny Tayanita, her options had not exactly improved. Between reporting and running the paper, she never had time to go to any of the local bars, that being about the only place single men congregated in Tayanita. Assuming she could even find anybody there whose name she didn't regularly see on police reports.

Maybe she should get Reynolds to fix her up with a cop.

Nah, that'd never work. Cops viewed reporters with all the warmth Octopussy reserved for yappy little French poodles.

A firefighter, maybe. She liked firefighters.

Jane sighed, imagining warm, strong arms to wrap around her, a sympathetic ear to listen to her gripe about the school board or the mayor. Someone to hold her while she cried for a murdered woman she'd never met.

Somebody to ward off killers.

Paws thumped frantically in the hallway floor overhead. Jane looked up, pausing on the stairs as Octopussy flung herself from the top of the steps. She caught the cat automatically, wincing as her pet dug every claw she had into her shoulder.

Staring into Jane's eyes, Octopussy began complaining furiously in a mix of meows, growls, and hisses. Like most Siamese, she was convinced she could talk.

"What's got you in such a tizzy?" Jane asked, trying to give the animal a soothing ear scratch that was foiled when the cat jerked her head away. "Are you hungry, or do you want to go outside?"

Octopussy's feline gripes rose in volume and bitterness.

Jane's mouth quirked as she stepped up into the bedroom. "Or is little Timmy trapped in the well?" The Siamese swarmed up her shoulder and leaped off to head back down the stairs in desperate bounds. As Jane blinked in bemusement, the cat shot under the couch, leaving not so much as the tip of a chocolate tail visible. "Guess Timmy's on his own."

Muttering about inexplicable feline mood swings, Jane walked down the hall into her bedroom, reaching for the buttons of her shirt. All she wanted was to crawl back into the sheets with her book. She'd just gotten to the good part when she'd heard the murder call over her scanner.

"Jane Colby?"

Jumping with a muffled shriek, she stopped dead in the doorway, her heart stuffing her throat.

There was a man sitting in the armchair across from her bed.

In that first instant of startled terror, Jane saw only size and black clothing and some sort of vivid paint running along one side of his face. "Who the hell are you?" she demanded, clutching her chest with one hand as her heart banged against his fingers.

"I'm Baran Arvid," the man said, uncoiling from the chair. "You're in danger, Miss Colby. I've been sent to protect you."

Protect, hell, Jane thought, staring wide-eyed as he straightened to a height of at least six-foot-five. *If I'm in danger, it's from him.*

He wore a black cable-knit turtleneck that stretched across impressively broad shoulders. Black pants hugged his long, muscled legs, and soft dark boots covered his feet. A long black duster that smelled like leather fell in folds around his massive body, putting her uncomfortably in mind of Dracula's cape.

"Protect me from what?" She licked dry lips and remembered Tom's gruff warning earlier this evening: *Jane, everybody in this town has a reason to be worried.*

Oh, God, was this the killer? No way could she fight him off, not judging by the width of those shoulders. Hell, she wasn't sure Arnold Schwarzenegger could fight him off; the man looked like a human tank. Jane backed up another step. "And how did you get in my house?"

"I broke in." He studied her, his expression dispassionate, no doubt reading the terror that was probably written all over her face. "Don't look so frightened. I'm not the threat you need to worry about."

"Yeah, well, personally I don't accept reassurance from burglars."

He lifted a dark brow. "Even if their only intention is to protect you from a killer?"

Jane blinked. "Well, that's certainly preferable to *being* the killer."

The burglar smiled slightly. "I thought so."

"Just for curiosity's sake, which killer are we talking about?" she asked cautiously.

"Is there more than one?"

"You never know."

The smile expanded, flashing white and charming across his tanned face. Damn, a housebreaker with a sense of humor. "Actually, I'm referring to the man responsible for the murder you covered tonight."

"How do you know about that?" Jane thought of at least one way he could have gotten that information—he could have committed the killing himself. She took another step back.

"I have my sources." The burglar shrugged. "In any case, we believe the same man will eventually try for you." His eyes were wide and dark, long-lashed, startlingly beautiful. And hard. Very hard. "I intend to stop him."

Apropos of nothing, a thought pierced Jane's unease: *Damn, he's gorgeous*. Not in a *GQ*-pretty kind of way, but in a primal, utterly masculine sense enhanced by his square-jawed face, aggressive cleft chin, even the beard stubble darkening his angular cheeks. Adding a startling touch to all that rough masculine beauty, a strange design in iridescent red and blue swirled down one side of his face from forehead to cheekbone. Not paint, she realized. A tattoo, though she had never seen one so bright and vivid.

His hair added to the impression of elegant barbarism, falling straight and black around his shoulders. Something glittered against the midnight silk; small jeweled beads, braided into a single dark lock that swung beside one high cheekbone.

Staring up at him, it hit her suddenly that he was standing a lot closer than he had been. While she'd been gazing at him in besotted fascination, he'd been subtly stalking her.

Oh, God.

As Baran watched, the fear deepened in Jane's eyes again. He almost growled in frustration. For a moment there, he'd seen a trace of feminine response in her gaze, but now the panic was back. She had reason to be afraid with Druas after her, but her best protection from that threat was Baran himself. Which was why he couldn't let her run from him.

"I appreciate your sense of civic responsibility," she told him in an elaborately polite tone as she edged away, "but I think I'd rather depend on the local cops."

"That wouldn't be wise."

She pointed toward the stairs. Despite her firm tone, her hand shook slightly. "Let me put it another way: Get out."

He shook his head and tried a wry smile. "I wish I could. I did have other plans for the next few days." Like the General's assassination, but he didn't think she'd find that particular detail reassuring. "Unfortunately, my superiors have ordered me to protect you, so it seems both of us are going to have to make the best of it."

"What superiors?" Her small pink tongue slipped out to moisten her full lips.

Baran was instantly reminded of that dangerously erotic red nightgown and its clinging scent of sex. A bolt of lust took him by surprise. He suddenly wanted to taste that mouth. And work his way down. He had to fight to keep his gaze from dropping to those pert, tempting breasts.

"What superiors?" she repeated, her tone sharpening, voice rising as her fear visibly increased.

"I can't discuss that." And he couldn't. The Enforcer had warned him repeatedly to keep Jane in the dark. Unfortunately, that presented him with a problem, since evasion wouldn't exactly win her trust.

Then again, neither would tying her up, but if she didn't start cooperating, he might have to try that next. And whatever her taste in reading matter, he doubted she'd like that at all.

Three

Baran edged closer, making up the distance she'd put between them as his mind ticked through his alternatives. He had a set of force restraints in his pocket, but he'd rather try to charm her first.

Jane, however, was not in the mood to be charmed. "Yeah, well, I think the only one I need protecting from is you," she told him, obviously doing her best to hide her nerves under a shell of cool courage. "I'm not bluffing. Get out, or I'm calling the cops."

Baran frowned. He couldn't allow her to contact the authorities. Arousing their suspicions would make his job even more difficult. "That's not a good idea."

"Let's find out." Jane whirled and bolted for the stairs.

Baran growled a curse and lunged forward, grabbing her wrist and spinning her around. "No."

"Let *go*!" she snarled, and went directly for his eyes with her free hand, fingers curled into claws. She had to reach up to do it.

He snatched her hand out of the air and curled a lip in warning. The ferocity in his gaze would have instantly quelled a woman of his own time. Jane just bared her teeth and tried to knee him in the balls.

He barely sidestepped in time. "If you don't stop this, I'm going to put you in restraints!"

"Try it and draw back a nub!" She darted her head toward his hand, evidently planning to sink in her teeth.

Baran jerked out of range and put her wrists together, transferring them into the grip of one fist. "Fine. Restraints it is."

Jane threw herself back, trying to drag free of his grip, but he held her easily. Given his enhanced strength, there was no way she could escape. She struggled anyway, brown eyes blazing at him. "You can't do this, you son of a bitch!"

"Watch me." Maybe after he tied her up, she'd see sense. Baran reached for a back pocket.

"No!" she spat, and launched her knee at his crotch again. This time she actually made contact with his thigh, though she was the one who grunted in pain at the impact. "What are you, the Man of Steel? Dammit, let go!"

"That's it!" Before Jane could kick him again, Baran used his grip on her wrists to snatch her off her feet, swing her around, and force her back toward the bed a few feet away. Ignoring her shrieks and kicks, he pushed her down on the mattress and dropped on top of her, flattening her with his greater weight. "Now. You'll listen," he growled, riding her slim body grimly as she bucked and fought.

"Do you have any idea of the kind of time you'll get for this?" she gritted through her teeth, glaring into his eyes. "And don't think I won't press charges!"

Despite his anger, he felt a niggle of admiration. She might not know what a Warlord was, but she was perfectly aware he outweighed her by a hundred pounds. It was hard not to admire a woman who wouldn't give up even when she was so obviously overmatched. "Calm down, Jane. I'm only trying to protect you."

"Yeah, right, you've got my best interests at heart!" She squirmed. In contrast to her rage, her full, soft breasts pressed against his chest so tightly he thought he could feel the bumps of her nipples through her clothing. His cock hardened as he lay in the cradle of her long legs. "That's obvious from the way you broke into my house and threatened to tie me up!"

His irritation took on an edge of heat. "Judging from your taste in reading material, I'd think you'd like that."

She froze under him, her eyes going wide at the taunt. As he watched, a mortified blush spread up her face. "You read my book?"

Frustrated and aroused, he gave her his darkest grin. "Oh, yeah. Want to act any of it out?"

Great. Just great. Break-and-Enter Boy had been flipping through her romance novel, and now he thought she was easy pickings.

Jane fought angry tears. Her legs hung off the end of the bed, and the burglar's powerful torso rode between them. He felt so damn big, so damn strong, so damn *hard* as he pressed her into the mattress. If he was the killer, she was dead.

But she still wasn't a coward. "Creep," she growled, feeling completely helpless, but damned if she'd show it.

He took a deep breath, visibly trying to rein in his temper. "I realize you're frightened. I don't blame you, but you're in no danger from me."

She licked dry lips. His dark gaze flicked to her tongue, tracked it with hot male interest. "Then get off." To her shame, a quiver of arousal shimmered along her nerves. *Damn,* she thought. *What kind of sick bimbo would find this a turn-on?*

"Stop fighting me." He let more of his weight settle between her thighs. "Otherwise I'll have to restrain you." The heat in his gaze intensified, mixed with a cool calculation.

Staring into his handsome face, Jane suddenly noticed glowing striations of bright red ringing the soft, rich sable of his pupils. She stared. She'd never seen anything like that fiery shimmer in anyone's eyes before. It was as if he wasn't quite human.

He lowered his head until she felt his breath against her mouth, warm and spiced with some scent she couldn't identify. "Do I have your word on it?"

Was he getting hard? Oh, God. *Distract him,* Jane thought. *Stall.* "Okay. Okay." If she could lull him into believing she'd given up, maybe she could get a chance to escape. Her chances were certainly better than if he bound her to the bed. Or did whatever it was he was thinking about that put that look in his eyes. "You said . . . you said earlier you had orders. From whom? What's going on?"

He paused. "I was sent by the government."

"Which government? I know every cop in Tayanita County, and you're not local. Are you state? FBI?"

He hesitated again as if he didn't even recognize the terms. Then his expression cleared. "I'm an FBI agent."

So the Bureau's new look is facial tattoos and shoulder-length hair? I don't think so. But she had to convince him he had her fooled. If she stayed pinned under his massive body much longer, he might decide to do something about it.

She licked her lips again. He tracked the movement like a cat watching a mouse just out of reach. The red striations in those dark irises brightened, sending a shiver down her spine. *Definitely time to get out from under him.* "Okay. Let me up and we'll talk."

That hungry cat gaze flicked back up to her eyes. She tried to look defeated and submissive. Evidently she pulled it off, because he nodded slightly and levered off her. She sucked in a deep, grateful breath. He backed up a pace, watching her, his big body loose and combat-ready.

Jane eased off the bed, watching him right back. No way in hell was she going to get away with him eyeing her every move. She had to find a way to put him down before he decided to drop whatever game he was playing and get rough.

Unexpectedly his gaze softened. "I'm not going to hurt you, Jane."

Damn, she wished she could believe that. At five feet eleven, Jane wasn't used to dealing with men who were six inches taller.

Her height had always made her feel she could hold her own with most men, but her captor's sheer size did not permit that illusion.

She needed a weapon. Scanning the room covertly, Jane spotted a cluster of bottles on her mirrored bureau. To distract him, she said, "This killer you mentioned." She took a deep breath. His attention instantly flicked to her breasts. Jane fought the instinct to cover them. *You're wearing a perfectly adequate shirt, you twit,* she told herself. *You are not naked, no matter how he looks at you.* "Who did you say you were sent to protect me from?"

He shook his head. "I didn't say. His name is Kalig Druas."

Okaaay . . . Play along, Jane. "From the sound of that, I assume he's not from around here." She moved toward the bureau, trying to look casual.

"He's not. What are you doing?"

She glanced warily over her shoulder. Crimson striations burned a bright warning in his hard, suspicious gaze as he watched her. "Brushing my hair," she improvised, picking up the silver-backed brush. *Yes, I'm the kind of bimbo who'd fight you one minute and primp the next. Work with me here. Think gullible.*

Giving the brush a pass through her curls as if to restore them to order, she turned back toward the mirror and surreptitiously checked out the bottles. Beaning him with one would obviously be a waste of time, but maybe . . . "So what does this Caleb Druis have against me?"

"Kalig Druas. He's got nothing against you, other than that you're female. He's"—he hesitated, as though searching for the correct phrase—"a serial killer. He murders for entertainment. And profit."

A chill slid over her. His expression was so intense and demanding, she almost found herself believing him. But if he was from the Bureau, why the hell hadn't he told any of this to the local cops?

True, it was possible he had and Tom Reynolds just hadn't mentioned it, but she didn't buy that. The detective would have been a lot more specific in his warning if he'd thought Jane herself was a target of the killer.

No, this guy was playing some kind of sick game with her, because it was for damn sure he was no cop. She knew cops, knew the vibe they gave off, and he was something altogether different.

So if he wasn't law enforcement, that made him the killer. And if she didn't get the hell away from him . . .

Forcing her fear into a tight, controllable ball, she picked up a tube of lipstick, bending close to the mirror to apply it. His attention never wavered. Pretending to study the results, she reached for the big bottle of White Swan that had been a Christmas present from an old boyfriend. Casually she uncapped the perfume. "So the Bureau sent you to protect me. Why do you think the killer is targeting me specifically?" She daubed the cap against her pulse.

"We've seized evidence that . . ." He stepped closer.

Jane spun and tossed the perfume into his face. His hand snapped out to snatch the bottle from her hand, but too late. The liquid splashed directly into his dark eyes. He fell back with a startled roar, both hands going for his face in an attempt to wipe away the burning perfume.

Jane shot past him and out into the hall to bound down the stairs three at a time. She sprinted across the living room for the front door. If she could just get to the SUV . . .

Something black and snarling sprang out of the darkness. She yelped and leaped aside, but it caught the hem of her flared jeans anyway, bringing her crashing to the carpeted floor hard enough to see stars.

Jane looked down to see what held her. And screamed with all the air in her lungs.

The biggest dog she'd ever seen clenched her jeans hem in fanged jaws. It looked more like a wolf than anything else—if wolves grew to the size of Saint Bernards. With another screech, she drew back her free foot.

"If you kick me," a deep male voice said, "I'll bite you. And then

I'll eat your cat." Impossibly it seemed to be coming from the wolf, or dog, or whatever the hell it was.

She looked around wildly, but nobody else was in the room; the burglar was still upstairs.

"I've got her, Baran!" the voice called. Jane thought she saw blue light flash in the fur around the wolf/dog's neck.

"Good," the man growled back. "Hold her."

Hell. She considered planting a kick across the wolf's furry black head despite the voice's threats, but one look into that feral canine stare stole her courage. She licked her dry lips. "Who are you? Who's talking?"

"Who do you think?" The wolf/dog's mouth didn't move when it spoke—its jaws remained firmly clamped on her hem—but she saw lights flash again in its fur. Looking closer, she saw what appeared to be a ring of glowing gems implanted directly into the animal's skin. LEDs for some kind of speaker, maybe?

Her heart was pounding so hard, she could feel her pulse in her ears. She felt sick. "What the hell is going on here? What kind of game are you playing with me?"

"This is not a game, Jane," the burglar said, stopping to flick on the light as he descended the stairs. "Not for us, not for you, and not for the man who wants to slit your throat."

Feeling sick and hunted, Jane watched his approach. His eyes were swollen, the whites bright red and bloodshot. The glowing striations in his pupils had expanded until it seemed twin flames burned in his skull. The fury on his face turned her blood to ice. *Oh, God,* she thought. *He's going to kill me.*

And those eyes . . . human eyes just didn't glow like that. What *was* he?

"Damn, Baran, you stink," the wolf/dog said, Jane's pants leg still gripped in his jaws. "What did the little bitch do to you—and why did you let her do it?"

"I think she hit me with some kind of chemical weapon." The burglar moved to stand over them. Even Jane wrinkled her nose at the choking floral stench. She must have splashed the entire bottle on him. "I underestimated her," he said grimly. "I won't do that again."

He reached into a pocket of his leather duster. Instinctively Jane tried to jump up and bolt, but the wolf/dog jerked her hem so hard, she fell back on her butt. Opening her mouth, she drew in breath to scream.

"Shut up," the burglar said, his voice so low and deadly she found herself obeying. She watched in suspended terror as he lifted something in one hand.

Even as Jane instinctively shrank against the floor, he pointed the object at his own face. A blue light shot out to play over his features. He waved it back and forth several times before running it over his chest and arms next.

"What's that?" Her shaking voice sounded far too high.

"A chemical neutralizer," he told her, his tone emotionless despite his molten stare. "It analyzes the weapon you used and renders it harmless."

Inhaling, she realized the overwhelming smell of White Swan had disappeared. How had he done that? "It wasn't a weapon. It was just perfume."

The wolf/dog gave her a look of astonished loathing. "You *wear* that substance? On purpose?"

"Well, I don't wear quite that much of it." *And I'm having a conversation with a talking wolf.*

Baran reached down a big hand and grabbed her collar to pull her to her feet as the animal released her leg. Her bubble of paralyzed disbelief popped. With a choked scream, she went wild, fighting like a rabid mink to get away.

In two strides he dragged her to the nearest wall and banged her back against it so hard the impact shocked her still again. "I am not the killer!" he roared. "If I were, I would have butchered you by now!"

For an instant they stared at each other. Until, slowly, a realization crept over Jane: He had a point. After the perfume trick, even a psycho bent on playing head games would have slit her throat.

Maybe he wasn't the killer.

But he wasn't FBI, either, not with those eyes. So what *was* he? Had he been sent to protect her? And if so, by whom?

"What do you want from me?" Her voice shook.

He lifted the corner of his handsome mouth in a snarl. "I want to catch Druas. And you're going to help me whether you like it or not. Turn around and brace your hands on the wall."

Jane stared at him, wide-eyed. "What? Why?"

"I'm going to search you." Catching her by one shoulder, he turned her around to face the wall. "I don't have the patience for any more surprises."

"And I don't have anything to surprise you with!"

He thrust his face close to hers, the pupils of his bloodshot eyes glowing. "Do you honestly expect me to take anything you say on faith?"

"What did you expect? You broke into my house!"

"And if you don't start cooperating, I'm going to do a lot worse."

At the lethal note in his voice, a shudder shook her. She slowly lifted both hands, flattening her palms against the cool plaster.

The first touch of his big hands on her ribs made her flinch. As if reading her fear, he hesitated. Then briskly he ran his hands up her sides and along the length of her braced arms.

Jane had seen cops pat down subjects before, though male officers rarely searched women if they could help it. Despite his evident fury, the frisk her captor conducted was just as professional and impersonal as the ones she'd witnessed. At least at first.

Until he kicked her ankles just hard enough to knock her feet apart. The kick didn't hurt, but something about the way he did it struck her suddenly as a gesture of pure sexual dominance.

He went still behind her. A moment of silence spun out, almost thrumming with tension. Suddenly that sizzling mutual awareness was back again, rushing in to fill the air between them with heat.

He crouched behind her. She heard the rustle of his leather coat as he moved. He put his hands on her thighs. Even through the fabric of her jeans, she could feel the heat of his long fingers as he slowly ran his palms down the length of her legs. To her horror, Jane felt her nipples peak.

Instead of his earlier cool professionalism, there was now something darkly possessive in his touch, even when he paused to pull up the cuffs of her jeans and explore inside her boot tops for weapons. Yet on the surface there was nothing improper in his technique.

So why did she feel . . . claimed? Like a slave girl being explored by her master?

Don't be so damned ridiculous, Jane, she snarled at herself.

But when he rose to his feet again, his sheer, brawny size added to her sense of helpless femininity.

His coat rustled again as he stepped closer. He seemed to surround her in heat. The rich smell of leather blended with his own clean musk as he cupped her bottom. Jane stiffened, but his hands didn't linger, sweeping around over her abdomen and upward to her breasts. As if the careful restraint had worn thin, his hands hesitated just a beat, then blatantly cupped her, lifting the soft mounds.

His thumbs brushed the tight, erect peaks of her nipples. She sucked in a breath to curse him, but the heat bolting along her nerves made the words seem hypocritical. She found herself longing to lean back, to ease into his arms.

Dammit, Jane! "Let go," she gritted.

To her relief, he did, dropping his hands and stepping away. But when she looked around at him, she saw dark male satisfaction in his strange, hot eyes, as if he'd tested her somehow. She didn't think she wanted to know the results.

Jane fumbled for a topic that would put them back on safer ground. "You said . . . you said you wanted me to help you catch the killer. How?"

"Isn't it obvious?" the wolf/dog said, moving to look up at them.

Its jaws gaped, revealing an impressive set of very sharp, very white teeth. "You're going to be the bait."

Jane looked down at the animal, perversely grateful he'd broken the erotic tension. The intelligence she saw in those pale canine eyes was far more human than animal. A sense of vertigo swept over her. "What *are* you? And don't bother with the FBI bull, because I don't think even the Bureau has a talking K-9 corps."

She looked over her shoulder at her captor just in time to see him pull out a length of what looked like thin gold cable. He reached for her right wrist.

"What are you doing?" Jane started to whirl, but he calmly stepped in and leaned a broad shoulder into her back, pinning her to the wall as he wrapped the cable around her wrist. Like a snake, it instantly coiled tighter. "Stop it!"

"I warned you, Jane." His deep voice was grim and cold. Using his grip on the cable, he dragged her right arm down even as he seized the other wrist and pulled it back. She squirmed, but he kept her mashed against the wall. To her disgust, she felt another potent snap of sensual awareness at the feel of his hard, muscular body pressed to hers.

"You've got no right!" she spat, struggling against both his grip and her own potent reaction. The effort did her no good in either case. He was so damn strong she couldn't break his hold no matter how she twisted and jerked. She might as well have been a toddler for all the effort he expended controlling her.

Fear slid through her fury. Granted, she didn't make a habit of struggling with men, yet even so his strength seemed somehow abnormal. As if he wasn't quite human. Instinctively she covered her unease with a snarl. "This is illegal!"

He simply ignored her, looping her other wrist in the cable. The thin metal seemed to coil around her arms like a snake, binding her hands. "They call this kidnapping, you son of a bitch!"

"Yes, and I don't care." He stepped back just enough to grab her shoulder and pull her around. The glowing striations in his pupils were still hot and burning, though the bloodshot red of his eyes had already begun to fade. "I'm going to do whatever it takes to catch Druas and keep you alive. So don't push me. You won't like the results."

She tugged futilely at her bonds. Impossibly, the restraints squirmed around her wrists like something alive, maintaining their grip. She'd never even heard of a metal that could do that. It was impossible.

Impossible. Like the talking wolf/dog. Like her captor's glowing eyes and amazing strength. Like the device that had instantly eliminated her perfume from the air.

The hair rose on the back of her neck. "What the hell are you?"

His handsome mouth took on a mocking twist. The iridescent tattoo on his cheek shimmered. "What do you think I am?"

Jane studied him, taking in the erect carriage, the fluid way he moved, the cold determination on his face. During her stint in Atlanta, she'd interviewed her share of soldiers, sailors, and Marines. He showed all the signs. "Military. Some kind of commando. Maybe."

His eyes flickered in reaction. "Good guess."

She relaxed slightly. That would explain all the James Bond toys. God knew what the government had cooking in the depths of some top-secret lab somewhere.

But what about the glowing eyes and the Big Bad Wolf? Not to mention the hair and beads, which sure as hell didn't look like any recruiting poster she'd ever seen. And . . . "What does a Navy SEAL—or Delta Force or whatever the hell you are—care about serial killers?"

Just for an instant he glanced down at the wolf, which tilted its head in a gesture curiously like a shrug. It wasn't the kind of look a man exchanged with a pet, or even an animal outfitted with a speaker as part of some elaborate masquerade.

It was the sort of glance you gave a partner when you wanted advice.

No matter what Wolfie looked like, he wasn't an animal. And

she'd be willing to bet that turning out sentient timber wolves was beyond even the United States government.

Which left . . .

"Are you some kind of aliens?" She felt ridiculous the minute she blurted the words.

Baran looked up at her, startled and amused. "Do I look like an alien?"

"I don't know." She glanced down at the animal, who watched them with sardonic intelligence. "But he does. He's sure as hell no dog, whether that's a speaker around his neck or not."

"*Dog?*" The wolf drew up in an affronted reaction that couldn't be anything but genuine. "I'll have you know I'm a genetically engineered timber wolf. There are no dogs anywhere in my family tree. And that's a vocalizer around my throat, not a 'speaker,' you ignorant hick."

Her lips tugged upward in reluctant amusement at his outrage. "So what's a vocalizer?"

"My body isn't designed for speech," the wolf told her with an outraged sniff. "My internal computer picks up my thoughts and sends them to the vocalizer, which turns them into sound."

"Which is my point exactly," she said to Baran. "Nobody has technology like that in the twenty-first—" Jane broke off, eyes widening as a new and even wilder idea occurred to her. "Are you from . . ." Damn, she couldn't believe she was saying the words. She took a deep breath and forced them out anyway. "Are you time travelers?"

Baran's brows lifted in an expression of startled interest. "What makes you say that?"

"The wolf. Your eyes. Your equipment. Like I said before, nobody on Earth has anything like this stuff. Yet aliens wouldn't look like anything that had evolved on this planet." Jane felt her tension building, stretching out, as if she were riding a roller coaster toward the top of a grade and the plunging drop on the other side. She took a deep breath and went right over. "But if you're from the future . . ."

Baran stared at her a long moment, but not like a man inventing a good lie. Like someone who was calculating how much truth to tell. "Yes," he said finally. "We're from the future."

A rush of goose bumps spread over her skin as Jane experienced a rush of the familiar quivering excitement she felt whenever she was on the trail of a hot story. And it didn't get any hotter than this.

Unfortunately, this situation also had implications that were far more personal than any story she'd ever covered. Terrifying implications. Swallowing, she asked the question that was gnawing at her consciousness. "Is that . . . is that how you know this guy is going to come after me?"

"Yes." Her captor said it so starkly, so simply, she had no choice except to believe.

"And he really is a serial killer?"

Baran's sensual mouth tightened. "Yes."

Jane licked her lips. "But you'll stop him. If you're from the future, you know what happens. Right?"

"Not necessarily."

"What does that mean?" A chill rolled over her skin. "You don't necessarily know or you won't necessarily stop him?"

He drew his big body to its full height and looked down at her. "I don't know if I'll be *able* to stop him."

Four

Jane's heart pounded as she stared at the handsome invader who'd just turned her life upside down. "But you said you're from the future!"

Baran sighed and dragged a hand through his hair. "Do you know everything that happened centuries before you were born?"

"You know this guy's coming after me!"

"Temporal Enforcement told me only as much as they had to. Which, unfortunately, wasn't much."

"Temporal . . . ?"

"Enforcement. They're the agency that regulates time travel."

"In the future." A new question occurred to her, and she asked it cautiously. "How far in the future?"

He shrugged. "Three hundred years."

"Yeah, that's definitely the future." She blinked, studying her brawny captor. Weren't future people supposed to be scrawny eggheads with big eyes? This guy looked as if he'd just stepped out of the cover of an old Viking romance, the kind where the hero tied the heroine up and pillaged her repeatedly.

Which, she had to admit, sounded like much more fun than it had any business being.

Baran watched as she rocked back on her heels, both hands still bound behind her back. The pose thrust her high, pretty breasts into prominence and drew his attention to the hard pebbled nipples behind her bra. He found himself battling the completely inappropriate urge to pull up her shirt and suck and tongue and tease those luscious points until they flushed red.

Sometimes his Warlord libido had a rotten sense of timing.

But perhaps the timing would improve. He'd scented her response more than once tonight, particularly when he'd kicked her feet apart. A seduction wasn't out of the question.

But since she'd apparently decided to cooperate, he'd have to explore that avenue another time. And he would. Now, however, she was too busy trying to process what she was learning—while he tried to decide how much information to give her.

He hadn't intended to tell her even this much, but she'd seen through the cover story those sloppy bastards from Temporal Enforcement had given him. They apparently hadn't anticipated how well Jane knew her own government and its workings. And Baran didn't have enough knowledge of her time to come up with a more believable lie.

So he was stuck with the truth, or at least as little of it as she'd let him get away with telling.

"So this . . . time agency . . ." Her brows drew down in concentration over her dark, narrowed eyes.

"Temporal Enforcement."

". . . sent you. What do they care if there's a serial killer in Tayanita County?"

"This particular serial killer is also from the future."

Her full lips parted. "Oh." For a moment she looked rattled. Then she rallied enough to manage an indignant snort. "What, they don't have women he could kill back in his own time? He's got to come back three centuries to find somebody to butcher?"

"Evidently."

"Why me? Why would somebody from three hundred years in the future want to target a reporter at a small-town weekly?" Her soft, sweet mouth curved down in a puzzled frown. "And I still don't understand why you'd care enough to come all this way to stop him."

He glanced from her rich brown eyes to her tempting lips, then down to the lush, promising contours of her breasts. "I can think of a number of reasons."

She blinked. "Umm." A flush heated her cheeks. "Well."

Baran smiled, watching those tempting nipples slowly peak under the soft fabric of her shirt. This mission was definitely looking more interesting all the time.

How did he do that?

One look, and he had her feeling as if she was about to burst into flames. It was humiliating.

"TE gave me a skull jack crystal on this time," the wolf announced, breaking into Jane's embarrassed arousal. "There are a couple of image files of the Jumpkiller in it. Could make things a bit more clear."

Baran glanced at his furry partner and nodded. "Let's see them."

"What's a skull jack . . . whatever?" God, her life was beginning to sound like an episode of *Star Trek*.

"Crystal. It's a memory unit I insert in my skull jack—that's the implant at the base of my right ear I can use to access data," the wolf added, seeing her open her mouth to ask.

"Where is this implant?" She moved cautiously closer and started to kneel, but her bound hands threw her off-balance. Impatiently, she looked at Baran and held her arms out straight behind her. "Look, can we lose the bondage? I get it now: You're the good guys. I have no intention of running away." She grinned. "In fact, you couldn't drive me off with a stick. I'm dying to learn more."

He gave her an appraising look, then nodded slowly. "But the minute you start giving me a hard time, I'm tying you up again."

Promise? her libido whispered. She told it to shut up. It quivered anyway as her handsome captor stepped behind her and went to work on her bonds. As the cable fell away, she stepped quickly away and turned, rubbing her wrists.

He tucked the restraints into a pocket of his coat, giving her a level, warning look.

Ignoring it, she crouched beside the wolf. "Okay, now about that implant . . ."

Freika helpfully angled his head, giving her access to the ear in question. Something that looked like a glowing blue gem glittered against his dark fur.

"So this crystal is some kind of recording medium?" She touched it. It felt warm and smooth under her fingers. "And it plugs directly into your head?"

"Right."

"Didn't that hurt?"

"Nah. I was just a pup when they did the procedure. Don't even remember it."

She looked up to find Baran watching her steadily. "Do you have one, too?"

He shrugged. "Not a skull jack, no. Any data I need, I get by downloading it from Freika."

"That way he doesn't have to worry about viruses," the wolf told her.

She sat up. "They still have computer viruses in the future?"

"Yeah, and they can be fatal."

Jane blinked, feeling more than a little boggled. "Fatal?"

"My computer controls my autonomic nervous system," Baran explained. "If I downloaded the wrong virus, it could stop my heart or paralyze me."

"Owwww." She winced. "That doesn't sound like fun at all."

He looked grim. "Believe me, it's not."

She was opening her mouth to ask for details when a man appeared in midair, floating a foot above the wolf's head.

Jane jumped, but when everyone else studied the figure calmly, she realized he wasn't real. Curious, she rose to examine the image. It was so sharp and three-dimensional, the man looked solid. Which pretty well finished off her last lingering doubt about whether they really came from the future. "Who the hell is that?"

"Kalig Druas," Freika said. "The Jumpkiller."

"He's the one who wants to kill me?"

"Evidently." Baran's face was utterly expressionless, his body so still he could have been carved out of ice.

Looking at him, Jane felt a chill skate her spine. *That,* she thought, *is a man with a very long fuse. But I don't think I want to be anywhere around when he blows.*

She turned her attention to the image that had inspired such cold hate. "Huh. Somehow I don't think we're going to have any trouble spotting *him* in a crowd."

A series of metal rings placed on edge appeared to sink halfway into the man's skull, forming a thick ridge across the top of his shaved head like a steel Mohawk. A second set of rings were implanted around the back of his head, stretching from temple to temple.

"And I thought nose rings were bad," Jane said.

"Skull implants are considered high fashion on Xer." Baran curled his lip. "Among other things."

"What's a Xer?"

"A planet." He moved closer, staring up at the floating figure. "About twenty years ago the Xerans invaded my world, Vardon. It took us five years to evict them."

Jane studied him, reading the cold anger in his eyes. "I'll bet that was unpleasant."

"You have a gift for understatement." He squared his shoulders.

"Recently we found out they were planning to have another try at taking us over. We've launched a preemptive strike."

"So what happened?"

He shrugged. "I don't know. The battle hadn't begun yet when the Temporal Enforcement agent showed up and took me off my ship." Baran's gaze turned brooding. "When this is over, I've got to go back and complete the mission he interrupted."

Something about the way he said the word *mission* sent a chill down her spine. It also thoroughly deterred her impulse to ask for details.

Dragging her attention away from Baran's grim face, she looked back at the Xeran. Despite the gothic hardware in his skull, the Jumpkiller's features looked human enough. In fact, the bone structure of his angular face was almost handsome, though his eyes were a bit too narrow and a bit too small. The color of his irises, though, was a distinctly nonhuman and very demonic red, complete with slit pupils. Add that hawk nose and tight, thin mouth, and you had the poster boy for meanasasnake.com.

Enhancing the reptilian effect, he wore a one-piece suit covered in what looked like tiny black scales. From what she could tell about the body under the suit, he was almost as thickly muscled as Baran. *What do they feed them in the future, anyway?* Jane wondered.

On second thought, she really didn't want to know the answer to that one, either.

In one fist he held a knife with a long curving blade that widened toward the point, almost like a machete. "What *is* that? It looks like a bowie knife on steroids."

"A Xeran *sevik*," Baran supplied.

"He's good with it, too," the wolf said, twisting his massive head around to gnaw at a patch of fur over his haunches. "At least judging from the trid he made for his subscribers."

"Subscribers?" Jane frowned. "What kind of subscribers? And what's a trid?"

Frieka gave his butt a lick. "A tri-dimensional recording."

"And the subscribers are Xerans who pay to see women murdered," Baran added.

She gaped at him. "People *subscribe* to things like that? And it's legal?"

"Xerans have a . . . flexible legal system." His tone was so intensely bitter, she wondered what they'd done to him. "The more money you have, the more flexible it is. These men have a lot of money."

"But—"

"If you'd just let me go on, we'll all find out everything we want to know," the wolf interrupted with an impatient rumble.

"Be my guest, furball," she muttered.

Freika chose to ignore the crack. "His name is Kalig Alrico Oth Druas . . ."

"Doesn't exactly roll off the tongue, does it?"

". . . a Xeran cyborg mercenary with a very bad temper and a tendency to kill those who irritate him. Including his commanders, which would probably explain why he hasn't worked in several years."

"So why isn't he in jail?" Jane asked. "Or on a penal colony, or whatever the futuristic equivalent is?"

Baran shrugged. "As I said, it's Xer."

"Aka Planet of the Psychopaths."

Evidently refusing to dignify her comment with a response, Baran looked at Freika. "Capabilities?"

"Basically, he's got enough nano-cybernetic muscle implants to match your strength."

"Even in *riatt*?"

"I doubt it, but it'll be close."

"Can I make a request?" Jane demanded, thoroughly frustrated. "Can we go five minutes without using futurespeak?"

Baran contemplated the question. "Probably not."

"Smartass. So how did the twenty-fourth century's answer to Jeffrey Dahmer get into the entertainment business?" If she asked enough questions, maybe all this would start making sense. Maybe.

The wolf cocked his black head, studying the image. "Basically, he needed money. From assorted records TE managed to acquire, it seems he supported himself the last few years working for various criminal enterprises. However, he must have been too unpredictable even by underworld standards, because that finally dried up, too."

Baran frowned as if a question had suddenly occurred to him. "Where did he get the temporal armor he uses to make his Jumps?" To Jane he added, "Access to T-suits is very tightly controlled. Possessing a suit without authorization is a capital crime. And TE is not picky about legal niceties when they catch you at it."

She digested the concept and wrinkled her nose. "So where *did* he get it?"

"The short answer is, TE has no idea," Freika said.

"But I'll wager they're working very hard to find out," Baran said, stretching his long legs out in front of him and lacing his big hands together over his flat belly.

"You'd win that bet." The wolf moved to lean against his knees. "Do you mind? That damn jack itches every time I access it." Baran reached down and scratched the spot obligingly. "Thank you. Where was I? Oh. However he got the suit, Druas quickly started using it in a series of temporal thefts, bringing back two previously unknown Da Vincis and one of Shakespeare's first folios—"

"Wait a minute," Jane interrupted. "Are you saying that people go back in time to *steal*?"

"Why do you think there's a TE?" Freika yawned, displaying a set of intimidating dental work. "Anyway, in the course of one of his thefts, he ended up murdering the wealthy female owner. Rather spectacularly."

"And probably raped her while he was at it," Baran noted, absently running his long fingers through the wolf's fur.

"Exactly. And either for his own amusement, or because there's a market for that kind of thing on Xer, he used his computer implant to record the crime. He gave a copy to a distributor, who put him in touch with other sick bastards with the same tastes and a great deal of money."

"Ewwww," Jane said.

"Indeed. Soon afterward, somebody came up with the bright idea of actually paying Druas to jump through time and commit well-known but historically unsolved crimes. This is his latest release."

The killer's image was replaced by a six-foot hole in the air. Inside it, a woman in a long dress walked through a narrow arched doorway built of rough brick.

Taking a closer look, Jane realized it wasn't really a hole, just another of those three-dimensional images. This one, however, was projected in the shape of a globe. When she tried to walk around it, the angle of the image seemed to follow her, giving the impression that the globe was rotating. "That's a really weird effect." She cocked her head and considered it. "So, is he carrying some kind of camera around, or what?"

"He has a computer implant in his brain," Freika explained. "It records what he sees."

"Through his eyes," Jane said, the light dawning. "That's how you get the three-dimensional effect. And why the angle doesn't change no matter how you move."

In the image the woman pushed open a door and stepped inside, then smiled flirtatiously as the killer moved after her. She was plump, pretty, and young, probably in her twenties, with dark hair piled on top of her head. Judging from the unsteadiness in her step, she was also more than a little drunk.

Jane frowned. The brunette wore a long shabby wool gown and a red jacket. "When is this? That dress looks Victorian."

"Very good," Freika said, his eyes shuttering with pleasure as Baran absently rubbed the top of his head. "According to the file, this trid was recorded in 1888."

Jane frowned. There were several famous Victorian murders

that immediately leaped to mind, of course, but it couldn't be one of those.

At least, she hoped not.

The brunette lit a candle, revealing a tiny room. It couldn't have been more than twelve feet square—there was barely room enough for a narrow bed and a small, rickety wooden table.

A male voice spoke from the trid, sounding very English and upper-class. "Sing for me, pretty Mary Kelly."

The little brunette smiled and unbuttoned her coat. "Wouldn't you like me to do somethin' a little more interestin' than sing?" There was a hint of Irish music in her accent that gave it a sweet lilt.

"Wait a minute," Jane said. "Why is she talking to that freak? I'd think a Victorian woman would take one look at those things sticking out of his head and run screaming."

"He must be using an imagizer," Baran said.

"Which is what, exactly?"

"His computer projects a three-dimensional image around him that makes him look like someone else."

She frowned. "If he can do that, how are we supposed to spot him?"

"I have sensor implants," Baran explained. "Xeran metabolism is different from the original human rootstock, so I should be able to detect him despite the visual shield."

"Besides, it's not a particularly effective disguise," Freika added. "The first time you touched him, you'd know something was wrong. If you'll notice, he's a lot taller than she thinks he is."

Jane looked closer and saw that the girl's eyes were aimed roughly at chest level, as if that was where the man's face was.

"You have such a pretty voice," Druas said. "What was that you were singing earlier?"

"It's just a little ditty," the brunette said, a dimple winking in her cheek. Despite the slight slur in her voice and the fact that she was visibly tipsy, there was a flirtatious charm about the doomed woman that made Jane wince. "It's called 'Sweet Violets.'"

"Sing it again. I want to hear it."

"Oh. All right." Softly at first, then more loudly, she began to sing, "Scenes of my childhood—"

"Undress for me," Druas interrupted. There was a note of menacing anticipation in that cultured voice the brunette was evidently too drunk to recognize. "And keep singing."

That girl is about to be murdered, Jane realized, as the reality of what was happening sank in. *Oh, God, I don't think I want to see this.*

Obediently Mary went on singing as she unbuttoned her shabby dress in the flickering light of the candle. ". . . This small violet I pluck'd from mother's grave . . ."

"This is sickening," Jane said, looking away.

"Granted," Baran said, his eyes cold and grim. "but I've got to review it anyway. I need to know as much as possible about the way this bastard operates."

She subsided. He had a point.

Mary lifted the gown over her head, leaving only a thin linen chemise that was stained and torn in places. Folding the gown, she put it on the chair before going to work on the buttons of her chemise. Work-roughened fingers busy on the horn buttons, she turned toward Druas, still singing. ". . . They all have left me in . . ."

There was a blur of movement, so fast Jane almost missed it. The girl's eyes widened as she made a choked, helpless sound.

Two enormous hands were wrapped around her neck, hoisting her into the air as her feet kicked helplessly.

Druas was much, much taller than she was.

"I always like this part best," the killer told her, his voice bright, laughing.

She kicked at him, clawing at the hands that were slowly choking her to death. Her open mouth gaped as she fought to breathe, her face darkening.

"You're going to be famous, Mary Jane Kelly," Druas purred, holding her effortlessly. "For hundreds of years the photograph of what I'm going to do to you will make people stare in horror, wondering what you used to look like before I sliced away your face."

Her blue eyes widened helplessly in terrified realization.

"That's right, Mary, sweet Mary," he said. "You're Jack the Ripper's last victim."

Jane stared at the trid in helpless horror as her head began to swim. "Sweet Jesus God."

Mary's face darkened still more, the whites of her eyes going red as tiny capillaries burst. Her frantic kicks weakened.

Finally Druas tossed her on the bed to flop bonelessly. Something silver flashed, followed by a spray of red flung by the knife as he made his first cut.

Baran stepped toward Jane as she swayed, looking as if she was about to fall in a heap. He caught her elbow, and she sagged against him. "Stop the playback, Freika."

"But we need to—"

"Later."

Before the wolf could argue, Jane tore herself from his arms with surprising strength and bolted across the room. Baran strode after her as she raced into a small alcove and collapsed on her knees in front of a shiny porcelain chair his computer identified as a *toilet*. Flinging her head down over the hole in its seat, she began to retch violently.

Baran watched for a moment, instinctively trying to maintain his emotional distance, but her misery was too much for him. With a sigh he knelt beside her and helped her gather her long hair out of the way. She ignored him, heaving in helpless rolling spasms. "Jane, he's not going to get the chance to do that to you. That's why I'm here."

She looked up at him, wild-eyed, her face tinged green. "You mean"—she stopped to gasp—"I really am a target for Jack the fucking Ripper?"

She jerked her head down and started heaving again, more violently than before.

Wincing, Baran could do nothing for her but support her head. He'd seen so much bloodshed and suffering over the years that normally he was able to maintain a certain detachment.

Yet though he'd done his share of killing, there'd been something different in the way Druas had attacked Mary Kelly, a vicious joy that was deeply disturbing.

And then there was Jane. Watching her struggle to control her rioting stomach, he felt a twist of pity. She'd fought him with such clever bravery, it hurt to see her reduced to this helpless, sick horror.

Finally the spasms were over. She climbed wearily to her feet and wiped her mouth with the back of her hand. Refusing to meet his eyes, she mumbled, "Thanks."

Baran shrugged, battling the uncomfortable impulse to put his arms around her. That, he knew, was a very bad idea. It was one thing to feel a healthy lust for her, but anything more was an emotional trap he couldn't afford to fall into.

So he hung back as she stepped to a small counter with a basin in the center and twisted a knob. Water poured from a metal projection over the basin as she picked up a small brush and started a procedure his computer called *brushing her teeth.*

Finally she turned to look up at him again. Her skin was still tinted a faint, unhealthy green. "All right, I'm ready. Let's finish looking at the recording."

Baran frowned at her. Knowing the Xeran taste for overkill, he suspected it would only get worse. "That's not necessary. I'll review the rest."

She shook her head, that delicate chin taking on a stubborn angle. "No, we need to stop this guy. He can't be allowed to go on doing this."

"Granted, but that's my job." Leaning a hip against the countertop, he studied her. "You don't need to be involved in it. Especially considering that the trid is only going to get worse."

"Yeah, I know." Jane swallowed and took a deep breath. "But I have to understand this guy, what motivates him. What his M.O. is. And the only evidence we've got is what's on that recording."

"You'll be running in here again in five minutes," Freika said from the doorway. "He starts getting artistic next."

"Then I'll run," she snapped. "And I'll come back and I'll watch the rest."

Any other civilian woman he knew would have been glad to let him handle the whole bloody, revolting mess. "Jane, it's not necessary."

"Yes, Baran, it is. Look, you guys don't know this time, and you don't know this culture. You need my help, and that means I have to know as much as I can about that sick bastard."

Baran sighed, caught between admiration for her courage and irritation at her stubbornness. "Actually, I'm more than capable of handling the hunt without your input. Whatever I need to know about your time, my computer implant can tell me." And if the recording did get worse than what they'd seen already, she didn't need to be exposed to any more of it. He didn't want her nerve to break completely. Not when she was supposed to be the bait.

He frowned. What if something went wrong? A chill rippled over him as his mind instantly supplied a terrifying image of pretty, delicate Jane confronting that sadistic bastard. All her courage, all her beauty and intelligence, all destroyed, flayed away by Druas and his knife. Like Liisa.

No, he decided, straightening his shoulders. Not Jane.

This one he was going to save.

Five

Jane glowered at Baran, unaware of his newfound resolve. "Look, it's my life that's on the line here! I'm the one that bastard wants to slice like bacon. I deserve to know—"

"Only as much as I think you need to," he told her, striving for patience. "You're a civilian, Jane. And I'm not. My job is to hunt Druas. . . ."

"And mine is to be the bait." There was a hot, angry glitter in her dark eyes, a bitter set to her mouth. "Just writhing on the end of the hook, waiting for that creep to take a bite. Screw that. If you were in my shoes, would you want to be kept in the dark?"

She had a point. Maybe she did need to know.

And maybe once she found out what Druas was capable of, she'd obey orders. He'd already discovered just how difficult Jane could make things when she chose, despite his Warlord strength and cybernetic implants. They'd both be a lot safer if she stopped questioning him. "All right."

Mouth open as if to launch another argument, she blinked. "What?"

"Maybe a good look at what Druas does for entertainment would convince you to let me do my job."

Two minutes into the rest of the recording, Jane bitterly wished she hadn't insisted on seeing it. She forced herself to endure anyway.

At first she tried to pretend it was some poorly made B-movie she had to review. But no director would have kept the camera focused on what Druas did to Mary Kelly. She'd seen cows butchered with less vicious brutality.

In sheer self-defense she tried to think like a cop, noting which hand he used and how deeply he cut. She wasn't a forensic scientist, but it was obvious from the easy way he hacked into the body that the man's strength was terrifying.

Yet no matter how Jane fought to stay detached, her stomach heaved with every slice. Her head began to pound in deep, rhythmic surges in time to her heart. She felt dizzy. Locking her spine into a rigid column, she concentrated on staying upright.

Every time Druas did something particularly nauseating, Jane was conscious of the cool, assessing gazes of Baran and the wolf. *They're wondering how long it will take me to pass out.*

She told herself savagely that she'd been exposed to carnage before. There'd been that shotgun murder last year, when she'd beaten the cops to the scene. She'd held it together then, despite the boneless sprawl of the body in the middle of the street, surrounded by blood and skull fragments. Yeah, it had haunted her, but she'd dealt with it.

And God knew Jane had covered so many traffic fatalities she'd gone numb in sheer self-defense. Then there were all the murder trials she'd reported on. After hours spent listening to gruesome expert testimony about wounds and the suffering of the victims, she should have been inured.

But none of that had prepared her for actually seeing it happen, listening to the killer hum in absent pleasure like a workman singing to himself over some pleasant task.

As the endless seconds ticked past, Jane realized that watching this would leave scars she would carry in her mind until the day she died.

It was only when Druas started cutting Mary's heart out that she jumped up and whirled away. "When you catch this guy . . ." She had to stop to swallow bile. "Are you going to kill him, or just arrest him?"

"I'm going to kill him." Baran spoke with such utter emotionless conviction, she knew he meant every word.

Jane took a deep breath. "Good."

None of the usual moral arguments about the rule of law or the value of even a murderer's life meant anything when it came to Kalig Druas. He had to be eliminated just as a rabid dog has to be put down. Not for vengeance or even for justice, but simply because he was a threat to every other human being he met.

When he finally rose from his kill—Jane could feel that last image of Mary Kelly's mangled body searing itself into her brain—Druas turned and picked up a mirror standing beside the bed. The face he saw reflected there was smeared with blood, flecked with crimson bits Jane had no desire to identify.

He addressed the mirror in a foreign language, the words incomprehensible, the triumphant, gloating tone all too clear. She realized he must be talking to his perverted subscribers. His mouth was twisted into a feral grin, his eyes wild in the mask of gore surrounding them.

Then the image, at last, winked out.

"What did he say?" Jane managed. She was standing at the other end of the room as far from the trid as she could get. Her lips felt cold and numb. She suspected she'd recognized a word, and found herself hoping she was wrong.

For a long moment, neither man nor wolf answered. "He said, 'Wait until I get to Tayanita,' " Baran said.

"That's what I was afraid of."

He barely got to her before her knees buckled.

Jane felt . . . strange. She knew she should be asking questions, making plans, but all she could seem to do was sit on the couch, staring sightlessly into space. It was a comfortable couch, thickly padded in cream leather. It had cost her a thousand dollars. She tried to concentrate on the feel of that very expensive couch, tried to lock her thoughts on it instead of . . . other things. She closed her eyes. And saw blood spray across the soft pale leather.

Her eyes flew open.

Baran was talking. Jane struggled to listen to him, but it was difficult when she could hear Druas humming to himself as he sliced. . . .

Stop that. Freika turned off the trid. It's over.

But it kept playing in her mind, flashes of red horror, seconds of incomprehensible evil caught in an endless feedback loop.

". . . been fighting Xer since I was sixteen," Baran was saying. She tried to switch her attention to his words, to the movement of his mouth. It was a very nice mouth. "I know how he thinks. . . ."

"I very much doubt that," she said, her voice low.

He rubbed a thumb across an eyebrow. "All right, I don't. But I am more powerful than he is, and anything he tries, I'll be ready for."

How could anybody be prepared for the kind of mind that could conceive of the things Druas had done to Mary Kelly?

And how could anybody want to watch him? That was the question her mind kept circling back to. People had subscribed to his recordings, had effectively paid him to butcher Mary Kelly the same way men in her own time would subscribe to an Internet porn service.

God, she was cold. Shivering, she looked around dully until she spotted the colorful crocheted throw lying over the back of the couch. Its expanse of warm reds and yellows looked like a spill of sunlight across the pale leather. Jane reached up, tugged it down, and wrapped it around herself, moving slowly, clumsily.

She still felt cold. She wondered if she was in shock.

The question emerged so suddenly even Jane was caught off guard. "Why didn't you save her?" Baran and Freika, engaged in an intense low-voice conversation, looked up as if surprised she was capable of speech. "You could have stopped him before he murdered Mary Kelly. Then that woman he killed here tonight wouldn't have died, either. And I wouldn't have had to see—" She stopped, vaguely ashamed that she'd even mentioned herself in the same breath as the others.

Baran sat down beside her. There was a tightness around his mouth, a shadow in his eyes. Futuristic warrior or not, the trid had shaken him. She was glad. She wasn't sure she'd want to be around a man who could watch that kind of butchery without being affected. "I couldn't have saved Mary Kelly, Jane."

"Why not?" If he couldn't save Mary, did that mean . . . ? "You said you were stronger, faster. . . ." Her voice rose. Jane could hear the edge of panic in it and knew she should reign in her fear. She also knew that kind of control was currently far beyond her meager resources.

"I couldn't have saved her because I didn't."

"Yeah, but why? Why didn't you?"

"For one thing, because TE didn't transport me back to 1888. But even if they had, it wouldn't have done any good. Druas murdered Mary Kelly, and there was nothing I could have done to stop it. If I'd tried, I would have failed."

"How do you know that?"

He shook his head. "Because humans have been time traveling for sixty-five years, and none of them have ever changed history. I'll only be able to save the victims I'm supposed to save."

There was a strange, high buzzing in her ears. She swallowed hard. "Are you supposed to save me?"

"Yes." His gaze was fierce and certain.

"You said before you didn't know." Jane licked her lips and fought the impulse to scream. She was afraid she wouldn't be able to stop. "You said they hadn't told you. Unless . . . I'm supposed to die?" Oh, God! To end up like Mary Kelly . . .

"No, you're not going to die." Something in his determined gaze steadied her. He closed a big, hard hand around hers, encircling her chill fingers in strength and warmth. "I swear to you, I will save you, Jane Colby. Druas is the one who's going to die."

The confidence in his voice made the fear recede. She felt her thoughts clear slightly. "So you're saying, what? You couldn't have stopped it because it was fate? We have no real control over what happens to us?"

Baran waved a strong hand in dismissal. "No, you misunderstand. Look, time travelers are not suddenly inserted into history. They're part of the time plane even before they make their Jumps. Hell, before they're even born."

Jane stared at him, wondering if he really wasn't making sense or whether her battered mind simply wasn't processing the logic. "What are you *talking* about?"

"Let me see that." He reached out and gently tugged the throw from around her shoulders. "My computer says that people in your time see time as a river. But it's more like this."

"Time's a giant blanket?" She blinked, puzzled.

"More or less." He spread the throw across their laps, then picked up one of the tassels that fringed its edges. His long fingers separated the strands down to one. "Let's say this piece of yarn is a life." He pointed at the knotted base of the tassel. "This is the moment of conception, and at the other end is the instant when decay ends and the body ultimately vanishes. Take a cross section of the string at any point, and that's the *now,* the instant you're in right at this second. Does that make sense?"

She frowned. "Not sure. Go on."

"Everything has a time string, a series of 'nows'—this couch, you, me, the Earth, everything. All of the different strings weave together as they extend forward into time."

She felt her fear drain even more, banished by the academic tone of the discussion. "So your people see time as a physical dimension—like width, length, and depth." Jane rubbed a hand over her belly, where the sore muscles still protested her bout of vomiting. "Okay. So?"

"Let's say when we made the throw, we took one string from here"—he pointed at one end of the throw—"and looped it around to here." He pointed at a spot in the middle. "Then wove it back in for a few inches, and then we looped it back to the point it came from."

"So if that string is a time traveler . . ."

"Everything he did during his Jump happened before he was born."

She dug her fingers deeper into a particularly stubborn knot of aching muscle. "So that old paradox about going back in time to shoot your own grandfather so you'd never be born . . ."

". . . couldn't happen, because you *didn't* shoot your own grandfather. Your gun would misfire, someone would wrestle you to the ground, something would stop you. That's why I couldn't prevent Mary Kelly from being murdered. One theory has it that the only possible paradox is when someone doesn't go back in time when they're supposed to, to play whatever role they're supposed to play. TE makes sure that doesn't happen."

"What if they don't?"

Baran shrugged. "There have been a couple of times TE has decided not to transport somebody, only to have a TE agent from the future pop in and Jump the individual anyway. But theoretically, if you didn't end up where you were supposed to go and do whatever you were supposed to do . . . it would create a ripple effect. Every action has consequences that affect other actions, which affect other actions, and so on. So if you're not there, the things you don't do cascade into the future, getting worse and worse. Almost instantly, the entire time plane would rip itself to shreds. Everyone who'd ever existed would die, past and future."

She stared at him, blinking at the image of such sudden, incomprehensible destruction. "But what about the real Jack the Ripper?"

"What real Jack the Ripper?" Freika asked, tilting his head in a gesture of canine puzzlement.

"The original Victorian guy who did those killings. If Druas killed Mary Kelly before the real Jack got a chance, then wouldn't that have caused one of these paradoxes?"

Baran shook his head. "That's what we've been trying to tell you. There was no Victorian Jack the Ripper. It was always Druas. He went back in time and killed those women, just as he killed the one tonight."

"That's why they call it 'time travel,' Jane," Freika said, and twisted his head around between his hind legs.

Jane eyed him as he went to work. "You know, if you're smart enough for sarcasm, you're smart enough to know it's rude to lick your own genitals."

The wolf looked up. "You're just jealous."

She opened her mouth to deny it, then stopped. "Well, yeah." Shrugging, she turned to Baran. "Let me get this straight—Druas went back in time to commit the crimes of Jack the Ripper. But if there really had been a Victorian Jack, Druas would have killed not only the first victim, but triggered the destruction of the entire universe—including himself?"

"Basically."

"What a lunatic."

Freika glanced up at Baran. "My. She is clever."

"I think I like you better when you're licking your own backside." To Baran, she continued, "So it's not really me TE sent you here to save. It's the universe."

He shrugged. "Basically. But the end result is the same. *I will save you.*"

Jane frowned as a new and unpleasant thought struck her. "How do you know that, Baran? What if they just sent you back here because this is where you're supposed to be?" Her voice rose. "What if that bastard gets his hands on me anyway, and does to me what he did to Mary Kelly?"

"He won't."

"What do you care?" She stood up, unable to sit still any longer, red nightmares spinning through her mind. "I'm nothing to you, any more than I mean anything to those sick bastards who're paying Druas to kill me for their entertainment. I'm just a victim. Just like that poor lady tonight. Just like Mary Kelly."

Anger stirred behind his eyes. Apparently he didn't like having his word questioned. "When I say I won't let you die, I mean it. I don't make empty promises."

"How do you know you can even stop it, Baran?"

"How does anybody ever know they can do anything? You just do it."

"What are you, a Nike commercial?"

"Protecting people is what Baran does," Freika said. "It was what he was created to do: He's a Viking Class Warlord. He can no more fail to protect you than he can stop breathing."

Jane snorted. "I'd probably find that a lot more comforting if I knew what the hell a Viking Class Warlord is."

He and the wolf exchanged a long look, as though in silent communication. Finally Baran said, "Like Freika, I'm genetically engineered. Almost a century ago, genetic designers on Vardon created a warrior class called Warlords, designed to act as the planet's protectors. They made us several times stronger and faster than an ordinary human the same size. And I've got cybernetic implants in my brain and muscles that enhance my natural abilities even more."

"And he's instinctively protective," Freika added. "They breed the desire to defend into the Warlords. He would literally die to protect you, without any hesitation at all."

Looking into the wolf's crystalline blue eyes, she found herself believing him. Jane swallowed and looked away, finding the moment too intense for comfort.

Warm fingers closed around her wrist, drawing her into a warm, dark gaze. "Trust me," Baran said quietly.

"It's not as if I have much choice."

He stood in a smooth rush of muscle and rustling leather. The top of her head barely came to his shoulders. "You're right. You have no choice—except to trust me and do exactly what I tell you to do. Not if you want to live."

"And what exactly are you telling me to do?" She folded her arms. Perversely, it felt good to challenge him rather than let herself be borne helplessly along on his strength.

"Cooperate. I'll have to be with you every minute. And I do mean *every* minute. The fact that Druas can Jump means he could simply transport wherever you are and kill you before I even know what's happening—unless I'm right there. At all times."

Oh, *that* was going to be fun. "How are you supposed to fight him?" she asked, frowning as she considered the implications. "I mean, if the guy can just teleport or Jump or whatever the hell you call it, how are you going to catch him? Can you Jump, too?"

"No. I don't have a suit; TE transported Freika and me here. But I can keep him from Jumping." He lifted a big hand and spread it. She blinked, focusing on the long fingers, the broad, square palm. It looked intensely masculine, that hand. Intensely skilled. ". . . power pack neutralizer," he was saying.

She shook her head. "What? I didn't hear that."

The wolf snickered. "No, you were wondering if the size of his hand matches the size of his—"

"Freika," Baran interrupted in cool warning. He stepped in closer to her, and this time she managed to focus her attention on the gold ring he wore. The band was filigreed, incongruously delicate on such a big man, and the red stone seemed to glow against his tanned skin.

"TE gave me this ring," he explained. "If I can get close enough to Druas, press it against his temporal suit and hold it there for several seconds, the pulse it generates will wipe out his suit's power pack. He won't be able to Jump."

Jane frowned. "Several seconds is a long time in a fight."

"True." He shrugged. "I'm going to have to pin him down somehow."

"Which puts you back in the same boat—getting close enough for long enough." She dragged her hands through her hair in frustration. "So what are we going to do, just wait for him to show up and kill me?"

Baran's ringed hand came to rest on her shoulder, radiating strength and warmth. Startled, she looked up. "He's not going to kill you, Jane." His eyes were so dark, so rich, like pools of dark chocolate. . . .

"At the risk of interrupting your mating ritual," Frieka said, "it's been three hundred years since I had anything to drink. I have three choices—I could go outside and look for a stream, I could drink out of the nearest toilet, or—"

"I'll get you something." Jane turned away from Baran, fighting the niggle of regret as his comforting hold dropped away.

"Food would be good, too," Freika added. "Though I suppose I could hunt for myself—if you don't mind losing your cat."

She eyed him. "Octopussy is not wolf chow, furball. I'm sure there's something in the freezer."

"Don't put yourself out." Raising his voice, he called, "Here, kitty, kitty. . . ."

"All right, already!" Jane stalked toward the kitchen. What the hell was she going to feed him? She didn't have any dog food, even assuming he'd lower himself to eat it.

Steak. There were a couple of rib eyes in the freezer.

She pulled it open and reached inside, found the package, and grabbed it. Out of habit she started to check it for freezer burn.

A chunk of meat, dark red, traces of frozen blood on the plastic . . .

An image rose in her mind—Druas, digging Mary Kelly's heart out of her chest. . . . Her ears began to buzz. She stared sightlessly at the steak, fighting to stay upright. It felt as though her throat was swelling shut. *Breathe, dammit,* she ordered herself. *Don't pass out on the floor in front of them. They already think I'm* . . .

Gutless, her father's voice whispered in her mind. *I always said you were gutless.*

No, she thought, fighting the well of tears. *No, you're wrong.*

He's going to kill you because you're too incompetent to save yourself.

Dammit, no. She blinked the tears away. *I'm not incompetent. That may have been what you told me for twenty years, but I proved you wrong. I'm aggressive, I'm tough, and I will survive this.*

Only if that big hunk of muscle in there saves you. Otherwise you don't have a prayer.

Anger flooded her, welcome and hot, chasing away the chill. *Yes, I will. I'm going to beat this.*

I'm going to beat you.

Baran and Freika watched as Jane started opening cabinets and rattling crockery. Because he didn't care to be heard, Baran used his computer's com unit to speak silently to his partner. *She's beginning to function.*

For the time being, the wolf replied. *Would you care to bet on how long it'll take her to collapse again?*

If she does, she won't stay down. She's got courage.

She'd better. Freika let his tongue loll in a lupine grin. *Speaking of going down, when do you plan to spread her? I haven't smelled so much pheromone in the air since the last time you took leave.*

Voyeur.

Hey, somebody should get a little pussy on this trip.

Leave the cat alone, Freika.

Spoilsport. The wolf padded toward the kitchen. "Well, I'd better make sure she isn't dumping horsemeat in a bowl," he said, pitching his voice loud enough to make sure Jane could hear him. "I keep telling her I'm not a dog, but I don't think it's sunk in yet."

"A little Mister Ed tartare, anyone?" Jane's voice sounded overly bright, as if she was working hard at being cheerful and unaffected. "Never mind, you wouldn't get the joke. This is steak, hairball. Rib eye, three bucks a pound. You should be very happy together. It's frozen solid, so I'm nuking it for you. You want it thawed until it's just bloody, or do you want it cooked?"

"I certainly don't want it radioactive. Nuked?"

"Not nuked as in bombed. Nuked as in microwaved. Cooked in a microwave oven. You stick it in the box, push the button, and magic waves of energy bombard it until it's hot enough to scald the roof of your mouth." Something began to hum. "See? You're not the only master of technology in this house."

Baran found himself grinning despite his concern. Jane's effort at humor made him feel a bit better about her chances. She was a fighter. She wouldn't give up, no matter how bad things got. That determination made it easy to like her.

Maybe a little too easy.

His smile faded. Charming or not, she was still a civilian, and that meant she had limits he couldn't afford to ignore. Baran could protect her, joke with her, even seduce her, but he didn't dare forget that when it came right down to it, she couldn't be trusted.

Trusting a civ was a good way to get killed.

*O*kay, Jane thought, watching Freika devour his dinner, it was time to start taking a proactive approach. "What other information do we have about the killer?"

"Not much," the wolf said, tearing off a chunk of meat with his teeth. Since he didn't use his mouth to talk, he could eat at the same time. "Basically what I've already told you."

"Then let's take it from another direction. What do we know about Jack the Ripper?"

"Freika, what do your files say?" Baran asked, moving to join them.

The wolf lifted his head and swallowed. "There is no other mention of this Jack the Ripper other than the Mary Kelly trid."

Baran grunted. "More TE games."

"Not a problem—I know where we can get all the information on the Ripper we could ever need." Jane turned and headed through the living room to the back room that held her home office. It was nice having something constructive to contribute. "People in this time are fascinated by his murders. There are books and Web sites galore."

"Which may be why TE didn't waste crystal space on it," he observed, trailing her. "They're nothing if not efficient."

"Unlike Jane's computer," Freika said, having reluctantly left his dinner to stick his head around the doorframe. He eyed the P.C. as Jane sat down at her desk. "What a primitive piece of junk."

She considered flipping him off; it was a top-of-the-line machine, brand-new, with enough power to run all the graphics and layout programs she needed to put the paper together. Of course, by the standards of your average cybernetic talking wolf, it probably *was* a primitive piece of junk.

No doubt about it, Jane thought, turning the computer on and waiting for it to boot up. *My life is getting really, really strange.*

Six

When Jane's fingers hit the keyboard, Baran moved to her side to watch. "What are you doing?"

"Hmm?" She used the mouse to click on the icon for Internet access. At least she had a cable modem.

"With your hands."

"Typing on the keyboard. It's the only way to interface with this kind of computer."

He frowned. "Why not just tell it what you want it to do?"

"It doesn't listen very well." She keyed *Jack the Ripper* into the search engine. The resulting list contained thousands of entries; she clicked on the most likely looking selection on the first page.

The site was loaded with an astonishing amount of information, everything from morgue photos to police statements to transcripts of newspaper articles of the time. There was even the lyrics of "Sweet Violets," the song Mary Kelly had sung to Druas. Jane printed it all out and went to the next site. Baran picked up the printouts, sat down in the second office chair, and started scanning them, Freika standing on his hind legs to read over his shoulder.

More than an hour later she turned off the computer and sat back in her seat, scrubbing her hands over her face. "Well, now we've got the opposite problem—too much information, most of it unreliable, and no way to tell what Druas actually did. We can't even be sure he killed the five that are usually attributed to the Ripper."

The Whitechapel killer was thought to have murdered five women in London between the dates of August 31 and November 9, 1888: Mary Ann "Polly" Nichols on August 31, Annie Chapman on September 8, Elizabeth Stride and Catherine Eddowes, both on September 30, and Mary Jane Kelly on November 9. But some researchers believed he'd killed other women as well, and there was considerable disagreement whether Eddowes was actually a Ripper victim at all.

"For what it's worth," Freika said, "the file TE gave me indicates they do think Druas murdered all five of the women."

"That makes sense," Baran said. "If the point is to enact the historical murders, he'd do all of them."

Jane picked up a pencil and tapped it restlessly on the desk. "What about all those letters that were supposedly from the killer, including the one they took the Ripper name from—did he write any of them or not?" Even at the time, police believed most of the letters were frauds, written by unscrupulous journalists.

Baran shuffled through the stack. "Who knows? Though the package sent to this George Lusk with part of a kidney in it certainly might be genuine."

"Judging from my file on him, it does sound like the kind of thing Druas would do," Frieka said.

"Eeewww." Jane put the pencil in her mouth and bit down, sinking her teeth in the wood while she thought. "I didn't know the Ripper strangled those women first, but all the autopsies do seem to indicate that. The mutilations were done postmortem, getting progressively worse as he went along." She grimaced and tossed the pencil aside. "Which doesn't sound good for the women of Tayanita County."

Including Jane herself. *Better not think about that.* She'd rather not have to race to the bathroom again.

Baran was still flipping through the stack. "What's really ironic is all these elaborate theories about his identity. An English prince, a writer named Lewis Carroll . . ."

"Off with her head," Jane muttered.

". . . an artist, a doctor, even a woman. And each and every theory was dead wrong."

"Funny how a time-traveling cyborg mercenary never made the list." She rolled her eyes. "What were they thinking?"

They sat discussing the murders until even Jane's vibrating tension couldn't withstand the need for sleep any longer. She suggested calling it a night.

Baran nodded. "That's a good idea. We'll all be able to think a little clearer in the morning." He stood, plainly waiting for her to lead the way.

Ohhhhh, boy, Jane realized. *He'll have to sleep in the same room with me.* The sensual awareness that had dogged her rose on a gentle wave of heat. Even the horrors of the night evidently hadn't managed to kill the attraction she felt. "The bedroom is upstairs."

"I know." He said the words briskly, without a trace of innuendo.

"I'll stay down here and keep watch," Freika said. "Druas may surprise all of us and actually use the door."

Jane glanced at him. Despite his bland offer, the look in those lupine eyes was knowing and amused. *Damn*, she thought, *even Wolfie expects us to get it on.*

And he was probably right, she thought as she led the way upstairs. At least judging by the warm tingle spreading through her breasts. After the night she'd had, who'd have thought her battered brain could even produce that much hormone?

Battered or not, though, she was acutely aware of Baran's potent male presence as he followed her into the bedroom. Fighting to ignore it, she tried to decide what to wear to bed that wouldn't make her look as if she were inviting a bout of Warlord love.

Despite her body's interest, she knew she wasn't up to entertaining his libido. From the looks of that big body, it would be an exhausting proposition.

On the other hand, she didn't care to bed down in the jeans and shirt she was wearing, either. It would be hard enough to get any rest as it was.

Pretending to ignore her brawny houseguest, Jane crossed to her cherry dresser, hoping to find something unattractive. The first thing she saw when she opened the drawer was a skimpy lace teddy. She buried it a little deeper and dug out a sleep shirt that was so big Baran could have worn it himself. After excavating a pair of baggy gray sweats to complete the keep-your-distance look, she started for the bathroom.

A hand caught the door before she could swing it closed. Baran stepped into the room after her.

"Hey, back off," she protested. "I need to change and . . . stuff."

"Didn't we cover this downstairs? I go where you go."

"Baran, you can't follow me into every ladies' room in Tayanita County. That's just not going to work."

"Why not?"

She sighed with elaborate patience. "Because the other ladies will not like it."

"I don't see any other ladies here, Jane."

"Baran . . ."

He folded powerful arms and lifted a dark brow.

She threw up her hands. "Fine, whatever. Can you at least turn your back?"

"Why?"

"Okay, now you're being a pain in the butt." She reached for patience and gritted, "I don't want to take off my clothes in front of you!"

That eyebrow climbed another fraction. "I hate to destroy whatever illusions you cherish, but I have seen naked women before."

"Yeah, well, you haven't seen *this* woman naked."

Baran sighed at her surly tone. "Jane, I'm a soldier. Half my fellow soldiers are female. In combat conditions you quickly learn you don't have to have sex with every woman you see without her clothes." He smiled slightly, rubbing his jaw like a man remembering a right cross. "When I was sixteen, I had a female sergeant once who . . . Well, I didn't make that mistake again."

He was in combat when he was sixteen? She shook her head, deciding to explore that topic some other time. "Regardless of your experience, I don't undress in front of men I don't know. And I'm going to change this sweater. It smells like . . . never mind what it smells like, I'm not wearing it another minute."

Baran leaned back against the door and looked amused. "Go ahead. I'll try to control my lust."

Something about that silent get-over-yourself air ignited her temper. "Fine," she snarled, grabbing the hem of her top. "You want me to undress? Okay, I'll undress." In a single violent gesture she jerked it up and over her head and threw it directly at his face.

He caught the shirt out of the air and tossed it into a corner. His indifferent gaze didn't even flicker.

She snarled. Suddenly the helpless fear that had battered her all night morphed into full-blown, defiant rage.

Jane twisted her arms behind her back, unfastened her bra, and stripped it off. She was too furious to feel embarrassed when her full breasts sprang free, nipples instantly pebbling. From, of course, the cool air.

Baran lifted a bored brow. *So?*

Jerk. Jane reached for her waistband and ripped open the button of her fly. Her zipper hissed loudly as she tugged it down and started squirming her way free. Her bare breasts bounced. She could almost feel him watching. Despite her anger, something heated low in her belly.

Her own reaction making her even angrier, she gave her butt a gratuitous wiggle as she struggled free of her pants and kicked them viciously aside. Dressed only in a silky thin pair of scarlet panties, she straightened to her full height and glared at him.

He couldn't have looked more indifferent if he'd been watching a commercial for feminine hygiene products. He wasn't even hard. Except . . .

His eyes were glowing again.

If Baran hadn't instructed his computer to keep him from becoming erect, he would have had a hard-on up to his rib cage.

Yet he'd meant what he'd said. He was used to seeing women— and other men, for that matter—walking around in various states of undress. He barely noticed anymore.

But those were battle-toughened fems, lithe, muscular warriors who could hold their own, whether in a brawl or in bed. If they were unbonded and you expressed an interest, they'd sleep with you as casually as he'd scratch Freika's skull jack when it itched. They always gave good sex—he'd never had bad sex—but it wasn't anything to get worked up about.

But Jane Colby's deliciously full, pointed breasts were a different matter altogether. He wanted to taste one of those tight pink nipples so badly, his balls ached.

Unfortunately, the look she was giving him was pure, unadulterated go-to-hell. Despite his powers, he strongly suspected if he touched her, she'd make him pay.

But those pretty nipples might just be worth it. . . .

Blithely ignoring how close Baran was to losing control, Jane curled a delicate lip at him and turned her back with a mocking roll of her ass.

His gaze followed the long, sweet indentation of her spine down to her narrow waist and rounded behind. Her butt was clad only in something thin and silky and bright red, and there were two tempting little dimples right above her waistband. He pictured cupping that pretty butt in his hands while he lowered her onto his shaft. . . .

She picked up the shirt she'd brought in with her and started dragging it on over her head. Her long, silken back curved and twisted with the motion, as if daring him to reach out and touch. He controlled his hungry hands with an effort.

She put on the pants next, sliding in one long leg at a time before slowly pulling the baggy fabric up over her thighs. Her firm behind flexed as she twitched the loose bottoms into place. Baran seriously considered bending her over that marble countertop and pulling them down again.

Throttle back, Warlord. Keep it together.

It didn't help that every breath he took was scented with arousal—his own, and hers. Despite her irritation, she was getting just as hot as he was.

Unfortunately, he'd made such a point of being immune to her nudity, he couldn't afford to indulge in any of the things he so badly wanted to do. She needed to trust him, and he needed to remain firmly in control. He knew he'd seduce her eventually, but now wasn't the time.

Maintaining his blank expression, he set his jaw and clamped a grip over his lust.

"I need to use the toilet, Baran," she said, sounding reluctant, as if it galled her to ask. "Step outside a second. I promise to scream if Druas beams in like Captain Kirk."

He grappled for his fraying patience. "Jane, every minute is *every minute*. I'm not going to risk getting you killed to preserve your twenty-first-century concept of modesty."

True, the chances that the killer would Jump into the bathroom at this particular instant were pretty slim. Unfortunately, Baran knew those odds would increase as time went on and the killer took up sensor surveillance. He had to establish standard procedure now so Jane wouldn't balk over it later.

She whirled to glare at him. "This is embarrassing, dammit!" Her breasts rose and fell behind that too-big shirt that didn't hide nearly as much as she thought it did. "It's one thing to do a strip tease, but there are certain bodily functions I don't like to share. Period. And somehow, I don't think women three hundred years from now feel any differently."

"People do all kinds of things in combat they wouldn't normally do."

"This isn't combat!"

"Actually, it is." But he turned his back anyway, the gesture designed to silently underscore that he'd gone as far as he intended to.

He knew he'd made his point.

Jerk.

Jane was still simmering when Baran led the way back into the bedroom a few moments later. He could have stepped out of the room for sixty seconds; he didn't have to be such a dominant schmuck about it. He . . .

Slid out of the leather coat and tossed it over the armchair, then grabbed his sweater and pulled it over his head. Muscle rippled up and down his long, powerful back with the movement.

She gaped at the sudden expanse of deliciously bare Baran as he bent to pull off his boots. He looked as if God had sculpted every ridge, muscle, and hollow personally as an illustration to lesser mortals.

That, or the Devil had done the sculpting in order to tempt vulnerable females into sin. . . .

Then he started pulling his pants down his long thighs, and Jane roused from her hypnotized shock. "What the hell are you doing?" She knew exactly what he was doing, of course.

This was payback.

Very effective payback, too. The man had the most gorgeous male butt she'd ever seen, particularly clad only in a pair of tight, white jockies.

Baran calmly turned, folding his pants. The view from the front was even more stunning. His broad, V-shaped torso looked as if it belonged on the cover of a romance novel, the kind good Southern mothers threw in the trash. Most powerfully built men tended to look a little short-legged, but Baran's were as long as the rest of his body. And in between . . .

Well, he didn't strike her as the type to stuff a sock in his shorts, so that bulge had to be real. Considering that he wasn't even erect, the man had to be hung like a Brahma bull.

And the grin he was wearing as he watched her check him out reminded her of his furry partner downstairs—all white, wicked teeth and dishonorable intentions.

Yeah, this was Operation Payback, all right. "What are you doing?" she demanded again.

The wicked gleam in his eyes intensified. *What would you like me to do?* But if he was thinking the question, he didn't ask it. "Getting ready for bed."

Jane folded her arms, ignoring the hot, eager trickle she felt somewhere south of her waistband. "You'd better not be about to tell me you sleep in the nude," she said. "Because your butt is going to need some padding when you bunk down on the floor."

"What I've got on now is sufficient," he said coolly. "And I have no intention of sleeping on the floor. I need to be close to you."

"You know, somehow I get the impression you're milking this," she said, eyeing him. "But I've got to be wrong. You couldn't be that big a jerk."

He propped big fists on his hips, silently tempting her eyes back to that intriguing bulge. "Is that any way to talk to a man who came three hundred years to save your luscious . . . neck?"

"That depends on what you're planning to charge me for it."

"I don't charge."

But you're not above enjoying whatever fringe benefits you can get, either. She clamped her lips shut before she could say the words. "Fine. Whatever. Just keep your distance."

Jane waited for some silken comeback, but he made no reply. Pointedly ignoring him, she stalked to the bed and flipped back the covers. Her copy of *Dark Passion* flew out of the covers and sailed through the air. He snagged it in midflight and handed it back to her.

"Interesting reading." The purr in Baran's voice was a perfect match to the predatory grin on his face.

Her own face heated as she remembered the scene she'd been enjoying when she'd heard the murder call earlier that evening. The hero had just tied up the heroine and . . .

"If you'd been any kind of gentleman, you would have kept your nose out of my book!"

He contemplated the point, then grinned that slow, wicked grin again. "Actually, if I understand the term—I don't believe I *am* a gentleman."

"I noticed!" With a huff she tossed the paperback on the nightstand, climbed into bed, turned her back on him, and curled tightly into a defensive ball.

He laughed softly. The mattress sank as he slid onto it. "Do you normally sleep with the lights on?"

She hissed and jumped up to flip the switch, then turned back toward the bed.

And stopped dead, the hair rising on the back of her neck. His eyes were glowing again, shining in the darkness like a special effect in a horror flick. And after viewing that recording, she didn't need anything else gnawing at her fragile composure. "Could you not do that?"

"Do what?" His voice was a velvety male purr, intimate and seductive.

"The glowing bit with the eyes." Trying not to look at him, she hurried back to the bed and slipped between the covers. "It's unnerving as hell."

"Unfortunately, that's one of the few body functions I have no control over. They're designed that way."

"Sounds like a serious drawback in battle." Small talk. Yeah. Get him thinking about something other than sex. Get *herself* thinking about something other than sex.

"I normally wear an armored helmet. The visor hides them."

She rolled over to face him and propped her head on her palm. "So why do they? Glow."

He sighed. "Jane, I thought the idea of going to bed was to sleep."

"I just wondered."

"Let's talk about it tomorrow."

"Fine."

But half an hour later Jane was still awake, her burning eyes fixed on the ceiling. She could hear Baran's steady breathing in the bed next to her, feel his sold, comforting presence.

But every time she closed her lids, she saw a flash of silver and a spray of red, heard Druas humming that snatch of song as he . . .

She felt so damn cold.

Curling on her side, Jane drew her legs up and wrapped her arms around her body. She shivered. She'd been all right as long as Baran had been awake to fight with, but now in the silent darkness the horror came rushing back.

It suddenly hit her the killer had been humming the same song he'd made Mary Kelly sing.

Jesus. Jack the Ripper intended to turn her into the star of a pornographic snuff video for a gang of perverts three hundred years in the future. And she was sleeping next to a time traveler who'd come back all those centuries to protect her.

When had her life become an episode of the *Twilight Zone*?

She was so tired her eyeballs ached, but the idea of going to sleep made her heart pound. She knew she'd find Druas and his knife in her dreams.

If only Baran would wake up and distract her again with one of those mind-bending lectures on time travel delivered with those hot bedroom eyes. Even if they did glow in the dark.

God, she was cold.

Had it hurt when Druas slit Mary Kelly's throat, or had she already been dead?

Cut it out, dammit.

She shivered again, but this time she had trouble stopping. She curled tighter, hugging her knees. And slowly became aware of a sense of warmth at her back.

Baran.

He seemed to radiate heat like a big male furnace. She found herself inching in his direction.

She tried to think of what she would do in the morning, how she'd protect herself. Her father's old .38 revolver was packed away with the rest of his stuff up in the attic, but she hadn't practiced with it in years. Maybe she should go to the firing range. . . .

Damn, Baran was warm. Jane edged a little closer and bumped into his hard, muscular side.

She slid away.

Practice. She needed to dig the gun out and practice with it. And what was she going to tell Tom Reynolds? She might know who the killer was, but she'd never be able to tell the police. God forbid they actually catch him—from what Baran had said, Druas would rip them apart.

Hell, she'd be lucky if he didn't rip *her* apart.

Don't think about that, Jane. Go to sleep.

She curled tighter into herself and tried to ignore all the man-shaped pools of blackness in the room her imagination wanted to turn into serial killers. Temptingly close to her back, Baran slept, big and warm, breathing quietly. Stranger or not, she wished her pride would let her curl into his arms.

She was so tired, so wrung out from the terror and rage that had filled her night. Her eyelids slid closed, only to snap open again. She didn't want to sleep, didn't want to dream, but she was tired. So tired. So . . .

T hey were fighting again.

Jane crouched under the dining room table, hidden by the drape of the linen tablecloth. Ducking her head, she cupped shaking hands over her ears as her father screamed insults at her mother. Her heart was pounding inside her Cabbage Patch Kids pajamas. They'd fought before, but this was worse. So much worse.

She felt sick.

"If you walk out that door, Jeanine, I swear to God you'll never see Jane again!"

"You can't do that! She's my child. I'll sue for custody."

"You won't get it. People in this county owe me, and don't think they won't pay their debts."

"And don't think I won't tell them what you've done to me!"

His laugh was dark and ugly. "You can't prove anything."

"Don't bet on it. I've got photos, Bill."

The silence that stretched between them jangled until Jane began to cry, stuffing her pajama top into her mouth to stifle any noise.

"Where?" Her father's low, deadly snarl made her freeze like a rabbit.

"Where you'll never find them. I've got a friend you don't know anything about. I told her everything. She'll—"

"She? Or he?" Jane heard the familiar sound of a slap and squeezed her eyes shut. "Is it a he?"

"No!"

"Who?"

"I'm not telling you! But she'll testify, and the photos . . ."

His laugh was mocking. "They won't care, Jeanine. This is South Carolina."

"And I'm Jane's mother, and South Carolina judges think ten-year-old girls belong with their mothers. Particularly if their fathers are abusive, *wife-beating . . . Hit me again and I swear I'll go to the police. How will that look in your precious paper?"*

Jane could hear him breathing.

"Jane!" Her mother's shout almost startled a scream out of her. She clamped both hands over her mouth. "Jane, come on. We're leaving."

"All right, bitch, you can go. But she's staying."

"I'm not leaving without—"

"She's a Colby, Jeanine. I'm leaving the paper to her, just like Colbys have for a hundred years. You're not taking her out of this town."

"I'm not leaving without her."

They went quiet again. Jane, too terrified to move, swallowed hard and fought against the need to throw up.

"If you don't leave without her," her father said, in a low, deadly voice, "I'm going to kill you."

A hot tear plopped onto Jane's bare foot. She stuffed her pajama top deeper into her mouth.

Her mother laughed, her voice too high, too wild. "They'd catch you, Bill."

"I've covered a lot of trials, Jeanine. You think I don't know how to create reasonable doubt?"

Jane fought not to sob. She knew she didn't dare give herself away.

"Get out, Jeanine," her father said, his voice soft and cold. "And you'd better not apply for custody."

Jane heard the door slam. Something hit the wall with a crash. Glass broke. Her father began to curse, his voice vicious with rage.

She curled tighter into a ball and quivered. If he found her . . .

Jane jolted awake to find herself standing in darkness.

"Jane?"

She whirled, stifling her scream from long habit. Moonlight streamed in the window, silhouetting the big male figure sitting up in the bed.

Seven

"Are you all right? You jumped out of bed as if someone shot you, but my sensors say you're uninjured." Recognizing Baran's deep, sleep-roughened voice at last, Jane slumped.

"I'm fine. Just a nightmare." The oldest one in her collection. She supposed it wasn't surprising she'd had it, given the circumstances.

Particularly since after Jeanine Colby had walked out the door that night, Jane had never seen her again. Her father had told people for years his wife had left to take care of her sick mother. When Jane had questioned him as a teenager, he'd produced letters addressed to Jane he'd claimed were from Jeanine. The handwriting had matched what she'd found in the family Bible, so Jane had decided her mother had simply gone into hiding.

But the doubts had lingered, so as an adult, she'd hired a private detective to search for her mother. He never found anything.

Maybe Jeanine had done a very good job of covering her tracks from the husband who'd abused her. Then again, maybe William Colby had carried through on his threats. A year ago Jane had finally decided to tell the police about her suspicions, but before she could go through with her plans, he'd suffered his fatal stroke.

Now she'd never know if her father had been a murderer.

"Is there anything you need?" Baran asked, jolting her out of her preoccupation.

"No." She laughed shortly. "Well, maybe a good therapist."

"Why don't you come back to bed?"

She eyed him as he sat against the head of the bed, his glorious bare chest silvered in a shaft of moonlight. He looked big and strong and safe. And just then, she was in desperate need of safety.

Jane crossed the bedroom to slide under the covers he lifted for her. He curled onto his side facing her, silently offering her the shelter of his body. His skin seemed to radiate a seductive heat, as though his natural body temperature was high. She felt too battered to refuse. She eased into the curve of one muscled arm. A hand came up to rub her back, so big it almost spanned the width of her torso.

"Your skin is cold," he said softly, drawing her farther into his arms as he rolled onto his back. The movement draped her over his chest like a scarf. "Let me warm you."

Yeah, I'll bet you'd be good at that, she thought with weary cynicism. The thing was, she felt so traumatized she'd probably let herself be seduced, if only for the illusion of safety she'd find in his arms.

But he made no further advances, instead rubbing her back in slow, gentle strokes. His chest felt broad and strong and hard under her cheek, and his heat enveloped her. Gradually she began to relax.

As she settled into him, Jane realized he had an erection. The long shaft pressed gently against the curve of her belly through her sweatpants. She tensed, but he did nothing more. Demanded nothing more.

And he felt so safe. Jane had experienced so damn little safety in her life, she found it difficult to resist. So she stayed where she was, despite that silently tempting erection, and savored his warmth.

She could feel the sculpted ridges of his muscles, the faint tickle of his body hair against her skin. He even smelled delicious. Every time she inhaled, her head filled with the spicy male musk of his scent. His arm lay curved around her shoulder, a comforting weight. She let her eyes close. Surely now . . .

Red splattered the walls. Eyes opened wide in shock, a screaming mouth . . .

Jane's screaming mouth.

Or was it Jeanine's?

She jerked upright out of his loose hold. Sitting up with a gulping sob, she buried her face in her hands. "You were right. I shouldn't have looked at that damn recording. I've tried, but I can't stop thinking about it. . . ."

"Yes, you can." Sheets rustled and the bed shifted under his weight. Warm hands closed over her wrists, pulled hers away from her face. "I'll help you."

Jane looked up blindly in the darkness, saw the shimmer of his eyes an instant before his mouth came down over hers. She tried to pull away, startled, but long fingers tangled in her hair and held her still. The kiss was an easy, practiced slide of his mouth against hers, carefully undemanding.

Jane had expected skill, but Baran's tenderness took her by surprise. His tongue caressed her lower lip, then entered her mouth in a long erotic stroke. His mouth tasted of a sweet, spicy something she couldn't identify. Strong hands closed gently around her shoulders, turned, and lowered her to the mattress. She cupped her palms around the curve of his shoulders. They more than filled her hands. "We shouldn't do this."

"Probably not," he murmured. "But it seems we're going to do it anyway."

"Yeah," she said, and sobbed in a breath as he cuddled her breasts through her shirt. "Just help me not to think. Just keep me from seeing . . ." Mother. ". . . Mary die."

"I can do that." Strong teeth closed gently over her lower lip, gave it a cool tug, then scraped softly against the curve of her jaw until they found a tendon. Stopped to nibble. "Just concentrate on this."

His hands slid up under the hem of her T, pushed it upward. She felt the cool draft on her erect nipples for only a moment before Baran's warm, long fingers covered one breast. Cupped lightly.

You don't know him, sanity whispered.

I don't care.

His long hair tumbled across her skin as he lowered his head to find one nipple. The heat of his claiming mouth made her spine arch.

"I've been wanting to do that for hours," he rumbled against her skin, and licked the pointed tip. "Ever since I scented your heat in that pretty red silk gown." He groaned. "God, that book of yours made you wet."

She inhaled sharply. He gave her nipple a delicate rake with his teeth. Pleasure danced up her spine. "You . . . you could smell that? On my clothes?" She knew she should be outraged, but just now she was too grateful for the distraction.

"Mmm," he said, and laughed, soft and dark. "My nose is almost as good as Freika's. In fact, it tells me you're creaming now." He suckled, making her squirm.

"I can't believe you sniffed my nightgown"—she had to stop to gasp—"when you'd never even met me."

That dark laugh rolled over her again, making her shiver. "I not only sniffed it, I seriously considered wrapping it around my cock." Another wicked almost-bite sent delight throbbing through her nipples as his long fingers squeezed and teased. "It's been a very long time since I've ridden a woman, and you tempt me."

Something about the rough, dark way he phrased it sent a quiver through her. "Yeah," she managed through the flood of heat, "I did pick up on that part. Your eyes glow whenever you're—"

"Aroused. Or angry." He swirled his tongue over one tight point, then lowered his head to find the curve where her rib cage met her waist. "You've got a talent for making me both."

He laved her belly button until she squirmed. Her giggle was cut off by his fingers hooking into the waistband of her sweats.

"I don't like these," he said. "Don't wear them again." Before she could work up any outrage at that blunt order, he started pulling them down. "I want to feel your bare legs wrapped around my ass."

Her head spun. "Okay," she panted as he stripped them ruthlessly off. "But just so we're clear, you're not telling me what to wear."

Baran's eyes flashed at her through the darkness, red and bright as coals before he turned to toss the pants across the room. She heard the soft thump as they landed. "Oh, yes, I am. You're going to do every last thing I order you to do."

"Not when you're just being a sexist jerk."

"Every last thing, Jane," he insisted, leaning close until his breath gusted warm on her ear. "Instantly. Without stopping to parse out whether you agree. Because it's the only way I can keep you alive." A big hand wrapped in the fragile fabric of her panties and twisted. The silk pulled at her hips and the tops of her thighs before it ripped.

"Hey!" She glared up at his dark shadow looming over her. "You didn't have to do that!"

His eyes gleamed as he moved back down her body like the erotic predator he was. "No, but I wanted to. Just like I want to do this." He dipped his tongue between her outer labia, a wet, tempting stroke along sensitive flesh and soft hair.

She was still gasping at that sensation when she felt him move between her thighs, broad shoulders forcing them wide. His mouth descended to the lips that had grown steadily more creamy with every stroke and lick and hot male purr.

She groaned, instinctively fisting the sheets on either side of her hips. To her shock, his hands clamped down over hers, pinning them to the mattress. "What are you doing?" she gasped.

"Making sure you don't go anywhere." That clever tongue flicked between her labia and over her clit, burning hot as he lapped her up like cream. She squirmed helplessly, gasping. With a satisfied rumble, he closed his mouth over her tender lips and drank from her before using his teeth on the delicate flesh.

It was all she could do to form words as he bit and sucked and nibbled. "Just because I . . . read a book with a bondage scene, it . . . AH! . . . doesn't mean I want to be held down!"

"No, but I want to do it anyway. And where you're concerned"— he paused to do something wicked with that long, clever tongue—"I do exactly what I want."

A cascade of fire raced up her spine, tearing a gasp from her lips. She writhed as the orgasm swamped her consciousness, instinctively trying to pull away from his overwhelming mouth. His hands tightened their grip, keeping her ruthlessly pinned as he sucked so hard her every nerve detonated in an erotic Fourth of July.

Jane screamed, convulsing against his mouth, grinding her hips against his face.

The fire took a long, long time to die. She was still quivering when he sat up, grabbed her hips, and flipped her onto her belly.

She opened her eyes, dazed, and looked around at him as he pulled her onto her knees. He didn't even take the time to remove his briefs—just tugged them down enough to free his jutting cock into the spill of moonlight.

"Now," he said, in a dark voice rich with male anticipation, "it's my turn."

Something hard brushed Jane's slick opening. Her head jerked up in shock at the diameter of Baran's shaft as he slowly impaled her, one mind-blowing inch at a time.

"Oh, you *are* tight." He came down over her, covering her back in hard, sweaty muscle as he purred in her ear. "And slick. Have a little more of me."

"Jesus, Baran!" She gasped as he drove in even deeper, slow, thick, and endless. Moaning, she fought to brace her hands beneath her and rise to all fours, but he caught her wrists and pinned them again, trapping her on her elbows with her ass lifted into his stroke.

Finally he was all the way in. "Mmmmm. How does this feel?"

Jane could only pant. She could feel her own slick interior stretching around his impaling shaft. Stuffed almost to the point of pain, she whimpered. She'd never been so turned on in her life. "Good. God, it's good. You bastard."

He rumbled a laugh in her ear. "I'll take that as a compliment."

Then he started to pull out. Slowly. Silk and width and heat, sliding from her deliciously. Out. And out. And out.

And in. And in. And in.

"Just so you . . . oh, GOD . . . know, just because I let you do this to me . . . in bed," she gasped, "that doesn't mean I'm going to . . . AH! . . . let you dominate me anywhere else."

He laughed, low and wicked, and started stroking out. "Oh, yes, you will. I'll make sure of it."

"No. No, I . . ." Out. And out. She whimpered.

"Darling, you won't be able to stop me. Not that you'll want to. I'm told I've got a talent for it."

The velvet amusement in his voice barely registered in the hot rise of another climax. The only response she could manage was a scream.

The pleasure spiraled tighter and hotter until it exploded, twisting her into convulsions in the cage of his arms. He kept pumping, hot and hard, in short, ruthless strokes that drove everything else out of her head.

Her orgasm built even higher under that merciless stoking, burning and ferocious, unlike anything she'd ever known in her life. Helpless in the grip of it, Jane yowled, mindless, forgetting Druas and her father and everything else but Baran Arvid's demanding body.

She was still drowning in the fire when she heard his triumphant roar as he came, deep in her pulsing sex.

R*eluctantly Baran slid out of Jane's hot, delicious clasp. As he* collapsed on his back, panting, he heard her whimper once. "Oh, God, that was . . . I never felt anything like that."

He felt his lips twitch in an automatic male smile that felt distinctly smug.

Though come to think of it, she'd been more than he'd expected, too. There'd been something in the way she'd responded, a pure female heat mixed with a curious . . . innocence? Wonder? Something very different from what he was used to.

Desperation, a cynical mental voice suggested.

Well, yeah, that was part of it. He'd had some pretty incredible sex the night before a battle. There was nothing like the possibility of death to add a rough power to passion.

Yet somehow, taking Jane had felt more . . . personal than that.

The mattress sank under him, kicking his senses instantly to alert, but it was only Jane rolling onto her side. Her arm encircled him as one small, cool hand came to rest on his chest. He heard her sigh once before her breathing deepened into sleep.

Good. With any luck, he'd done such a good job wearing her out, she wouldn't have any more nightmares.

He only hoped he could say the same.

Her fingers felt so cool and delicate against his hot flesh, so small. Her palm felt like silk, without the callouses of weapon use or combat he was used to in the Warfems he'd bedded.

Vulnerable.

She was so helplessly vulnerable. If he'd tried to hold down a Warfem the way he'd pinned Jane, he'd have had a fight on his hands.

Oh, he could have done it. His partner might even have decided to submit as part of the game. But fems were never truly helpless; their strength was two or three times that of a normal human male. A Warlord was even stronger, of course, but a really determined Warfem could still turn the tables.

Jane couldn't. She couldn't have broken his hold no matter what he'd chosen to do to her.

And if it had been Druas who'd pinned her . . .

He couldn't move. They'd ordered his computer to lock his body on his knees. Helpless. He heard laughter, then Liisa's voice. Screaming. The sound ripped at him. He struggled desperately to move, to break out of the paralysis, but his computer wouldn't allow it, wouldn't release him.

Then he felt . . .

Shit. Baran shut the memory down and rolled out of bed in a convulsive burst of motion, barely aware of Jane's slim hand dropping limply away. Adjusting the briefs he'd tugged down to take her, he strode to the window, automatically positioned himself out of the path of fire. *Scan, computer. Check for Xeran life indications.*

The response came back an instant later. *No Xer detected.*

He stared out at the darkness, his jaw clamped tight, his hands curled into fists. He shouldn't be here. He should be on Xer with Freika, stalking General Jutka and waiting for his chance to put his ghosts to rest. The General's bodyguards would probably execute him afterward, but he really didn't care. He owed it to Liisa, to Lieutenant Ullock, to Thorp and Ive.

The team he'd failed to die with.

"Wait," he whispered to the darkness. "I'll get it done."

But first he had to take care of Jane.

He glanced back at the bed. She lay curled in a defensive ball on top of the sheets. One of her feet twitched. He hoped she wasn't having yet another nightmare.

Not that he could afford to care.

It was fine to spread her, to play hot games that taught her his strength and conditioned her to yield to him. The obedience he built in bed might pay off later when she followed some crucial order at some crucial moment. If she became obsessed with him, so much the better.

But he couldn't afford to become obsessed in turn. She was a job, no different from the rescue of the admiral's daughter, or that Vardonese scientist, or any of those he'd saved. Just another mission on the way to the only one that counted: looking into the eyes of General Gavoni Jutka and watching the bastard's life drain away.

Baran had gotten all the others who'd tortured and killed his team, or at least all the ones whose names he'd been able to discover. He'd stalked them patiently, challenged them one by one.

All except the bastard who'd murdered Liisa. He'd never been able to discover that one's name. But Jutka knew. He had to. And he'd give Baran that final name before he died.

One way or another.

But not tonight.

With a sigh Baran moved back to the bed and stood looking down at Jane. With his enhanced senses, he could plainly see the way her lashes fanned over her cheeks in the dark, her mouth relaxed in a full pout. He thought about kissing her again, tasting those velvet lips.

Keep your distance, warned a mental voice. *Don't get too close. Don't let her get too close.*

He moved around the bed, pulled free the sheet that was trapped under Jane's sleeping form. Climbing in beside her, he covered them both and started to reach for her. He wanted to feel her delicate warmth against him.

He stopped the gesture in midmotion. Better not.

Instead he rolled over on his side until he faced away from her, leaving a comfortable distance between them. His back felt cool. For a moment he imagined what she'd feel like spooning him from behind, all curves and silken warmth.

Then he shut down the thought and closed his eyes. *Computer, enable sleep. Scanners to full. Alert me if you detect anything.*

Engaged, the comp said. He felt the tension drain from his body as the comp flooded his brain with the slow, deep wave patterns of sleep.

He knew nothing else.

Jane snapped her eyes open with a choked whimper and stared wildly at the wall bathed in the golden glow of morning sunlight. For an instant she had a memory of bloody dreams. Then the memory fled, and she was left with nothing but an impression of terror and violence.

She was glad. Her current reality was bad enough as it was. Except for . . .

Baran.

She turned over quickly, half hoping to discover he'd been nothing but a dream himself. Along with the concept of Jack the Ripper bouncing merrily through time killing people . . .

No. There he was, handsome and sound asleep, long hair tumbling around his tattooed face as he lay on his side facing her. His chest seemed to loom like a muscled wall, soft chest hair curling in a tempting cloud across its breadth. He was so damn gorgeous, she wanted to touch him just to see if he was real.

Which was no reason to *sleep* with the man mere hours after he'd broken into her house. Damn, that was the kind of thing romance heroines did, not real, living people who paid bills and ran a newspaper. She couldn't believe she'd let him seduce her like that.

Then she looked at the soft line of his mouth, the fan of his long eyelashes over his cheeks, the truly outstanding width of his shoulders. . . .

Okay, maybe she could believe it.

She sighed. And promptly grimaced at the nasty taste in her mouth. If Baran woke up and decided to give her one of those incredible kisses, he'd be appalled. Time to brush the teeth.

Among other things, she mentally added, noticing the pressure in her bladder.

Jane started to roll out of bed, then stopped. He'd told her he had to be with her at all times. But what was she supposed to do— wake him out of a sound sleep and say, *Hey, wake up. I have to pee?* She didn't think so.

She'd make it quick and be back in bed before he—

A strong male hand snapped out to wrap around her wrist. She looked down to see Baran had opened one eye to look at her. "Where are you going?" his voice was sleep graveled. And astonishingly sexy. It just wasn't fair.

"I didn't mean to wake you. . . ."

"You did anyway. Where are you going?"

"Bathroom break."

He lifted his head from the pillow, yawned hugely, let her go, and rolled smoothly to his feet. "One more time, Jane—you don't go *anywhere* without me."

"For God's sake, Baran, the Secret Service isn't this paranoid!"

His gaze turned abstracted. She realized his computer was probably feeding him the meaning of the term—and probably the complete history of the Service, all the way back to the day it was created. Growling, she bent to snatch her sleep shirt off the floor, then jerked it down over her head. She looked around for her pants and found them on the other side of the room.

As she recovered them and put them on again, she looked around to see him watching her, mouth flattened with displeasure. "Unlike you, your President doesn't have Jack the Ripper after him."

"No, just every other nutball on the planet." Janet turned and stomped toward the bathroom, resentfully aware that Baran dogged her heels. "I know what this is about, by the way. I lived for twenty-two years with a dominant jerk, and I know all the games. Daddy played them, each and every one. 'I'm the man, and you'll do what I say. Or else!' No wonder Mom made for the hills." If she had. If her father hadn't . . .

"What *are* you talking about?"

"My father, alpha male of the universe." She plopped down on the toilet. "Turn your back, dammit."

Baran obeyed. "What has he got to do with this?"

"He thought women were naturally inferior, too. An old-fashioned, Southern-fried, sexist . . ." Wife-abuser, but Baran didn't need to know that part. "So you can imagine how thrilled he was when his only offspring turned out to be female."

Baran turned back around to gape at her. "Naturally inferior? Women? I never said that."

"Yeah? So what's with the 'You're going to obey my every command' crap? Turn your back, dammit."

"That's not about your being a woman! That's about your being a *civilian*."

Finished, she rose and stalked to the sink to wash her hands. "Same difference."

"No. It's not." Baran angled his head down until he was nose to nose with her. His eyes were beginning to glow again. "I will fight Druas for you, Jane. That's a given. But it's not going to be easy, because from what Freika said, he's at least my match in strength. He may even be stronger. And considering what we both know he's capable of, that may not turn out well for me."

Jane had to fight the impulse to step back from the red-hot threads of rage burning in his irises. Instead she grabbed a towel and started drying her hands. "Yeah, I'm aware of that. I really am. And I'm grateful. But that still doesn't give you the right to push me around!"

"The point is, I'm willing to die for you." He bared his teeth and gritted, "But I'm not willing to die for your stupidity!"

For a moment she stared at him in shock. Then her rage exploded. "Fuck you, Baran." Throwing the towel into his face, she stormed from the room.

Eight

Baran grabbed her wrist, jerking her to a stop just outside the door. She looked down at the hand that gripped her, then slowly raised her eyes to glare at him. In her mind's eye she saw every time her father had ever grabbed her mother, every time he'd pushed, every time he'd slapped. "Let. Go."

He glared. Jane peeled her lips away from her teeth as her fury burned hotter. She knew in that moment that if he lifted his free hand, she was going to hit him with everything she had, no matter how much bigger and stronger he was.

Slowly a faint alarm replaced the rage in his eyes, as if he realized just how close she was to the edge. Carefully he released his grip and stepped back.

That backward step was one her father had never taken. Somehow it pricked Jane's fury like a bubble. She slumped, deflating as the rage drained away, leaving only weariness behind. "I won't be abused, Baran. Not even by a man who promises to protect me from Jack the Ripper."

"It's not my intention to abuse you." His voice was just as low and tired as hers.

"Then you need to work on your delivery, because you're getting awfully damn close." She walked over to the bed and lowered herself to the mattress, the sudden exhaustion weighing at her.

Baran moved to sit down at her side, broad shoulders slumping. "I'm sorry."

"Huh." She snorted. "I've heard that before."

He eyed her, frowning. "Not from me."

"No. From my father. He was always sorry." She laughed shortly. "Every single time he beat the hell out of my mother, he was sorry. Not that it ever stopped him."

"Your father beat your mother?" She saw that she'd somehow shocked him.

She shrugged. "Until she . . . left."

He frowned. "And you thought I was about to hurt you?"

Jane lifted a brow at him. "Well, you were pretty pissed."

"But I wouldn't have *hit* you." He tilted his chin, visibly offended. "I'm a Warlord."

She waited for him to elaborate, but he just looked indignant. "And? Unlike some people I could name, I don't have a computer implant to tell me what that means."

"No Warlord would use his strength against those he's sworn to protect," he explained, still visibly offended. "Particularly women. It's . . . dishonorable."

"Yeah, well, you didn't seem to have a problem with holding me down while you were—"

"That," he informed her, "was sex."

She stared at him. "I feel so much better now."

"Now you're being deliberately obtuse." The beaded braid swung against his cheek as he gestured sharply. "There's a great deal of difference between playing erotic games and hurting someone under my protection. The only reason I'd ever use force against you is if you were trying to do something that would get you killed. Even then, I wouldn't beat you. Tie you, possibly . . ."

"Which sounds awfully damn patronizing," she interrupted. "I'm an adult, Baran. I don't need to be restrained for my own good."

"In principle, I agree. But I've been in this kind of situation before, and I found out the hard way that principles and reality do not always coincide." He sighed. "Which is basically why this argument began in the first place."

"Oh?" She lifted a brow at him.

"I've been in this situation before. Or one like it."

"Ah." Suddenly his earlier fury began to make sense. She turned to stare out the window at the bright morning sunlight. Outside, one of the neighbor's kids zipped by on his bike. "I gather it didn't end well."

"No. No, it didn't." Baran braced his elbows on his knees and clasped both big hands between them. "When I was sixteen, the Xerans invaded Vardon, my home world."

She nodded. "I think you mentioned that."

"Yes." He looked down at his broad, scarred palms. "They tried to wipe out the warrior class, the Warlords and Warfems, all of us who'd been genetically engineered to defend the planet. They killed many of us, but I was one of those who survived. We headed for the highlands and lived as guerillas, striking out of the mountains, killing and running."

Jane looked at him, trying to imagine the life he must have led, all those centuries away. It was incomprehensible.

Just as incomprehensible as the fact that this wild, alien man had just given her the best sex she'd ever had in her life. *Damn,* she thought. *I really am in trouble.*

And she wasn't just thinking about Druas.

"It sounds as if your childhood was worse than mine," Jane said, dragging her mind away from its hot memories of Baran in bed. "And you grew up like that?"

"Yeah. It was . . . difficult. There was never enough to eat, and we lived like, well, predators. And our prey was the Xerans." His gaze turned grim. "We were so savage we eventually made the price too high for them. They put a puppet government in place and left. The puppet lasted about a week before one of us assassinated him." He shook his head. "The Vardonese had a hell of a time civilizing the Warlords again after it was over. Me in particular."

"Oh?"

He shrugged. "The Femmats who run our world are pacifists. They had no frame of reference to understand what torture does to you."

"Torture?" She felt her eyes widen. "You were tortured? When?"

Instead of answering, he said, "Back when I was sixteen, I was in a combat unit. I'd grown up with them. Lieutenant Ullock, and Thorp, who did demolitions, and Ive . . ." Baran smiled slightly at the memory. "Ive cheated at cards like nobody I've ever met, but he was so damn charming you had to forgive him for it. And Liisa. She was . . . I . . ." He stopped and shrugged. "First love. You know how it is."

"Yeah. I've got a pretty good idea." Oh, this did not sound good.

"Central Command sent us on this mission to rescue a Femmat scientist the Xerans were holding in this compound out in the mountains. It wasn't supposed to be all that tough a target. We'd done that kind of thing before. Should have been in and right back out. But it didn't work out that way."

Jane studied his profile. He'd drawn himself very straight, head up and shoulders back, staring sightlessly out the window. When he didn't speak for a moment, she prompted softly, "What happened?"

"Liisa and I were supposed to go in and get the scientist out while the others created a distraction. Only when we popped the cell open, the Femmat wouldn't come with us. Said we had to get her data crystal first. She said it held top-secret results from some kind of experiment, and we couldn't leave it in the hands of the enemy. I told her that wasn't the mission, that we were on a timetable and we had to get her out now, no detours."

"But she didn't go along with it."

His mouth took on a hard, bitter twist. "No. No, she told me I didn't understand, that I was just a child in the body of a human tank, good for nothing but killing people. She said I didn't have the intelligence to grasp the importance of her work. And she said she wasn't moving one foot until I got her crystal back for her."

"Bitch." She paused to consider the term. "No, that doesn't do her justice. *Stupid* bitch."

"If she'd been anybody else . . ." He shrugged. "But she was a Femmat. You don't even have the concept. They're . . . I suppose the closest term is *aristocracy*, the ruling class on Vardon. I'd been taught to obey Femmats. I'd been created by a Femmat geneticist, raised by Femmats, taught by Femmats in the Warlord Creche." He shook his head, the colored gems in his braid swinging. "I didn't know what to do. She wouldn't move and I couldn't manhandle her, because a Warlord doesn't even touch a Femmat without her permission." His lip curled in sudden anger. "One punch. One punch, and they'd all still be alive. But I couldn't make myself do it."

Jane swallowed. "What happened?"

He laughed shortly. "I went to get her crystal. Liisa was going to try to get her out, but they ran into trouble. I wasn't even all the way back down the hall when I heard the beamer blast. The Xeran guards had caught them. I turned around and went back, but it was too late. The next thing I knew, Xerans were coming out of the walls. Liisa and I fought them, but they overwhelmed us."

His face was almost expressionless, his tone coolly professional, but there was something in his eyes, a shadow of loss and despair that made Jane's heart clutch in pity. It was starkly painful to watch such a powerful man torture himself over his inability to save those he'd loved.

Particularly when she knew there was nothing she could do to comfort him.

"I used my computer to com the lieutenant, tell him how

everything had gone to hell," Baran said. "He in turn commed Central Command and reported what had happened. Then he and the others tried to rescue us. He should have left us to rot."

"They were captured, too," Jane guessed.

"Yes. And the Xerans . . ." His voice trailed off. "By the time Central Command sent in another team to get us out, the others were dead, and I was . . . injured." His eyes fixed on some ugly vision. Baran said softly, "What the Jumpkiller did to Mary Kelly . . . I'd seen something similar before. It's not really all that far outside the norm of Xeran behavior. If you allow yourself to be taken, they think you deserve whatever you get."

"Jesus."

What in God's name had they done to him? Somehow she couldn't bring herself to ask. As a reporter, Jane was no stranger to dealing with people who'd suffered profound emotional and physical trauma. Yet she found herself totally unable to think of anything to say in the face of such pain.

She took a deep breath and blew it out. "I'm sorry. God, that's inadequate, but I'm sorry."

He turned his head and looked at her, his eyes blasted with such desolation she instinctively put a hand on his shoulder. He flinched.

Then anger flooded his gaze. "Don't make the mistake of pitying me." His voice was low, dangerous. Faint red striations began to glow against his dark irises. "I don't need your pity. I need your obedience."

"Baran, I'm not like that woman scientist. I'm not an idiot."

He rose in a rush of angry muscle. "She wasn't an idiot, Jane. But she wasn't a warrior, either. Are you?"

She sighed. "Well, no."

"You can't understand combat until you've been in it. And the Xerans are like nothing you've ever encountered. You don't know how they think, what they're capable of. I do. I've been fighting and killing them for twenty years."

Jane stood, finding it to uncomfortable to sit with him looming over her, all angry male strength barely held in check. "You made your point, Baran."

"You'll obey orders?" His eyes were narrow, burning like flames in his skull.

"Yeah. Aye aye, sir. Whatever." She turned away from him, suddenly needing breathing room, time to think. "I'm going to get something to eat. You want anything?"

"Not particularly, but I'm coming with you." He moved to the bag he'd dropped in a closet the night before and dug in it for something to wear.

"Somehow," she said dryly, reluctantly admiring the muscular curve of his butt clad only in briefs, "I didn't expect anything else."

You smell like sex, Freika commed to Baran as they watched Jane bustle around the kitchen. *Why don't you look happier?*

It makes more than sex to make humans happy, Freika.

Which pretty well sums up your whole problem. The wolf flicked his left ear lazily. *You all think too much. If you thought less, you wouldn't make yourselves so miserable.*

Baran's lips curled in an wry smile. *You've got a point.*

Freika nodded regally. *Of course.*

Jane walked over and plopped a bowl down in front of his paws. "Breakfast is served. You ate the rib eye, so it's hamburger for you until we can go shopping."

He sniffed the bowl. "There's not enough meat in there to keep a Chihuahua alive."

"Yeah, well, I didn't expect to have the Big Bad Wolf for a houseguest. That's what you get when you drop in on people unannounced."

Suddenly something furry shot past to leap on the kitchen counter. Baran whirled, automatically dropping into a combat crouch.

Only to find himself almost nose to nose with a tan and black house cat. It meowed loudly, looking neurotic. Chagrined, he straightened.

"Perhaps I'll just have an appetizer," Frieka said, eyeing the animal.

"Touch my cat and die, hairball." To her pet, Jane added, "Where have you been all night?"

"Hiding under the couch." The wolf took a fastidious bite from his bowl. "She's lucky I didn't just flip it over and snack." To Baran, he added, "And you say I have no self-control."

"Leave the cat alone, Freika."

"Certainly—if Jane starts buying a better cut of meat."

She looked up from operating something astonishingly loud; Baran's comp identified it as an *electric can opener*. "Keep it up and you'll be munching on the cheapest kibble I can find." Dumping the can's smelly contents into a bowl on the counter, she added to the cat, "Here ya go, Octopussy. Can you believe these guys? They think just because they come from the future, they get to eat us."

Baran grinned. "I didn't hear you complaining last night."

"You caught me in a weak moment." She grinned at him, then sobered. "Speaking of time travelers, I've been thinking. Would Druas be staying in Tayanita, or is he Jumping back and forth from the future?"

Baran leaned against the counter and folded his arms. "It's possible, but I doubt it. Charging the suit's power packs after a Jump that long is time-consuming. And frankly, Druas doesn't strike me as that patient."

"Think he'd get a hotel room in the present?"

He asked his comp for data on twenty-first-century hotels, then paused to consider the results. "It's a possibility. Though there are a lot of woods in this area. He could have established a camp out there."

Freika looked up from his bowl. "Assuming he doesn't just kill somebody and commandeer their house."

Jane opened a cabinet and got out a bowl, then started rummaging in her refrigerator. "Those are possibilities, but it'd be hard to check them out. On the other hand, there are only three motels in Tayanita County. We could see if he's at one of them. At least eliminate them as possibilities."

Baran considered the idea, frowning. "I don't think I want to confront him with you in the line of fire."

"I don't intend to get in the line of fire. I can hang back with Cujo here if we find anything. The furball can protect me while you go . . . do whatever it is you're planning on doing."

"Kill him."

"Yeah." She took a deep breath. "Killing him is good." She shook herself and looked over at him. "So. What do you want for breakfast?"

Jane was heading upstairs to clean up, Baran on her heels, when she realized the implications of taking her clothes off in front of him again. She cleared her throat. "I'm going to need a shower."

He smiled, slow and wicked. "What a coincidence. So do I."

She swallowed, remembering the dizzying warmth of his hands, the heat of his mouth. Among other things. "Oh."

His eyes started to glow.

Well, she thought as her nipples peaked, if my life has to turn into an episode of The X-Files, at least there are fringe benefits.

Jane walked into the bedroom ahead of him with every nerve quivering and alert. This is so not a good idea, the voice of sanity said. The man has more issues than Dad's National Geographic collection. And that's aside from the whole business of going back to the future as soon as he kills the bad guy. Assuming Druas doesn't get us first. . . .

On the other hand, she'd always had a secret fantasy about no-strings sex with a gorgeous stranger. They didn't get any more gorgeous than Baran.

Or, come to think of it, any stranger.

The only catch was, she had to keep it light. This was the equivalent of a shipboard fling—or at least a doing-battle-with-a-psychopath fling. It would be way too easy to get hung up on Baran, and that would be bad. She'd have enough psychological scars out of this episode as it was—that damn recording alone would probably give her nightmares for years. She didn't need a broken heart on top of it.

Stepping into the bedroom, Jane looked around just in time to watch him strip off his T-shirt, baring that magnificent chest. Hot eyes met hers over that wicked grin.

On the other hand, what's life without a little risk?

Baran stared into Jane's big, dark eyes as he stripped. They got even bigger when she saw the size of his erection. She licked her lips and gave him a nervous smile. And, typically, tried to defuse the rising tension with a joke. "Why, sir, whatever are your intentions?"

He gave his best feral smile as he pitched his jeans across the room. "Actually, I thought I'd rip your clothes off, pin you against the wall, and fuck you until you scream."

Jane blinked twice. "Uh, yeah. That's what I thought," she said, and fled into the bathroom.

He eyed her retreating back. And grinned.

Baran grabbed the door just before she managed to slam it in his face. Shouldering through, he purred, "Are you running from me?"

She retreated quickly to the glass stall that took up one side of the room. "Who, me?" There was a definite squeak in her voice. Whirling, she started fumbling with a set of chrome knobs that made water shoot from a nozzle in the wall of the stall. "Why would I do that?"

"Maybe because it's a good idea?" He strolled over to snatch her against him, grab the hem of her T-shirt, and jerk it over her head. She hadn't bothered with a bra that morning, and her bare breasts bobbed with the motion. Those pretty nipples were delicately erect, pink, and tender. He swooped in to sample one, sucking it into his mouth as he grabbed the waistband of her baggy trousers and started pulling them down her thighs. "I thought I told you not to wear these ugly pants again," he growled between nibbles.

"And I don't . . . AH! . . . take fashion advice from a guy with beads in his hair. Baran!" The last word was a yelp of protest as he snatched her off her feet, one hand around her backside, the other arm circling her torso. He bent her back, nestling his erection against her velvet soft nether lips as he attacked both tight nipples in turn, licking and nibbling until she squirmed, giggling.

"All the hot water's going to run out!" she protested, writhing deliciously against him in a way that made his cock throb.

"Primitive plumbing," he growled, and stepped into the stall with her. Warm water pelted his skin as he moved to pin her to the ceramic tile wall. He settled against her, savoring her soft, yielding body, the way the silken hair over her sex caressed his hard shaft, the cushion of her tempting breasts.

"Put me down," she said breathlessly, giving her legs a kick of protest.

Baran smiled down at her darkly, tightening his grip on her tender butt. "No." She felt so damn luscious. So helpless. Perversely, he found her vulnerability made him want to both protect and ravish her at the same time. "Now what are you going to do about it?"

A grin teased the corners of her mouth. "Apparently," she said dryly, "not a damn thing."

Jane squirmed again, testing, but his powerful hold didn't even falter as he cradled her. Held like this, feet off the ground, immobilized against the cool tile by so much muscle and heat, she felt completely at his mercy.

And wildly aroused.

He stared down at her, the angles of his face stark with desire, his eyes glowing, a hungry smile on his face. The shower stream bounced off his muscled body as if it were rock. And it felt like rock, too, in more ways than one. If any other man had held her like this, she'd be worried that he'd drop her, yet Baran's grip was so strong, she felt utterly secure in his arms.

But not at all safe.

"Now that you've got me, what are you going to do with me?" She'd intended the question to sound flirtatious, but it came out breathless.

His slow, dark grin was not reassuring. "I thought I'd find some tight, wet entrance and force my cock into it."

Jane swallowed. Perversely, his dominance turned her on even as it irritated her. And she knew he knew it. "You're really not a nice man."

Baran bent his head to study her nipples with predatory interest. "No." Slowly he raked his teeth over one pink tip, sending pleasure bolting up her nerves. "But then, I don't think you want a nice man."

Gasping, she let her head fall back against the wall and closed her eyes. "Not right now, no."

He began to pleasure her breasts in earnest, licking and sucking. He knew just how to do it, too. It was as if he could read her mind, sense when she wanted a hard, drawing pull, when she wanted a gentle scrape of his teeth, when she wanted a swirling pass of his tongue. She'd never had a lover so utterly aware of her—or so determined to use that knowledge to drive her out of her mind. Moaning helplessly, she felt herself going limp in his arms, surrendering to whatever he wanted to do.

One of those moans became a muffled shriek as he shifted his grip and reached one hand beneath her to begin a leisurely exploration of her sex. His thumb strummed her clit as a long, strong forefinger slid deep, stroked.

Her flesh was soaked and ready, swollen tight with need. "Mmmm," he purred against her breast. "Now, that's tempting." She felt his cock jerk in lust against her belly.

For several long, delicious moments, he played with her, his mouth busy on her breasts, his fingers delving, first one, then two, stretching and stroking. She fisted both hands in his wet hair and wrapped her thighs tighter around his hips, bucking against him, craving everything he did to her.

He lifted his head so he could press his full length against her belly. His shaft felt long enough to reach her heart. "Ready for more?" he purred in her ear over the sound of the shower spray pounding their bodies with a pleasant sting.

"Yes," she whimpered. "God, yes."

"Good." It was a growl, soft with sensual threat. He wrapped both hands around her backside, lifted her and settled her over the straining head of his cock. And slowly, slowly lowered her as he rolled his hips upward, impaling her by delicious increments on his thick shaft.

"Jesus, Baran!" Jane dug her nails into his wet back and rested her head against his shoulder, gasping at the sensation of being stuffed by him, one aching inch at a time.

He stopped. Only half of his length was inside her. She groaned and squirmed, hungry for the rest, but he held her suspended, helpless.

"Baran, please!"

He looked down at her, droplets beading on his long hair and high cheekbones. His smile held a taunting edge. "What do you want, Jane?"

"More. God, more!"

He lowered her another fraction, but not enough. Her senses clamored. She wanted to be full of him again, the way she'd been last night.

"Is that enough?"

"No! Oh, oh, you've got a sadistic streak, you know that?"

His smile was slow and deadly. "I have heard that a time or two."

And he rammed in to the hilt.

She screamed in startled delight. Skewered on his long, thick cock, she writhed in his arms, overwhelmed, trembling on the knife edge between pleasure and pain.

"You okay?" he asked roughly.

She clung to him, raking his broad back with her nails. "Oh, God! Yeah, yeah, I'm fine. More!"

With a dark, tight smile, he obeyed, rolling his hips. The momentary discomfort faded with his slow, careful thrusts, teased into full pleasure.

Panting, she rested her cheek on his shoulder and closed her eyes, concentrating on the unbelievable feeling of his body against her, inside her. The merciless pleasure was so intense, she might as well have been a virgin again.

"More?" His voice rasped the question. She realized he was afraid of hurting her.

Jane shuddered. "God, yeah. You feel so—" She broke off, panting, words no match for the raw sensation.

Reassured, he increased the pace. She realized he'd made himself just as hot as he had her.

And she was burning.

Baran gasped at Jane's tight, slick grip, struggling to control the need to ram into her. She felt so small and delicate in his arms, even as her creamy sheathe milked his cock. He didn't want to hurt her.

"God, you feel so good," she gasped in his ear. He could feel those sharp little claws of hers raking his back again, pricking him on like spurs.

He yielded to her silent demand, pinning her against the wet wall of the shower and bracing her there so he could fuck her harder.

As many times as he'd had sex, he knew he must have had a woman as good as Jane. He just couldn't remember when. Her soft breasts pillowed his chest, hard nipples teasing his skin as those endless legs tightened over his butt. Her slender arms gripped him with a surprising strength, matching the demanding clasp of her hot cunt.

"Dammit, Baran," she gasped in his ear, "I won't break!"

He laughed even as his head spun. "Apparently not."

Letting go at last, he gave both of them exactly what they needed—long, driving strokes that ground her against the shower wall and stripped his sanity away. The pleasure coiled like a powerful spring, forced tighter with every impact of his body on hers.

Until she convulsed in his arms, screaming out her orgasm in his ear. "Baran! Oh, God!"

"Jane!" he roared back, and stiffened, slamming against her with one last ferocious dig that threw him right over the edge. The orgasm crashed him and out of him, exploding from his cock in jets of heat.

Limp, they collapsed together against the wall with the shower still pelting them.

Nine

Baran zipped his jeans, watching with possessive male interest as Jane squirmed into hers. Her pretty breasts quivered with the movement in the cups of a delicate lace bra.

He found himself wondering again what it was about sex with her that was so much hotter than anything he'd had before. It was nothing short of overwhelming, so different from the casual encounters he'd had with various Warfems and civilians over the years.

Maybe it was her delicacy; with his strength, he had to be very careful not to hurt her. He'd never particularly enjoyed using that much restraint in the past, but with Jane, the tension seemed to add to the eroticism of taking her.

And she was so sweetly responsive. Every time he touched her, he could feel her body arching into his touch, writhing for each caress, each stroke, each thrust. His own hypersensitive senses responded to her with just as much intensity—the taste of her skin, the scent of her arousal, the sound of her erotic moans. He smiled, knowing he could easily become addicted to sex with Jane.

Then the smile faded. He wasn't sure he liked the sound of that. . . .

"That's it!" She stopped with her knit shirt halfway over her head, then jerked it the rest of the way down and grinned at him. "I've figured out how to explain you to everybody."

He lifted a brow, watching her as she hurried over to an armchair sitting in one corner. "Explain me?"

"Well, I can't exactly tell people you're my bodyguard from the future, can I?" She bent over a small black bag sitting in the chair. The sweet curve of her butt did a very good job of distracting him, but he somehow managed to follow the conversation as she continued, "You've got to have some kind of cover story. I've been talking about hiring a photographer for months, but I never did anything about it. I take adequate shots myself, so I didn't think I could justify the expense." She opened the bag and pulled out a black object his computer identified as a camera. Reaching in again, she got out a short, cylindrical object—a lens?—and inserted it into a round opening in the device's body. "I don't suppose you know how to use a Nikon?"

Baran opened his mouth to say no, but his computer interrupted. *Skill file present.* His brows lifted; it struck him as a fairly esoteric bit of knowledge to have. Knowing Temporal Enforcement, they probably gave him the file because they'd seen pictures he would take sometime in the future. Being TE, however, they hadn't mentioned it.

"Actually, I do know how," he said slowly. "Or I will, as soon as my computer uploads the information into my brain."

Jane eyed him. "Well, that's convenient."

He grimaced. "If you discount the general discomfort of the process."

"Discomfort?" She frowned, dubious. "And how does that work, anyway?"

"My comp can use my neural network to implant a skill directly into my brain, the same way you'd program a computer. That's how I learned English."

"Yeah, I'd wondered about that. You don't have any accent at all, and your slang is dead on. You sound like an American network news anchor."

He snorted. "Probably because TE used news recordings to create the file."

"So how do they get these files into your head? You don't have one of those skull-jack things Freika was talking about." She grinned impishly. "I looked."

"I don't need one. Freika's my database unit. His computer's a lot more powerful than mine; it has to be, because it provides so much of his intelligence. He keeps data files I don't use all the time, so he needs a way to access big chunks of information more quickly. Sticking in a crystal's faster than a download." *Transfer ready,* the comp interrupted. "Excuse me a minute."

He braced himself. He always hated this part.

A wall of information and images slammed into his mind like a tidal wave. It was all he could do not to scream.

B*aran's big body jerked as his eyes widened.* His mouth contorted, opened, but all that emerged was a strangled gasp.

"Shit!" Jane tossed the camera on the chair without a thought for its two-thousand-dollar price tag and ran to catch him. She knew even as she did that there was no way she could support his greater weight.

She needn't have bothered; he remained rigidly erect, his body quivering. "Baran!"

He didn't answer. She put a finger to the big pulse under his jaw. It pounded furiously, but he didn't react to her touch. "Baran, talk to me!" Hell, was he having some kind of seizure? Was this some weird Druas attack? Should she call 911? "Baran!" It was a wail.

His eyes focused. He blinked at her, registered her panic. His body instantly coiled into a combat crouch as he scanned the room, his eyes hard. "What? Where's the threat?" he barked.

He was all right! Relief flooded her, followed almost instantly by anger. She thumped him hard in the chest. "You *jerk!*"

He straightened and looked down at her. "What? What did I do?"

"You scared the daylights out of me! What was that all about? It looked like you were having some kind of attack!"

"I told you, I had to download the skill file."

"Yeah, but you didn't mention the flipping epileptic seizure! Next time you have to do some weird future crap, warn me!"

He lifted a brow at her and strolled over to pick up the camera. "You really were worried, weren't you?"

"Yes, I was, you biped rat. By the way, aren't you the same guy who won't even let me out of his sight to use the john? But it's okay to check out for five minutes to jerk around?"

Baran examined the camera, then reached into the bag and pulled out the flash. "My computer was keeping watch. It would have stopped the data transfer if Druas had Jumped into the room." He slid the flash into its hotshoe, then cradled the camera, pointed it at her, and started clicking off shots with the skill of an experienced photographer.

She glared at him. "I repeat: You could have warned me."

He sighed and crouched, moving around her to find another angle. "Yes, I should have. I'm sorry I didn't realize you'd be alarmed. I'll keep that in mind in the future."

Jane deflated, drawing a frustrated hand through her dark curls. "You do that. Okay, I'll bite, let me see what you shot."

He stood and walked over to hand her the camera. She flicked a switch to display the digital images on the view screen. And whistled soundlessly.

He'd captured her every expression, starting with angry frustration and finishing with the rake of her fingers through her hair. Each shot was expertly, perfectly framed.

"Damn. You're good. The computer taught you how to do this

just now?" Jane looked up and shook her head. "Where can I get one of those things?"

Baran grinned back and pointed at the ceiling. "About three hundred years from now, eighty light-years that way."

She looked at him. "Don't think I want to go quite that far. But . . ."

Just then a feline yowl sounded downstairs, followed closely by a startled canine yip.

"My nose!" Freika bellowed in outrage. "You clawed my nose!"

Something crashed. Paws thudded on the floor, accompanied by vicious snarls and the sound of breakables shattering. "That's it, cat! I'm chewing you into pâté and spreading your ass on a cracker!"

Jane whirled and raced for the stairs. "Stay away from Octopussy, you fuzzy psycho!"

As she hit the steps at a run, she heard the deep rumble of Baran's laughter. "One thing about this mission," he called, loping after her, "At least I'm never bored."

"Can't you hitch this thing to a horse or pour in another scoop of coal and get it to move faster?" Freika demanded.

"We're going sixty miles an hour as it is," Jane gritted out. "Get your head back in the window before a truck comes along and knocks it off."

"Sixty?" The wolf was leaning out so far from the backseat, his nose almost level with Jane's as she drove. His tongue whipped in the wind. "I can run faster than that."

"Yeah, right. Baran, tell your partner he's shortening his life expectancy."

"Freika, get back in the . . . whatever this thing is."

"SUV. Do it, Cujo. It's always fun until somebody loses a head." She hit the power button for the rear passenger window, rolling it up and forcing the wolf to pull back inside.

"What's a cujo?" he asked. "My comp doesn't have a definition for that term."

"It's a character in a book by Stephen King," Jane told him. "I'd lend you my copy, but I'm afraid it would give you ideas."

The wolf snorted in disdain. "I don't need some twenty-first-century scribbler to 'give me ideas.' I'm more than capable of coming up with my own. You—" He broke off as static blasted from Jane's dash-mounted police scanner. "Do we have to listen to all that human babble? It's annoying."

"Yes, because it'll tell us if the cops find another body. Or Druas himself, God forbid, since he'd probably eat them." She slanted a look at Baran, who was belted into the front seat, looking as if he, too, wanted to go faster but was too polite to complain. "Does Fur Boy always whine this much?"

Baran smiled slightly. "Yes."

"I do not whine," Freika said in a tone that dripped offended dignity. "I'm simply trying to give you hapless bipeds the benefit of my superior intellect."

"No, you're trying to give me a giant, throbbing pain in my—"

"Ten-fifty with PIs and entrapment. Southbound I-85 at the ninety-third mile marker," the scanner interrupted. "Car versus eighteen-wheeler."

"Shit." Jane threw a quick look over her shoulder, saw nothing behind her, made sure there was nothing in front, and whipped into a U-turn, bumping onto the grass shoulder to do it.

"Where are we going?" Baran asked as she hit the gas and shot in the opposite direction back down the highway. "And what's a ten-fifty?"

"A car's crashed with an eighteen-wheeler—that's a very big truck. All that dispatcher jargon means somebody's trapped and hurt. Could be really, really ugly."

He looked at her so sharply, the beads on his braid tapped his cheek as his head swung. "Jane, we need to search for Druas. We don't have time to run off investigating random police calls."

"We can take twenty minutes to cover this."

"Jane . . ."

"I'm a newspaper reporter, Baran." Face grim, she concentrated on the road. "I'm not going to stop doing my job just because Jack the Ripper's in town."

They entered the interstate at the northbound on-ramp closest to the scene; Jane had known traffic going southbound would be backed up for miles behind the crash, and she was right. As with every other traffic accident she'd ever covered, the scene was chaos. Fire trucks, law enforcement and ambulances blocked the road with lights flashing, while behind them, a line of cars waited for the mess to be cleared away. She'd learned to judge how bad a crash was by the number of emergency vehicles in attendance.

This one was pretty damn bad.

After parking the SUV on the broad grass median behind two fire trucks, she grabbed the Nikon out of the back and thrust it into Baran's hands. "You shoot the wreck. I'll talk to the cops and bystanders, see what I can get." Usually she had to do it all at one time; it was nice to have help from someone she could depend on.

As they got out of the SUV, Jane noticed Freika hopping between the seats to follow Baran. "Fuzzy, get back in the truck. Nobody's going to want a dog on the scene."

He gave her a pale-eyed lupine glare. "For the last time, I am not a dog! And I'm coming with you."

"Keep your voice down, dammit!" she hissed. "And you'd better be a dog, because people around here would shoot a wolf. Which would be a very bad thing, considering that each and every one of these cops has a gun."

Freika sniffed. "As if they could even hit me."

"Take my word for it, they could hit you. These are Southern boys. They grew up shooting the four-legged and furry . . . Oh, hell." She spotted a big, boxy truck with a huge antenna and a colorful logo.

"You'd better not be a talking *anything*, because I see a TV live truck, and that kind of media we do not need!" Without waiting to see whether Freika obeyed, she started up the median, grumbling under her breath. "Frigging television poachers. How'd they get in my county so fast? They must have been passing by, because it's for damn sure they couldn't have beat me here otherwise. Just my luck. . . ."

Baran strode past on his longer legs, his attention focused on the cluster of men and emergency vehicles. Freika trotted at his heels.

Jane sighed and lengthened her stride to catch up. "Well, at least they're getting into the spirit of the thing."

Just ahead, Tom Reynolds waved violently at a driver in the northbound lane, who'd slowed down to stare at the mangled car sitting at a right angle to the jack-knifed semi. "Quit rubbernecking and drive before you cause another wreck, you"—he spotted Jane—"citizen."

"Nice save," she said, pulling her notebook out of her purse. "What are you doing here? I figured you'd be off trying to catch . . . the guy who killed that lady." Dammit, she'd almost said Druas. Not good. Tom was far too sharp to miss a mistake like that, and she didn't want to have to answer the questions he'd ask.

"I was on the way to talk to the victim's relatives when the crash happened right in front of me," Tom told her, thoroughly disgusted. "Jerk driving the eighteen-wheeler did an illegal lane change and drove right over the lady. Who the hell is that?" He stared at Baran's profile as the Warlord raised his camera and squeezed off a shot.

"Uh, my new photographer." Which was the truth. "From Atlanta." Which wasn't. She hid a wince of guilt at the lie.

"He looks like a fruit."

Jane choked, remembering what Baran's massive body had felt like driving into hers in the shower. She grinned. "Well, he's not."

Tom eyed her shrewdly, no doubt reading that grin. "You do realize your daddy's rolling over in his grave right now—you taking up with some guy in a tattoo and beads."

Jane clamped her teeth shut against the impulse to tell Tom just how little right her father had to serve as an arbiter of morality. Bill Colby had been far too good at hiding behind a good ol' boy pose. At least with other men.

Before she could shatter his illusions, Tom's eyes widened as he noticed Freika loping along at Jane's heels like the furry bodyguard he was. "What the fuck is that?"

"It's an . . . Irish wolfhound."

"Hound, my ass. That's a wolf, period. Get it out of—"

"She's dying," Baran interrupted, turning back toward them as he lowered his camera. The muscles in his powerful shoulders visibly knotted under his white T-shirt. "The woman in the wreckage."

"No shit, Sherlock," Tom snapped. "Get that animal out of—"

"She needs treatment *now*. What are they waiting for?" Baran glanced over at Jane, who silently cursed and reminded herself to buy him a pair of sunglasses. The red striations had appeared in his eyes again. Fortunately, Tom was too busy glaring at Freika to notice.

Glancing at the car, she winced. The little blue Toyota had been crumpled like a beer can in a redneck's fist. "They probably can't get the doors open—the car's too badly damaged. They're going to have to cut her out of the wreckage." Giving him a significant glance, she pretended to scratch beneath her own eye. Baran looked back at the mangled car and quickly raised his camera to hide his glowing irises.

He clicked off a shot as a firefighter climbed gingerly on what was left of the car's mangled roof. Someone handed a power saw up to him. "She'll be dead before they can get to her."

"Probably. And there's not a damn thing any of us can do about it," Tom said. "Look, I'm sure you've been at this long enough to know dogs—or whatever—do not belong at accident scenes. . . ."

Baran tuned out the rest of the man's protest. *I've got to get her out of there*, he commed to Freika. Even through the noise of idling firetruck engines, his acute hearing picked up the woman's thin, hopeless cries of agony, more animal than human.

You don't know if you're supposed to save her, the wolf replied. *You don't want to cause a paradox.*

TE said anything we do now that we're here is supposed to happen anyway. Which means if she's not supposed to live, she'll die. But I can't just stand around. Everything he was rebelled against doing nothing while any civilian endured such agony.

No, I don't suppose you can.

I've got to get closer. Distract those men for me. To his computer, he gave a silent order: *Begin riatt.*

Initiating riatt, the comp responded. Baran barely braced himself in time as heat blasted through his veins and his heart began to pound in heavy, frantic lunges. With the fire came a dark, feral joy, a product of *riatt* neurochemicals. He felt his lips stretch into a wild grin.

How a man could kill as many people as you have and still be so softhearted . . . The wolf commed as he moved off to circle the oblivious firefighters.

I'm not softhearted. Baran laughed, endorphins flooding his brain. *I just love doing this.*

Oh, yeah, and the metabolic crash afterward is so much fun. Without warning, Freika launched himself at the rescue workers, snarling and growling, his sharp, white teeth snapping together like castanets.

As one, they jumped back away from him. "What the fuck!"

"Somebody shoot that goddamned . . ."

His own teeth bared in a grimace of euphoria, Baran shouldered between the startled firefighters, thrust both hands through the shattered car window, clamped down on the door frame, and heaved backward. Steel groaned as something popped with a shower of glass. The door tore free.

He turned to find himself the focus of an astonished ring of eyes. "All you had to do was pull," Baran said, managing to give his voice a disgusted inflection as he quickly lowered his gaze to the ground. He knew his eyes would be blazing with the effects of *riatt.*

After thrusting the car door into the hands of the nearest

astonished firefighter, he grabbed the camera still hanging around his neck by its strap. He turned around and started snapping away at the moaning victim, knowing instinctively how the rescue workers would react.

"How the hell did you . . . ? Hey, you can't take pictures of that." Somebody grabbed his shoulder. He let himself be shoved back as the firefighters closed in on the woman and prepared to get her out.

A skinny man dressed in a padded protective jacket glared at him. "Who the hell are you anyway?"

"Photographer," Baran said, and pointed the camera into his interrogator's face. The man threw up a hand and backed off.

"Who was that asshole?" one firefighter asked another. "How'd he do that? I tried that door. It was jammed tight."

"Must not have tried hard enough. Where'd the dog go?"

"Hey, you," somebody said behind him. "Clear a path."

Baran backed up another pace to give the paramedics room to bring the stretcher up to the vehicle. He framed a shot of the firefighters tenderly lifting the woman from her vehicle, the faces under their yellow helmets tight with concentration.

For an instant the woman's eyes met his, filled with a sort of desperate gratitude even through her pain. He nodded back.

End riatt, the comp said.

Baran winced as the battle neurochemicals drained away, taking with them the momentary high. A deep, racking quiver rolled through his muscles, and his stomach twisted with such force, he had to battle the urge to vomit.

The worst thing about going to *riatt* was the aftermath, as the body reacted to the wild biochemical swings it had endured.

Suddenly he was aware of a hot throbbing in his shaking hands as they cradled the lens of his camera. Blood rolled down his forearms. He wondered when he'd cut himself. *How bad is it?*

Lacerations to fingers and palms, but no tendon damage, the comp replied. *Healing acceleration procedures initiated. Estimated duration five-point-six hours.*

Well, it could have been worse. And had been, any number of times.

The heat in his hands intensified as the healing began, pain rolling in behind it. He sighed in disgust. Normally he wore protective battle armor when he went to *riatt*, since the berserker state multiplied his strength by a factor of ten even as it killed his ability to feel pain. But TE had not allowed him to bring the suit here, and his twenty-first century jeans and T-shirt offered no protection to vulnerable flesh.

Suddenly a huge black barrel thrust itself into his face. Baran jerked and almost knocked it flying before he realized it was a lens even bigger than the one on his own camera. As he recoiled, a black tube his computer identified as a microphone was shoved under his mouth.

"Bill Clarkson, WDRT News," the man holding the tube announced as his partner focused the videocamera on Baran's startled face. The reporter's expression was avid. "That was amazing. How did you do it?"

"Do you mind?" Jane snapped, shouldering past the cameraman. "Quit harassing my photographer and go do your job, Bill. Maybe you can even get the story right for a change."

"*Your* photographer?" Clarkson lifted a brow and curled his lip. "Since when can a triweekly rag like the *Trib* afford a shooter? Especially one that can rip the doors off a Toyota."

Baran tightened his grip on his own camera and licked his dry lips, trying to squelch the racking quiver he could feel building in his body. "Impact ripped the door off," he lied. "It was just hanging there. I only gave it a tug."

"Oh," the reporter said, the gleam in his eyes fading. "Well, that explains it. Why didn't the firefighters do that?"

"Hey," Jane said loudly, "isn't that the driver of the semi over there?"

Bill turned, following her pointing finger toward a tubby, bloodstained figure. "Sir!" he called, and strode away, leaving his videographer to scramble after him with the heavy camera.

She watched them go. "Some people in the electronic media are really, really good. And then there's Bill Clarkson, the human hemorrhoid." Jane turned to stare at him. "*Was* that door just hanging there?"

"No."

"Didn't think so. Oh, hell." The last was muttered as a short man with a badge clipped to his belt stalked up.

"I told you to get that fucking dog off this scene," he growled, thrusting his face as close to Baran's as he could manage, given that he was seven inches shorter. "I thought it was going to take a chunk out of one of those firefighters. I should run your ass in. . . ."

"On what charges, Tom?" Jane demanded. "You know County Council never passed that leash law. Besides, Baran got the door open, didn't he?"

The man's eyes narrowed. "And what the fuck is he, anyway—Superman?" His gaze flicked down, attracted by the bright scarlet dripping from Baran's fingers. "Jesus, you're bleeding like a pig. You must have gashed your hands wide open."

Jane's eyes widened. "Damn, Baran! What did you do? You're . . ."

Ahhhhh, a voice purred through his comp, drowning out her words, *I was right. It is you.*

Baran jerked. That definitely wasn't Freika, and the only other person in this time capable of comming him was . . .

That's right, Druas said. *It's me.*

Ten

Freika!

Yeah, I hear him.

Stay with Jane. Barely aware that the wolf had moved to join them, he thrust his bloody Nikon into her hands and turned to scan the area. *Sensors,* he ordered his computer. *Pinpoint the Xeran's location.*

A flashing bright red X suddenly appeared across the highway from him, covering a human figure standing at the edge of a stand of trees. Baran started toward the man his computer had targeted, mentally cursing himself for coming out of *riatt* so soon. He couldn't go back into the berserker state again until his computer had rebuilt its reservoir of neurochemicals. And the synthesizing process would take another half hour at least. *Send me back into* riatt *as soon as possible,* he ordered.

"What's with him?" he heard Tom ask.

"I don't know. Freika, dammit, get out of the way!"

Baran didn't look around, but he knew the wolf was deliberately blocking her path. The last thing they needed was for her to get within striking range of the Jumpkiller.

Baran Arvid, Druas commed as Baran crossed the interstate. *The Death Lord himself. Now, this is more like it. I knew it was you three hundred years from now, when I saw the vid footage those humans just shot of you ripping the door off that car.* The killer's tone was hearty, familiar, as if they were old friends meeting again after a long separation. *You do realize the mystery around you is the reason these killings will become so famous? Which is ironic, when you think about it.*

Do we know each other? Damn, he wasn't up to a fight with the Xeran right now, but it looked as if he was going to get one anyway. Maybe if he could stall the bastard long enough, his computer would be able to throw him back into *riatt.*

And luckily, he still had the suit neutralizing ring the Enforcer had given him. If he could tag Druas with it long enough, it would knock the suit offline and he'd be able to beat the bastard to death.

Unfortunately, there was no guarantee Druas would let him get close enough. He had to keep the Xeran talking.

Druas began moving away, retreating slowly even as Baran approached. *You have no idea how famous you are among the Xerans. Everyone talks about the Death Lord—all those wonderful duels, all the men you killed. And General Jutka's put a very high price on your head, by the way.*

So I heard.

I do believe you've got him shaking in his battle boots. I assume he is one of your targets? You've killed almost all the others who were present when your team was tortured.

At the moment I'm much more interested in you. Baran lengthened his stride. The man his computer had pinpointed grinned at him. The Xeran must be generating an image field; the figure staying just out of reach was short and potbellied, nothing like the mercenary's true build.

That's refreshing to hear. The man sauntered away again, keeping just ahead of his slow pursuit. Baran thought about breaking into a run, but he didn't want to drive the killer into Jumping.

I was starting to get bored, Druas commed, circling him. *The Ripper killings were entertaining, but hardly challenging. It's not like the little bitches could fight back, could they? Though they did squeal well. . . .*

Baran snarled, remembering Mary Kelly's helpless struggles.

Still, the killer continued, *I was thinking of giving it up until I saw the archival footage of you while I was doing a little research. I recognized you the minute I saw you.* Even at a distance the smile on the round, bland face was chilling. *That's when I realized the Tayanita killings were my work. I must have come here, and TE sent you after me. Now, there's a challenge, I thought. Me against the Death Lord. Gave me a shiver.* He beamed. *And now here you are.*

Eyes narrowing, the Warlord stopped in his tracks. Maybe the bastard would come closer if he didn't follow. The question was, would Baran be able to put the Xeran down at normal strength? Not that he had a choice, with Jane's life at risk. *If you want a fight, I'll be more than happy to oblige you.*

But not yet, I'll wager. You just dropped out of riatt, *so you can't power up again for a good half hour or so.* Reading Baran's expression, Druas grinned. *Don't look so surprised. I did a little research on Warlords when I decided to play this game. But I wonder—how much research did TE let you do on me?*

They gave me all the data I need.

Oh, I doubt that. Knowing Temporal Enforcement, I'll bet there's a great deal they didn't tell you. Though why they're so afraid of causing a paradox, I have no idea. If the universe doesn't die when you make the Jump to begin with, you can do whatever the hell you want. The grin on that round, ordinary face took on a thoroughly inhuman cast. *And there's a long list of things I want to do to sweet Jane.*

Baran fought to keep his rage from showing. *You'll never lay a hand on her.*

Won't I?

No. Because I'll kill you before you get that close.

The killer sauntered closer until he was just out of Baran's reach, bland human eyes studying him with cruel interest. *You're fucking her already, aren't you? I wondered about that. Is she good?*

You'll never know. To his computer, he thought, *How much longer to riatt?*

Twenty minutes.

Too long. Too damn long.

Actually, Druas said, *before this is over I'll find out exactly how good she is. But not yet. If you'll excuse me, I have women to kill, police to mystify . . .*

Hell. Baran lunged for the killer. He risked getting caught in the backwash of the Jump, but if he could just pin him long enough for the ring to do its work . . . He clamped a hand around the man's wrist.

"Idiot." Druas's fist slammed into Baran's head so hard he saw stars, but he didn't let go. "You're going to get fried, you fool!" And he was right; Baran could feel the energy of the Jump building as the killer's armor began to glow.

Warning! Temporal field building! The comp blared, its voice seeming to echo in his skull. *Step back!* Baran ignored it, blocking another hard punch, intent only on holding on. The ring was heating on his hand. . . .

Too late. A blinding white light exploded in the center of his vision as an electric jolt tore though his body. Something picked him up and threw him with an eardrum-shattering boom.

He never felt the ground come up and hit him.

Jane, trapped behind the furry barrier of Freika's body, saw a lightning bolt knock Baran ten feet like the slap of a giant's hand. He hit the pavement flat on his back as a thunderous boom drowned out her scream.

Freika whirled and raced toward his fallen partner, a black streak faster than any dog she'd ever seen. Jane sprinted after him, her heart in her throat, dimly aware of Tom pounding at her heels.

Baran lay sprawled on his back, his eyes closed, his face so pale his scarlet tattoo looked like blood. His brawny arms and legs were

flung wide, lacerated palms upward. Freika nuzzled his face, whin-
ing like the dog he wasn't. Jane fell to her knees beside him, reaching desperately for the pulse in his strong throat. It throbbed
comfortingly against her fingers, but he didn't move. "Baran! Baran,
wake up!"

She'd known him less than twenty-four hours. How had he become so damn important to her so damn fast?

Jane looked wildly at Freika. The wolf jerked his head, but she
couldn't tell what he was trying to communicate. Unfortunately,
they didn't dare talk in front of Tom.

"Paramedics!" the detective bellowed, but the standby ambulance crew was already pounding toward them.

"What the hell happened?" Jane heard one yell.

"Dunno," Tom called back. "Looked like maybe a lightning
strike, but there's not a cloud in the sky, and I don't see any power
lines nearby."

"How is he? What's going on?" Jane whispered fiercely to Freika
while the detective was distracted.

The wolf pressed against her and whispered back. "His comp
says he's okay. He just got in too close when Druas Jumped."

"Druas was here?" She looked around wildly, remembering
Mary Kelly's blackening face, the silver flash of the knife, the spray
of blood and tissue. . . . Instinctively she covered Baran's big, helpless body with her own.

"He's gone now."

"Is he conscious?" Tom demanded, kneeling by Jane's side as she
slumped in relief.

"No." She picked up one of Baran's bloodied hands, examined it
anxiously. The wound was already crusting over.

Tom frowned. "Then who were you talking to?"

Damn, he'd heard Freika. "He was babbling," she improvised.

"Get back, miss." The paramedic pushed her aside. She sat back
on her heels. He put two fingers to Baran's throat, then lifted one of
his eyelids. Jane craned her neck anxiously, but the Warlord's irises

were simple human brown. "Pupils reactive, pulse is good," the man said. "Don't see any sign of electrical burns."

The second EMT pulled a blood pressure cuff out of his bag and reached to wrap it around one of Baran's thick biceps. Jane sensed rather than saw the blur of motion. The EMT yelped.

One of Baran's huge hands was wrapped around the paramedic's throat in a stranglehold as he held the man stiff-armed, half off his knees. As she watched in horror, the man's face began to darken. He gagged, clawing helplessly at Baran's choking fingers.

Brown eyes blazed as Baran peeled his lips back from his teeth, snarling at the EMT in an alien language. The words might be incomprehensible, but the tone of murderous threat was crystal clear.

"Baran!" Jane cried as both she and Tom grabbed for his hand and fought to pry away his choking fingers. "Let him go! He's trying to help you! It's okay!"

Baran's gaze flicked to hers as the paramedic gagged.

"Let him go, mister!" Tom snapped.

The big hand released its hold. "Sorry," he said gruffly, and sat up as the paramedic choked in a breath and fell back on his butt. "Didn't know where I was."

The EMT steadied his gagging partner and eyed him warily. "Lie back down and let us have a look at you, sir. You were unconscious for more than a minute. You may have a concussion."

"I'm fine," he said, and proved it by getting to his feet. Jane scrambled up, ready to steady him. She thought he swayed, but caught himself almost instantly.

"Beg to differ, son," Tom said, stepping in close to study him. "Looked to me like you just got struck by lightning. You need a ride to the emergency room to get checked out."

Where, Jane realized, an X ray might reveal entirely too much about the Warlord's genetically engineered body. But if he really was hurt . . .

"I don't have time for that," Baran said crisply. "I don't know what you saw, but I didn't get hit by lightning." He glanced skyward.

"Obviously. There's not a cloud in the sky." Dark eyes turned to Jane. "Let's go."

"Your hands are badly cut, mister. You need stitches. . . ."

"Let him go, Dave." The paramedic rubbed his throat and coughed. "Man wants to leave, you don't want to stand in his way."

Baran started off across the highway, Freika trotting at his heels. Jane stared after his broad back, worried, then hurried after them.

Behind her, she heard Tom say, "That was thoroughly fucking weird."

The paramedic coughed again. "Tell me about it."

"You should have at least let them clean those wounds," Jane said, running to keep up with his long strides.

"My computer will take care of it," Baran said. "I just have to get the glass out."

"There's glass in the wound? Idiot. Why didn't you—"

"Because right now Druas is somewhere in this town, deciding who to kill," Baran interrupted, shooting a quelling glance at her over his shoulder. "And I need to get to him before he makes up his mind."

Jane cursed and absently clicked her key fob so she could open the door for him, sparing his lacerated palms. "Didn't your time cops identify the targets?"

"No. Evidently, they don't want me to save at least some of them." He shrugged. "The paradox problem."

"Bastards."

"That does sum it up." He eased into the seat.

She caught the shoulder belt and leaned over his lap to fasten it. "I've got a first-aid kit in the back. . . ." Jane looked up and found herself face to face with him. Suddenly she realized her hands rested in his lap, inches from the swelling bulge of an erection. His mouth was close enough to kiss. Baran's eyes kindled into a hot male blaze that made her swallow. She froze, hardly daring to blink, like a woman afraid of goading a tiger into attack.

"He always gets horny after he's been in *riatt*," Freika told her, sticking his furry head around the door. "After he quits wanting to puke, anyway. Hormones . . ." He nudged her wrist with his muzzle, jolting her out of her hypnotized fascination with Baran's blatant lust. "Hey, either step aside or open the back door for those of us without opposable thumbs."

A hot blush rolling over her cheeks, Jane took a hasty step back and slammed the passenger door on Baran's feral interest. With a relieved breath, she opened the back to get the first-aid kit and one of the bottles of water floating in the cooler's melted ice. Freika jumped past her and settled himself in the seat. "You know, I hope this thing has better safety equipment than the one that woman was riding in."

"Not really."

The *thunk* of the closing door drowned out the wolf's next grumble.

Horny. The man's hands were sliced to ribbons, and he was horny. Hell, he'd directed so much erotic heat at her, she could almost hear her own body sizzle.

There isn't time for this, Jane told herself sternly, striding around the SUV to the driver's side, carrying the bottle of water with the kit tucked under her arm. *We've got to figure out where Druas is going.*

She opened the door and hopped up into the driver's seat, dumping the water and first-aid kit into Baran's lap. "I'll find a place to pull over so we can tend your hands. Though I still say we should let the paramedics—"

"I don't want them getting a closer look at me than they already have." Evidently having flipped off his lust as quickly as he'd turned it on, he opened the kit to assess its contents. He pulled out a pair of tweezers.

"What's this *reeatt* thing?" Jane asked after she'd pulled onto the highway into the northbound traffic. The cars in the southbound lane were just starting to edge past the woman's crumpled Toyota under the direction of cops and firefighters. The victim herself had long since gone off in the back of an ambulance.

Jane glanced over at her passenger and almost ran off the road when she realized he was using the tweezers to dig into his injury. "Jesus, Baran, let me take care of that! Or at least wait until I pull over."

"I can do it," he said, pulling something from his palm she realized was a bloody chunk of safety glass.

"Doesn't that hurt?" She pointed the SUV for the nearest exit.

Baran shrugged his broad shoulders. "My computer dulls the pain."

"Well, that's something anyway." Sighing, Jane drove up the off-ramp and turned left on a less-traveled street. "So what's this *reeatt* thing again?"

She asked the question as much to distract herself as him. Jane didn't ordinarily consider herself particularly squeamish—not in her line of work. But somehow it made a difference that it was Baran bleeding all over her front seat, Baran in pain, Baran digging into his own skin with a pair of tweezers. . . .

"Not *reeatt, riatt,*" he corrected absently, depositing the glass sliver in the empty trash bag hanging from the SUV's central floor hump.

"It's kind of a computer-induced berserker state," Freika explained, thrusting his head between the seats. "Increases his strength by a factor of ten. The drawback is that his judgment goes to hell. He doesn't feel pain in *riatt,* and without combat armor to protect him, he tends to break bones and cut himself all to hell doing something the human body isn't designed to do. Here, let me lick that. . . ."

"Ack!" Jane planted an elbow under his jaw and pushed his head back. "Get away from there. You want to give him an infection?"

"Freika's computer secretes antibiotics in his saliva when I'm hurt," Baran explained, raising his hand for the wolf's swiping tongue.

"Which taste nasty," Freika noted, licking.

Jane fastened her eyes firmly on the road. "Y'all are making me sick. Anyway, can't your own computer do the antibiotic thing?"

"It does, but Freika does a better job on topical treatment." He lifted an eyebrow. " 'Y'all'?"

"My Southern accent comes out under stress." Spotting a likely place to pull over, she whipped the SUV off onto the shoulder. Deciding it was time for a subject change, Jane asked as she opened the driver's door, "What are we going to do about Druas?"

"Personally, I think killing him's a dandy idea," Freika observed.

"Duh," she said, getting out of the truck and leaving the door open as she started around the SUV's massive hood. "I mean, how are we going to stop him from killing whoever he's planning to kill?"

"I have no idea, but I'm damn well going to try," Baran told her as she opened the passenger door and stepped to his side. "There's another piece in my right hand. I can't seem to get it out with my left. Can you try?"

She flinched mentally, then gave him a determined smile. "Sure. So what are we going to do now?"

"Exactly what we were doing before our little detour—check the hotels. If he's at one of them, I should be able to sense him." Baran handed her the tweezers as she cradled his hand in one of hers.

"What if he's not there when we go by?"

"Then we're out of luck, and his next victim's dead. She may be already. Or close to it." He clenched the other fist on his knee. "If I hadn't dropped out of *riatt* . . ."

"If you hadn't, you wouldn't even have gotten that close to him," Freika pointed out. "Druas knows better than to allow a berserk Warlord within striking distance."

Jane's delicate probes with the tweezers discovered something hard buried in his bloodied flesh. "You've got it," Baran said.

"Joy," she muttered between her teeth and tried to close the tweezers around the tiny object. "So in *riatt* you're stronger than Druas, right?"

"Possibly," Baran said.

Her tweezers slipped. She growled.

"Then again, possibly not," Freika observed, leaning around Baran's seat. "He's got cybernetic implants that increase his strength, but it's not clear by how much. He could be weaker than Baran, but then again, he could be a lot stronger."

The Warlord nodded. "We won't know for sure until I fight him."

Jane clamped her lower lip between her teeth and jerked the piece of glass free. "Has anybody ever heard of the concept of firearms?" She tossed the piece into the trash bag and looked at Baran. "Is that it for the glass fragments, please, God?"

"Yeah." He extended his hand to Freika. "But nobody but an idiot would try to make a Jump with an energy weapon. The Tachyon power packs would react with the temporal field and blow you to hell and gone." Jane looked away as the wolf started cleaning the injury. Taking the water bottle out of his lap, she dumped part of its contents over the tweezers, washing them off. After tossing them back in the first aid box, she rummaged around in it for the roll of gauze to wrap his wound with. When she found it, she ripped it open and took his hand again.

"So what about weapons from this time? Like a gun, for instance." Jane remembered her father's pistol, buried in his stuff somewhere in the attic. "Couldn't you just shoot him?"

He shrugged. "Yeah, but it probably won't do any good. According to the sensor readings I just took, that T-suit Druas is wearing is armored. I doubt one of your contemporary firearms could puncture it."

Still thinking, she wound the gauze around his hand. "So does he wear a helmet?" She knew from covering cops that all the body armor in the world wouldn't protect you against a head shot.

"No, but his skeletal system is reinforced, so I doubt a bullet would get through his skull, either."

"On the other hand, they still haven't managed to do a damn thing about the fragility of gray matter," Frieka pointed out. "If you battered him enough, you could bounce his brain around in that thick skull until he died of cerebral swelling."

Baran shrugged. "If he didn't manage to kill you in the meantime."

Jane sighed. "Damn. It just can't be easy, can it?" The Warlord's hand felt deliciously warm in hers. Suddenly she found herself uncomfortably aware of him.

An image flashed through her mind: Baran moving over her, his head thrown back so the cords stood out in high relief in his powerful throat.

Then she flashed on the sight of his big body, sprawled and helpless on the pavement. Her grip tightened convulsively on his hand. She'd thought she'd lost him.

She still could. If he fought Druas and lost . . .

You don't have him to lose, Jane told herself fiercely, tying off the bandage. *He's not going to stay with you, you idiot. As soon as this is over—one way or another—he's going back to his own time.*

And she couldn't afford to let him take her heart with him when he did.

Clamping her lower lip between her teeth, she started wrapping his other hand. Despite the injuries he'd suffered, his palm was broad and square and solid, his fingers long, beautiful. She remembered how skilled they'd felt, teasing her nipples into tight points, sliding into her sex in deliciously seductive strokes. Something hot gathered below her belly button.

Cut that out. We don't have time for this.

Which was when she glanced down at his lap—and the thick bulge that swelled behind his fly as she watched. She looked up to find his eyes were locked on her face again, heavy-lidded and hungry.

And glowing.

Jane started to draw back, but a gauze-wrapped hand lifted to cup the side of her face. The touch made her breath catch. Slowly he leaned forward until his mouth touched hers in a velvet-gentle kiss that made her heart pound. His tongue slipped over her upper lip, tempting her into opening for him. When she gasped, he slid inside slowly, taking his time. She heard a helpless, needy moan and realized it was her own.

"Well, if you're going to do that, I'm going to go catch squirrels," Freika announced. He slid between the seats and hopped out the open driver's door. "Maybe *I'll* get a little tail."

Jane didn't even register the quip. Her every sense was focused on Baran—the taste of his mouth, the warmth of his gauze-wrapped hand.

So even though she knew it was the wrong place, the wrong time, and the wrong man . . .

She didn't care.

They didn't have time for this.

He knew it. Knew he should cage his growling hunger and get back to work. Normally he'd be able to do just that, despite the hunger *riatt* had touched off. All it would take is a single order to his comp, and neuronet would chemically cool his ardor and let him concentrate again.

But she felt so damn fragile.

Every time Baran remembered Druas's smug voice spewing those poisonous threats, rage and desperation rolled over him, and he felt the driving need to touch her, reassure himself that she was alive.

So very hot and alive.

She shouldn't mean this much to him. She was, after all, only another mission. He'd protected women before in situations every bit as dangerous, and it had never affected him like this.

But there was something about Jane.

Maybe it was the fact that she didn't know enough to back down from him. Every other woman of his acquaintance would have hesitated to challenge, infuriate, or tempt him the way Jane did. A Warlord was not, after all, someone to take lightly. Particularly him. The Xeran did not give a nickname like "Death Lord" for no reason.

Yet he strongly suspected that even if Jane had known what he was capable of, she wouldn't have acted any differently. After all, she was already well aware of his greater size and muscle, but that had never stopped her, either.

Which was why keeping her alive was not going to be easy.

Sweet goddess, what if Druas hadn't been lying when he said this would end in her death? What if Baran really couldn't save her?

No, damn it. *No.*

With a low, desperate growl he twisted in the seat until he could drag Jane against his body, feel the giving warmth of her belly against his stone-hard erection.

Soon women would be dying, and Baran knew with a black, hopeless despair he'd fail to save at least some of them.

But Jane was here, warm and soft, so deliciously soft, and he was going to protect her no matter what he had to do.

She was his. And right now he was going to claim her.

Even if, one way or another, he'd eventually have to give her up.

Eleven

Baran had taken her before in calculation and in heat, but this desperation was new.

Jane could taste it in the way he kissed her, openmouthed and fierce, his long fingers curling around the back of her skull, angling her head just the way he wanted it.

He took her in a long, sweet stroke of tongue and lip, hot and wet and hungry. Somewhere in the endless tumble into delight, she heard the rumble of a passing car, accompanied by the short, mocking toot of its horn. A tiny measure of sanity returned. Prying her mouth away from his, she panted, "We can't do this on the side of the road, Baran!"

"Yes, we can," he growled, and captured her mouth again, the kiss drugging, hungry.

Jane wrestled free and threw a desperate glance around them, trying to determine if they were being watched. She realized she knew the area from her wild teenage years. "There's a spot down by the woods. A stream. We could . . ."

He looked down at her. The lust in his eyes was so intense, it didn't seem quite human—and not just because of the fiery glow.

His lips pulled back from his teeth in a slow, erotic smile. "Run. Before I take you on the hood of the truck." His powerful hands reluctantly relaxed their hold.

It wasn't an idle threat. Jane whirled and fled as if chased by something that would eat her. And with a little squirt of heat, she knew he intended to do just that.

She ran flat out, recklessly, plunging through the tangle of brush and trees, leaves crackling and flying around her booted feet. Throwing a glance over her shoulder, she saw Baran still standing by the truck, almost crouched, anticipation hot on his face. Even from yards away she could see the erection tenting his jeans.

Then he exploded after her.

Jane sucked in a desperate breath, whipped her head back around, and ran for all she was worth.

Her heart banged in her chest as she ducked between a stand of trees and jumped a bramble bush. She could hear him gaining already.

God, he was fast.

Her nipples hardened as she imagined just what he'd do when he caught her.

Every running step Baran took chafed the massive erection throbbing behind his fly. He had to consciously drag back on the instinctive need to leap across the distance separating them and take her down. Spread her. Fuck her.

He couldn't remember ever wanting a woman with this much hunger.

And every deep breath he took carried the growing scent of her desire, carried on the cool April wind. She was creaming for him, as turned on by this impromptu game as he was.

Breathing hard from lust more than exertion, he watched her round little ass roll with every step, the flash of her long, jeans-clad legs, the desperate pump of her arms. She was running with everything she had.

But she wanted to be caught almost as much as he wanted to catch her.

His hunger growled, dark and feral, demanding an end to the game. He lengthened his stride and reached for her delicate shoulder, meaning to jerk her off her feet and into his arms.

But to his amazement, she twisted with the instinct of something small and delicious and shot behind a tree, eluding his lunge. He growled and spun after her. For an instant their gazes met. Hers was bright with desire and humor, until whatever she saw in his made those brown eyes widen in feminine alarm. She yelped a giggle and took off again, ducking and dodging, using the trees as barriers to slow him down. He growled and charged in her wake, ignoring the brambles that dug into his shins as he shot through a bush instead of around it.

It was time he stripped that pretty little body and got those long legs spread.

Running for everything she was worth, Jane heard the chuckle of the stream over the crackling crash of the chase. She burst into the clearing with a sense of triumph, skidding into the wide, flat area beside the snaking creek. The spot hadn't changed from the days when she'd been a teenager and it had been the favored make-out spot.

Before she could stop, a big bandaged hand clamped over her shoulder, whirled her around, and snatched her against a hot, rock-hard body. She barely had time to register the raw lust on Baran's face before he was kissing her so hungrily, all the strength ran out of her knees.

One hand tunneled into her hair, holding her still for his mouth.

The other clamped boldly over her butt, dragging her lower body into his. His erection felt thick as a baseball bat against her belly.

Heat snaked through her as he claimed her with lips and tongue, licking, sucking at her mouth, gently biting her chin, strong fingers tugging her head back by the hair so he could rake his teeth across her banging pulse.

"Jesus, Baran," she managed as he lifted her off her feet and took her down into the crunching leaves.

No sooner had her back touched the ground than he was dragging up her shirt, then jerking her bra over the curves of her breasts to get at her hard nipples. Before she could even gasp, he was suckling one, teeth scraping and teasing as his tongue flicked the hard, pink point.

She grabbed at his massive shoulders to steady her spinning world. He went on feasting even as one big, impatient hand plucked at the button of her jeans, got it open, worked the zipper down. Reached inside. Tested her swollen outer lips.

"Mmmm. You're slick."

A thick finger slid inside, tore a gasp from her mouth. "Oh, God, Baran, you make me . . ."

He grinned darkly. "I noticed. You liked being chased, didn't you?" With his free hand, he pinched and rolled her nipple. "Didn't you?"

"Yeah. Oh, yeah." She whimpered softly.

His glowing eyes narrowed as he studied her with predatory calculation. "You do realize I can do anything I want to you?" The question was asked in a velvet purr that would have made her wet even without the stroke and slip of those possessive fingers. "You're totally helpless."

Jane swallowed at the jolt of desire that sliced through her at the dark promise in those words. "Not totally," she managed, as feminist instincts rebelled.

"Totally." It was a soft growl. The hand tormenting her sex slid away. She looked down just in time to see him reach into a jeans pocket and pull out a familiar length of gold cable. "Or you're about to be."

"Oh, no, you don't!" Jane started to sit up.

"Oh, yes," he purred, "I do." Before she manage more than an outraged yelp, he grabbed her shoulder and flipped her over on her belly. She tried to push up, run, but he slung a leg over her butt to pin her. Grabbing one wrist, he whipped the cable around it.

She gasped as he captured her other hand and pulled it down to join her captured wrist, then looped it in cable. The cool, slick metal tightened its grip, binding her hands at the small of her back. As her spine arched helplessly with her position, dried leaves teased her erect nipples. "You big jerk!"

"The operative word there is *big*," Baran said, a dark chuckle in his voice. He grabbed the waistband of her jeans and jerked downward. Cool air flowed over her backside as he bared her. "And getting bigger by the second."

He pulled her jeans down to her knees, trapping her legs in denim as effectively as the cable had bound her hands. Sliding an arm around her waist, he lifted and manipulated her body until he had her arranged the way he wanted—on her knees, ass thrust out, head pillowed on the leaves. She was so wet and hot, the air felt cold on her spread labia.

He made a deep, rumbling sound of satisfaction. Leaves rustled. Jane squeaked in surprise as warm fingers spread her lower lips and his tongue slipped into the creaming seam. She quivered in pleasure as he licked her like a man enjoying something hot and melting. His tongue played over her flesh with a wicked skill that had her thigh muscles jumping.

He drew away a moment, then slid a forefinger deep inside her, testing her readiness. "Very nice," he murmured as she writhed helplessly. The dry, papery leaves rasped over her nipples, and she moaned in need.

"You're driving me insane!" she managed.

Baran laughed softly. "Good."

Then his mouth sealed over her clit, and she jerked at the sudden, intense pleasure as he began to circle the wet nubbin with his tongue.

Baran angled his head slightly until he could slide two fingers deep into her core while he tongued her. The combination of those thick fingers and that wicked tongue sent pleasure whipping up her spine. Jane, wrists bound and legs trapped in her own jeans, could do nothing but shiver.

Eyes squeezed shut, she gasped, inhaling the rich, loamy scent of the leaves. Birds sang overhead, warbling background music for the tiny wet sounds Baran made as he licked and sucked.

She could feel a climax blooming just out of reach when he suddenly pulled away.

"Baran!" she wailed in protest.

"Ready to be fucked, Jane?"

The rough question in that deep, velvet voice was almost enough to make her come all by itself. "God, yes."

His zipper rasped. She waited, suspended, for that first ruthless thrust.

It didn't come.

"You sure?"

"Do you want to die?" she snarled in frustration.

He laughed. "Just checking." The round, smooth head of his hot cock brushed the fine hair over her desperate sex.

Jane whimpered in need. She'd never been so turned on in her life.

"You know what happens to pretty little civilians who let themselves get chased into the woods by hungry Warlords?"

"I've got . . . AH! . . . a pretty good idea." She shuddered at the incredible sensation of that slick head beginning to work its way past her lips and into her tight opening.

"Just so you're ready for it."

He worked in another inch. Jane gasped. "I'm . . . definitely ready."

"Good." And he rammed to his full length, all the way to the balls.

She screamed at the sensation of being filled so utterly. It was too much, too intense. She squirmed instinctively, but his strong hands held her still as he began to pump.

And she lost all interest in escape.

He rode her hard, his big shaft spearing her in long, delicious thrusts. Each jolting impact teased her nipples across the rasping leaves as he held her bent, arms bound helplessly behind her.

She shouldn't be so damned turned on. The arrogant bastard had chased her down and tied her up. It was kinky and uncivilized and not at all the kind of treatment a modern woman should tolerate.

And she loved it. Loved every hot, wicked thrust of that powerful cock, loved the feel of his hands gripping her hips, hauling her back into his ruthless banging.

The orgasm took her by surprise, kicked her screaming into pleasure. As she cried out, it kept right on pulsing with each slap of his body against her ass.

Baran sucked in a breath as she convulsed around him, her sheathe milking him in sweet pulses. She felt so good, the skin of her behind like silk against his groin. When he swallowed, he could taste her on his tongue, salty and hot. Each inhalation carried the scent of her musk. He shuttered his eyes and drew it deep as he stroked in and out of her, savoring the essence of sex and pleasure and Jane.

Her pale, narrow torso twisted as she writhed in the leaves under him, her chest left bare when he'd pushed her shirt up to her shoulders. Her delicate wrists were bound in restraint cable at the small of her back. Dark curls cascaded around her head in a river of sable silk. She moaned his name over and over as he fucked her, the breathy gasps arousing.

His own orgasm rose as her tight inner muscles rippled along his shaft. Spurred, Baran ground against her, reaching as deep as he could, trying to pound his way that last glittering increment into the climax hanging just out of reach.

Then he was there, bursting into light.

Ramming himself to full length, he held himself deep in her creaming grip as the heat poured into him and out of him in a pulsing erotic circuit.

When the storm passed, Baran collapsed over her, bracing his bandaged palms on the leafy ground. Sweating and gasping, he tried to remember the last time he'd fucked anybody this damn good.

Long moments passed before Jane felt her IQ rise enough to manage a whimper. Slowly she lifted her head and shook the mane of her hair aside until she could see her Warlord lover.

Baran knelt braced over her on his hands and knees. She was pleased to see his muscular arms were trembling. At least she wasn't the only one who'd gone completely out of her mind.

"We've got to quit doing this," she groaned.

"Why?" Leaves rustled as he sat back on his heels and pulled out of her tenderly. She groaned at the lost connection. He started unwrapping the cable from around her wrists.

"Because anything that feels that good has to be bad for you. It's a rule." Released, her arms flopped limply to the ground. Whimpering at the delicious soreness between her thighs, Jane rolled over onto her side. The breeze on her bare butt reminded her that her jeans were still pulled down, but she lacked the strength to pull them up again.

"I don't think there's an actual rule," Baran told her, zipping his pants.

"You must not have been raised Southern Baptist. There is. Believe me." She considered the mechanics of dressing herself. And stiffened as a thought occurred. She was on the Pill, but . . . "STDs." She stared wildly at him. "Oh, God, please tell me you don't have some little Martian whatzits that have now migrated to my—"

"What are you *talking* about?" He eyed her as she sat up convulsively.

"STDs," she told him grimly.

"What's an . . ." His eyes widened, then narrowed in offense. "I do *not* have a sexually transmitted disease!"

"That you know of." She scrambled around until she managed to jerk her jeans up and her shirt down. "I can't believe we had sex three times already, and it never once occurred to me . . . How do you make my common sense take a lunch break?"

Baran folded his brawny arms and glowered. "Evidently, it's a common occurrence."

"Hey!"

"To begin with, venereal diseases are highly uncommon in my time, and if I did get one, my neuronet comp would discover it and take appropriate action. Just as it has since I arrived and started encountering all the other microbes this medically backward time seems to breed. In other words," he concluded coolly, "I'm a lot more likely to get something from you than the other way around."

"I," she snarled, "do not sleep around. Which, considering the stories you've been telling me—"

"Perhaps it would be wise to drop this particular line of conversation."

"Fine!" Turning on a booted foot, she stomped through the trees. *Three hundred years*, Jane thought, simmering, *and men still haven't evolved beyond the need to kill a mood.*

When they finally made it back to the SUV, they found Freika sitting in the back, wearing a white, toothy grin.

"I caught two squirrels and told a stacked redheaded jogger I was the Big Bad Wolf. Scared the hell out of her," he said to Baran as they slid into their respective seats. "What did you get?"

"That," Jane said firmly, picking a leaf out of her hair, "is none of your business."

Looking across at Baran, she caught him grinning smugly over his shoulder at his partner. He didn't say a word.

He evidently didn't need to. "That's what I thought," Freika said, jaws gaping in a silent lupine laugh.

"Didn't your mother ever teach you not to kiss and tell?" Jane growled, and started the SUV.

"Why is he being so stubborn?" she demanded half an hour later, staring at the entrance to the Sleep Inn Motel. Baran had gone in to question the manager twenty minutes before, leaving her under Frieka's protection in the SUV.

"Because he's a Warlord," the wolf told her with a huge, toothy yawn. "That's the way he's programmed."

"Well, programming or no programming, Danny Jackson isn't gonna tell him a damn thing," Jane growled, sitting back in her seat. "He can't. He doesn't know Baran from Adam, doesn't know what he wants or why. For all he knows, Baran's planning to cap the guy." Which, come to think of it, he was. "If Danny gives him information about a guest, the hotel could get sued."

"Huh," Freika snorted. "I think it's safe to say Druas won't be suing anybody."

"Danny doesn't know that!" Her eyes narrowed. "But I'll bet he'd talk to me. I went to school with him. Hell, I did a story on his mamma's collection of vegetables shaped like Elvis." The wolf poked his head between the seats and stared at her. She shrugged. "Human interest feature. You'd have to be Southern to understand. Point is, I'll bet I could get him to give me the information, whether he's supposed to or not. But Baran wouldn't even let me try."

"You're a civilian," Freika told her, and angled his head toward her. "My implant is itching. Would you mind?"

She reached over and dug her nails behind his ear to give it a thorough scratch. "He doesn't trust me." The idea stung.

"Trust is not one of Baran's best skills," the wolf agreed. "Over a little. Besides, where we come from, most people take one look at his tattoo and his command beads and tell him whatever the hell he wants to know."

Intrigued, she shifted her target and scratched some more. "Why?"

"Ohhh, yeah. Right there . . ." The wolf produced an astonishingly human moan before continuing with the topic. "Because they either want to be helpful or don't want to piss him off. Either way, he's not used to refusals. That's enough, thanks."

She stopped scratching and began to stroke his head absently, enjoying the texture of the thick, coarse fur. "So the tatt and the beads mean something?"

"Right. The color stands for the House of Arvid, the Femmat clan that birthed, raised, and educated him before giving him into military service. The section of the design above his eye is the personal signature of his genetic creator, while the part over the cheekbone signifies he's a Viking Class Warlord. The empty circle at the bottom means he's an unbonded male; when he marries, the circle will be filled in."

Jane stopped stroking to reach into her handbag and pull out her notebook.

"If you start taking notes, I'll bite you."

She looked up into the wolf's hard blue-white gaze. "Oh, come on! I'm just trying to make sense of this."

"You want to cause a paradox? TE told us not to tell you a damn thing, and if we did, not to let you write it down. You don't know who will get his hands on those notes."

"Oh, all right!" Disgusted, she stuffed the notebook back into her bag. "So what's a Viking Class Warlord?"

"*Warlord* is a really rough translation of the actual term," the wolf explained, hopping up front to sit comfortably in the passenger seat. "It means a genetically engineered warrior. There are different classifications based mostly on weight and specialized skills. Comanche Class Warlords are scouts, built for endurance and speed, while Samurai are mostly bodyguards, specializing in hand-to-hand. Crusaders are good with weapons and make up the bulk of the infantry . . ."

"All of those are historical warriors renowned for their skill," Jane murmured to herself. "And Vikings . . ."

"Break things and kill people."

She eyed him. "You're making that up."

"No, seriously. They're the heavyweights of the military, the shock troops and raiders. The bitch Femmat civilian who accused him of being a human tank was pretty close to the mark."

"Hmmm." Jane digested that idea. "What about the beads?"

The wolf lifted a hind leg and scratched briskly at his left ear. "Rank and combat decorations. One of 'em also designates his status as a military assassin."

Jane gapped. "He's an *assassin?*"

Freika stopped scratching as though registering her instinctive revulsion. "It's not like in your time—grassy knolls and sniper scopes. Baran and I slip into guarded military camps and take out enemy commanders during wartime."

She frowned. "That sounds dangerous."

The wolf angled his head in his version of a shrug. "It's the stuff of suicide missions, sweetheart. We're good at it, mostly because Baran doesn't give a damn whether he lives or dies. And hasn't for a very long time."

"Not since the Xerans got his team," she guessed.

"Possibly. I only joined him when he volunteered for the assassination unit six years ago." He rested his head on her knee and looked up at her, something sad in his eyes. "My orders were to keep him from committing suicide by enemy, but he hasn't really attempted that, despite some close calls. Unfortunately, I have a feeling that will change when he finally goes after General Jutka."

"Who's General Jutka?"

The wolf was silent so long, she had to prompt him. "Freika? Who's Jutka?"

"I think you'd better ask Baran that. But I will tell you he's the man we're supposed to go after when we return to our own time." Before she could interrogate him further, Freika said, "Whoops, there comes Baran. And he's not happy."

Jane looked up to see him striding across the parking lot toward them, his braid swinging angrily against his cheek. She'd stopped off and picked him up a pair of sunglasses before they'd gone to the motel, but she was willing to bet that behind their protection, his eyes were glowing with rage.

He walked over to her car door and pulled it open. "Okay," he growled, his tone savage. "You try."

Simmering, Baran watched Jane charm the doughy desk clerk who had coldly refused to tell him a damn thing a few minutes before. He'd done everything he could think of to get the information he wanted, short of hauling the little bastard over the counter and planting his fist in that smug round face. He'd considered that, too, but his computer had warned him there was a ninety-eight percent chance the clerk would call local law enforcement. And he couldn't afford to go to jail, not with Druas after Jane.

Who, at that very moment, was leaning her elbows on the counter and hanging on to the doughy little bastard's every word.

The man temporized. She wheedled. He wavered.

Finally the clerk sat down at the primitive computer behind the counter. "There's only one guy that's checked in within the last three days without family members in tow," the man said, fingers tapping on the keys. "Tony Anderson. Atlanta address. He told me he sells farm equipment. I think he's talking to the guy with Sanders Tractor and Farm Supply. . . ."

"Oh, yeah. Jimmy Sanders. I interviewed him when his guard unit got called up for Operation Iraqi Freedom."

Was there anybody she hadn't interviewed?

"What's his room number, Danny?"

"Now, Jane, you know I can't tell you that." At her pleading expression, he hesitated. "Uh, would you like a cup of coffee? I just put on a fresh pot."

She looked at him a second before a dazzling smile spread across her face. "Sure, Danny. That'd be great."

The clerk got up and ducked through a doorway behind the counter. Jane stood on tiptoes and craned her neck to check out the computer screen. "Our boy's in Room 104," she told Baran and made for the door. "Come on, let's check it out."

He caught her wrist as they stepped outside. "No, I'll check it out, you wait with Freika. If it is Druas, I don't want you in the line of fire."

Jane frowned at him, her rich brown eyes concerned. "I don't like that idea, Baran. "What if you need backup?"

"I won't." He eyed her a moment from behind the awkward sunglasses she'd given him. "Why was he willing to give that information to you when he wouldn't tell me anything even when I all but threatened him?"

Jane shrugged. "Tayanita is a small community, Baran. Everybody knows everybody. But nobody knows you, so nobody's going to talk to you. You'll be seriously hampered if you try to investigate this thing by yourself. Like it or not, you need me."

Baran frowned heavily, watching as she got back into the truck. He was beginning to see that.

And he didn't like it. Not one bit.

Twelve

B ut when Baran stalked back to the SUV five minutes later, it was to say that Tony Anderson was not Druas. He hadn't even had to talk to him—just scan him through the door. The man was definitely not Xeran.

Their luck was no better at the other two motels, though Baran did allow Jane to do the talking. She was able to get the information they needed at the Avon, but even she struck out with the clerk at the Journey's Inn. Baran was forced to circle the entire motel, scanning each room for signs of the Xeran or twenty-third-century equipment. He came back simmering with frustration.

"So where the hell is Druas?" Jane said as Baran got in the SUV and slammed the door. She could make out the glow in his eyes even through the sunglasses.

"Probably killing somebody," he snarled.

On the dashboard the scanner crackled and popped.

* * *

They ended up stopping at a Burger King drive-through for a late lunch. At Jane's suggestion, all three of them got out of the SUV to eat at one of the restaurant's cement tables in the shade of a huge, colorful umbrella.

The scanner at her elbow, Jane munched a french fry and watched Baran sniff his burger dubiously while Freika worked his way through a pile of Whoppers on the grass at their feet. "Who's Jutka?"

Baran put down his food and looked down at the wolf, who gazed up at him guiltily. Then he shrugged and went back to eating. "A Xeran general."

"Whom you're supposed to kill."

"It *would* simplify the war considerably."

"If you don't get killed trying."

He munched and considered the question. "There's always that."

Jane dragged another fry through a blob of ketchup and frowned. "Freika's worried you won't be as careful as you should be. Why? What's so special about this guy—I mean, considering you've evidently been assassinating people a while now."

He looked up at her and chewed, his face expressionless. She was beginning to regret buying him those sunglasses. At times he looked entirely too much like the Terminator in them. "Freika talks too much."

"Well, yeah, but sometimes he does have a point."

"Thank you," said a voice from under the table.

But before Baran could answer the question—assuming he intended to—a short horn toot called their attention. Jane looked up to see a familiar champagne Crown Vic whip into a parking space not far from their table. Tom Reynolds got out.

Normally Jane would be delighted to see the primary in a murder investigation, particularly when she hadn't interviewed him yet. This time, though, there was something in Reynolds's calculating expression that made her uneasy.

"Taking a break from harassing hotel clerks, Jane?" he asked pleasantly, plopping down on the cement bench across from her and Baran.

Hell, Jane thought. *Busted. Maybe literally, judging from the look on Tom's face.* She shrugged and pasted a bright smile on her own. "Just working on a story."

"Yeah, and I know exactly what story you're working on," he said, his eyes hard. "Stay out of my case, Nancy Drew." Tom flicked a gaze at Baran. "By the way, exactly when did the Hardy Boy here come to town? He wasn't with you Friday night at the murder scene. In fact, you didn't even mention you'd hired him."

"The subject didn't come up," Jane drawled. Oh, God, Tom was suspicious of Baran. She thought fast. "He flew in early this morning."

"Yeah?" His eyes flicked to the bigger man's face. "You already found a place to stay?" His smile held a distinct edge. "You're not registered at any of the motels."

Baran leaned an elbow on the table and lifted a dark brow. "Actually, I'm staying with my good friend Jane."

"Uh-huh." The look he gave Jane was so coolly disapproving, she felt her cheeks heat. "Your daddy wouldn't much like that."

"Daddy didn't like a lot of things," Jane snapped back. "But since I'm twenty-nine years old, he wouldn't have had much say even if—" She clamped her teeth shut over *he wasn't a dead wife-beater.*

"Guess not." She was surprised at how much the disappointment in Reynolds's eyes stung. He flicked his attention back to Baran. "How you feeling after your little run-in with that lightning bolt?"

"It wasn't a lightning bolt. And I'm fine."

"Even the hands? Gashed 'em up pretty well, looked like. Get 'em tended?"

Baran shrugged and displayed a broad palm. He'd pulled off Jane's makeshift bandages after the trip to the second hotel. Now the wound showed as nothing more than a healing red line. "They looked worse than they were."

Tom frowned at his palm in astonishment. "Damn, I could have sworn—"

"How about the woman in the car wreck?" Jane interrupted, pulling out her notebook more as a means of distracting the detective than anything else. "How's she doing?"

The detective's expression turned grim. "She didn't make it."

Baran stiffened. Jane glanced over at him. His face was blank, but she could sense his helpless anger at the news. He'd tried so desperately to save her. . . .

"That's too bad," she said softly. Straightening her shoulders, she assumed an expression of cool professional interest. "What can you tell me about the crash?"

Tom lifted a sandy brow at her. "I just directed traffic, Jane. You need to talk to the Highway Patrol to get the details. You know that."

Of course she did, but she also wanted to keep him from grilling Baran. "Oh, yeah. So what about the murder? Can you tell me anything about it?"

Tom hesitated, then sighed. "Let me go get my paperwork out of the car." He got up and headed back toward his Crown Vic.

As he walked away, Jane looked at Baran, taking in his stony expression. "You tried," she said softly.

He shrugged, but something in the movement communicated pain. "Evidently I wasn't supposed to succeed."

Thirty minutes later Jane tucked her notebook back in her purse as Tom drove away. He'd given her the formal details of the case, including the victim's identification. She'd have to get the details of the cause of death from the Tayanita county coroner, but she already knew what he'd say: Jennifer Moore had been strangled, then methodically butchered.

She sighed and looked over at Baran, who'd listened patiently during her conversation with Reynolds. "So where do we go from—"

". . . Alpha six, caller reports stabbing at 534 Cherokee Lane," the scanner interrupted.

All three of them froze, looking at the rectangular device as the tension rose, almost vibrating in the air between them. "Is that . . ." Baran began.

". . . white male victim, blond hair, blue eyes. Caller said she stabbed him in the buttocks when she caught him with another woman."

Relieved, Jane grinned at the Warlord. "Ten will get you twenty the butt in question was bare and between the other woman's thighs at the time of the stabbing."

Baran's lips twitched as he relaxed, sitting back on the cement bench. "In any case, I doubt Druas was involved."

"Not unless he was the victim, anyway." She snorted. "Now, there's a mental image to cherish."

"We're not that lucky."

"Not judging by recent events, no." Jane sobered. "So, as I was saying before our butt-stabbing friend interrupted—where do we go from here?"

Baran shook his head, beads tapping his cheek. "I have no idea. Unless you want to drive around Tayanita County while I scan every house."

"God, please no," Freika said from underneath the table. "I don't think I could take being cooped up in that truck with both your libidos that long. I'm traumatized enough as it is."

Jane picked up a cold french fry and threw it at him. He snapped it out of the air. As he swallowed, she looked over at Baran. "Much as I hate to admit it, I don't care for that idea, either."

He shrugged and drummed his fingers on the cement table. "It does sound like a waste of time."

"Besides," she added, picking the scanner up and tucking it back into her purse, "I've got a newspaper to put out tomorrow, and right now I don't have a damn thing to put in it. Well, nothing anybody would believe anyway, assuming I could even print it. . . ."

"Which you can't," Frieka said, popping over the lip of the table to lick up a couple of surviving fries with his long pink tongue. "You know, these are good."

Jane aimed a swat at his pointed ears. He dodged, giving her a dirty look. "As I was saying," she continued to Baran, "I need to do a couple more interviews."

He lifted a questioning brow. "With whom?"

She grimaced. "Jennifer Moore's family."

Which, she knew, wasn't going to be any fun at all.

Cars were lined up on both sides of the street in front of the neat brick colonial that belonged to Jennifer's sister, Rebecca Rogers.

Jane pulled the SUV into an empty spot and got out as she draped the chain of her press card around her neck. Opening the rear door, she reached for the huge peace lily that occupied the seat next to Freika. She'd had to pick it up at the grocery store, since all the florists were closed on Sunday.

Reporters didn't usually give flowers to survivors, but Jane had gotten into the habit years ago. It was a multipurpose gesture, showing she both sympathized and regretted intruding. Families seemed to get the message; she got cussed out a lot less now, and people were more inclined to talk to her.

"You're going to have to stay in the car," she told the wolf when he started to jump out past her.

"I've got a better idea," he said. "Let me out to terrorize the neighbors."

Jane snorted. "This is South Carolina, furball—even the little old ladies are armed. Somebody'd shoot you." Turning, she found Baran eyeing the line of cars with a frown.

"I don't understand why this is necessary," he said. "They can't tell us anything about Druas."

"No, but they can tell me something about Jennifer Moore," she said, fluffing the plant's emerald leaves. "And like it or not, talking to the families of victims is part of my job."

Jane hadn't even bothered to ask Tom where to find Jennifer's family—she'd known he wouldn't tell her. But when she'd driven by the *Trib* office, she'd discovered that, as she'd hoped, the funeral home had already faxed in the obituary. As was customary, the obit had listed where Jennifer's family could be reached.

The plant in her arms and Baran at her heels, Jane started toward the brick two-story. Her stomach twisted with that ugly, sick feeling she always got when she had to conduct this kind of interview. She knew families of murder victims often seethed with impotent rage—a rage for which reporters made the perfect guilt-free target.

Unfortunately, without a human glimpse of the victim's personality, it was too easy for readers to view this kind of story as more titillating than tragic. So Jane gritted her teeth and sought to ignore the knots assembling themselves in her stomach.

Then Baran took her elbow as she started across the neatly trimmed lawn. There was something so comforting about his solid male presence, she felt the knots ease.

This was, she thought, so much easier with a partner.

A number of people were sitting out on the house's screened-in front porch. One of the traditions of Southern grief was that friends and family always gathered as soon as they heard the news of a death, to sympathize, cry, and bring food. The crowd usually ended up spilling out on the porch; Jane had lost count of the number of interviews she'd done standing on the front stoop.

A pale, subdued young woman came to push the screen door open and take the peace lily from her arms. "Thank you for coming," she said in a soft upper-class drawl, probably assuming Jane and Baran were friends of the family.

Jane lifted her laminated press badge and met the woman's eyes. "I'm sorry to intrude on your grief. Jane Colby with *The Tayanita Tribune*. We were wondering if you had a photo you wanted to run of Mrs. Moore in the paper tomorrow." Usually the funeral home took care of that detail, but then again, they might not.

The brunette's expression cooled. "I'll check," she said, and turned around to step back into the house.

Jane, with Baran behind her, instantly found herself the focus of five pairs of hostile eyes. "I want to tell you how sorry I am for your loss," she said, letting the sympathy she felt show in her own gaze. "This is"—she couldn't think of a word that did it justice and settled on—"horrible."

A tall, thin girl spoke up from the wooden porch swing. "Did the police tell you anything? Do they know . . ."

Somebody hushed the teenager, but Jane answered her question anyway. "At this point, they're still investigating, trying to find witnesses."

"It wasn't Barry," a haggard, potbellied man said. Grief and anger seethed in his voice. "People are going to think it was Barry, but he was at work. Second shift at the Triad plant. This is killing him. And the kids . . . Her little kids . . ."

She had two, according to the obit. They were six and four; Tom had said they'd been spending the night with their grandmother when it happened. Jane winced at the thought of what Druas might have done to them had they been home.

"It's good you're all here. They're going to need all the support they can get." Taking a deep breath, Jane added, "I wondered if anyone has anything they'd like to say about Jennifer, about the kind of person she was. As a tribute to her." She took her notebook out of her purse by way of making clear anything they said would be for the paper.

A silence fell while the little group digested the question. They'd either throw her out now or talk to her.

"She loved her kids and she loved her husband," somebody said.

In the next fifteen minutes a picture emerged of a bright, pretty young woman who did pastel sketches of her friends' children and homeschooled her own. She'd taught Sunday school and told corny jokes and had evidently never met a single human being she didn't try to make friends with.

Her husband thought she'd hung the moon. He was somewhere inside, sitting in dazed shock. Yesterday had been their tenth wedding anniversary; they'd planned a romantic dinner that evening. Instead one of the neighbors had called him at the textile plant where he worked third shift to tell him his house was surrounded by police. He'd raced home in a panic only to find his wife dead and himself a suspect.

While Jane was gently extracting her quotes, the woman emerged from the house with Jennifer's photo and handed it to her. "I couldn't find one of her by herself," she said. "All I had was the group shot they took at Christmas."

"That's okay," Jane said. "We can crop it." She looked down and felt her heart clutch.

Jennifer and her husband sat side by side in the professional studio shot, two cherubic blondes standing in front of them. The two little girls had their mother's warm, broad smile and their father's hazel eyes.

Druas had destroyed that idyllic picture, butchered that pretty woman simply because he could. But Jennifer wasn't his only victim. He'd shattered the lives of her children and her husband, too. Her little ones would grow up with the scars of trauma and loss, and her husband would feel the ache until the day he died. To make matters worse, there would always be whispers, questions, rumors that he'd murdered the woman he'd loved.

"Pretty family," Jane said to Baran, a knot in her throat.

"Yes," he said, looking down at the photo from over her shoulder.

She looked up at him. He wore the carefully blank expression she'd come to realize meant he'd locked down his emotions. Somewhere behind those dark glasses, she knew, hell was banked in his eyes.

Without another word the Warlord pivoted and walked out the screen door. It banged shut behind him.

Jane stared at his retreating back, then shot a wide-eyed look at the bewildered group on the porch. "Thank you for your time."

Tucking the photo in her purse, she hurried out after him.

"He's stolen so much from them," Baran said as they got back in the truck.

Jane thought of the photo, of Jennifer Moore's shattered family. All her life, she'd lived with the gnawing suspicion her father had killed her mother. Yet she'd never been sure. Maybe that's why she'd been so driven to become a reporter—so that others would never have to wonder what lay behind a shield of lies.

For the first time, she wondered if the truth was such a blessing. Jennifer's little girls would never even have the dim, faint hope their mother might be alive. They'd know exactly how she died; every detail of her murder would be laid out in newspaper and television stories. Hell, if the Tayanita killings did gain the notoriety of the Ripper murders, they'd find themselves sought out for anniversary interviews from now on. Endlessly tormented.

They didn't deserve that.

Yet not knowing . . .

Had William Colby killed her mother? If he had, how? Did he use that .38 that even now waited back home in Jane's attic, or had he simply used his fists on her one last time? Had she suffered?

Or was Jeanine Colby alive and well somewhere, daughter and abusive husband forgotten?

Damn, Jane would like to believe that. Unfortunately, everyone who'd ever known her mother couldn't believe Jeannine would simply abandon Jane.

Was it better not to know? Who was luckier—Jane or Jennifer's little girls?

She . . .

The cell phone rang in its pocket in her purse.

One hand on the wheel, Jane reached into her purse with the

other and fished the phone out. "Jane Colby," she said, as she always did when she was working.

"She's got the most lovely legs," a male voice said. "Not as long as yours, of course, but not bad."

Jane frowned, distracted and puzzled. "I think you've got the wrong number."

"Oh, I don't think so. Tell me—have you been enjoying your handsome visitor from the future? Or should I say—has he been enjoying you?"

A wave of ice seemed to roll up the back of her neck. "Druas."

"Very good."

Baran reached for the cell. "Give me that."

"Do it and I'll kill her now," Druas snapped. "I want to talk to you, Jane."

She licked her lips. Shit. She had to stall him. Waving Baran off, she demanded, "Where are you?"

"Ohh, some Tayanita landmark. Laughing children, dancing water—and a pretty girl, running as if her life doesn't depend on it. But it does."

Laughing children? Oh, hell. Jane fought panic as she tried to figure out what he was referring to. "Leave her alone, Druas."

"I can't do that, Jane. Wouldn't want to cause a paradox, now would we?" His laugh was low and taunting. "When you think about it, I'm not committing murder, I'm saving the universe."

"Oh, yeah, you're a big hero," Jane growled, fighting to think where he could be. Dancing water, laughing children . . .

Her eyes widened. There were bronze statues of laughing children around a fountain in Cherokee Park—along with jogging trails.

The son of a bitch was about to murder a jogger.

Jane stomped on the gas and shot toward town. Luckily the park was close by. If they could just make it in time . . . "Why are you doing this, Druas?" she demanded, hoping to stall him long enough for them to arrive. "You're a mercenary, a warrior. Those women can't be a challenge for you."

"No, but your handsome fuck buddy is. Now, *there's* a killer. You do know his body count is higher than mine?"

Baran had whipped off his sunglasses to stare at her, listening hard with his Warlord hearing. His eyes shone as red as a couple of coals. Jane ignored him. "I'm a lot more interested in you at the moment."

"You should be. I'm going to kill you, Jane."

She almost lost control of the SUV. "No. You're not. Baran—"

". . . Is going to be too late, just like he was too late to save that bitch in the car this afternoon. My face is going to be the last thing you ever see. And my dick is going to be the last thing you ever feel—after my knife, of course."

"You're the one who's going to die, Druas," Baran snarled, lifting his voice so the phone would pick it up.

"If I do, it won't be in time to save you, bitch. You're going to squeal for me, just like all the others. Just like Baran squealed for my comrades back on Vardon. He was such a pretty boy. I'll bet he hasn't told you about that."

"Yes, he did." Her skin felt curiously numb, cold. She fought to concentrate on her driving, on getting them there in time. "He told me all about what you sick Xeran bastards did."

Druas laughed. Something in the sound made her skin crawl. "Oh, I doubt that. I doubt that very much. Some things a man just doesn't tell the woman he's screwing."

"What are you talking about?" Ice slid over her. He couldn't mean what she thought he meant.

Not Baran.

"Sorry, Jane, you're just not going to be able to stall me that long. I've got to go kill her now."

The phone went dead.

"Shit," Jane spat, slamming the gas pedal all the way to the floor as she dialed 911. "Shit shit shit shit."

"What's your emergency?" the dispatcher said.

"A woman's about to be murdered in Cherokee Park. Send everybody you can dispatch. Now."

"Wait a minute, who is this? How do you know that?"

"Jane Colby with the *Trib*. The killer just called me on my cell."

"Ma'am, we'll send somebody to check it out, but it was probably a prank."

"It wasn't a prank, damn it! It was a fucking serial killer, and if you just send one deputy, that girl is not going to be the only one bleeding out on the ground. Your cop is going to end up dead!"

"It's not necessary to use that kind of language, ma'am."

"Do you want to be on the front page in fifty point type, lady? 'Dispatcher refuses to send adequate help: woman murdered.' How does that sound, huh? 'Cause I can do it!" She hit the End button and slung the phone back in her purse. "Stupid bitch." Zipping around a minivan, she screeched up to the curb in front of the park.

Near the entrance, a fountain sprayed a plume of water skyward from the center of a ring of dancing children.

Baran threw his door open and jumped out without bothering to close it behind him. He took off at a run. "Freika, stay with Jane! I've got Xeran sensor readings!"

"I'm going with . . ." She blinked, watching his retreating back as he raced toward the trees. She'd never seen a human being move so fast in her entire life; he was almost a blur. She started after him.

"No!" Freika's teeth closed on the hem of her pants, dragging her to a stumbling halt. "He's right. If Druas gets you out in those woods away from Baran, you're dead."

She looked down at him helplessly. "But . . ."

In the distance a woman screamed, her voice ringing with terror.

Then there was nothing but the sound of the fountain's spray pattering on brick.

Thirteen

Baran went to *riatt* as he ran, neurochemicals roaring through his body in a molten flood, power pumping in after them. This time he would be in time. This time he was going to kill the bastard and end it.

He could see them in his mind, his computer generating the image from sensor data since they were out of direct view. The girl ran easily, not realizing she was in danger as Druas closed in from behind in a leisurely jog. As if he had all the time in the world.

Baran poured on the speed, dodging around the trees that blocked his path.

As if sensing him, the Xeran glanced back over his shoulder. He began to run. The girl turned, evidently hearing him. Her scream rang high and shrill over the trees.

The Jumpkiller didn't bother with the slow strangulation that might have given Baran time to reach them. The computer image painted the flash of steel as he drew the knife, the arch of his arm swinging, the spray of hot blood. The girl crumpled; Baran was close enough now to glimpse the movement through the trees with his own eyes.

Close, so close, but not close enough. Not close enough to be in time.

Druas stepped back. With his sensors engaged, Baran could see the temporal field building around the murderer's T-suit in waves of warping time.

BOOM!

And the killer was gone, leaving only the girl dying in the leaves as Baran skidded up.

Her eyes met his, wide with horror over her ruined throat, begging him silently for help. Druas might not have taken the time to strangle her, but he hadn't cut deep enough to render her unconscious, either. He'd meant for her to suffer, to know she was dying without being able to do anything to save herself.

Death in 2.3 minutes, Baran's comp told him.

How can I save her? he demanded as he fell to his knees beside her crumpled body. *Apply pressure?*

Ineffective. She'll die before medical assistance can arrive.

He had to try anyway. Jerking the T-shirt off over his head, Baran wadded it up and pressed it against the wound, trying to avoid cutting off her breathing as he did so. She lifted a shaking hand and wrapped it around his, fighting feebly to help.

"Hang on," he ordered roughly, watching the white shirt turn red as she bled out into it. "Stay with me."

As if in answer, she made an awful, strangling sound. The bewildered pain in her glazing eyes choked him. It was all so vicious, so pointless. Savagery for its own mindless sake.

"I'm going to kill him," he gritted as he smoothed her blond hair back from her face with his free hand.

She blinked up at him once. Her mouth moved, but no sound emerged. He struggled to read her lips. Something about "husband" and "love."

Then the life bled away from her eyes, and her hand fell limply to the leaves.

And Baran, who'd killed more men than he even cared to think about, felt his shoulders began to shake.

Jane heard the temporal boom roll out over the trees over the wail of sirens. "Son of a bitch." She started toward the sound, but Freika grabbed her again.

"We don't know where Druas transported," the wolf said. "In those trees he could Jump right in behind you before I could do a damn thing."

"Fuck." She was tempted to run in after Baran anyway, but she knew if she didn't wait to tell the police he'd gone to help, they might shoot him by mistake.

The first car roared up with shrieking sirens and squealing brakes. The door flew open and an officer scrambled out, gun already drawn. She knew him from a previous crime scene: Tony Garrison. He'd been a deputy barely a year.

"That way!" Jane yelled, pointing in the direction Baran had gone. "They're in the woods. My photographer went after them."

"Gonna get himself killed," the cop grunted, holstering his weapon as he grabbed his shoulder mike to radio it in before running toward the tree line.

"Now we can go," Jane told Frieka, and sprinted after the officer.

"Jane—"

"Find Baran," she snapped, cutting off his protest. "One of these cops could shoot him if I'm not there to defuse the situation."

The wolf hesitated, then growled something and shot ahead of both of them. Jane brought up the rear, pouring everything she had into every stride she took.

"Stay back!" the cop yelled at her.

"The wo . . . dog belongs to my photographer!" Jane yelled back.

"Freika'll track Baran. Since he went in after the girl, if we find him, we'll find her."

Garrison muttered something that was probably obscene, but didn't protest again as the two of them crashed on through the woods.

They found Baran cradling a limp figure in his arms, his broad, bare shoulders hunched, head bowed. His braids trailed in the blood that covered her chest. He'd pulled off his shirt; it lay forgotten in a gory bundle in the dead leaves beside him.

"Put her down and back away," Garrison ordered, drawing his weapon.

"It's my photographer!" Jane protested, her stomach twisting as she stepped between Baran and the cop. She'd been afraid of this. "I told you, he came in to help her!"

"I've only got your word on that," the deputy gritted. "And I'm not taking chances. Get out of the way, lady, or your ass is going to jail!"

She knew he was just pissed off enough to do it, but she had to make him listen. "Baran was only trying to save her!"

"But I didn't." She looked back over her shoulder and caught her breath. The Warlord's lethal gaze was fixed on the deputy's gun. "Get that weapon out of my face." He still had his sunglasses on, thank God, but he'd been in *riatt*. She remembered how he'd taken her in the woods and realized just how shaky his control over his emotions really was. If the cop got too aggressive, Baran just might slam him through a tree.

Hell. That was all they needed.

"Put the girl down, sir!" Garrison set his feet apart and steadied his aim.

"If you don't shift your aim, I'm going to make you eat that gun." His voice was utterly toneless, matter-of-fact, but something in his face made the cop back up a pace.

Then Garrison stopped himself and steadied his aim. "Sir, I will shoot you."

And he would, Jane knew. Especially since he'd only gotten out of the Academy a few months before—and this might be the first time he'd ever faced a man over the body of a murdered woman.

Or seen anything like the killing rage in the Warlord's eyes.

"Put her down, Baran!" she said, raising her voice just short of a yell, trying to penetrate the Warlord's *riatt* frenzy. "He'll do it. And you're not thinking clearly."

He stared at her for a long moment before he gently lowered his limp burden to the ground. "She's already gone. I didn't get here in time."

"Down on the ground!" the deputy snarled. "Hands behind your head."

"Deputy Garrison, he didn't hurt her!" Jane raised her empty hands to show she wasn't armed. "The man who did this called us on my cell phone and told us he was about to attack her, and Baran ran in here trying to help."

"So where is this killer, huh?"

"Getting away while you wave a gun in our faces!"

"My job is to secure the scene," Garrison snapped. "I'm securing it. Get! Down!"

"Tony, I'm a reporter. You know me!"

"And you should know better than to interfere with a police officer! Down on the ground! Both of you!"

"Do it, Jane." Baran said heavily, and stretched out beside the body of the woman he'd fought—and failed—to save.

She looked from Garrison's furious eyes to the bore of his gun, sighed, and obeyed. As the deputy began to pat Baran down, she pressed her face into the crinkling leaves and tried not to wonder who Druas was planning to kill next.

It might just be her.

"Lose the shades," Tom Reynolds said to Baran as they sat in the detective's car. "It's like talking to the Terminator."

He had no idea who the Terminator was, but Baran obeyed the detective anyway. For lack of anywhere else to put them, he held them in his lap. It was a good thing enough time had passed to give his body time to recover from *riatt,* or his eyes would have given him away. Unfortunately, he still felt raw, and he knew his control over his simmering rage wasn't the best. Law enforcement agents on his own world would have understood, but these deputies obviously found his reaction to the aftereffects suspicious.

One of them, watching the tremors shake him, had asked if he was under the influence. Baran had asked, "Of what?" For some reason, the man had not seemed to appreciate the question.

Now Baran eyed Reynolds and hoped he could get through this interview quickly. Jane was being questioned in another car, and Baran did not particularly like having her out of his sight. Freika was sitting patiently by the vehicle she occupied, standing guard, but that wasn't enough. The wolf was deadly in a fight, but it was doubtful he could hold Druas off in any extended combat.

The facts were brutally simple. If Baran was arrested, Jane was dead.

His fists clenched. He couldn't afford to be taken. If he had to fight these men so he could snatch her and run, he'd do it. He would not allow Druas to butcher her as he had the woman Baran had just watched die.

"It's been a bitch of a day, huh, Hoss?" the detective asked in a low, quiet voice, watching his face. "You've tried to save two women and fucked up both times."

Baran's head snapped toward the detective so hard the beads slapped his cheek. It took him a moment to cool his helpless rage and blank his expression. "So it would seem."

"Pisses you off, doesn't it?" The cop settled back in his seat and wrote something down on the little notebook he held. "You cut yourself all to hell trying to get the first woman out of the car, then you go tearing through the woods after a killer, only to get there too late. All you can do is watch her die in your arms. Sucks to be you, huh?"

He almost told the deputy he'd had to watch people die before, but remembered the photographer he was supposed to be. "I've had better days."

"So tell me what happened."

"I have already told you what happened," Baran said, restraining his flare of irritation at hearing the question yet again. "Just as I told the three other officers who asked."

"We just want to make sure we get the details right," Reynolds said blandly. "So when was the first time you met this girl?"

Baran frowned. "What girl?"

"The girl that just died."

He shook his head and drummed his fingers on the car's dashboard, staring at Jane's silhouette in the back of the other patrol car. He wanted to be done with this so he could get her to safety. "As I said before—repeatedly—I didn't know her. All I did was try to . . ."

Suddenly a plump, motherly woman ran past the front of the car. Even through the closed window, Baran could hear her sobbing screams of denial.

A cop ran to meet her. She tried to push by, but he stepped to block her. She screamed something and flung herself at him just as a middle-aged man ran up to drag her back.

"That would be the momma and daddy," Reynolds said. Baran could almost feel the weight of his coolly analytical gaze, dissecting every expression, every twitch. "That's the thing about a small town. Somebody dies, and two minutes later the family knows it. Poor bastards." Softly, cruelly, he added, "You want me to introduce you? I mean, you did try to save her, right?"

For an instant Baran considered planting his fist in the man's face. Unfortunately, he still had so much *riatt* left in his system, the blow would probably kill the detective. He forced his muscles to relax.

The detective smiled slightly. "That's better. Thought for a minute

I was going to have to shoot your ass right here in the car. You're a scary bastard when you want to be. Your eyes ... I could have sworn . . ." He shook his head and closed his notebook with a tired sigh. "Okay, you can go. I gotta start looking for this son of a bitch."

Baran lifted his brows, wondering if this was some kind of trick. "That's it?"

"I've talked to a lot of people who just killed somebody, and you don't have the look. You've got the eyes of a guy who's blaming himself for not being thirty seconds faster."

Baran smiled slightly, dryly. The detective was far too perceptive.

"Besides," Reynolds continued, "I've known Jane since she was twelve years old and coming to crime scenes with her daddy. If she says you didn't do it, you didn't do it."

His muscles cautiously unknotting, Baran reached for the door handle. "Thank you."

"Don't forget your blanket." Reynolds had handed it to him so he wouldn't have to walk past the crowd of onlookers bare-chested and covered in gore. "None of us needs the kind of rumors *that* would trigger."

He nodded and pulled it up around his shoulders again as Reynolds radioed the other officer to let Jane out of his car.

As he got out, Reynolds leaned over and looked up at him. "By the way, tell her she needs to get a new cell number. And don't give this one out to everybody in town, dammit. The wrong guy definitely got hold of it this time."

The Warlord nodded. "I'll make sure to pass along the message."

"On the other hand, don't." Reynolds frowned. "We may need to put a tap on her phone. Might be useful if he calls again."

With an effort, Baran kept his opinion of that idea off his face. All the police needed to do was listen to one call, and they'd realize he and Jane knew far more about their mystery killer than they should. *That,* he thought, *we definitely do not need.*

Baran pushed the door open as Jane get out of the other car and hurried toward him, Freika trotting at her heels.

"Let's get the hell out of here," he growled.

"God, yes," she said, glancing toward two men, one armed with a video camera, who were working through the crowd of onlookers toward them. "There comes that jerk Clarkson from WDRT News. We *don't* want to talk to him—particularly not with you covered in blood." She led the way back toward the SUV at a speed just short of a run.

As they pulled away from the curb a moment later, she glowered into her rearview mirror at the camera pointed at their truck. "I never thought I'd ever be the one running from reporters. Usually I'm at the head of the pack." She turned her attention to the road, a grim set to her mouth. "Damn, I don't want to end up as that bastard's lead story."

Glancing at him, she read his puzzlement. "There's an old saying in television journalism, Baran—'If it bleeds, it leads.'"

An hour later Jane realized she was a slut.

It was, she decided, the only possible explanation. No decent Southern belle would get this turned on after the day she'd just spent. Not even watching Baran Arvid take a shower.

Dry-mouthed, she gazed through the bubbled glass door at the muscle shifting in his powerful arms as he washed all that long, black hair. She barely noticed the beads biting into her hands. He'd handed them to her when he'd taken down his bloody braids; now she clenched her fingers around them and fought to control the impulse to join him.

Yep. Slut. She had to face facts.

White runnels of soap ran down the rippled planes of pectorals and washboard abs, painting slow and sensual trails that Jane would love to follow with her fingertips.

Yet even through the glass, she could see the tired slump in his body, could tell from the slow movement of his hands that he felt drained, weighted with guilt and failure.

Jane frowned at the surge of tenderness she felt. Lust somehow seemed less complicated than this sudden need to comfort him.

It was hard to believe that this time yesterday, she hadn't even known him at all. The hours they'd spent together had been so crammed with terror and passion they'd felt elongated into weeks. Now it seemed she knew more about the elemental core of Baran Arvid than she'd learned about her college lover in the entire year they'd dated.

Jane frowned, shifting on the lowered toilet seat. She had offered to shower with Baran, knowing his desire should be running high after spending so long in *riatt*, but he'd declined. He'd claimed washing away blood was not considered a romantic activity even in his own time, but she suspected the real truth was that he wanted to punish himself.

"You weren't supposed to save her, Baran," she said, knowing his keen hearing would pick up her words even over the hiss of the shower. "Don't torment yourself."

He looked at her over the edge of the door. His hair was slicked tight to his head, shining and black. His gaze was brooding. "And who else am I not supposed to save?"

The bottom fell out of Jane's stomach. "Do you think . . ." She had to stop to swallow her rising gorge. "Do you think he's going to get me?"

With a sharp, violent gesture he cut off the water. "No." His determined voice rang on the tiles. "No, he's not going to get you."

She tightened her grip on the beads until her fist went white. "How can you be so sure?"

Baran swung the shower door open with a hard thrust of his palm and stepped out, gloriously naked. "Because I'm not going to let him." Grabbing the towel from its rack, he rubbed it roughly over his gleaming tanned skin, his face set as cold and hard as iced steel. "I'm not going to give him the chance."

She knew he meant every word. Baran would die before he let

Druas touch her. A cold knot of fear inside her loosened. "Sit down and I'll do your hair."

He took her place on the commode seat as she went to get her comb. He was toweling his black mane when she returned.

She stepped close and pushed his hands aside so she could begin. His hair was surprisingly long; she wondered how many years he'd been growing it out.

Picking up a silken fistful, she started gently working the comb through a knot that had formed while he'd been scrubbing out the blood. The activity was so mindless, so sensual, that she felt her anxiety beginning to fade.

He, however, seemed immune, judging by the way he was restlessly rubbing the towel up and down his belly and wet thighs. "I've killed people, Jane," he said suddenly, his voice sounding strained.

She hesitated, then went back to tugging the comb through the knot. "Yeah, I think you mentioned that."

"Other soldiers, enemy commanders. Mostly with a beamer, some with a knife, some bare handed." He leaned forward, the towel hanging limply from one big hand. She dropped the handful of smoothed hair and picked up another tangled hank. Patiently she began working out the knots.

"I watched their eyes when they died," he said. "There's a look they get—you never forget it. Sometimes I close my eyes, and they're there, looking back. . . ."

Jane wasn't sure she wanted to hear this, but she sensed he needed to say it, so she kept her mouth shut and kept combing.

"With a couple of them, I felt a sense of triumph, but most of the time I didn't feel anything at all. Nothing. Just dead inside. It was a job, one the high command said needed doing. So I did it."

"I'm sorry." The phrase felt inadequate, but she couldn't think of anything else that wouldn't be.

"I've known a few who got a taste for it. There was a soldier in my unit once . . . I never liked having him at my back. I often wondered if there'd been a moment when he got the hunger."

Jane stopped in midmotion as she processed the idea. "Druas is like that," she decided.

"Yeah." He sat up. "I want to kill him, Jane. For that girl today, and for Mary Kelly, and Jennifer's family. And most of all, because he put fear in your eyes." His voice dropped to a low, deadly register. "I think I'm going to like killing him."

"You afraid you're going to like it too much?"

His shoulders stiffened, then slumped. "Yeah. Yeah, I am."

Jane moved around in front of him and knelt between his spread thighs. "Baran, you're not like Druas. Men like that—there's something missing in them. Something that makes the rest of us human. But you've got it."

His expression was bleak. "The Femmats always said Warlords aren't human. Not really."

Jane snorted. "The Femmats are full of bull." She reached out a hand and laid it across his high cheek. "Look, I don't care if you can rip the doors off a Toyota, you're still human in all the ways that count. If you weren't, you wouldn't be doing this to yourself because that girl died in your arms. If you weren't, you wouldn't care."

Jane tilted her face up toward his. "If you weren't, I wouldn't want to do this."

Slowly, with exquisite tenderness, she took his mouth in a slow, deep kiss.

Fourteen

Baran groaned as Jane settled into the kiss, her mouth hot, wet, and silken. Her slim body came to rest against his, all velvet curves and gentle heat. He went still like a man approached by something small and wild, instinctively afraid to do something to scare her off. Before, he'd always been the one to seduce her. To have her reach out to him now struck him as a sweet, dark gift.

Her long hands cupped the sides of his face, fingers threaded through his wet hair as she kissed him, drinking from his mouth, tasting him, filling him with the taste of her. She drew back, just slightly, and his arms tightened in protest around her slim back. He hadn't even been aware of wrapping them around her.

Against his lips she murmured, "Come to bed. I refuse to make love to you sitting on a toilet."

She stepped back, her eyes sultry with invitation. He rose as if hypnotized to follow her as she turned with a roll of her slim hips and sauntered for the bedroom. His erect cock pointed longingly at her sweetly curving backside as he strode after her.

When Jane peeled her top off over her head, Baran felt the breath catch in his throat at the long, sensual line of her torso stretching upward. She tossed the shirt aside with a careless flip of her wrist, then bent to pull off her jeans. His cock jerked in lust. He squelched the impulse to stride to her and snatch her off her feet. Normally it wasn't in his nature to let a woman take the lead, but he wanted to feel the quiet acceptance in Jane's touch.

He hungered for it.

For a moment he started to wonder why, then pushed the thought away. He didn't want the distraction.

She stepped from her jeans and reached behind her back to open the catch of her bra, her elegant spine twisting with the movement.

When she turned toward him, lust stabbed him at the sight of her bare breasts, perfect pale hemispheres topped by long pink nipples drawn hard with need. Saliva flooded his mouth. He swallowed hard.

She stepped up to him dressed only in tiny silken pink panties he was seriously tempted to rip away. Before he could yield to temptation, she touched him, raking her nails delicately across the arch of his chest. He inhaled sharply as she swirled her fingers through the wiry curls covering his chest, then traced the muscled ridges of his rib cage.

Closing his eyes, Baran let his head drop back, savoring the sensation. Then she stepped closer until the head of his erection nudged her flat stomach, and his eyes popped open again. Her breasts were temptingly close to his eager hands. He managed not to reach for them, wanting, needing, to see what she'd do next.

She bent forward as her hands moved to curve around his hips. Slowly, delicately, she pressed a kiss to the center of his chest, right over his heart. The heat of that delicate touch seemed to spear through him. He gasped.

Jane made a purring sound and began kissing her way to one tight male nipple. He shuddered as her hot, swirling tongue danced over his skin.

Then long fingers closed gently around his balls, and his body jerked. She stroked. He moaned. She raked her teeth softly down the ridges of his ribs, stopping only to flick his skin with her tongue. He resisted the impulse to grab her, knowing where that soft, teasing mouth was headed, inch by delicious, maddening inch.

Then she was there, her soft little hand wrapped around his shaft, holding the head of his throbbing cock steady for her mouth.

She used just her tongue at first, swirling it over the velvet flesh until he had to battle the need to force his entire greedy length between her lips. The battle grew fiercer as she gave him more by slow degrees, sucking the very tip first, then a fraction more, then a fraction more.

"God, Jane, you're playing with fire!" he groaned as she nibbled delicately.

He felt her smile around his cockhead. "I know."

Suddenly she swooped her head forward and engulfed half his straining shaft, ripping a started gasp from him. Shuddering, he wondered how much of this he could take.

God, it was intoxicating, playing with him like this, taking the lead for once, feeling the tension in his big, male body as she toyed with him.

Jane worked him in deeper and felt him quiver. Savoring the taste and feel of his broad cock, she decided it was like teasing a tiger.

Sooner or later, you'd get eaten.

The thought sent wicked heat blooming through her as she remembered just what it was like to be at the mercy of this particular big cat. Smiling, she drew her mouth completely off his cock to swirl her tongue lazily over its velvet head.

Sometimes it was fun to live dangerously.

"God, Jane, deeper!" The low male growl held a faint note of threat.

She smiled and gave him a teasing lick. A powerful hand came to rest in her hair, capturing a handful of curls in silent warning.

"Jane . . ." The growl was deeper now, rumbling as if his control was straining to the breaking point.

She nibbled, feeling herself cream. Finally drawing back, she purred, "Is there something you want?"

The sound he made was closer to a snarl than anything else. Big hands closed around her shoulders, jerked her off the floor, and tossed her lightly on the bed behind her.

Jane shrieked out a giggle as he loomed over her, grabbed the waistband of her little pink panties in both hands, and ripped the silk in two. Without pausing, he snatched her up so only her head and shoulders rested on the bed as he braced a knee on the mattress.

Then it was her turn to gasp as his massive shaft speared between her swollen, cream-slicked lips. He lifted her into his thrust as if she were a doll, nothing more than stuffing and air. Yelping at the depth of his entry, she fisted the bedspread in both hands and held on for dear life.

Standing beside the bed, he held her thighs draped over his powerful forearms as he cradled her butt, pulling her body into an arch while he fucked her in long, deep strokes.

Wide-eyed, she looked up at him from the mattress and writhed with every delicious entry. He felt so damn big, so damn merciless as he took her. And he looked so triumphantly feral as he stared down at her, his eyes blazing red fire, a dark smile on his handsome mouth.

Just the sight of him made her hot. She twisted as he impaled her. "God, Baran, you're so deep!"

"That's what you get for cockteasing a Warlord," he said with a low, wicked laugh.

The orgasm caught her by surprise, swamping her in heat so intense, it dragged a scream from her throat.

He came a heartbeat later, hauling her against his hips as he spilled himself into her, roaring.

★   ★   ★

Much later they shared cartons of Chinese in the living room, watching television and feeding Freika bites of sweet and sour chicken. Jane's scanner sat crackling on top of the set, but though they looked up every time the dispatcher's voice came on, the police did not get called out on another murder.

Later, Jane carried the scanner into the bedroom with them and set it up beside the bed. She fell asleep to its constant chatter, curled in the warm, muscular shelter of Baran's big body.

She jerked awake from a blood-drenched, confused dream when she felt him jolt against her. "No!" he groaned in her ear. "No . . ."

Blinking, Jane looked over her shoulder at him. She could see nothing but his broad silhouette against the moonlit window behind him. "Baran?"

"Get away from me!" he roared, bolting upright in bed, one powerful fist drawn back, ready to take somebody's head off.

She rolled over quickly and started to grab his shoulders, then thought better of it and turned on the bedside lamp instead. "Baran, you're dreaming!"

He glared at her, fear and rage on his face. She knew from the look in his eyes he didn't recognize her.

"Baran, it's me," she said carefully, clearly. "Jane. You're all right. You were just dreaming."

Slowly recognition flooded his eyes, followed by chagrin. He slumped and raked a big hand through his tangled mane. "Jane. I'm sorry, I just . . ."

"Must have been a pretty bad nightmare," Jane observed carefully, taking in the faint quiver in his hands. What could have been bad enough to make Baran Arvid shake?

He swallowed. "Yeah, you could say that."

"Want to talk about it?"

"No." He lay down again and turned his back.

Jane eyed its muscled width and frowned, then turned off the lamp and curled into a ball, back to back with him. For a long moment she listened to him breathe in the soft darkness.

Then abruptly he turned over, encircled her waist with a massive arm, and hauled her tight into the spooning curve of his body. She tensed, waiting for another of his delicious sensual assaults.

Instead he sighed in her ear, settled her more fully against him, and relaxed. Something about the way he did it reminded Jane of a small boy cuddling a teddy bear—an incongruous association to make in connection to a man who could bench-press a Buick.

Almost as incongruous as the wave of tenderness she felt.

She settled against the warm width of his body as his breathing deepened and the scanner crackled and droned. It wasn't long before she joined him in sleep.

After the terrorized pace of the previous day, Sunday was almost ridiculously quiet. Jane carried her scanner and cell phone around the house with her, but there were no calls on either.

"Wonder if the creep's taking the day off?" she said to Baran as she fixed lunch for them and their furry companions.

"Maybe," he said grimly, watching Octopussy lunge headfirst into a bowl of tuna. "Or maybe they just haven't found the bodies yet."

Jane gave him a sour look. "You're such a cheery soul, you know that?" She took a ferocious bite of her ham sandwich and stalked into her office to call the Highway Patrol about the previous day's fatal accident. She spent the rest of Sunday harassing Tom and writing copy, in between listening to the scanner and waiting for the other shoe to drop.

But it didn't.

Normally, she'd have been relieved, but unfortunately she knew a little too much about the way Druas operated.

What was the bastard planning now?

* * *

Jane opened the door on blackness. Her heart gave a single hard thump, and she fumbled quickly for the light switch. Harsh white illumination flooded the attic, but still she hesitated.

"Jane?" Baran asked behind her, sounding puzzled. "What's wrong?"

"Nothing." She swallowed and stepped onto the rough plywood floor, picking her way past boxes of Christmas ornaments and the thick white box that held her artificial tree.

Off in one corner, isolated from the Rubbermaid tubs of winter clothing, stood a pile of cardboard boxes.

Somewhere in one of those boxes was her father's gun, Jane told herself. And it was past time she got it out. They might need it. After all, they had a living killer to worry about. That should outweigh the lingering presence of a dead one.

She forced her feet to carry her closer to the stack. Looking down at them, she felt her stomach clench.

Coward, her father's voice whispered in her mind.

Jane took a deep breath and knelt, aware of Baran's puzzled gaze as he stood watching.

"You're afraid," he said suddenly. "Your heart is pounding. What's got you so frightened?"

She swallowed past the stale taste in her mouth. "Memories." She reached out and grabbed a box at random, popped apart the folded cardboard flaps to open it. Looked inside.

Notebooks. Piles and piles of old reporter's notebooks, jumbled together with ancient floppy disks. She picked one up at random. Her father's spidery scrawl sprawled over the pad's narrow cardboard cover: "County Council, January 30, 1986." Notes from an old meeting.

"Reporters aren't supposed to keep these," she told Baran, tossing the notebook back in the box, feeling subtly contaminated. "If you get sued, they subpoena them."

"I didn't know that." There was compassion in his voice.

Jane reached for another box, opening it as she began to talk, trying to drown out the voice of her fear. "I really should have thrown all this stuff away, but I kept hoping I might find answers here sometime." She pried the flaps apart. "When I could stand to look."

"What answers are you looking for?" Baran asked, moving to kneel beside her.

She didn't even hear the question. The box was filled with neat stacks of her father's clothing. And on the very top lay a leather belt.

Jane felt the blood drain from her face. She could remember the slap that belt made, the bite of the metal cutting into her skin. "He used to wrap the leather end around his fist and hit me with the buckle."

"What?" Baran sounded startled.

Her stomach churned at the memory. When she'd cried, he'd beat her even harder. If she dared look as if she disapproved of anything he did or said, that bought another beating. He had taught her a perfect doll-like poker face, complete with plastic smile.

And somewhere in these piles of boxes was his gun. The gun he had probably used to murder her mother.

She jumped to her feet and ran from the attic.

"Jane?" Baran said, startled. She didn't stop.

"I thought we were going to look for that gun." He descended the attic stairs, sounding puzzled.

She found she couldn't look at him. "There's really no point. You said he was bulletproof anyway."

"Yes," he said slowly. "I did."

Dogged by a nagging sense of shame at her own cowardice, Jane settled in front of the television to brood. Baran joined her, shooting a look at Freika.

The wolf turned and silently trotted out.

A moment later they heard crashing overlaid by an offended

feline yowl. "Here, kitty kitty kitty!" Frieka called, sounding remarkably like Jack Nicholson playing a psychotic.

"Leave her alone, Cujo!" Jane roared, leaping from the couch. She shot Baran a fulminating look. "Dammit, help me get him before he turns my cat into Octopussy pâté."

She plunged from the room at a dead run, never even noticing the Warlord's satisfied smile.

Panting, her body still quivering with the aftermath of a savage orgasm, Jane slowly came to the realization that her hand was planted squarely in the middle of a slice of pepperoni pizza. Luckily, it had cooled. Baran had bent her over the kitchen table about five minutes after the delivery boy left.

"The thrill is gone," she wheezed as he slowly withdrew his softened shaft from the swollen grip of her sex. "You only fucked my brains out once today."

"The night is young," he said, leaning down to nip her ear. "There's still time to get in my quota."

She whimpered softly.

Baran grinned. "At least you're not brooding anymore."

On the table, the scanner crackled.

The Tayanita Tribune offices were housed in a former National Guard armory building Jane's father had bought and renovated years before. The staff worked in the warren of postage-stamp–sized offices, while the big three-color press reigned over what had once been the main hall.

Most of the employees had at least ten years with the paper, hired in the days when Jane's father had run the operation like a combination good ol' boy and despot. Most of them had known Jane since before she was even tall enough to see over his desk.

So when she walked in with Baran Arvid and his wolf in tow, all three of them became the instant center of attention. And it wasn't approving.

Jane took Baran around and conducted the introductions anyway, ignoring the speculative glances he collected.

"I thought you said we couldn't afford a photographer," said Jeff Low, director of the paper's three-man advertising team.

Baran, expressionless behind his Ray-Bans, said in a cold, deadpan tone, "I work cheap."

"You bring your dog to work?" Lillian Russell asked him later, eyeing Freika dubiously.

"He gets lonely by himself," Jane said hastily, half afraid the wolf would tell the obituary clerk he, too, worked cheap.

"What is he, some kind of faggot?" one of the pressmen demanded of another, *sotto voce,* as Jane showed Baran the press. "No straight guy wears beads in his hair."

She winced, and was deeply relieved when she, Baran, and the wolf finally escaped back to her office and closed the door.

"Well, that went every bit as badly as I thought," she said, pulling a floppy disk out of her purse and booting her Mac. Pulling the scanner out next, she plugged it into its wall charger.

"Your employees are stupid," Freika informed her over the pop and crackle. "Two of them called me a dog! Do I look like a dog?"

"No, you look like a loudmouthed timber wolf." She turned up the scanner, hoping to confuse any eavesdroppers who might wonder who was talking. "Hold it down, Rin Tin Tin. We've started enough rumors as it is."

"Why is everyone so interested in my hair and sexual preferences?" Baran settled into one of the chairs Jane reserved for interviewees.

She sighed. "It's a Southern thing. You wouldn't understand."

Visitors from the future or no visitors from the future, she had a paper to get out.

Jane went to work pulling stories up and positioning them on each page of layout, flicking periodic glances from her computer viewscreen to the clock on the wall. The paper needed to be in the mailboxes of Tayanita County before everybody got home from work and started flooding the office with irate phone calls. Fortunately, she'd already done most of the interior pages on Friday, so all she had to worry about were the obits and ensuring the breaking news fit on the front and the jump page.

She was toying with the placement of the photo Baran had taken of the firefighters clustered around the woman's mangled car when there was a tap on the door. It opened a crack, and Billi Weaver stuck her bleached-blond head in. "Jane, may I have a word with you? Privately?"

Despite the formal tone, there was a gleam in her best friend's eye that made Jane's lips curl in a reluctant smile. She knew what was coming—and it would be just as well if Baran didn't hear it. She glanced at him. "Excuse us a minute."

He shot Freika a look. When Jane got up to walk out, her furry bodyguard trailed silently after her.

"Ooooh, what a beautiful . . . animal." In the hall Billi dropped to her knees and started to reach out to pet the wolf. Hesitating, she lifted a brow at Jane. "Does he eat reporters?"

"Not so far."

"Good. You're a doll baby, you know that?" A seasoned canine-lover, Billi knew just the spot behind Freika's ear to attack with her manicured nails until the wolf leaned into her hand with a low whine of pleasure. Her busy fingers slowed as she discovered the jeweled implants in his skin. "What an unusual collar."

Jane winced and spoke quickly, hoping to divert her attention before she realized the gems were sunk directly into Freika's skin. "I know what you're going to say, and no, Baran is not gay."

Billi looked up at her and stood, attention successfully diverted. "Honey, it never even crossed my mind. I see the way he looks at you. Where did you find him, anyway? And are there any more left?"

Jane shifted her feet. She hated lying to Billi, both on general principals and because she was so rotten at it. "Atlanta. I worked with him at the *Times*."

"You never mentioned him." Billi studied her, blue eyes sharp in her angular face. They'd been friends since grade school, and they'd hashed through every crisis in their respective lives for the past twenty-two years. Jane wished suddenly, violently, she could talk to her about this one. "And you really, really should have. Honey, he looks at you like you're a bowl of homemade peach ice cream and he wishes he had a spoon." She lifted a blond brow. "*Does* he have a spoon?"

Jane flicked a glance down at Freika, who stared up at her blandly. "Yeah," she admitted.

The wicked gleam intensified. "Are we talking demitasse or soup spoon here?"

She couldn't help it. She grinned. "We're talking ladle."

Billi's eyes widened. "Do you mind if I *lick* the spoon?"

Jane laughed. "One, the implications of that are kind of disgusting, and two, don't you think George would object?"

"We have an open marriage."

"You do not."

"Okay, we don't, but I'm also not dead. And you've got this whole cat-in-a-cream-bowl smile when you look at the guy that's driving me insane with curiosity."

She grinned. "Suffer."

"Bitch. Okay, I've got to ask—does he know what to *do* with his spoon?"

Jane thought back over the weekend. "Oh, yeah."

"There it is again—that cat smile. So, as far as culinary skills, are we talking the guy at Bill's Stop N' Chow, or are we talking Emeril?"

Jane laughed. "Bam!"

Billi gave a mock shiver. "That's what I thought."

After listening to her friend segue into a complaint about her teenage son, Jane returned to her desk.

As she slipped past Baran, he purred in a deep velvet voice, "The best thing about cooking is eating."

Jane's eyes widened as color flooded her cheekbones. She stared at him, feeling her jaw drop.

"If you'll close the door," he continued wickedly, "I'd be delighted to whip something up."

"Newspaper," she squeaked. "I've got to get out the newspaper."

Baran chuckled in a sensual rumble that made feminine things quiver low in her belly. "Ah, well. Maybe when you break for . . . lunch."

"Warlords," Freika observed, curling up by the desk, "have really good hearing."

"I'll keep that in mind," Jane said weakly.

It took her another ten minutes to get her mind back on the layout, but finally she sent the last page off through the system for output as a negative that would then be used to burn a flexible metal printing plate.

Jane was about to massage her temples in a vain effort to relieve her habitual post-deadline headache when the phone rang. She reached for it absently. "Jane Colby, *Tayanita Tribune*."

A male voice said over a loud crackle she at first took for a bad connection, "Better get to 604 Parris Street, Janey. She's starting to brown."

And Jane recognized the crackle. It wasn't static. It was fire.

In the background a woman screamed.

Jane banged the phone down and ran for the door, Freika and Baran lunging after her. They didn't even ask for explanations; they must have overheard the conversation.

As the three sprinted into the parking lot, she reached into her purse, grabbed her cell, and dialed 911. "There's a fire at 604 Parris Street. A woman's trapped, and the guy who murdered those girls is inside with her."

"What?" the startled dispatcher demanded. "Ma'am, slow down! What are you talking about? Who are you?"

"Jane Colby. The killer called me again. He's set fire to a woman's house, and she's trapped in there with him. Send fire trucks and police to 604 Parris Street!" Jane hit End as she unlocked the SUV with her key fob. The three of them piled in. A moment later, she was burning rubber down Main Street.

She just hoped this encounter with Druas ended better than the last.

Fire flooded Baran's mind as his computer pumped the synthetic hormones of *riatt* into his body until his muscles jumped and coiled under his skin. He knew the feeling from a thousand battles, but with it came an emotion that was new: a cold, sick doubt.

Was he going to fail this woman, too?

Never mind that succeeding when he wasn't supposed to could theoretically cause a universe-destroying apocalypse. If he failed, she died. And for Warlords, failure was simply not acceptable.

Even less acceptable was the idea of failing Jane.

He glanced at her as she drove. Her delicate profile was set and grim, her hands white-knuckled on the steering wheel. He remembered the pleading eyes of the woman who'd died in his arms. The fear of seeing Jane look at him with that same terrorized despair made his gut clench into a fist.

He had to kill the bastard.

"There's the smoke," Jane told him. There was fear in her eyes, but something told him it wasn't for the woman they'd come to save, or even for herself.

It was for him.

That realization sent another sensation rolling through him—not fear or even anger, but warm pleasure that she cared.

And that, he knew, wasn't good. A warrior could not afford to feel too much, care too much. That kind of emotion could cloud thought, make you prone to fatal mistakes. *Shut it down,* he thought.

Besides, it wasn't as though they had a future. He thrust the thought aside.

The SUV rounded a corner. His eyes locked on a small wooden house off to the right, surrounded in a cloud of smoke pouring from under the eaves. The heat had not yet shattered the windows; he could see the leap of flames through the glass.

Baran unbuckled his seat belt and threw the door open before she'd even brought the truck to a halt. He didn't allow himself to look back.

Is the Xeran inside? he demanded of his computer.

Yes. Along with a human. Sensors indicate she has been injured. Fire burning at multiple locations, indicating arson.

Guide me to them.

Fifteen

Baran was halfway across the yard before Jane got the truck parked, running with that inhuman speed she knew meant he was in *riatt*. As she watched, he jerked the screen door open and found the front door locked. Without hesitating, he kicked it in so hard she heard the wood crack from the curb. Smoke billowed out in gray, choking waves.

"Dammit, he needs an air pack and protective gear!" She'd worked fires long enough to know how deadly smoke and heat could be for an unprotected human, genetically enhanced or not.

"Well, he doesn't have them," Freika said as she flung open the driver's door and leaped out. He loped after her as she ran across the yard. "And where the hell are you going? We've been through this. You can't go in there. He doesn't need the distraction."

Maybe not, but she was damned if she'd let him go into a burning house after that psychopath by himself. With no gear, if Druas didn't get him, smoke inhalation would. Jane put down her head and ran harder.

The next instant something massive hit her back, sending her flying. The world tilted as she plowed into the grass in an impact that drove the air from her lungs.

"Sorry," Freika said grimly, settling his considerable weight on her back, "but you're not going anywhere."

All she could do was fight for enough air to curse the wolf.

Though it was daylight, the inside of the house was pitch black and flooded with choking clouds of smoke. Baran couldn't see a damn thing, but his computer painted a sensor image behind his eyes, picking out the shapes of furniture and walls and the glowing heat signature of the flames Druas had set as a blazing obstacle course.

He looked around. Just beyond the next wall, his sensors showed a pair of glowing blue images: a male silhouette standing over a female shape curled on the floor. Druas and the hostage, both in the kitchen, surrounded by a ring of flame.

Baran knew he had less than a minute to get the woman out. The heat would sear his lungs as thoroughly as it would hers, killing them quicker than even the smoke inhalation could.

Took you long enough, Druas commed to him as he leaped a flaming coffee table. Evidently the killer had sensors of his own. *I was getting bored. And she's getting crispy.*

As if to punctuate his taunt, a female scream ripped through the air, ringing over the roaring crackle of the blaze.

Baran swore silently. His sensors told him the bastard was wearing combat armor, a helmet and a breathing unit. With that kind of equipment, Druas could swim in molten lava without breaking a sweat. The Jumpkiller could easily trap Baran in the house until the heat finished him off.

That wasn't a game Baran had any intention of playing. He had to snatch the woman up and get out, even if he had to punch his way through a wall. They didn't have time for anything else, not even the seconds it would take to disable Druas's suit with the ring.

What, no pithy reply? No chilling threats?

The kitchen doorway was blocked by flame. Baran dived through it, feeling the heat singe his skin. Without breaking step, he lunged for the woman on the floor. At least lying down there, the air was cooler. Maybe she would sur . . .

Druas caught him with a vicious kick to the jaw that slammed him into the wall behind him. The entire house shook with the impact.

Somehow he managed to hit the floor on his feet, despite the stars that flooded his vision. So much for taking the bastard off-guard.

Not that easy, Warlord, Druas mocked. *You disappoint me. I've been looking forward to this fight.*

You want a fight, come outside and face me, Baran commed back. *Without the T-suit and the armor—and without a woman as a shield.* He snapped into a spinning kick that could have taken the bastard's head off even with his helmet, but Druas somehow jerked aside at the last minute.

But the move had done what Baran intended—created an opening. He swooped down and snatched the woman, then wheeled toward the back door.

You do know Liisa was my first kill? Druas stepped through the smoke to block him, shooting a fist toward his head.

Only training let him duck in time, the woman still cradled in his arms. He didn't dignify the Jumpkiller's ridiculous lie with an answer.

I loved the way she squealed for me. And she was so tiiight. . . . Despite the smoke, Baran could almost hear the sneering grin on his face. *None of the others have been as good. But Jane . . . Jane has possibilities.*

Kakshit! Baran commed, goaded into a reply. *You weren't there. You only heard the stories.* Even in the deep, hot well of his rage, he felt the woman stir and moan. He had to get her out before the heat killed her. The back door . . .

Perhaps. Everybody knows why the Death Lord kills.

He ignored the mocking words and turned. The heat burned his lungs with every inhalation. He'd have to kill the bastard later.

But do they know what Gelar did to you just before you killed him and escaped?

Baran froze. Unable to help himself, he looked back at his enemy, at the cold, blue gleam that was all his sensors could show him in the choking smoke.

They'd paralyzed you with your comp. I was in the next room, finishing Liisa, when I heard him say he wanted your mouth next. Then I heard him scream. Did the fool free you for that one second? Did he . . . ?

You're lying. Even as he commed the words, he rammed his foot into the door so hard the flimsy wood seemed to explode. *If you'd heard, you'd have stopped me.* He leaped, carrying the woman out into the blessedly cool air.

I never liked Gelar.

You weren't there. I'd have seen you. Gritting his teeth, he ran, forcing himself to carry his limp burden to a safe distance from the house. Glancing down at her in the sunlight, he winced at the burns. *And I'd have killed you.*

Oh, you'd have tried. The commed words slid into his brain like snakes. *Which is why I had no desire to run into a Warlord in* riatt *after I'd just butchered his girlfriend. But I did take a trophy before I left . . .*

As he bent to lay the woman on the cool grass, Baran looked up to see Druas standing in the doorway. Something gleamed dully through the billowing smoke; a thin gold chain wrapped around the killer's gloved fist. A locket dangled from the chain.

Just as Baran realized he recognized that locket, Druas caught it between his thumb and forefinger.

From its center appeared a hologram image of Baran. Not as the man he was, but as the sixteen-year-old boy he'd been when he'd given Liisa the necklace.

With an incoherent roar of rage, Baran rose from the woman and started toward his enemy. If he could just pin the bastard long enough to disable his T-suit, he could take the Xeran apart.

BOOM! Wood splinters flew as the sonic boom from Druas' T-jump blew out the doorframe.

Leaving Baran staring in helpless fury at the spot where his enemy had been. "Fuck," he snarled, just as a man in a bulky gray and yellow suit ran around the corner, Jane and Freika at his heels.

"Fire trucks just got here," she said breathlessly as the suited man dropped to his knees beside the woman.

The man looked up. "Anybody still in the house?"

Baran clenched his fists. "Nobody."

The SUV was filled with the smell of smoke as Jane drove them all home after yet another interrogation. The silence from Baran's side of the truck was so leaden with fury, even Freika seemed subdued.

The woman had been medevaced to a burn unit in Georgia that was the closest facility available to treat such severe injuries. Baran had miraculously escaped any serious burns, though his face and hands were bright red. He'd seemed grateful for the oxygen the fire fighters had pressed on him, though. He kept coughing, and the lining of his nose was black with soot.

They'd been lucky the first paramedic had been too busy with the woman to notice the hot coal blaze of his eyes. Jane had barely managed to slip him a spare pair of sunglasses before anybody else noticed.

She'd wanted to take him home, but Tom had other ideas. The detective had grilled them mercilessly yet again.

Before he'd let them leave, he'd told them he was ordering a tap on Jane's phones, both at home and at the paper. She didn't dare protest.

Baran had answered the cop's questions in a low, deadly monotone that made Jane nervous. Judging by the way Tom eyed him, she suspected they were lucky they had an entire newspaper office full of people who could alibi the Warlord for the time the fire was set.

Baran hadn't said a word since.

"You want to tell me what the hell's wrong?" Jane said, unable to endure the icy silence any longer.

He shrugged his powerful shoulders. His face could have been chiseled from granite for all the emotion he showed. "I went in, I got the girl out, Druas played his games. There's not much else to tell."

"Yeah, right. That's why I feel as if I'm sitting next to a nuclear bomb, waiting for the explosion. What happened?"

"Nothing I have any intention of discussing with you." The snarl was so low and deadly, Jane felt her courage desert her.

Maybe, just this once, she should leave well enough the hell alone.

Baran had never known who'd murdered Liisa. It wasn't for lack of trying; he'd interrogated every Xeran he'd hunted down for the torture and murder of his team. Even those who'd participated in her rape seemed to have no idea who'd butchered her. He suspected they'd have given the killer up if they had. The Xerans were a vicious lot, but even so, many of them had been disgusted at the sick brutality of her murder.

In retrospect, Baran should have realized Druas was the killer when he'd seen what the Xeran had done to Mary Kelly. Her body had been mutilated the same way as his lover's had been.

The mystery had haunted him for more than two decades. Now it was solved, but he felt no sense of relief, no sense he was close to the revenge he'd thought would bring him peace and lay Liisa's ghost to rest.

Oh, he knew he'd eventually either kill Druas or die in the attempt.

What terrified him was the very real possibility that the Jump-killer would get to Jane first. And he knew the Xeran had every intention of doing so.

Baran also knew exactly how it felt to be at the mercy of a man like that. Gelar had told him in great detail exactly how he intended to kill him while he was paralyzed and helpless.

He'd never had any interest in having sex with another man. The idea wasn't an anathema to him, but neither did it have any appeal. Yet being raped, having another man take from him what he had no desire to give . . .

Baran was a Warlord. He'd been raised to fight, trained to die rather than surrender, taught that failure was never an option. By capturing and torturing him—by raping him—the Xerans had rubbed his face in his failure. And by using his comp, the source of his complete control over his body, they'd stripped away his identity as a Warlord.

And in a way he'd never gotten it back, even though he'd successfully tricked Gelar into freeing him. The fact was, he still hadn't been in time to save the rest of his team. Not even Liisa, who'd believed in him.

As the years passed, he'd hunted down each and every one of the Xeran murderers he could identify, and he'd killed them—most through challenge and combat, a few by simple execution. Yet no amount of Xeran blood could ever change the fact that he'd failed the team.

Failed the woman he loved.

He'd never allowed himself to be a permanent member of another team again. That was why he'd volunteered to become a military assassin, a job most Warlords considered dishonorable. He'd thought it would allow him to work alone. Instead, the High Command had assigned Freika as his partner. By rights, working with an animal should have been safe, but the wolf had refused to let him keep his distance. Slowly, relentlessly, Freika's intelligence and humor had seduced him into caring again, had broken through his cold emotionless shield.

Yet bright as Freika was, Baran could tell himself the wolf was still only an animal, still as much artificial intelligence as living being.

He couldn't fool himself about Jane.

To make matters worse, she was not only human, she was even more delicate and fragile than Liisa had been. At least Liisa had been a Warfem. Jane was just prey. If Druas got his hands on her, she was dead.

He turned his head to study her as she drove, and was struck again by the clean, delicate lines of her profile. Her full lips seemed to pout slightly, as though begging a kiss. Her breasts rose and fell under her silk blouse as she drove. Looking at them, he thought he could see the gentle contours of her nipples beneath the fabric.

The sudden rise of hunger took him by surprise. He knew it shouldn't have. He'd been in *riatt,* after all; the downslope from the hyper state was at least part of the reason he was in such a foul mood.

The other part was his fear that he'd fail her. As he'd failed Liisa and his team and all the women Druas had murdered.

It would have been so much easier if she'd been what she was supposed to be: just another human female. Someone to protect and fuck, but without the ability to touch him on any level other than the physical.

Jane was so much more than that. She was as bright and fiery as she was beautiful. What was worse, she was also maddeningly un-aware of her own vulnerability. She'd seen what Druas could do, yet she kept insisting on taking a role in the hunt, even if it meant putting herself in harm's way.

And she'd made him care about her as he'd been careful not to care about anyone else in decades.

It was all going to end in pain. Even if he did succeed in protect-ing her, he was going to have to leave, and he'd never see her again. Never even have the possibility of seeing her again; she'd be cen-turies dead the minute he got back to his own time.

The thought sent a shaft of grief shooting through him. Damn her anyway. She was going to make him suffer for the rest of his life. How had she done this to him? He hadn't even known her that long.

Eyes fixed on her face in a dark combination of hunger and angry despair, he watched her turn the wheel to send the SUV into the driveway of her house. His eyes drifted down to the rise of her breasts again. A hot, angry lust rose.

If he had to suffer, he was damn well going to enjoy himself in the meantime.

Jane turned the key and sat slumped as the SUV's engine growled into silence. She shot a look at Baran. He smelled of smoke, and his face was soot-streaked and red from the radiant heat burn. That ticking-bomb feeling she had about him had not gone away.

She knew why when he reached up and pulled off his sunglasses. His pupils blazed in that particular way she'd come to recognize as a combination of lust and rage. Perversely, she felt her body tighten.

Oh, that's sick, she thought, and jerked the door handle of the SUV. *The man wants to give me another dominance fuck, and instead of being pissed, I get turned on.* Aloud she said, "Forget it," and thrust the door open.

"Forget what?" Baran said in that low, hot voice he used when-ever lust was simmering just under the surface.

She swung out of the truck and strode for the front door. He opened the passenger door and followed, Freika at his heels.

"You're not pinning me against the wall and screwing me be-cause you're in a bad mood." She dug the keys from her purse and reached to unlock the door.

Before she could swing it open, he stepped up behind her and low-ered his head. His teeth closed over the lobe of her ear in a gentle erotic bite that made her knees weaken. "Why not?" he breathed, and cupped her breasts in big hands. Long fingers found and squeezed her nipples through the satin of her bra. "You like it when I pin you against the wall. When I pull down your pants. When I start working my cock into your tight little cunt an inch at a—"

"Now you're being a bastard," she managed, the keys rattling desperately as she struggled to get the door open before he seduced her on the front steps in front of half of Tayanita. *Though that would probably put the whole gay rumor to rest,* she thought wildly.

The key finally slid in and turned, and she shoved the door open. Freika slipped past her, blocking her path for an instant as he scooted inside.

That instant was all Baran needed. He bent smoothly, hooked an arm under her thighs, and scooped her neatly off her feet. "But, Jane," he said, carrying her inside without missing a beat, "I thought you knew—I *am* a bastard."

At her height Jane had never had a man pick her up and carry her. Baran did it as easily as if she weighed no more than Octopussy. Perversely, she found the sense of helplessness arousing.

And that pissed her off. She squirmed. "Put me down, dammit!"

He looked down at her with a slow, dark smile. "No."

She glared into his eyes. Her nipples were hardening, and that made her even madder. "Are you going to rape me, you son of a bitch?"

Stepping into the living room, he spilled her back onto her feet. "Would you like me to?"

"Asshole!"

"I think we just covered that," he said, stepping in closer as she backed away until he crowded her against the wall. She would have ducked aside, but he extended both brawny arms to cage her between them. The sense of being surrounded by heat and masculinity was dizzying.

His voice dropped. "I also think you know me well enough to know I wouldn't force you to do anything you don't want to do." He met her eyes, his gaze steady. "Are you really telling me no?"

She looked up into those glowing eyes and felt a quiver roll across her skin. "No."

His face shuttered. He pulled away.

Jane reached out and cupped his face in both hands. "No, I mean—no, I'm not refusing you." Slowly she rose on her toes and pressed a kiss to his lips.

When she drew back, a hot white smile spread across his face, and the glow in his eyes leaped into a blaze. "Good."

Before she could pull her hands away, his hands flashed up and wrapped around her wrists. He stepped fully against her body, pinning her to the wall as he lifted her arms over her head, around a curving light fixture that thrust out from the wall above her. Trapping both her hands in one of his, he reached into his pocket and pulled out the gold cable.

She gasped out a laugh as he bound her wrists to the fixture. "Do you carry that for a reason other than tying me up?"

His mouth flattened, and something deadly leaped behind his eyes. "Yes."

"Oh." Wide-eyed, she decided she wasn't going to ask him to elaborate.

He gathered the hem of her knit shirt in both big hands and jerked it up over her head and behind her neck, leaving her torso bare but her arms still in the sleeves. Deftly he reached between her breasts and opened the front catch of her bra. Her breasts spilled free into the cool air and the heat of his gaze.

She blinked at him. She could feel herself getting wet.

He reached down to unbutton her jeans, then caught the tab of her zipper. The hiss of its descent sounded loud against the counterpoint of their rough breathing. Dropping to his knees, he caught the waistband and began to pull it down over her hips, taking her panties with it. The legs of her jeans were just wide enough that he was able to drag them off without removing her boots.

He threw them aside. Jane looked down at him, twisting her bound hands together, feeling the cool air on her nipples. She'd never felt so deliciously, erotically helpless.

Sitting back on his heels, he was eye level with her sex. He inhaled once, sharply. "God, you're wet." He licked his lips. "I can smell it."

Swallowing, she set her feet a bit farther apart in silent invitation. He took it, reaching between her thighs, touching the soft nest of hair. A long, thick forefinger brushed the tender seam of her lips, slipped between. Inside.

She moaned and let her head fall back against the wall at the delicious sensation.

"I was right." His voice was rough, deep. "Wet."

Slowly, gently, he pumped his finger in and out of Jane's tight entrance. His thumb found the erect nub of her clit, stroked delicately. She whimpered. He drew out his finger, added a second, screwed them deep inside.

"God, Baran," she moaned, arching her back against the wall. The plaster felt cool and smooth against her bare back. "You make me so hot."

"Just wait." He leaned forward. She inhaled sharply as his breath gusted warmly over her wet sex.

His tongue slid across creamy flesh as a third finger joined the ones delving deep inside her. "Baran!" Her body pulled into a hard arch over his head. He reached up a hand and cupped one full, shivering breast.

Barely aware of what she did, she lifted a leg and hooked it over his brawny shoulder, spreading herself more thoroughly for him. He gave her exactly what she wanted, fingering, stroking, licking, thumb and forefinger working her desperately hard nipple until her heart thundered in her ears and the heat coiled tighter and tighter and . . .

She screamed, coming in long, endless waves, drowning in fire.

The silken pulses hadn't even begun to fade when he growled, dragged her leg off his shoulder, and rose to his feet with the speed of a man in rut. She heard the hiss of his zipper. Then he grabbed her thighs, spread her wide, and stepped between.

"Baran!" she gasped.

He impaled her. It seemed he drove his entire massive length all the way to her belly button in one stroke. She yelped and grabbed the light fixture over her head.

"Now," he said against her mouth, buried in her to the balls. "Let's find out how fast I can make you come again."

He drew out of her slowly, the plunged back in again. Jane could feel his massive shaft stroking its way up her core. She shuddered and gasped, wrapping both hands around the light fixture.

He pressed against her, all heat and working muscle as he rolled his hips, pulling out, plunging in, fucking her mercilessly. "That's it," he said, tightening his grip on her butt and angling her so he could reach even deeper with his long, hard cock. "Let it go. Surrender to me."

He picked up speed, bucking his shaft in and out in powerful, dizzying strokes. She could only wrap her calves around his muscled ass and hold on for dear life as pleasure battered her like a storm.

"God, you feel so good," Baran gritted. "So wet, so tight." His voice lifted into a roar. "I'm coming!"

He shoved deep and stiffened. She screamed as the long, hot orgasm she'd began under his mouth trip-hammered to an explosive finish. "God, Baran," Jane cried, "I love you!"

It was minutes later as they rested against each other in the exhausted aftermath that she realized what she'd said.

Sixteen

Baran was trying to remember if anyone had ever said the words to him before. He finally decided they hadn't, which might explain why such a simple sentence held such dizzying power for him now.

As a child, he'd been raised in the Warrior's Creche by paid caretakers who stayed only a few years before leaving. They had too many children to oversee to get emotionally involved with any of them. His relationships with the other cadets had been no warmer; the Creche was an environment where competition was as ruthlessly encouraged as discipline and achievement. Open affection was nowhere in the curriculum.

Baran's emotional horizons had expanded when he'd joined the team. With only five members, his unit had bonded with the kind of desperate intensity combat can foster. Then he and Liisa had become sex partners, and he'd fallen for her as only a sixteen-year-old can. Yet he'd never told her he loved her. Somehow it wasn't the kind of thing one warrior told another.

The closest he'd been able to come to admitting his feelings was giving her the necklace. In turn, Liisa had presented him with a locket embedded with her trid, then added one of him to her own. For both of them, it had been a silent declaration of love. It was the best they could manage.

After she'd died—after they'd all died—Baran had been left feeling that a hole had been scooped out of his chest. He had sex with women when his Warlord body demanded it, but he never slept with the same woman twice. In the end, he'd become a skilled fucker, but he was coming to realize he'd never been a lover.

Until Jane. Who'd just said she loved him.

Even in the midst of a shattering orgasm, it had felt as though that gasped, "I love you!" had lodged in his soul. He'd almost felt the words expand inside his chest.

Who'd have thought such a simple phrase could hold such majestic power?

He should say something. He knew he should say something, but he had no idea what. Opening his mouth, Baran started to say "I love you" back to her, only to realize he couldn't. The phrase felt too naked, too vulnerable.

Besides, he wasn't sure it was true. Surely it would be worse to say such a thing in error than to fail to say it when it was expected.

And he would be leaving soon. There was a promise implied in "I love you" that he wouldn't be able to keep.

So instead he stood there, breathing hard as he cradled her slim, soft body against him. Like the words she'd given him, she seemed so fragile, so precious.

And she was in so much danger.

Well, that, at least, he could do something about. He had no intention of letting Druas take *this* woman away from him. He'd kill the bastard first.

The thought held an odd, serene certainty, as if there was no longer any possibility of failure.

Resting his chin on the top of her head, Baran closed his eyes. And for the first time in his life, let himself just feel. Feel the silken brush of her hair, the soft, sweat-slick skin under his hands, the full breasts pressed into his chest.

For the first time in decades, another human being cared if he lived or died as other than a military asset. The euphoria of that thought was stronger even than the sense of invulnerability *riaat* always gave him.

She stirred against him. It came to Baran suddenly that he reeked of smoke and soot, and she was still tied to the light fixture. Somehow that embarrassed him, as if he'd rewarded a precious gift with boorishness.

"Let me get you down from there," he said softly, and lifted her so she could pull her linked arms from around the light. When he put her on her feet again, her legs trembled visibly. The sight sent a curious male satisfaction through him.

Never mind that his own muscles were jumping just as hard.

Odd. Normally in the aftermath of a long session in *riatt,* he wanted only to collapse in a quivering heap. Now he felt energized.

Carefully Baran unwrapped the cable from Jane's bound wrists, rubbing his thumb over the indentations it had left in her delicate skin. "I'm sorry about that," he said.

She shrugged.

"Are you all right?" he asked.

"Fine." Her tone was brusque.

He frowned and silently ordered his computer to do a sensor scan. He'd taken her hard; he knew she'd been ready for him, but had he hurt her anyway?

No, according to the comp's readings, she was probably a little sore, but that was all. Baran relaxed. Everything was fine.

Caught up on a wave of buoyant pleasure, he bent, swept her into his arms and carried her toward the stairs.

Jane stiffened in his grip. "Wait—what are you doing?"

"I don't know about you, but I could use a shower," he said, smiling down at her.

"I don't . . . I'm not—not really up to making love again right now," Jane said. "I'm a little sore."

"I know." His smile broadened. He suspected the tenderness he felt showed in his eyes, but for once, he didn't try to hide it. "Don't worry, I'm not planning to attack you again. I just thought you'd feel better after a bath."

And it would give him a chance to pamper her, he decided.

It was the least he could do.

Fifteen minutes later they were soaking in her big garden tub together. After examining her collection of bath oils and bubble baths, Baran had picked one and dumped so much into the water that they were now surrounded in a cloud of foam.

Unlike every other man of Jane's acquaintance, he evidently felt no qualms about smelling like Passion Peach.

Now he sat slowly rubbing a cake of soap over and around each one of her fingers as she lay back against his powerful chest. She'd expected another flaming seduction; instead he gave her such tenderness, she felt her heart swell in her chest.

Too bad all that pretty warmth didn't mean anything.

It was obvious he'd taken her at her word when she'd blurted that she loved him. Any other man would have assumed she'd gotten carried away in the throes of orgasm, particularly given that they'd only known one another three days. Baran evidently believed she'd meant exactly what she'd said.

Worse yet, Jane suspected he was right. Oh, this was just not good. "I don't think we should do this anymore."

Having rinsed off her hand, he'd begun slowly rubbing his soapy palms over her breasts, cupping and squeezing with a breathtaking tenderness. "What, bathe?" He smiled slightly. "Wouldn't we get a little smelly after a while?"

"No. I mean, make love." She swallowed and corrected herself. "Have sex. We shouldn't have sex again."

He went still. "Why not?"

"I just don't think it's a good idea."

"Funny," he said, his tone going so chill that despite the warmth of the water, she shivered. "You seemed to think it was a very good idea when you were screaming that you loved me."

"That's what I'm talking about." Jane started to pull out of his arms and sit up. For a moment his hold tightened until she thought he wasn't going to let her go. Then he slowly released her. She stood, water sluicing around her naked body, and stepped out of the tub.

"We're getting too involved with each other," she said, reaching for one of the towels she'd hung over the rack. "You're going to be leaving after this is over, and—"

"Did you mean it?"

Jane turned to look at him. He lay in the bath surrounded by a cloud of bubbles. Yet somehow, he'd never looked more masculine as the delicate white foam provided an intense contrast to his big, tanned body.

"Mean what?" she asked carefully, though of course she knew.

"Did you mean it when you said you loved me?"

"No."

His nostrils flared and anger flashed in his eyes. "You shouldn't lie to a man with sensor implants. It's a waste of time."

"Baran, it's only been three days." She wrapped the towel around her body, using the process of tucking it in as an excuse to look away from him. "Nobody falls in love in three days. What I'm feeling—I don't even know if it's real. And you haven't—" She broke off.

"What?"

Jane swallowed. "You haven't said you loved me."

He closed his eyes and leaned his head back against the tile.

"And why should you?" she added hastily. "It's only been three—"

"Nobody has ever said they loved me." He didn't open his eyes as he spoke. "Ever."

That stopped her. She fought to regroup. "Liisa . . ."

". . . Never said the words. Our culture doesn't exactly encourage romantic attachments. Especially not in the middle of a war. It's bad luck. If the woman you love is in danger, you're going to be thinking about her instead of the mission and the safety of the unit as a whole." He smiled, but the expression held no humor. "In fact, my lieutenant lectured me on that topic more than once."

"Oh." She blinked rapidly. "Your mother and father . . ."

"Mother," he corrected. "A Femmat genetic designer who constructed my DNA and grew me in a uterine vat with ten other fetuses. I've never even met the woman. Well, once. She came to my graduation from the Creche when I was twelve, but somebody had to point her out to me. I got to shake her hand."

Jane winced. She realized that despite his cool tone, his bland expression, she had somehow managed to find the one spot of vulnerability he had. "Baran," she said softly, miserably, "you're going to leave."

"Yes." He looked at her steadily. "I can't stay. The chance of a paradox—"

"I know. But every time we touch, what I feel gets stronger."

A silence spun between them, so intense the faint foaming pop of the bubbles sounded loud. "So you're saying if we don't have sex again, you'll be able to stop loving me."

"No, it's not going to be that damn simple." Looking into those rich brown eyes, Jane realized she had to be honest. Somehow he needed it, and she needed to say the words to him. "I've had lovers before, been in love before, but this is different. You're different. I don't know if it's because you're . . . what you are, but this is so damn intense. It scares the hell out of me."

"It scares me, too."

She blinked at the revelation, then fumbled to go on. "I've been telling myself this relationship is just the equivalent of a shipboard fling—that we've bonded so fast and so intensely because of the danger we're in."

"I've been in danger before," Baran told her. "I've protected women before. It was never like this."

"So . . ." She took a deep breath, gathered her courage, and asked, "You do feel it. Are you in love with me?"

He rose from the bath in a sudden rush of restless power. Water sluiced down his hard contours, trails of bubbles sliding along ridges and hollows. She had the sudden, uncomfortable feeling she'd remember the sight of Baran rising from his bath when she was a very old, very lonely woman.

"I feel . . . something," he said as she mechanically handed him the towel she'd hung on the rack for him. "It's different than it was with Liisa. It feels deeper, a little less . . . giddy."

Jane couldn't help it. She grinned. "Giddy?" Somehow that wasn't a word she associated with Baran.

He shrugged. "I was a teenage boy." Flipping the towel over his head, he began to dry his damp mane. She watched the muscles and tendons shift in his round, hard biceps. "My computer says there are biochemical changes in my brain, but I don't have a baseline to compare. . . ."

"Damn, Baran, you *are* a romantic."

He lowered his towel. She could tell from the bewilderment on his face that he had no idea what she meant.

She took pity on him. "In my time, nobody consults a computer to discover if they're in love."

"In your time, nobody has computers implanted in their brains." He gave his head another brisk rub with the towel and sighed. "Something unusual is happening to me. I'm just not sure what it is."

Jane felt a little bubble of pleasure expand in her heart. He did love her, whether he realized it or not. Then she squared her shoulders and pushed the delight away. "Which is why I think we should back off. The separation is going to be bad enough as it is. Knowing I'll never see you again . . ."

He turned and threw the towel across the room with a sudden, violent flip of his wrist. "That's why I think we need to seize every moment we have together." Moving toward her, he took her shoulders in his hands. "Jane, in my profession, I've learned life can be snuffed out in an instant. It's stupid to waste it."

She gazed up into the pure, strong lines of his face. "Dammit, I know that. I'm a reporter—I've seen it. One minute you're going to the store to buy a loaf of bread, the next minute a train caves in the side of your Toyota, or some asshole shoots you from his car just for the hell of it. But you have to live as though that's not going to happen, or you'll drive yourself nuts." She sighed. "And frankly, I'm going to be in some serious fucking pain when you leave. I don't want it to be worse."

"And I think you'll end up regretting the chances you lost," Baran said, lifting his square chin at her. "I don't intend to allow that."

"So you'll . . . what?" Her heart began to pound.

He smiled slowly, darkly. "Seduce you every chance I get."

Jane swallowed. "That's what I thought you'd say."

For the next three days Druas made himself scarce. Once again, Jane found herself carrying around her scanner and cell phone, waiting for the next call that would mean somebody was dying.

Meanwhile, the tension grew thick enough to cut. Tom Reynolds carried through on his promise to install taps on her phones. Jane signed the paperwork giving her permission, inwardly reluctant, but knowing she couldn't afford to raise his suspicions.

But when so many days passed without a call from Druas, she soon realized they'd been raised anyway. The detective started dropping by the paper and questioning Baran, Jane, and her employees, grilling them over and over on the same details until he managed to get on everybody's nerves.

"Look," she finally exploded after he'd asked to speak to her privately in her office for the fourth time. Baran had allowed it only because Freika was curled up under her desk. "It's not Baran. He didn't do it. I've told you repeatedly, I was with him when the killings occurred, and *he did not do them.* Do you think I'm lying? Hell, the entire paper staff saw us leave after we got the tip on the fire. Do you think *they're* lying?"

Reynolds glanced up from his notebook, his gaze cool and accessing. "Maybe he didn't do that one."

"Dru . . ." Jane barely caught herself before she said the killer's name. ". . . The murderer called us. He told us it was happening. We did everything we could do to stop it. Hell, Baran charged into a burning building to save that girl. As she'll tell you when she regains consciousness." The victim was in an induced coma while her body healed from the burns she suffered.

"If she regains consciousness." Tom scrawled something in his notebook. "She may die."

Jane dragged her hands through her hair in frustration. "Why would I lie, Tom? Just tell me that. You've known me since I was twelve years old. Do you really think I'd protect the kind of monster who'd do these crimes?"

Suddenly the bland cop facade cracked. Tom sat forward in his chair to glare at her. "Dammit, Jane, I don't want to believe that, but I know you're hiding something. I can smell it, I can see it in your eyes. And there's a hell of a lot about this situation that stinks. I don't like the way Arvid never wants to leave you alone. I don't like the timing—he appeared the day after the first woman died. I don't like the fact that he keeps playing hero, but the people he 'saves' always die anyway. I don't like the fact that nobody, not even your best friend, has ever heard you mention this guy, and yet now he's grafted to your ass. It all stinks, Jane, and you know it!"

"He didn't kill those people, Tom!"

"Yeah? Well, who has he killed?"

She froze. Under the desk, Freika lifted his head from his paws.

Grim satisfaction gleamed in Tom's eyes, and he sat back in his chair. "Yeah, you know something."

"He's a photographer, Tom. He's just a photographer."

"Bullshit. I've met a lot of photographers in my line of work, and none of them moved the way he does, had the look in their eyes he's got—when he deigns to take those fucking sunglasses off so I can see his eyes. He smells like former military to me. Some kind of really nasty former military."

"He's not the killer."

Tom leaned forward and lowered his voice. "Jane, is he threatening you? Is he forcing you to cover for him? I can provide protection. . . ."

She laughed shortly. "No, he's not threatening me, and I'm not covering for him. I'm telling the truth. He's not the one who's doing these things."

"Well, somebody sure as hell is."

Her temper snapped. "Yeah, somebody is, Tom. Why don't you get out of my fucking office and go look for that somebody?"

Reynolds flipped his notebook shut and rose from his chair. His eyes locked on her. "You've got all my numbers, Jane. When you get tired of letting women die, give me a call."

He stalked out of the room and slammed the door behind him.

Jane slumped back in her chair, covering her face with both hands. "Damn. Damn damn damn."

"Well," Freika said from beneath the desk, "that did not go well."

She sighed. "You've got a gift for understatement, furball."

When Jane wasn't listening to the scanner, trying to get out a newspaper, or fencing with irate police detectives, Baran was teaching her just how thin her willpower was.

His promise to seduce her had not been an idle threat.

She might have been able to resist him if he'd approached her with his usual pose of erotic dominance, but he didn't make it that easy for her. There was a tenderness now in every touch, every kiss, every whisper. Where before he'd overwhelmed her with sheer, bluntforce sensuality, now he seemed to be saying with each brush of his fingers what he couldn't put into words: that he loved her.

And God help her, she found it impossible to say no.

Even knowing what it would eventually cost her.

The way he knew her scared her sometimes, such as the night she finally yielded to the urging of common sense and went back into the attic after her father's gun.

Baran had simply walked into the room, moved two boxes out of the way, opened a third and reached inside. He'd turned around and handed her the gun. "Sensors" was all he said.

Yet he didn't ask her what it was about that stack of cardboard that terrified her so. She had the feeling that somehow he knew.

Later that same night Jane lay sprawled across the width of the bed, limp and helpless, staring blindly up at a ceiling washed in gold light. Baran had collected every candle in the house and lit them one by one before arranging them around the bedroom and turning out the lights. He'd even turned on her CD player and set it to spill something soft and jazzy into the room. The singer's voice crooned past the snap and crackle of the police scanner as Baran's hair slid like silk over her thighs.

He was feasting on her sex, his tongue swirling lazily. One big hand teased and pinched her nipple, as two fingers of the other stroked slowly in and out of her core. He seemed to savor each creamy lick for its own sake, rather than just engaging in foreplay to get her hot enough for his pleasure.

Not that she needed any more foreplay. She'd already come twice. She knew he'd bring her with his mouth again in a moment.

WARLORD

And she didn't want that. She wanted him. In her. "Baran," she moaned. "Please. I . . . AH! . . . need you."

"You have me."

Somehow she managed to force her lax neck muscles to lift her head so she could look down at him. He watched her over the plane of her body, his dark eyes burning in the soft darkness.

But instead of the male triumph she'd seen before, there was a hint of something lost and desperate in his gaze, as if he was storing away the taste of her, the sight of her, the feel of her. Saving those sensations in some mental memory bank for the day she was gone. "Now," he whispered, "you have me."

He rose to all fours. Muscle flowed through his shoulders and arms as he crawled up her body like a great cat, the head of his erect shaft brushing her skin. She found herself unable to look away from his intent stare. He settled over her, his body surrounding hers in strength and heat, a blanket of hot muscle. His gaze never left hers as he lifted just enough to aim himself.

Then he sank inside, a long, slow thrust, and she caught her breath.

Baran lowered his head, his long hair curtaining her face. He reached up an absent hand to sweep it aside. Then he found her mouth with his and kissed her as he began a slow, teasing thrusting. His lips felt hot and soft and slick.

Jane kissed him back as the pleasure rose in a warm wave, swamping them lazily. Arching against him, she came with a moan even as he groaned and poured himself into her.

It was only later, as she lay curled in the cove of his body staring blindly at the dancing flame of one of the candles, that she felt a tear slide down her face. "Baran, when you leave, it's going to be . . ."

The hair-roughened arm around her waist tightened. "Yeah. I know." He pulled her closer.

The scanner crackled.

* * *

She woke from a light doze to the feeling of his tongue swirling over her nipple. Whimpering helplessly, she threaded her fingers through his silken hair and lost herself in him.

"Tayanita One-Eight," the scanner blared. "Reported stabbing, one-oh-two Bajor Lane."

Jane jerked up her head. "Shit. Baran . . ."

He lifted his head. "I hear it."

"Caller describes a white male, over six foot, long hair, wearing jeans and a T-shirt. Code five with a knife."

"May not be him," Jane said as he rolled off her and grabbed his pants off the floor.

"Female victim suffered a laceration to the throat."

"It's him," Baran said, jerked the slacks up his long legs. "He's using his imagizer to change his appearance again."

Jane shot out of the bed and started pulling on the clothes he'd stripped away. "Why didn't he call us this time?"

"I have no idea, but I don't like it. He's broken the pattern." He sat down to pull on his shoes. "Freika!"

"I hear you, boss." The wolf trotted into the room from the hall-way, where he'd been curled outside the door.

"Where the hell is Bajor Lane?" Jane jerked on her boots. "I've never even heard of it."

"TE gave me a map," he said, frowning. She looked up to see his eyes slide out of focus. "It's at the other end of the county, eighteen-point-two miles from here. Looks like a heavily wooded area."

"Hell, it's going to take us twenty minutes to get there." She jumped up, grabbed the scanner and headed for the stairs, Baran and Freika at her heels. "I wonder why the hell he didn't call us this time. . . ."

They were halfway there when she remembered the gun, tucked away in her nightstand drawer. Jane cursed; they didn't have time to go back for it.

Just as well. She didn't want anything to do with the fucking thing anyway.

*   *   *

It was a harrowing trip in the dark. Jane strongly suspected that without Baran's flawless directions, she'd never have found the place.

Bajor Lane was a gravel road that snaked through thick woods. Trees loomed on either side, ghostly in the SUV's headlights as she drove. Something about the whole scene made the hair rise on the back of her neck. That feeling was intensified by the knowledge that Druas was probably somewhere out there, watching. What the hell was he up to now?

Seventeen

They rounded a bend in the road to see the revolving blue-and-white glow of patrol car lights casting shadows on a lone double-wide mobile home. Jane spotted Tom's champagne Crown Vic and knew they were in for another grilling on their whereabouts during the time the woman had been murdered.

She spotted something lying under a bright blue plastic tarp in the center of the gravel road; the victim, waiting for the last crime scene photos before the coroner took her away.

"Too late again," Baran growled. Jane could almost feel his rage burning in the darkness like something molten.

After parking behind the farthest patrol car, she got out carrying her notebook, Baran and Freika moving around to join her. The Warlord had the camera looped around his neck, but his eyes flicked restlessly over the surrounding woods, and she knew he was scanning for Druas.

Then he stopped in midstep. "He's here," Baran murmured.

"Yeah, I see him," Freika said, pitching his voice too low for the cops to hear. "He's talking to Reynolds in that group of cops."

Startled, Jane looked toward the group as her stomach laced into knots. A tall, skinny blond man she'd never seen before was standing with the detective, the lights of the surrounding cars throwing grotesque shadows as he gestured violently. His lifted voice carried clearly up the street. "I don't know what the fuck happened. We'd just got out of the car when this guy walks up and grins at her, and then he fuckin' *cut* her, and she . . ."

"The blond guy?" she asked softly.

"Yeah," Baran said, his tone grim. "I don't like this. Let's get the hell—"

"That's him!" the blond shouted suddenly. Jane jerked, feeling her stomach plunge. He was pointing right at them. "That's the guy that did it! He had a tattoo on his face. . . ."

As if in slow motion, Jane watched the group of cops turn toward them, Tom's eyes narrowing. As their attention was diverted, something nasty and triumphant flashed across the blond's narrow face.

A couple of feet away, two deputies standing beside a patrol car pivoted in their direction. Jane registered the wariness flashing over the face of the nearest man, a burly black officer. The eyes of his fellow cop widened under a shock of carrot red hair. "Sir," the black deputy said to Baran, reaching for his sidearm as he stepped toward them, "we need to talk to—"

"Look out!" Druas shouted.

The Warlord grabbed the cop's shoulder and jerked, pulling him off-balance. The man staggered past them. Baran slammed an elbow in the back of his head. As he fell, out cold, the Warlord pivoted and punched the redhead in the face. The deputy collapsed in a boneless heap on the gravel road.

It had all happened too quickly for anyone else to react.

Jane heard Tom roar, saw several of the cops reach for their guns as the whole herd started forward. Druas, grinning maliciously over their heads, winked and blew her a mocking kiss.

Then the world flew sideways and something hard slammed into her stomach. Jane screamed before she realized Baran had jerked her off her feet and tossed her over one shoulder in a fireman's carry. One powerful arm clamped across the back of her thighs as he started running, bounding toward the woods.

"Stop!" somebody bellowed. "Stop or we'll shoot!"

Baran didn't even break step.

Something popped, sounding more like a child's cap gun than the 9mm Smith & Wesson Jane knew the cops carried. She cringed and covered her head with both hands.

"Hold your fire!" Reynolds bellowed. "You'll hit the woman!"

Thank you, Tom!

Her head almost slapped into Baran's butt as he leaped over something. Yelping, Jane flailed around until she managed to hook her fingers in the fabric of his T-shirt. Between bruising impacts with his shoulder, she gasped, "I've . . . got . . . a car!"

"They could catch us in a car!" Freika yelled back, racing through the dark at Baran's heels. "Nothing human can keep up with a Warlord on foot."

She realized he was right as they plunged into the trees. Jane had no idea how fast they were going, but even Freika was running like hell to keep up. How was Baran doing it? She wouldn't have thought it possible to carry a grown woman at a dead run through thick woods, yet Baran didn't even seem to notice her weight. *Must be in riatt,* she decided woozily as her stomach protested jolting against his rock-hard shoulder.

Clutching his shirt, she looked up to spot the swing and jitter of flashlight beams. The deputies had charged into the woods after them. She clamped her eyes shut and prayed nobody popped off another shot. Given her position, any bullet would probably end up in her head.

The flight through the woods seemed endless. Jane could barely see the trees Baran dodged around or the brush he either bulled through or leaped over. Yet he ran without breaking stride. With his sensors, the woods must have looked as bright as day, or he'd never have been able to do it.

She, on the other hand, jounced along in the center of a black, half-seen world with his shoulder pounding into her belly. It was all she could do not to vomit down his back.

Somehow Jane managed to hold it together until the shouts of the deputies faded behind them. Finally, unable to take any more, she yelled, "Baran . . . stop! I'm going . . . to . . . be . . . sick!"

He kept going.

"I . . . mean . . . it!"

Something in her tone must have told him Jane was serious. He slid to a halt and lowered her to her feet. She promptly collapsed onto all fours, swallowing desperately as she fought to control her gastric rebellion.

Freika flopped onto his side, panting like a bellows. Even Baran was breathing hard. Managing a glance up at him, she saw his eyes glowing in the dark like a pair of coals. "What the . . . *hell* are . . . we doing?"

"Keeping you alive," he gasped, and braced his hands on his knees.

"Yeah, well . . ." She rolled onto her back with a groan. "I can't decide whether . . . we're Butch and . . . Sundance or Thelma and Louise. Either way . . . it ain't . . . good."

"I have no idea what you're talking about."

"Movie references." She took a deep breath, blew it out, and managed an uninterrupted sentence. "Both from flicks with heroes who ended up dead after a run in with the cops."

He straightened to look down at her. She could see the burn of his eyes in his silhouette. "I can't go to jail, Jane. You'd be dead before they closed the cell door."

"Freika . . ." she began.

"Does not have opposable thumbs," the wolf said from the darkness. "I'm good, but I'm not that good. I can hold Druas off for a while, but he'd gut me eventually. And then it'd be your turn."

Jane sat up wearily and braced her palms behind her in the crack-ling leaves. "What the hell are we going to do, then? We can't stay on the run. I've covered manhunts before, I know how it works. They'll saturate the area with law enforcement. Cops'll come in from three counties, they'll have helicopters, dogs . . ."

"Huh. Any dog that comes after me is kibble," Freika growled.

Jane ignored him to focus on Baran's shimmering eyes. "As far as they're concerned, you've butchered three women and taken a fourth hostage. They won't stop until they get us."

"I've infiltrated enemy armies, Jane. I can handle a few twenty-first-century policemen."

"Of course you can." She braced her elbows on her knees and sighed. "If you're willing to let the situation blow completely out of control. You can't kill these people, Baran. One, they're just doing their jobs, and two, you could trigger a paradox."

He looked off into the darkness. "Anything I do here I was sup-posed to do." She felt him brush her shoulder as he extended a hand to help her up. "Come on. We need to get moving again. They're getting closer."

"Not that close. I don't hear a damn thing."

"That's the idea. If we stay far enough ahead of them, they won't hear us, either."

"So, now what?" She put her hand in his and let him tug her onto her feet. "We run around in the woods indefinitely, dodging cops? That's not going to work, Baran. Eventually, they're going to corner us."

"And I'll take care of them," he said, wrapping his fingers around hers and tugging her forward through the darkness. "Eventually Druas is going to get tired of playing games, and then we'll finish it."

"Baran, dammit, these men are my friends! I don't want them hurt."

"And I don't want you dead!" He reached up and pushed a limb aside for her to pass under. She was lucky he was there; she hadn't even seen it.

Frustrated, Jane stopped, pulling at his hand in an effort to get his attention. *"Look, this is what he wants!* Why are we following that bastard's game plan? That's not the way to win this."

The full red glare of his eyes focused on her face. "And what do you suggest?"

She blurted the idea that had been teasing the edge of her consciousness for days. "Work with Tom to set a trap for him. He could pretend to arrest you. When Druas shows up to come after me—"

"Forget it."

"It would work!"

"Jane, in case you haven't noticed, Reynolds is leading that pack back there. If he arrests me, it's not going to be 'pretend.'"

"If we told him the truth . . ."

"That he's after Jack the Ripper? Oh, that'll go over well. He's not going to believe us."

"He will if you show him the Mary Kelly recording. It's pretty damn evident that thing is not the product of contemporary technology. It sure as hell convinced me."

"Out of the question," he said coldly. "I'm not going to put your life in the hands of some human who could get us all killed. I've been that route before, remember?"

Jane winced, remembering the civilian scientist whose stupidity had resulted in the slaughter of Baran's entire unit. Which sounded like her cue for a change in tactics. "Okay, let's say it plays as you think it will. You lead the cops around by the nose until Druas gets tired of waltzing and comes out to play. You kill him. What happens then? Are you going to leave his body for the cops to find?"

"You know I can't do that. They'd do an autopsy. Given his implants and reinforced bones, that would raise too many questions."

"So as far as the cops are concerned, this case will be unsolved."

Leaves crunched as he shifted his weight. "It'll have to be. Otherwise Druas would have had no reason to come here—and that *would* cause a paradox."

"Okay, I'll buy that. But what about me?"

"You go back to your life."

She shook her head. "No, I don't. I'll end up under a cloud of suspicion I'll never escape."

"What?" Jane could almost hear the frown in his voice.

"Baran, as far as they're concerned, *I brought you here*. I vouched for you, I supplied you with an alibi while, they believe, you killed three women. I could be charged as an accessory."

"That's highly doubtful," Freika said. "There's no evidence."

"Which doesn't mean a damn thing. People will believe I'm guilty. Tayanita's a small town; that kind of public doubt would ruin me. The paper my family ran for more than a century will go under. And if the story goes national—and it could, given the serial-killer angle—I won't even be able to get work as a reporter anywhere. For the rest of my life, I'll be the woman who covered up for the Tayanita Ripper."

"Hell."

Hearing the sick realization in his voice, she knew she finally had her opening. She had to take advantage of it. "My only chance is to talk to Tom and get his help. He can clear both of us when this is over."

"He won't cooperate."

"Yes, he will," she said, praying she was right. "I'll convince him."

"Before or after he slaps me in jail? In either case, you won't have much time to convince him. Druas was back there, Jane. And I guarantee, the minute the cops take me into custody, he's going to be all over you."

"Not if I'm with Tom."

"Even if you're with Tom." His tone was grim and certain. "You'd outlive your cop friend by about two minutes."

She frowned. "But would Druas risk killing him? Wouldn't that cause a paradox?"

Freika snorted. "If Druas gave a damn about paradoxes, he wouldn't have started the whole Jack the Ripper scheme to begin with."

"For that matter, he doesn't even have to kill the cop," Baran pointed out, "just incapacitate him long enough to get at you."

They had a point, and yet . . . "Well, we've got to do something. This sure as hell isn't working."

There was a tense silence. In the distance Jane thought she could hear shouts.

Finally, reluctantly, Baran said, "I have an idea."

T*om Reynolds emerged from the woods five hours after he went* in, feeling as if someone had beaten him. He could hear the helicopter circling overhead, along with the bay of distant tracking dogs, but it wasn't looking good.

At first he'd thought it would be easy. The two dogs had picked up a scent quickly enough, following the trail Arvid and Jane and that damn wolf-whatever had left as they'd run into the woods.

Then suddenly the animals had stopped dead and begun casting around as though the trail had vanished. He'd seen that behavior before, of course; it usually meant the perps had gotten into a car and driven off. But it was the middle of the fucking woods. There wasn't room for a car. And there was no stream around the three could have used as a scent-free pathway. It was as if they'd somehow erased the trail.

Where the hell had they gone?

And how had Arvid run like a freaking gazelle carrying the weight of a full-grown woman—in the dark, in brush so thick even the cops had a hard time forcing their way through? What was the son of a bitch, Superman?

Tom sighed, rubbing his stomach as he trudged toward the victim's house. They had no choice but to continue the search, though the sheriff had grumbled he'd rather wait until there was more light. Unfortunately, they couldn't afford to do that, not with Arvid holding a hostage. Jane could be dead by morning.

Assuming he hadn't butchered her already.

None of this shit made sense. She must have been covering for him, but why? Tom would have bet his badge Jane Colby was not the kind of woman who'd turn a blind eye to murder. He'd known women who rationalized their lovers' crimes, up to and including the rape of their own children, but Jane just didn't fit the profile.

Yet she'd looked Tom in the eye and sworn Arvid wasn't the killer. He'd believed her, too, though he normally had a pretty damn good idea when he was being lied to.

So what the hell was going on?

Adding to the general fun and games, he now had to go talk to the victim's roommate, who'd been cooling her heels ever since she'd arrived more than an hour ago. All the poor woman wanted was for someone to tell her what the hell happened, and since the coroner was off talking to the vic's immediate family, the sheriff had sent him out to handle it.

The deputy had put the woman in a patrol car; they didn't want her going into her house until they'd had time to finish processing the scene. Cynthia Myers had been killed outside, but they still needed to go over the house, if only to close any loopholes Arvid's defense attorney might use later.

As he approached the car, the front passenger door opened and the woman got out. "Are you the detective?" she asked. "Can you tell me what happened? Nobody's talking. Who did this? They said Cynthia's dead. What . . . ?"

He sighed and gestured toward the open passenger door. "Why don't we sit in the car, Miss . . ."

"Terri Jenson." She knotted her shaking hands together and obediently got back in.

With a sigh, Tom walked around to the driver's side. He always hated dealing with survivors, but unfortunately, it was part of the job. And a good rapport with family and friends of the victims could be invaluable to solving a case. He got in the car, pushing aside the officer's clipboard and ticket book so he could sit down.

"I was at work when one of the neighbors up the road called and said there were police at my house," Jenson told him. "She said . . . she said Cynthia was dead." Her eyes filled.

Tom studied the woman sympathetically. She was a short, slender brunette, dressed in blue jeans and a T-shirt, both clean. Not quite thirty, he decided, scanning her haggard face. She was probably pretty, at least when not dealing with the murder of a close friend.

"I'm afraid your neighbor was right," he said gently. "Cynthia was attacked outside your house earlier tonight by a man with a knife."

She flinched. "Do you know . . . who did it?"

"Her boyfriend identified—"

Terri's eyes widened. "Who?"

"Her boyfriend." Tom reached into a pocket and pulled out his notebook, flipped it open. "Jason Anderson. He told us—"

"I don't know who you talked to, but it wasn't her boyfriend."

Tom blinked at her. The woman stared back at him with an expression of indignant alarm. "You seem pretty sure about that," he said cautiously.

"I should," she told him, her voice sure and cold. "Cynthia and I have been lovers for the past five years."

Shit. Shit, shit, shit. He dragged a hand through his hair, fighting the cold, sick feeling that was trying to take root in his guts. "Are you sure she didn't have a male friend you don't know about?"

"Cynthia did not date men," Terri gritted. "If a man told you he was her boyfriend, you were talking to her killer."

By the time Tom pulled into his own driveway, it was pushing dawn. His eyelids were gritty, and a headache was throbbing a relentless bass beat behind his forehead. He'd spent the past three hours trying to find Jason Anderson, who had mysteriously vanished.

As far as he could determine, Terri Jenson was right. Virtually every word in Anderson's statement had been a lie. The address he'd given them was a vacant lot, the phone number was a dummy, and they could find no mention of anybody named Jason Anderson in Tayanita County, either in the phone book or in criminal records, not even as an alias.

Tom had also done a computer search on the name with the South Carolina Law Enforcement Division. Half a dozen Jason Andersons had popped up, all in other counties, but the ages and descriptions hadn't matched.

It was beginning to look as if what Terri said was true. Anderson—or whatever his name was—had killed Cynthia Myers, and possibly the other women as well. He'd accused Baran Arvid to throw off the cops while he escaped. But why had Arvid run? Even if he hadn't realized it made him look guilty as hell, Jane damn well should have known.

The sheriff had called off the search for the two—a manhunt was ungodly expensive—but he'd still issued a Be On the Lookout for them. He hoped the BOLO would eventually bear fruit or they'd emerge from hiding on their own. Either way, Tom was going to question them thoroughly.

And then chew Jane out for stupidity above and beyond the call of duty.

Yawning, he pulled into the two-car garage of the brick colonial he and Christine had shared for the past fifteen years. It was dark in the garage, and he reminded himself to buy that replacement lightbulb he'd been meaning to pick up.

Wearily, he got out of his Crown Vic and trudged toward the cement steps that led up into the house.

He sensed the motion barely an instant before the hand closed over his throat, jerking him back against a body that was a lot bigger than his own. Another hand reached into his shoulder holster and neatly removed his gun.

"We want to talk to you," Baran Arvid said.

"What a coincidence," Tom gasped around the fingers circling his throat. "I want to talk to you, too."

Then he drove an elbow back into his captor's ribs in a blow that should have made the man keel over and gag. Arvid didn't even grunt.

"We had nothing to do with the murder, Tom," Jane Colby said from the darkness.

"That statement would fill me with more confidence," he wheezed, "if the Man of Steel here wasn't choking the shit out of me."

The hand around his throat disappeared, but he heard the warning click of his own gun being cocked. He rubbed his throat and glared in the direction of the sound. "Did it ever occur to you to just come to the sheriff's department and fucking *talk* to me?"

"I couldn't risk being arrested," Arvid said. "The killer has targeted Jane. If I leave her alone, she'll end up like the others."

"All you had to do was ask for police protection . . ." Tom bit back the "dumbass" he wanted to add to the end of that sentence. "Under the circumstances, the sheriff would be happy to assign the manpower."

Jane sighed. "Y'all can't protect me from this guy, Tom."

"And Bead Boy can?" His headache gave a particularly nasty throb. "Look, I would feel a lot more comfortable if I could see who the hell I'm talking to. Let's go to the Sheriff's Department."

"No." Arvid's tone did not invite debate.

Shit. He didn't want them in the house, not with his wife in there asleep. "Then let's go out on the deck. Christine left the lights on out there."

As he led the way out of the garage, he heard the distinctive ring of Jane's boots on the cement drive. "Just for curiosity's sake, does the phrase 'assaulting a police officer' mean anything to you?"

"Yeah, and I'm sorry about that, Tom. We just don't have a lot of options right now."

He grunted. This melodramatic shit was getting on his nerves.

Tom walked across the lawn and up the steps that led onto the deck. Leaning a hip against the railing, he watched as Jane followed, the big photographer on her heels. That damn wolf melted out of the darkness after them. He thought about protesting its presence, then decided that would probably be a waste of time.

Jane fell into the nearest lawn chair with a tired sigh as Arvid took up a post against the railing protectively close to her. The wolf sat on his haunches at her feet.

"So," Tom said, "you want to tell me what the fuck is going on?"

"That," the wolf said, "is a very long story."

An hour later Jane rubbed the throbbing spot between her eyebrows and eyed the detective. Tom was staring at the frozen playback of the Ripper recording with his jaw hanging open.

"Shit," he said at last, "I've died and gone to an *X-Files* rerun. Where are the fucking gray aliens?"

"About four hundred light-years that way," Freika said, tilting his muzzle skyward.

Tom shot him a wild-eyed stare.

"He's playing with you, Tom," Jane said.

"No, I'm not."

She ignored that. She really didn't think she wanted to go there. "You can see why we couldn't allow Baran to be arrested."

"Yeah." He shook his head and sat back in the lawn chair he'd dropped into about halfway through their explanation. "But what I don't get is why you're telling me all this."

"Because we need your help falsifying paperwork," Baran said.

Tom gaped at him. "What?"

"We need to make it look as though I'm under arrest for at least the next three hours."

"Aside from costing me my badge, what would that do?"

"We've got to lure Druas in. He needs to believe he has an unrestricted path to Jane, but he's not going to believe I'm going to just walk off and leave her."

"Because he's from the future, he's probably got access to the paperwork surrounding this case," Jane explained.

"Three hundred years from now?"

She shrugged. "Why not? Look at all the paperwork that survived from the Ripper murders. And record-keeping wasn't nearly as good in Victorian England as it is now."

Tom frowned, considering the idea. "So how would my falsifying a report help you?"

"If you leave a paper trail that shows Baran in custody during a particular period of time, Druas will think he's got a clear field to me."

Tom's eyes widened. "But that means the fraud would have to be rock-solid. If it ever came out that I hadn't had you in custody, the creep would know it was a trick."

"Yeah." Baran folded his arms, his expression grim. "You'd have to keep the secret until you died."

"Shit. It's not that easy, Arvid. Even at this hour, there are people at the department and people at the jail. They'd know you were never there. And I'd lose my badge."

There was a desperate, thrumming silence while they tried to figure out a solution to that problem.

"What if you were questioning him somewhere else?" Jane asked suddenly. "It doesn't have to be that you actually arrested him, just that you could attest that he was in a given location at a given time. Maybe you could say he attacked you here."

"But that wouldn't get you alone," Baran pointed out. "I'd never have let you out of my sight."

"Druas doesn't know that. Look, Tom could say I was horrified that you'd actually attacked him, so I ran off. You held him for a while, but then he escaped and you ran. It would create a window of time when I'd be left unprotected."

Baran shook his head. "Druas wouldn't fall for that."

"If it's in the paperwork and Tom swears it happened that way, why wouldn't he?"

"Neither of us would be that stupid."

"People are uncharacteristically stupid all the time," Jane said. "Besides, Druas believes he's smarter than the rest of the universe. He *wants* to believe we're that dumb."

Tom sat forward and braced his hands on his knees. "You have no way of knowing whether this guy is going to take the bait. You're asking me to put my career on the line on the off chance this is going to work. If it doesn't, I'm fucked."

"If it does, no other women will get killed," Baran told him. "Including Jane."

He sighed. "Shit, when you put it that way . . . But what if he does take the bait and you can't beat him?"

Baran's eyes narrowed. "That's not going to be a problem. One way or another, Druas is dead."

Tom sat back in his chair. "I'd object to that just on general principles, but practically speaking, I can't offer an alternative. Even if I arrested the bastard, I doubt a prison would hold him, not given the abilities you describe."

"And you'd lose a lot of cops during his escape."

"You sure I can't help take the fucker down?"

Baran shook his head. "Too risky. If he got his hands on you, you wouldn't have a prayer. I'm going to have my hands full keeping Jane alive as it is. I don't need to worry about triggering a temporal paradox by losing you."

"So how do you know telling me all this won't cause one of those paradoxes all by itself?"

"It won't," Baran said.

He lifted a brow. "You sound pretty damn certain."

"He is," Freika said from the floor of the deck. "We're all still alive, aren't we?"

Tom stared at the wolf. "You mean . . . Never mind." He sighed and looked over at Baran again. "So, have you got a gun? I figure if I'm committing career suicide, I might as well do it right."

"I've got one at home," Jane told him.

Baran shook his head. "Wouldn't do much good anyway." He told Tom about Druas's armor and reinforced bones.

"Huh." The detective contemplated the problem. "How about a knife?"

"That'd work." He shrugged. "I could always slit the bastard's throat. Better than being unarmed." He grimaced. "Actually, I should have picked one up earlier."

"I've got a bowie knife with a sheathe I use for deer hunting, if you want to use it."

"Are you sure, Tom?" Jane asked. "If Baran uses that knife to kill Druas . . ."

The detective waved a dismissive hand. "That asshole needs to go down. Whatever I can do to help, I'm going to do. Give me a minute." He got up to open the glass door and slip inside.

Baran took a deep breath and looked at Jane. "Well, you were right."

Jane shrugged. "Tom cares more about protecting people than career building." She looked at him steadily. "He'll keep the secret until he dies, Baran."

"Yeah." For a moment they fell silent. Baran stared off across the yard at the moon riding just over the trees. "This plan is risky as hell," he said, his voice low. "I don't like it."

She shook her head. "You know I'm the only one who can pull it off."

"Maybe, but it's so damn risky. . . ." He straightened from his pose leaning against the deck railing and walked over to her. His expression going even grimmer, he slipped the suit-nullifying ring off his finger. Then to her surprise, he knelt on the deck beside her and took her hand. Solemnly he slipped the ring on her finger. Its alien metal automatically shrank to fit. "I'll keep you safe."

Staring into the fierce vow in his eyes, Jane curled her fingers around his. "Yeah," she said softly. "I know."

Eighteen

Jane's heart thudded so hard it seemed to choke her, and her mouth was utterly dry. She fought to concentrate on the road and ignore the clawing terror she felt.

She was aware of Baran's eyes on her in the darkness as he crouched in the floorboard of the car, his big body coiled uncomfortably. Freika was stretched out across the bench seat in the front, his furry head almost in her lap. They were both sensor shielded—using their computers to generate a nulling field to keep Druas from picking up their life signs. But the field didn't work on visible light, so they had to stay out of sight.

For the purposes of the trap, they needed to make it look as if she was driving home alone in Tom's "stolen" patrol car.

The detective had decided to let them borrow the car, since that was the only way they could be sure of smuggling Baran and the wolf in past Druas. Unfortunately, since his report would claim Jane had taken it without his permission, there was a distinct possibility she could face charges for it later. She'd decided she'd worry about that problem if she managed to live through the next hour.

And she wasn't making any bets on that.

As they'd made their way toward Tom's house earlier that night, they'd decided Jane had the best chance of getting close enough to Druas long enough to use the ring. If she could distract him while she touched him with it, he might not realize what was happening until it was too late. As soon as the ring disabled the suit, Baran and Freika would attack.

Of course, the really tricky part of the whole plan was the period while the two were hiding just out of Druas's sight. Even though they'd be watching, if he went after her before she managed to disable the suit, she could get hurt before they could come to the rescue.

Fortunately—though that might not be the right word—Druas's M.O. was to strangle his victims before he used the knife, which should give Baran and Freika enough time to interfere. Unfortunately, as strong as Druas was, Jane could still end up dying slowly with a crushed larynx.

The whole plan was risky as hell. Baran hated it; it went deeply against his grain to take a risk of that magnitude with Jane's life. Unfortunately, every other option they came up with carried a virtual certainty that Druas would simply Jump to freedom and return to attack Jane later. And there was no telling how many women he'd kill in the meantime.

All of which had made perfect logical sense when she'd argued for the plan during that hike through the woods. But now, in the car on the way to face a monster, it seemed a hell of a lot less convincing.

He'll kill you, Jane, her father's ghost whispered, sibilant in the darkness. *You're not smart enough to fool him. He'll see through the act and slit your throat on the spot.*

No, she told herself. *I can do this. Baran will protect me.*

Glancing down at the ring gleaming dully in the light of the dashboard, she remembered the look in his eyes when he'd slipped it on her finger. The knot of fear eased fractionally.

Baran reached up from the floor of the car and cupped her knee, giving it a gentle squeeze. Jane looked over at him. He didn't speak, yet something in his gaze spoke of love and determination. Tears welled in her eyes. She blinked hard and returned her attention to the road.

Jesus, she realized suddenly, *I really am in love with him.*

Jane knew she should probably find that realization disquieting—after all, even if they all survived this fight, he was going to disappear from her life within hours. She'd never see him again. Yet as she contemplated the love that had been quietly growing over the past few days, she found herself grateful.

She needed all the strength she could get.

Baran watched the single tear roll down Jane's cheek and felt his heart contract in his chest. He wanted to take her in his arms. Hell, he wanted to tell her to turn the car around and forget the whole thing. There were a dozen ways this insane plan could go wrong.

Unfortunately, he also knew that in combat, you sometimes had to take a chance because it was all you had. This was one of those times.

He had every intention of minimizing the danger as much as he could. He and Freika would conceal themselves as close as possible, and they'd never take their eyes off Jane and Druas. But he still couldn't eliminate the risk completely.

The moment of greatest danger would come when she touched Druas with the ring. If the Jumpkiller realized what she was doing . . .

Baran would have to get to him first. And he would. That bastard was not going to hurt Jane. Baran had already lost Liisa to him; that was more than enough.

Odd. For years he'd been driven by the obsession of finding Liisa's killer and giving him as bloody and painful a death as possible.

Yet now Baran realized he would happily forgo his vengeance if it would mean keeping Jane alive.

Nothing he did would bring Liisa back to life—but it might prevent Jane's death. And that was all Baran really cared about. One way or another he was going to keep her safe. And he didn't much care what he had to do in the process.

Jane pulled into her driveway with her stomach coiled into a solid knot. "Is he here?" she murmured, scarcely moving her lips.

"Yeah," Baran whispered. "I've got him on sensors, waiting out in the trees."

She swallowed hard and lied. "Good."

Her hands so damp with sweat it was all she could do to turn the wheel, she backed the patrol car into the SUV's customary spot. She ordinarily parked facing the other direction, but she needed the driver's door next to the house. In that position the bulk of the car would block Druas's view while Baran and Freika got out.

It was a good thing she didn't have a porch, she thought; the extra elevation would have made them impossible to miss.

Jane got out and walked to open the front door, leaving the car door standing open. As Baran duck-walked inside with the wolf slinking at his heels, she pretended to remember to lock Tom's car.

A moment later she slipped back inside and closed the door behind her. "How long do we have before he comes in?"

"I have no idea," Baran said, straightening from his crouch to look toward the woods as if he could see right through the wall. Which, given his sensors, he evidently could. "He's maintaining position now."

"Okay. Let's head upstairs." There were several places they could conceal themselves up there.

She just hoped they had time to do it.

*   *   *

Baran and Frieka slipped up the stairs ahead of her. Jane, following, thought there was something dreamlike about anyone as big as the Warlord moving so silently.

When they walked into her bedroom, Freika immediately headed for the walk-in closet. Before he slipped inside, he shot them a long-suffering gaze. "Hiding in a closet—really, this is so undignified. Not to mention clichéd. You do realize I'm mortally embarrassed?"

Jane grinned despite her clawing nerves. She'd had no idea a wolf's face could even do disgruntled. "Yeah, it sucks. I appreciate your sacrifice, Freika."

He sniffed. "See that you do." He slipped inside and hunkered down on the floor, ready to spring.

Baran, meanwhile, eyed the closet's doors dubiously. Jane realized what he was thinking; they were designed to open by folding to either side, a process that might take too long. He shrugged and looked at her. "Hell with it. I'll be in *riatt*—I'll just smash 'em."

Jane nodded shortly. Her heart was pounding so hard she could feel the pulse in her ears. She badly wanted to run to the bathroom and throw up.

Baran's hard expression gentled. "You'll be fine," he said softly, and took her chin in his hand.

The kiss he gave her was hot enough to burn as his lips moved hungrily over hers, his tongue sweeping inside to stroke and claim. His body felt so big and warm against hers. She let herself lean into him, greedily drinking in the comfort.

As the kiss spun out, his mobile mouth seemed to make another one of those silent vows of protection and passion. Something about it drove back the fear beating at her.

Then they both heard the front door open downstairs. Baran deepened the kiss, then stepped into the closet.

Jane's heart gave a hard thump as the folding door slid closed. At least they'd be able to see through the slats, while Druas would be unable to see them.

She turned and moved quickly to the nightstand to open the drawer. Her father's gun lay inside, loaded and ready. For once, the weapon was a comfort instead of a symbol of doubt and fear.

Hearing a tread on the stairs, Jane pulled out an old romance novel and slid the drawer partially closed.

I'm not going to throw up, she told herself fiercely. *I can do this. All I've got to do is rest the ring against his suit for a few seconds. I can do that.*

You're going to die, her father's ghost hissed.

Fuck you, Daddy.

The bedroom door opened. Baran walked in. But he'd just stepped into the closet. . . .

For an instant, Jane was confused. Then it hit her. It was Druas. The son of a bitch was using his imagizer to look like Baran. He thought the Warlord was still back at Tom's house, as the report Tom would falsify would claim he was.

The killer smiled Baran's smile at her. "I decided you were right. I'd never be able to convince the detective I didn't do it. Taking him hostage was a mistake."

Suddenly Jane's fear was gone, washed away by pure rage. The bastard was playing a game with her, planning to use her love for Baran against her.

For once, years of hiding her emotions from her abusive father stood Jane in good stead. Her face automatically fell into the sweet, doll-like smile she'd learned under Bill Colby's belt. "I'm glad you saw the light," she said. "Once Tom gets an idea into his head, you couldn't pry it loose with a crowbar."

"Yeah," Druas said in Baran's deep voice. He tried a smile of his own, but now Jane realized how unlike her lover's it really was. Evidently the computer used the expression he was actually wearing on the face of the projected image. The result was like looking at a perfect mask of the man she loved—worn over the face of something cold and reptilian.

He moved closer to her. "I thought we might as well make use of what time we've got left together."

I'll just bet you do, you son of a bitch. But did he really want to have sex, or was he just trying to get close enough to kill her?

Either way, she had to play along just long enough to rest her hand on his chest until the ring disabled his suit.

If he didn't kill her before it could do its job.

Baran had never felt such rage in his life, not even when he heard Liisa's last scream. The idea that Druas had dared to wear his face while planning to murder Jane made him want to pound the killer to a bloody bag of shattered bone. He'd been about to drive right through the closet door when Freika had caught his hand in fanged jaws, jolting him back to his senses.

Now he crouched, seething in the darkness, watching through the door slats and praying to all his people's gods he'd be in time to stop whatever Druas was planning.

He had to go to *riaat* at just the right moment. If he entered the berserker state too soon, he wouldn't be able to maintain it all the way through the battle; too late and he might not have the strength to save Jane when he needed it.

At least she was playing her role to the hilt. He'd been afraid that she couldn't control her justifiable terror. Yet the minute Druas had walked in, she'd gone icily calm.

Now she was smiling into the murderer's face, projecting seductive warmth, almost glowing with sensuality as she flirted, quite literally, with death. Even Druas looked fascinated. Despite his fear, Baran felt the rise of admiration mixed with a curious pride. A week ago he would never have thought a civilian capable of such cool, brassy courage.

But then, Jane was no typical civilian.

He just had to make damn sure he was ready to snatch her clear when the killer made his move.

*   *   *

Jane decided she needed to work closer to Baran before she touched the Jumpkiller. Ideally, she wanted Druas beside the closet so the Warlord could take him in one easy lunge. The trick was maneuvering the killer without giving the game away.

Smiling that not-Baran smile, Druas reached for her. With a light, flirtatious laugh, she stepped back and slipped past him, giving her hips a taunting little sway.

"Oh, you do enjoy playing with fire," Druas said, dropping his reaching hand as he watched her saunter around the bed.

She shrugged and gave him a wicked smile. "What can I say—I like it hot. But then, so do you." *And you're about to get seriously burned, you bastard.*

"The hotter the better." He grinned and swaggered after her. How he thought anybody could mistake him for Baran with those empty shark eyes, she did not know.

"So," Jane purred, suppressing the instinct to step back as he stopped right where she wanted him. "Just how much heat can you generate?"

"How much do you want?" He reached for her again. She managed not to flinch under his touch. He might look like Baran, but his hands didn't feel the same as they rested on her hips. The shape and size were wrong—chunky palms, short, stubby fingers. If she hadn't already known he wasn't her lover, his touch would have told her.

Luckily, Druas thought women were stupid. And that was an advantage she could use to destroy him.

Stretching her lips into a feline smile and dropping her lids to hide the revulsion she knew filled her eyes, she reached for his chest. Pretending to study those illusionary Baran pectorals, she laid her left hand there.

And felt the scales of his T-suit under the illusion.

Hell. If he realized she should feel the suit, he'd know something was up when she didn't react.

To distract him, she rose up on her toes and took his mouth in a kiss that was as deep and sensual as she could make it. His mouth

had an odd, metallic taste, but she ignored it, ignored her own clawing revulsion, and pressed her body fully against his. One way or another, she had to distract him long enough.

The ring was growing warm around her finger. She hoped to
God that meant it was working.

He moaned into her mouth. Something about the note of perverted excitement in the sound made Jane's skin crawl. *You'd better
work, ring,* she thought grimly. *This bastard's about to kill me.*

Suddenly the ring spiked so unbearably hot she jerked back with
a startled yelp.

"What?" Druas gasped. He looked down at himself in shock.
"My suit! What did you . . . ?"

As she stared up at him, his eyes widened with stunned realization. He looked down at her, his face contorting in fury. He lifted
one hand. "You little b—"

The crash of rending wood and a roar of raw male rage drowned
out the rest of the insult. Jane fell back as Baran barreled into the
killer so hard the impact carried both men across the room to slam
into the wall. The Sheetrock cracked around their bodies.

"I hope you know a good carpenter," Frieka said to her, emerg-
ing from the closet as the two men fell to the floor.

His furious partner managed to roll on top and slam his fist into
Duras's face. The killer bucked in the Warlord's grip, but Baran ignored his struggles, jackhammering blow after blow into his head.

Then Druas twisted around and got some leverage, sending Baran
flying with a kick.

The Jumpkiller rolled to his feet even as the Warlord regained
his own. Druas snarled at Jane, "You're going to die for that, you little bitch!"

"No," Baran hit him so hard his head snapped back, spraying
blood. "She's not. But you are."

"Oh, she'll die all right." Baran's image wavered around the killer
and disappeared, leaving a hulking figure dressed in black scaled armor, a foot-long blade in his hand. "And so will you."

"You may be hell on unarmed women. . . ." The Warlord reached behind his back in a blur of motion and drew Tom's hunting knife from its sheathe at the small of his back. "But I'm neither."

"Oh, this should be good," Frieka said as the two big men began to stalk each other. He moved back toward the doorway. "Come on, let's give 'em some room to play."

Jane stared at him, outraged. "Play, hell. Go help him!"

The wolf shook his head. "Sorry, already got my orders. And they say my first responsibility is to keep you from becoming Jane Kabob."

Frustrated, she growled, but the wolf was right. As long as Baran knew she was relatively safe, he could concentrate on fighting for his life. And distracting him was a very bad idea. Reluctantly she joined Freika in the hall and poked her head around the doorframe to watch.

The fear and rage were gone.

Now that the battle had begun, all Baran felt was a cool, empty silence filled only with the flicker of Druas's eyes and the pattern his knife described as it moved. The comp whispered a constant stream of sensor data into his brain, but Baran was scarcely aware of processing it. He was in the killing space, and he wouldn't come out until one of them was dead.

The trouble was, his opponent was wearing armor and he wasn't. That gave Druas a lot more targets to work with, while the suit would turn away all Baran's knife attacks. He only had only two real ways of killing the bastard—either an attack to the eyes or cutting that thick bull throat under the jaw, where the protection of the T-suit ended.

But Druas was too strong and too fast to make either strike easy. Baran was going to have to wear the bastard down by hammering at him. The suit could absorb penetration impacts, but part of the force still got through. And in *riatt* Baran could generate a hell of a lot of force. At least for a while.

Unfortunately, he couldn't sustain the berserker state for long before his body ran out of reserves to burn. Too, he'd begin to spike in temperature as the body heat generated by his elevated metabolism overwhelmed the cooling system of his genetically engineered body. He was already streaming sweat, almost steaming as he circled Druas.

"You're not going to be able to save her," the killer hissed, his red eyes burning, the pupils contracted to narrow vertical slits. "She's mine. And I'm going to make you watch while I cut her open and fuck the cooling remains."

Baran's foot whipped out so fast even the mercenary's nano-injected muscles had no time to react. The scything kick slammed into the side of Druas's head and spun him around.

But before Baran could close in on him, the mercenary used the momentum of the kick to whip around again. His knife flashed out, slicing a bright red path diagonally across Baran's chest.

The Warlord snarled and drove his own blade right for one of those red snake eyes. Druas barely jerked back in time to avoid taking the point halfway through his brain.

"You don't really think you'll win, do you?" The killer danced away, blood smearing his face from his busted lip, one eye rapidly swelling shut. Baran was in no better shape. He could feel blood soaking his shirt from the knife wound, and half the side of his head felt numb. Something grated ominously in his chest; his comp whispered of a broken rib. And the room felt cold as an icebox as his body temperature rose.

"Oh, I'll win," Baran growled. "I'll win and I'll mount your head on a pike over Liisa's grave."

"Even if you do, it'll be too late to save your pet bitch," Druas taunted. "Jane's fated to die, Warlord. And if you don't let me kill her, you'll cause a paradox that will kill us all!"

Baran didn't even dignify that lie with a response.

"Think about it, Death Lord. If I knew she was supposed to survive, would I have strolled into this trap? Would I risk causing a paradox?" Druas smiled, cold and ugly. "Eventually she dies. If I don't kill her, you'll have to. Isn't it better to let me do it?"

Baran's only reply was a blurring attack that sent the killer scrambling back.

Jane stared in horror, then looked down at Freika. "Oh, God, please tell me he's lying!"

The wolf flicked a dismissive ear. "He's lying."

"But why? If he killed me when I wasn't supposed to die . . ."

"Jane, Druas doesn't give a cat's ass about paradoxes, or he wouldn't have decided to become Jack the Ripper in the first place. If he'd been wrong, he'd have caused a cataclysm the minute he arrived in Victorian England. So he's fully capable of trying to trick Baran into letting him kill you, just to see what happens."

A flurry of motion dragged her eyes back to the combatants. They moved so fast, attacking and blocking with such blurring speed the fight didn't look quite real. It was as if somebody had decided to stage a road show of *The Matrix* in her bedroom.

But the blood and sweat were real. Droplets of it flew with every impact, splattering everything in the room. And the snarls and grunts of pain were more animal than any soundtrack she'd ever heard.

For a moment they slammed together, body to body, straining against each other. Then there was a quick grunt and twist, and suddenly Baran had Druas on the ground. Each man had one bloody hand wrapped around his opponent's knife wrist.

Slowly, inexorably, Baran forced his own blade closer to the killer's throat, lips peeled back in a horrific snarl.

Then Druas twisted his right arm somehow. Baran's hand, slick with blood, slipped on the scales of the T-suit. He grunted.

The Jumpkiller shoved Baran's knife away from his throat and kicked him airborne. Jane and Freika barely ducked aside in time as he rocketed through the hallway door.

Druas barreled through the doorway after him, ramming into him as he lay on the floor. The two tumbled together, writhing as they fought, knives and fists swinging.

"Shit," Freika growled. "Druas tagged him."

"Baran?" Jane stared at them, feeling panic rise. "Where?"

"Through the right side." The wolf looked up at her, pale eyes grim. "He says for me to get you out of here. He's not going to be able to keep this up, losing that kind of blood."

"No!" Jane gasped. Now that Freika had pointed it out, she could see the bright red soaking from the wound in Baran's side as the two men fought. "I'm not leaving him!"

"Maybe not willingly." The wolf reared and slammed into her, knocking her back against the wall. Before she could struggle free, he sank his teeth into the collar of her shirt and dragged her to the floor, then started hauling her toward the stairs.

"No!" Frantic as a trapped mink, she batted at him, but he scrambled around so he was at her head and kept right on dragging her. "Dammit, Freika, let go!"

"There's nothing you can do for him, Jane!" the wolf said, his synthesized voice strained. "There's nothing either one of us can do."

Ninteen

Situation critical, Baran's computer whispered.

Fuck, tell me something I don't know, he thought back, straining to keep Druas's knife from his throat. The Jumpkiller sneered at him, snake eyes blazing.

The damage is too severe for conventional healing. I sent nanounits to clamp the bleeding and begin tissue repair, but you'll still lose too much blood.

How long before I crash?

Given Druas's strength, you have forty-eight-point-three seconds of effective combat time left.

It'll have to be enough. Blow the reserves, comp.

Inadvisable. Body temperature already too high.

Blow 'em!

"Bleeding out, Warlord?" Druas panted, struggling to drive the knife into Baran's chest as he fought to hold it back. "Let's see if we can speed it up!"

Then the power hit like an explosion of pain and fire, so hot and ferocious it tore a scream from Baran's throat. The Jumpkiller's eyes widened as Baran's hand clamped down convulsively on his knife wrist. Bones grated, crunched. Druas howled in agony as the Warlord's comp forced his body to pour out every ounce of power it had left, crushing his wrist despite the armor, despite the mercenary's reinforced skeleton.

Baran thrust Druas's broken arm away so violently the knife spun off to lodge in the wall. Maddened, he slammed his fist directly into the killer's face, once, twice, again. Druas fell back, stunned by the savage blows that jarred his brain even through his reinforced skull.

Baran exploded off the floor, grabbed him by the shoulder, and rammed his fist up into the Jumpkiller's gut so hard he would have slammed Druas into the ceiling if he hadn't had a grip on him. The knife fell from Baran's hand, but he didn't even notice. Frenzied by the biochemical storm racing over him, all he wanted to do was beat his opponent to death with his bare hands.

Halfway down the stairs, still dragging Jane, Freika stopped and stared upward as Baran began pounding Druas like Rocky assaulting a side of beef. "Oh, shit," the wolf said, "he's blown the reserves. If Druas doesn't go down now, Baran's dead."

Jane took advantage of his distraction to jerk away from his teeth, ignoring the ragged sound of her shirt ripping.

"Wait a minute!" The wolf lunged for her pants leg, but she dodged. "Where do you think you're going?"

"To get my gun!" She raced up the stairs with Freika at her heels, slipping past Baran as he methodically pounded his struggling opponent.

As fast as it came, the last of Baran's berserker reserves drained away. Druas's limp body suddenly seemed to weigh more than Jane's truck. Unable to hold him up anymore, Baran staggered back and watched the killer fall in a heap in the hallway floor. Black spots danced in front of his eyes.

Blood pressure dropping, the comp said.

No shit. "Gotta . . . kill you now," Baran panted, and looked around for the blade he'd had a minute ago.

His eyes fell on something sticking out of the wall. Druas's knife. He wondered vaguely how it got there. He tried to pull it out, but his bloody hand slipped on the hilt. Bracing his other palm on the wall, he fought to pull the blade free. It came loose so suddenly he reeled back, hit the opposite wall, and fell on his ass.

Blinking, he stared at his fallen enemy, who glared back at him with malevolent hate.

"Oh, that's rich," Druas said with a wheezing laugh. He coughed. A bubble of blood formed over his mouth and popped. "You used it all up. You don't have enough left to kill me."

"I do," Jane said, stepping into the hall. She held her father's gun in her hand.

Fear flickered behind Druas's snake eyes before the killer laughed again. "I'm wearing armor, you stupid slut."

"Maybe." Her face cool and grim, she stalked down the hall to stand over him and point the gun at his face. "But you're not wearing anything on your head."

"Won't do you . . . any good." He peeled his bloody lips back from his teeth. "My skull's reinforced."

"I'm not aiming at your skull."

Baran blinked, realizing the weapon was pointed at one of the killer's snake pupils.

The gunshot boomed, astonishingly loud in the confined space.

"Damn," Freika said, watching the body slump sideways to the floor, "I didn't think you'd do it."

"Neither did he." Jane turned and dropped to her knees beside Baran. He looked up at her, his eyes unfocused. They were bright red—not from *riatt* this time, but from burst capillaries. She laid a hand against his cheek. His skin was so hot it seemed to burn.

"Damn, your fever must be over a hundred!" she said, alarmed.

"One-oh-three," Freika said.

"I'll call 911 . . ." She stood.

A boom from the bedroom shook the house. "Don't bother," Baran said, his voice faint. "I think our ride's here."

Jane turned toward the bedroom just as Octopussy darted out at a dead run, fur on end from ears to tail. Without hesitating, the cat hurled herself into her arms. Jane caught the little animal automatically just as a figure appeared in the bedroom door.

"Well, you evidently lived up to your reputation, Warlord," the man began as Jane gaped at him. His skin was an inky black with shimmering blue highlights that was not even remotely human. The darkness stood in stark contrast to the fiery shimmer of red curls tumbling around his ethereal face. "You've completely wrecked this. . . ."

Then the man's metallic gaze fell on her, and he looked every bit as dumbfounded as she felt. "You're alive!" He look a half-step back. "You aren't supposed to be alive!"

"Shit," Jane said, clutching Octopussy so close the cat began to squirm. "I knew it."

Baran struggled to focus on the TE agent despite the hallway's slow revolutions around him. "What do you mean, she's not supposed to be alive? You told me . . ."

"You were supposed to *try* to keep her alive—you weren't supposed to succeed!" The agent gave him a wild-eyed look. "You have to kill her now!"

Baran looked at him, feeling even colder and sicker than he had a moment ago. "Fuck off."

Accurately reading his snarl, the Enforcer looked at Freika, who stood at Jane's side as she cradled Octopussy in one arm, the gun held awkwardly in the other hand. "Forget it," the wolf told him. "I wouldn't even touch her cat."

The Enforcer squared his shoulders, taking on a grim look. "Then I'll do it." He took a step forward.

Jane, standing on the other side of Baran, began to back up toward the stairs. Terror grew in her lovely eyes as she read the menacing intent in the agent's.

Hell, Baran thought. *Give me something, comp. I've got to . . .*

No reserves left.

The Enforcer started to step across his sprawled body. *Never mind, I'll use what I've got.* He lifted one leaden hand, wrapped it around the agent's ankle and jerked.

With a startled yelp the Enforcer went down as Baran forced his drained body to roll onto hands and knees and scrabble after him. He didn't so much pounce on the agent as fall across him.

"What the hell are you doing, Arvid?" the Enforcer roared, struggling to escape as the Warlord wrapped his legs around his body and curled an arm across his throat.

"You're not killing her!" Baran gritted, glad the bastard didn't have sensors. Otherwise he'd know how close he was to passing out.

"Do you want to cause a paradox! She's got to die!"

"Did they find a body?" He held on desperately as the Enforcer writhed in his grip. It was a good thing the little bastard was a standard human, or he'd be screwed.

"Yes!" The agent tried to tear loose, instead managing to roll Baran onto his back. The Warlord kept his grip, but it felt too damn good to lie there. He fought his body's need to collapse as the Enforcer panted, "She had a .38 bullet in her brain!"

Baran felt a spurt of relief as his comp reported the man's bouncing heartbeat. "Never lie to somebody with sensors, asshole. They didn't find a damn thing."

The Enforcer snarled, white teeth flashing against the blue-black of his lips. "All right, you bastard, she disappeared! But she was never seen again—she had to have died."

Baran looked up at Jane, who was staring down at them, frozen.

Disheveled, her shirt torn, clutching her cat and the gun she'd used to kill Druas, she'd still never looked more beautiful.

The realization hit him in an explosion of warmth and joy. Somewhere inside him a voice said, *Of course.* "That's because she goes back to the twenty-third century with us."

Jane's brown eyes widened in astonishment.

"Are you insane?" The agent's voice rose in outrage. "Or do you *want* to cause a paradox!"

"No, I don't." Baran tightened his grip. "Which is why I want her transported with us. She's *supposed* to go. It's fated." The black specks were dancing faster before his eyes. *Keep me conscious, dammit,* he ordered his comp. The specks thinned.

The Enforcer tried to wrench himself free. Baran barely managed to tighten his grip in time. "I'm not going to risk destroying the universe so you can have a piece of ass, Arvid!"

"She's not a piece of ass, you arrogant little prick," Baran snarled, and shifted his hold to wrap his hand around the curve of the other man's skull. "She's the woman I love. And if you don't bring her with us, *I'm going to break your neck.*" Ruthlessly he began to apply pressure, praying his strength wouldn't fail him.

The agent gasped in pain and subsided, panting. Suddenly he went still, staring hard at Jane. "Do you want to be responsible for the destruction of everything?" he asked her in a low, ugly voice. "Are you that selfish?"

She gaped at him. "No, I—"

"Use the gun, Jane," the Enforcer ordered. "End it. Die a hero's death and save us all."

Her pale lips moved. "Commit suicide?"

"No!" Baran roared, knowing he didn't dare turn loose his captive to try to stop her—even assuming he could make it to his feet. "We're supposed to be together!"

★   ★   ★

Jane clutched the cat and the gun, staring into Baran's wild bloodshot eyes. He was pale as a sheet, blood seeping across the carpet under him, yet the force of his will blazed out at her. *It's probably the only thing keeping him conscious,* she thought.

"If you cause a paradox, you'll die anyway," the Enforcer told her, his metallic eyes narrow and hard. "But you'll die knowing you killed everyone and everything that ever was."

Oh, hell. How could she take that kind of risk?

Jane looked down at the gun. It felt heavy and cold in her hand. She wondered once again if her father had used it to kill her mother.

"Don't do this to me, Jane," Freika said suddenly.

She blinked and shifted her gaze to his. "What?"

"If you don't come back with us, Baran won't return from our next mission. And neither will I. You can see it in his eyes."

Automatically Jane looked at Baran. There was such desperate pleading on his face, she felt her chest clench.

"Please, Jane," he said. "I love you."

"Love?" the Enforcer sneered. "He's off his head, high on *riatt* and blood loss. He's an assassin—what the hell does he know about love?"

Jane straightened. "You'd be surprised." She lifted the gun and pointed it at the Enforcer. "Take us to the future. Now."

The agent stared at her, incredulous. Then his eyes narrowed. "Kill me, then!" he spat. "Unlike you, you selfish little bitch, I'm not willing to risk a paradox to save my own life."

"*We won't be causing a paradox!*" Baran snarled, tightening his grip on the agent's jaw and bending his neck painfully back. "I know I will not allow Jane to die, so therefore she lives, so therefore"—he forced the Enforcer's head back another inch, tearing a gasp of pain from the man—"you're going to Jump us all back to our own time."

"I'm not Jumping you anywhere!"

"Do you know the sound a man's neck makes when it snaps?" Baran said, his tone so cold even Jane felt a chill. "I do."

The Enforcer's eyes rolled in their sockets. Jane could have sworn he paled even under that midnight-blue skin.

Suddenly he went limp. "All right, dammit. Let me go, and I'll do it."

"Uh-uh." Baran jerked his head another inch. "Now."

The agent closed his metallic eyes and reached for the belt of his suit.

"Come on, Jane," Freika said, stepping closer to the two. "Gather around and brace yourself."

Hurriedly she joined them, still clutching Octopussy and the gun. The cat squirmed. She dropped the weapon on the carpet and tightened her grip on her pet.

A wave of hot, burning energy suddenly slapped into her, as if she was standing too close to a furnace. Jane tensed, staring wildly down into Baran's wild, determined stare.

Just before the energy beam hit, she heard Freika say, "But do you have to bring the cat?"

Then the beam hit. As she felt it rip her apart, Jane screamed, "Baran, I love you!"

T*he beam assembled Jane inside out.*

Or at least, her stomach thought it had. Her guts went into such instant, violent rebellion that she dropped Octopussy and fell on her knees, clamping both hands to her mouth to avoid throwing up. Purple starburst explosions filled her vision until she couldn't see a damn thing. Desperately she fought to hang on to her stomach contents and remain upright.

She almost lost the battle when the starbursts faded and she realized she was looking at Druas's body. His one remaining eye stared sightlessly at her.

"Well," Frieka said, sounding a little strained himself, "we're all still alive. Guess Jane was supposed to come here after all. Huh, Enforcer?"

The agent replied in a foreign language, but from the tone, she could guess the content. Dazed, she watched him tear himself out of Baran's arms, get to his feet and stomp away, armor creaking, still snarling alien curses.

The Warlord didn't move.

Looking down at him, Jane froze in horror. Like Druas's, his eyes were fixed and empty, staring at the ceiling.

"Baran!" she screamed.

Life flooded his gaze again. He sucked in a desperate breath and began, weakly, to cough.

"Shit," Freika said. "Medtech! Oh, hell, wrong language." He paused, then bellowed something incomprehensible.

Glancing around wildly, Jane saw no one around. They were lying in the middle of a long, curving corridor. "Did anybody hear you?"

"They're coming."

"They'd better." She scrambled to her lover's side as he lay far too still on the floor, staring up at the ceiling with eyes that didn't seem to track.

"Baran?" Jane reached for his hand. In contrast to his earlier blazing heat, his fingers were ice cold. Slowly his head turned until he could look at her, but there was no recognition at all in his gaze. "Baran, it's me," she said urgently.

His expression warmed. His lax grip tightened. "Jane?"

She clamped her fingers over his, praying the contact would keep him with her. "What can I do? How can I help you?"

"Be . . . fine." His voice was slurred, weak. "Gotta . . ." His eyes slid closed.

"Freika!" Jane looked at the wolf desperately.

"The medtechs'll be here in a second." He moved over to look down at his partner. "They'll save him." He didn't sound nearly as confident as she'd like.

"It looked like he was dead," she said, squeezing the big, limp hand. "And he feels so cold."

"Shock," Freika told her. "And he probably was dead, at least for a few seconds. I've seen it happen before. His comp jolted his heart back into beating."

"Jesus. This happens a lot?"

"Well," the wolf said, sounding grim, "not a lot."

Running footsteps drew Jane's head around. A woman and a man towing something that looked uncomfortably like a floating glass coffin raced down the hallway toward them.

The woman snapped incomprehensible orders at them, waving her free hand. Reluctantly Jane stood and moved back with Freika so the two technicians could reach Baran.

The pair positioned the floating transparent box over his lax body. It began to lower over him like a lid. The moment it had him covered, it flooded with some kind of pink vapor before rising again, lifting Baran with it.

A glowing trid display appeared in midair over him, displaying what was evidently a schematic of Baran's body. Ominous sections were colored bright red. The two medtechs stepped in close and started touching parts of the trid with their fingers.

Jane watched nervously. At her feet Octopussy meowed pitifully. She bent absently and picked the cat up. The little animal felt warm and solid in her arms.

The skin of one of the medtechs was a bright emerald green. His hands seemed misshapen; she realized he had twelve fingers.

"Is he an alien?" she asked Freika in a low voice, cuddling Octopussy.

The wolf snorted. "Nah. If he was, he'd look much weirder than that."

"Oh."

The glass box began to float away. Automatically Jane started to follow. The female medtech turned toward her and gestured, her tone sharp. Jane shot a questioning look at Freika. The wolf said something back to the medtech in the same language. The woman replied over her shoulder as she followed the box off down the corridor.

"What was that all about?"

"They're taking him to the ship's hospital. He's going to be in regeneration for the next five or six hours. Then we've got a mission."

"A mission?" Jane gaped at him. "The man was *dead* a second ago, and they're going to just patch him up and send him back into combat?"

The wolf glanced up at her as he started down the hall in the opposite direction from the one the medtechs had taken. "Well, yeah."

"That sucks."

Freika flicked an ear. "Not compared to the situation we were in ten minutes ago."

Ten minutes ago, Jane remembered, they were all back on Earth trying to keep the Enforcer from executing her while wondering if the alternative would destroy the universe. "Okay," she said, "you've got me there."

Sitting on Baran's bunk several hours later, Jane looked up just as a muscular blond Warlord strode by, stark naked. Catching her stare of wide-eyed amazement, he looked puzzled, then glanced down at himself. When he realized what she was gaping at, the grin he gave her needed no translation whatsoever.

"I," Freika announced, "am going to tell."

Covering her burning cheeks with both hands, Jane muttered, "I'm in love, not blind. Jesus, Baran meant it when he said his people are casual about nudity."

The wolf yawned, revealing impressive fangs. "No reason they shouldn't be. You all look alike anyway."

"That was a racist comment. Or maybe a species-ist comment. I'd think somebody from this time would be more . . ."

Resting his head on his paws, Freika flicked an ear at her. "You're babbling."

Jane sighed. "Going nuts does that to me. Shouldn't Baran be back by now?

"Evidently not, since he isn't."

She eyed him as he lay on the bunk beside her. "You're disgustingly literal, aren't you?"

The wolf lifted his head and eyed her. "And you're terrified out of your mind. It's going to be all right, Jane."

"Yeah, right." Absently she stroked Octopussy as the cat coiled in a neurotic, shivering ball in her lap, a thoroughly traumatized Siamese. Jane knew just how she felt.

They sat in a huge round room filled with what looked like several hundred bunks. All around them, people talked, did incomprehensible things with strange bits of equipment, or watched trid images that danced in the air. Jane had never felt so lonely surrounded by so many people. The fact that they all spoke a language she didn't understand wasn't exactly a help, either.

Jane sighed. Her eyes fell on a brawny blond woman on the bunk opposite hers. The woman—a Warfem?—seemed to be making some kind of adjustments to something that looked like a weapon. For all Jane knew, it was actually the twenty-third century equivalent of a Salad Shooter.

"I'm three hundred years in the future, I don't speak the language, and two of my only three friends in the entire universe have tails," Jane said.

Freika grunted. "Do not include me in *any* category with that cat."

"Methinks the wolf protests too much." She grinned suddenly, unable to resist an opportunity to twit him, if only to distract herself from her misery. "You know, back home we say that anybody who professes to hate somebody that bad must have a secret. . . ."

"Forget it."

"Well, you know what Freud would say about all those jokes about eating pussy."

Freika gave her a look of such horrified revulsion it was all she could do not to fall off the bed laughing. "Sick. You're just sick. God, we've brought a pervert to the future."

She snickered.

"You take it back."

"I'm just saying—"

"Get away from me!" He jumped off the bed. "I can't believe you'd even think something like that. That's not natural!"

Jane hugged the cat and collapsed into giggles. Octopussy gave her an offended meow and struggled free before leaping onto an empty bunk.

"See?" Freika glared at her. "Even the cat is disgusted."

"Freika loves puss-y," she singsonged in a schoolyard chant, unable to resist. "Freika loves—"

"Here I hurry back, thinking you'll be heartsick with worry," interrupted a deep male voice, "and instead I find you in hysterics. I'm hurt."

"Baran!" Jane threw herself off the bed and into his arms.

"Just in time," the wolf growled, glaring at her. "You can hold her down while I bite her."

"Actually, I was planning to hold her down while *I* bite her," Baran said, pulling her tightly against him.

He felt so big and hard and safe. She burrowed into him, inhaling his clean male scent. No blood, no dirt, just Baran. Drawing back slightly, she looked him over anxiously. No wounds, either. "Boy, medicine in this time is amazing."

"As long as you're not dead for too long, yeah." He looked down at her, searching her face with hot, dark eyes. "God."

Then she was plastered against him, and he was kissing her with a passion that seemed to singe the roots of her hair. She moaned against his ravenous mouth and twined her body around his, arms around his neck, legs circling his waist.

"*Chi di rath ki,* Baran!" a strange voice called, and laughed.

"Roughly translated, that means 'Get a room,'" Freika told them. "Though personally, I wouldn't want to be alone with her, considering what a deviant she is."

They ignored him.

Jane finally came up for air while he strung nibbling kisses along her collarbone. "Isn't there somewhere we can go where we won't have a fascinated audience?"

"Yeah." Baran got in a last nibble and lifted his head reluctantly. "Unfortunately, we don't have time to go there. Frieka and I have to go kill Jutka."

"Now?" She drew back to study him in dismay. She realized he was dressed in some kind of futuristic black body armor. "But you just got out of the hospital, or sickbay, or whatever they call it here."

"There's a war on, Jane," Baran told her grimly. "And victory will be a lot easier with the general dead."

New anxiety attacked her. What if something happened to him? They finally had a future together, and now he had to risk it again.

But one of the things she loved about Baran was his devotion to duty. She knew she had to let him do his job, even when it terrified her. Fighting the impulse to cling harder, she pulled away from him and straightened her shoulders. "So kill the creep and hurry back."

He grinned, eyes lightening. "Believe me, I'm going to wrap this thing up as quickly as I can." He reached into one of the pouches attached to his belt and pulled out a small object. "By the way, I've got something for you." He took her hand and put it in her palm. "Had a hell of a time getting my hands on one. Finally just ordered the ship to synthesize it for me."

Jane opened her fingers and studied the small, curving piece of gold. "It's . . . nice." What the hell was it?

"It's a personal comp," he told her, taking it back from her and taking her chin in one hand. Tilting her head, he slipped the little device around her ear so it rested snugly against her skull. "When I get time, I'll reprogram it for English. Then it'll be able to teach you Galactic Standard."

"Oh!" Jane brightened. "That's neat. How does it . . . ?"

He winced. "Hell, they're calling us. Frieka . . ."

"Yeah, I'm ready," the wolf said, moving to join him.

"When will you be back?"

"As soon as we can." Baran dragged her close again for another hug. Something about the ferocity of it told her he was worried.

Suddenly she remembered Freika referred to the job he and Baran did as "suicide missions." She tightened her grip, feeling her heart leap in fear. "You come back to me," she said, her voice low and hard. "I lived for you, Baran Arvid. Now you live for me."

He drew away and looked down at her, his gaze just as determined as she felt. "I will." He turned his head, as if hearing a voice she couldn't. "I've got to go."

Baran turned and strode off down between the bunks, Freika trotting at his heels. Jane watched them go, feeling forlorn. "Bye," she whispered.

At the other side of the room, the doors slid closed behind them.

She sat down. Octopussy crept out from under the other bunk and jumped into her lap. Gathering the cat against her, she settled back to wait.

Twenty

Something loud startled Jane awake. She jerked upright on Baran's bunk and looked around, blinking hard. She couldn't see the source of the noise, and she had no idea what the hell it was. A warning of some kind?

But none of the people moving around the room reacted. Blinking, she fell back on the bunk and scrubbed her hands hard over her sandy eyes. Her heart still thumped hard from surprise.

Baran was still nowhere to be seen. Where was he? Was he back? Had he been hurt again?

Was he dead?

Calm down, she told herself sternly. *Don't borrow trouble.*

As she sat there curled in a ball, Octopussy suddenly jumped onto the mattress. She startled. "Damn, cat, don't do that to me."

The Siamese looked at her and meowed plaintively. She sounded hungry. Come to think of it, Jane wouldn't mind a bite or two, either.

And to make a bad situation worse, she needed to use the bathroom desperately. Unfortunately, she had no idea where it was—or even how to use twenty-third-century plumbing.

He's not going to come back, her father's ghost whispered. *You'll be stuck here, unable to speak the language, knowing no one, with no means to support yourself.*

Jane felt the rise of helplessness. It was bitterly familiar.

Incompetent. She was so damned incompetent. She'd stranded herself in a time long after everything and everybody she knew had disappeared, without a way to meet even her own most basic needs. And the man she loved was God knows where, fighting and perhaps even dying while she sat in bed and did nothing.

Incompetent, whispered her father's ghost.

So how did I kill Jack the Ripper?

Jane straightened, remembering the moment when she'd looked into those snake eyes and pulled the trigger.

If I'm so incompetent, how did I trap the most infamous serial killer in history, deliver him to Baran, and finish him off afterward?

For once, her father's ghost made no reply.

Jane swung her legs off the bed and stood. She could, by God, find a fucking toilet and figure out how to use it.

She looked around until her eyes fell on the brawny blond in the opposite bunk. This time the woman was working on what looked like a futuristic suit of armor, the parts of which were scattered all over her bed.

She'd know where to find a bathroom. The problem was, of course, communication.

Hell with it. Jane would figure it out as she went along. She stepped over to the woman's bunk as the Warfem looked up at her in surprise.

"I need to go to the bathroom," Jane announced, "Can you help me?"

"*Ke ta?*"

"Bathroom." Ignoring her instinctive embarrassment, she began making gestures, a couple of which felt remarkably lewd addressed to an utter stranger.

The woman, however, didn't look the least discomfited. An

expression of understanding entered her shimmering cobalt eyes. "Aaah. *Sherirqi daritho an dak. Av ka.*" She stood up and started across the room.

Jane followed her.

So much for you, William Colby, she thought. *I'm done with you now.*

She was three hundred years from the life she knew, and the man she loved was off trying to kill a tyrant. But suddenly Jane Colby felt like dancing.

Baran gulped a bottle of Charge as he strode down the corridor, Freika trotting at his heels. The drink was obscenely sweet, but it was loaded with all the nutrients his depleted body needed after that extended session of *riatt*.

The Xerans had damn near had his ass that time. He'd barely made it off the base before they discovered Jutka's body, dead with a neat beamer hole in his forehead. If it hadn't been for the knowledge that Jane was waiting back on the ship, Baran might have ended up taken prisoner.

But he'd been damned if he'd die and leave her alone and friendless, unable even to speak Standard. He'd been determined to get back to her, no matter what he had to do.

So he'd killed a Xeran transport crew, stolen their craft, and roared back to the ship, ducking and darting through Xeran fire in the greatest display of piloting skill he'd ever given in his life.

Now he was finally back home, and all he wanted was to feel her warm and silken body in his arms.

"She's probably starving," he said to Frieka. "I should have made sure she had something to eat before I left. That was thoughtless. Hell, I should have made sure she knew how to find the head."

"And a litter box," the wolf said. "That stupid cat's probably shit all over the ship by now. The captain's gonna shoot her furry ass right out the airlock."

Baran looked down at his partner and grinned. "Why, Frieka—you actually sound concerned."

The wolf glared up at him defiantly. "All I'm saying is, Jane wouldn't like it if they kakked her kitty cat. You know how she is about that useless little hairball."

Baran poked his tongue into his cheek. "Uh-huh. So you're not actually concerned about the cat."

"Of course not."

"Right."

"Why would I be? It's weak and stupid and it's a *cat*."

"And it's cowardly."

"Well, no. It got in a couple of really good rakes across my nose once, and I outweigh it by at least ninety kilos. You can't really say it's—" The wolf broke off and eyed him suspiciously. "You're grinning at me. If you're getting ready to imply I have some kind of disgusting sexual intentions toward that cat, I'm going to bite you."

"Well, of course not," Baran said honestly.

"Good." Freika sniffed and trotted ahead of him. "Step it up. They're probably hungry."

But when they walked into the dormitory deck, Baran realized his bunk was empty. His heart jammed into his throat.

"Where the hell are they?" Frieka said.

"Let's try the mess. Maybe somebody thought to give them something to eat."

They found Jane sitting over the remains of a meal with T'May Vajo. Baran felt that shiver of unease any man feels when he sees the woman he loves with a former bed partner. He pasted a bright expression on his face and walked over to join them.

Jane looked up at his approach. Her face lit with such joy he had to grin right back. "Baran!" She leaped up and threw herself into his arms.

Closing his eyes, he basked in the sensation of her body pressing against his, warm and solid and safe. His universe settled silently into place.

"Good Goddess," T'May drawled in Standard, cuddling Octopussy in her lap. "The Death Lord has been domesticated."

He considered flipping her off, but realized she wouldn't understand the twenty-first century gesture.

Instead he whispered into Jane's ear, "God, I missed you." His voice sounded hoarse.

"Yeah," she said, equally strained. "Me, too."

They fell into a mutual famished kiss, drinking in the sensation of holding each other again, tasting each other again. Being together again.

Dimly he heard Freika's voice. "So how are you, T'May?"

"Holding steady. Are they always like this?"

"Pretty much."

"It's kind of . . . sweet. That, or nauseating." She sighed. "So much for my fond hopes."

Reluctantly Baran drew away from Jane's mouth, silently promising his body it would get more of her very soon. "Hello, T'May," he said in Standard. "Thanks for taking care of her for me."

T'May waved a hand. "My pleasure. She picks up things fast." She pointed to one of the colorful mounds on her plate and said to Jane, *"Tere va."*

"Unidentifiable vegetable, presumably alien," Jane said to Baran in English. "Tastes kind of like asparagus with a hint of tangerine."

T'May shook her head. "I don't know what she just said, but it sounded like two cats fighting in a sack."

"That's English for you," Freika said.

"So," Jane said to Baran, "y'all used to sleep together."

He choked. "You discussed my romantic past between trying to learn Standard?"

She shrugged. "I could tell by the way she says your name."

"You," Baran said, "are frightening."

"The relationship wasn't all that serious though," Jane decided. "At least from your end."

He lifted a brow. "What makes you say that?"

"You don't look panicky enough."

"I'll take it back—you're not frightening."

"No?"

"You're terrifying."

She nodded, satisfied, and curled her arms tighter around his neck as she settled against him. "Good. Remember that."

He felt a wicked grin steal over his face. "And maybe *you* should remember that so am I." He bent and scooped her neatly into his arms, barely feeling the weight.

"Baran!" Jane protested, laughing. "What are you doing?"

"You'll see." He looked at T'May as she watched them with amusement, scratching Octopussy behind the ears. "Excuse us. I feel the need to show my future bondmate another area of the ship."

"Like, say, the pleasure chambers on the recreation deck?"

"Oh, yeah." He laughed and headed for the doorway, Jane kicking her feet in mock protest.

"So," Frieka said to T'May just before the door closed behind him, "I haven't had gevalope steak in a week. Mind carrying the plate for me?" To the cat he added, "I may even let you have a bite, you primitive hairball."

"You know," Jane said to Baran as he carried her down the corridor, "I am capable of walking."

"That's true." He kept going.

"You could put me down."

"I could." He smiled down at her, so handsome he made her breath catch. "But I'm too busy establishing erotic male dominance."

She settled happily back against his muscular chest. "Kinky."

He laughed wickedly. "Oh, love, you haven't seen my idea of kinky yet."

Jane lifted a brow at him. "This doesn't involve a riding crop or a rubber chicken or anything, right?"

"Certainly not."

"Good."

"I have no idea where to even get a rubber chicken."

She stiffened. "Baran!" Her tone of outraged warning made him laugh.

Until, as he looked down at her, the humor was replaced by something warmer, softer. "God, Jane," he said in a low voice, "I love you."

She blinked at the moisture welling in her eyes and cleared her throat. "We're in serious danger of getting gooey here."

"Well," he said, stopping before a door that obediently opened, "not exactly gooey. More like hot, wet and . . ." He tossed her into the air. "Creamy."

Jane yelped as she landed right in the midst of something that sank under her weight, then rebounded so gently she barely bounced. Whatever it was immediately cuddled around her, feeling warm and far too friendly to be inanimate. She struggled to sit up as Baran stepped into the room, the door closing with a whisper behind him.

"What the hell is this?" she demanded, eyeing her surroundings warily.

She lay on the biggest bed she'd ever seen in her life. In fact, there was no room for anything else in the chamber. The mattress stretched from wall to wall, except for a small space next to the door just big enough to allow entry.

The bed itself was covered with a thick silken blanket that reminded her of a comforter. She ran her hand over it cautiously.

"Not quite what I have in mind," Baran said. "How about . . ."

To her astonishment, the comforter began to grow hair. Jane yelped and recoiled, but before she could leap up, the whole thing had morphed into a huge expanse of black fur. She touched it warily. It was as soft as a kitten's pelt, though of course no kitten could ever grow that big.

She didn't think.

"It's not . . . real is it?" Half-hypnotized by the sensation, Jane found herself stroking the comforter/pelt/whatsit.

"You mean, am I holding some poor alien hostage and forcing it to grow fur on command?" Baran asked dryly. "No, it's not real. It's a . . . Well, you don't have a word for it. Call it a machine."

"Damn." She petted the silken pelt again. "You just want to get naked and roll around on it."

"That's the idea." There was a note of lustful anticipation in his voice that made her look up. And blink.

He'd stripped off his armor while her attention was diverted. And he was definitely happy to see her.

"Um." She licked suddenly dry lips. "Hi."

"Yes, I am." He put one brawny knee on the bed-thing and climbed onto it. All that fascinating muscle rippled under smooth, tanned skin as he crawled toward her. "I'm also hard, thick, and long."

"I've noticed that about you." Cautiously she backed up on the bed. His expression was distinctly predatory, and it made her nervous.

"You, on the other hand, are small, creamy and tight." He gave her a feral smile. "Not to mention overdressed."

Jane swallowed, feeling something melt deep inside her in the heat of his stare. "And what are you planning to do about all that?"

"Actually," he told her softly, "I thought I'd rip your clothes off and fuck you to a screaming orgasm."

She blinked again. Swallowed. "That's fair."

"Glad you approve." He pounced.

Jane yelped, discovering he'd meant the "rip your clothes off" part literally. "Hey, cut that out!" she protested as he shredded the rest of her top with the gleeful ruthlessness of a small boy attacking a Christmas present. "What am I supposed to wear?"

"Sleek, lovely Jane Colby **skin**," **he** told her, jerking the cups of her bra apart. "Always in **style, no matter** the era."

Ducking his head, he fastened his hot mouth on one eager nipple. In seconds he had her squirming from the pleasure he inflicted with nibbling teeth and swirling tongue.

Finally he sat back on his heels, grabbed the waistband of her jeans, and jerked. The tough denim stood no chance at all against his ruthless Warlord strength.

Neither did the delicate silk of her panties.

She was still gasping when he took her thighs in both big hands, spread her legs, and started driving her insane with his mouth.

God, it felt good. That tongue of his should come with a warning label. She writhed helplessly, gasping, as he fluttered the very tip of it over her most tender flesh, driving her mercilessly toward an orgasm.

"Stop!" she gasped, unable to take any more.

"I don't think so," he growled, and gave her another long, long lick.

"No!" she panted. "I want . . . I want . . ."

That got his attention. He stopped and looked at her, leaning his face against her thigh. "What? Anything you want me to do, I'll do." Turning his head, he gave her thigh a tempting little nibble.

"I want to be on top!" she gasped.

He lifted a brow. "Of course."

"No, I mean . . ." She drew in a deep breath and managed to bring her desperate pants under control. "I want to be in charge this time. Dominant."

He lifted his head in surprise, then shrugged. "Your wish is my command."

Jane managed a cheeky grin. "That's the idea." She sat up. "Lie down on your back. I want to tie you up this time."

Because she was looking directly at him, she saw his eyes flicker. "All right."

That moment of unease reminded her of that horrific story he'd told her of being paralyzed while the Xeran tortured him. They hadn't discussed it, but she strongly suspected the abuse had been even worse than he'd let on.

And yet, he was willing to allow himself to be bound if she wanted it that way.

"Just . . . extend your hands over your head," she said, hastily modifying the game. "Grab one wrist, and keep them there. Don't let go." She watched while he obeyed, slowly stretching his big body out, assuming the position she directed. His cock bobbed, its violently blushing head touching his belly button. She eyed it hungrily, remembering all the times he'd used his mouth with such hot, devilish skill.

It was her turn now.

Jane rolled onto her knees and moved to straddle the powerful arch of his chest. The muscle felt rock-hard between her thighs as she let her weight settle on her heels.

He looked up at her, his eyes shuttered. Lust made his pupils glow bright red as a hungry smile teased the corners of his lips. Delicately she reached out to thumb his tiny dark nipples with both hands. He caught his breath. She smiled.

Gently, slowly, Jane started running her fingertips over his skin, exploring the ridges and hollows of his powerful body, savoring the outlines of the hard male shapes. She combed her sharp nails through his silken chest hair, gently raking him with the tips. He made a rough, hungry sound.

That became a muffled snort of laughter as her delicate touch found the broad hollows of his armpits. He squirmed. She grinned, wickedly delighted. "Ticklish?" she purred.

He shot her a warning look. "Not as much as you are."

"Uh-uh-uh!" she chided. "Thou shalt not threaten Mistress Jane. She doesn't like it." Rising from her crouched position, she swung off him—but only so she could turn her attention on his deliciously massive cock. "Mmmm." She reached out and took it in one hand. He was so thick, her fingers couldn't close completely around the base. "What have we got here?"

"What do you think?" he asked in a rough growl.

"I think," she said, "it looks edible." Lowering her head, she ran her tongue gently up the flushed shaft, stopping just at the head.

He actually quivered.

Jane grinned, relishing the sense of erotic power she felt. Slowly she began to lick the thick rod, stopping now and then to nibble gently at the thick ropy veins that ran up its length.

"Jane," Baran gasped, and started to reach for her.

"Hands!" she snapped, fighting to sound stern instead of breathless and aroused. "Did I say you could move?"

He groaned and reluctantly stretched his arms over his head again.

She rewarded him for his obedience by gently cupping his full, tight balls, stroking and cuddling them as she worked him over with her mouth. She could feel his big body shudder with each slow lick and nibble.

And she loved every minute of it.

Finally she lifted her head, opened her mouth, and took his cock inside. His heartfelt groan of pleasure made her lips curl around his width. Bobbing her head, she squeezed his balls with careful delicacy.

"Jane!" he gasped, and began to pump his hips in short, shallow thrusts.

She felt so wet, so desperate to have him strong and hard and deep inside her. But first, she wanted to show him what she was capable of.

Baran clamped his right hand hard around his left wrist to keep from reaching down, grabbing her, and plunging himself in to the hilt. She felt so damn good as her mouth moved up and down over his shaft, sucking the sensitive head and rolling her tongue over it as though it were something juicy and she wanted to draw out every last sweet drop.

He groaned in need.

He was far too close to just shooting right down her throat. Briefly, he considered telling his computer to help him back off the pleasure, but it just felt too good to give up. Instead he gasped, "Jane, I can't last too much longer!"

She lifted her head, depriving his cock of her hot, sweet mouth. "No?" She smiled slowly.

Baran wanted to howl. "Jane!" Goaded, he started to grab her.

Her brown eyes flashed. "Hands!"

He considered showing her just what he could do with those hands. But God, it felt so good lying here, letting her use that incredible mouth on him. He growled and clamped a grip on his wrist again, suspecting he was leaving bruises. He didn't give a damn.

But instead of bending over him, Jane rose to her knees and straddled him again. She took his aching cock in those small, soft fingers and aimed it upward at her entrance. Feeling velvet lips even softer than the fur he lay on, he shuddered.

Then slowly, taking her time, she slid down over him, one bare fraction at a time.

She was so wet, so tight.

He tossed his head on the pillow. She came on, taking more and more, plunging him by fractions into the sweetest heat he'd ever known. Until, at last, her silken little butt rested on his thighs.

"There," she said. She was wearing that siren's smile again, but her eyes were very wide. As tight as she was to him, he must feel huge to her. He smiled smugly.

He lost the grin in a hurry as she began to rise, slowly, slowly, silk and cream and fire.

Too slowly.

He needed to plunge deep.

But her cheeks were flushed and lovely, and her eyes sparkled with triumph. He knew she relished being in control, feeling him yield, for once, to her.

He could stand this.

Maybe.

Still, Baran couldn't resist arching his spine, lifting her on his pelvis. She braced both hands on his tightly laced abdomen and threw her head back. Dark curls slid around her shoulders. Her pale, perfect breasts lifted and fell with her quick breathing. Her nipples were dark pink and stiffly erect.

"Let me taste you," he demanded hoarsely.

With a soft, arousing moan, she bent forward until Baran could reach one exquisite tip. He suckled it, caught halfway between the pleasure of her taste and the frustration that she'd had to rise half off his shaft to reach his mouth. Her hair tumbled around his head in a sweet silken cloud.

Suddenly she wrapped her arms around his head, gathering his hair into fierce little fists. "For a while there, I was afraid I'd lost you," she said. "I was afraid they'd taken you away."

He released her nipple and encircled her body with his arms in a hard, comforting hug. "You'll never lose me. I'll always come back to you."

Then he rolled her over on her back and plunged his cock in to the hilt.

It was all Jane could do not to scream as Baran began riding her. His strokes were long and strong and powerful, yet she had the impression he was carefully gaging their depth and force to make sure he wouldn't hurt her.

He'd taken her before, of course, but this was different. Before he'd claimed her, overwhelmed her. This time he seemed to be giving himself to her with every hot, mind-blowing plunge. With a whimper of pleasure, she lifted her legs and wrapped them around his muscular ass, opening herself, surrendering herself.

Returning his gift.

His gaze met hers. His eyes were blazing again, but the fire no longer seemed alien. There was too much love in them.

By rights, her own should be glowing right back at him.

"Jane," he said, his voice low, intense. "I love you."

"I love you," she gasped. Such common words, such simple words, but she realized suddenly she'd never really felt them, never really meant them, until this moment.

And she'd never felt so loved in return. Never *been* so loved in return.

Then he drove in his deepest thrust yet, and threw her headlong into fire. She screamed, barely aware of his simultaneous roar.

Writhing together, they tumbled into heat and light.

Jane lay draped over Baran's damp, heaving chest, limp as a scarf. Her entire body still twitched and vibrated like a plucked violin string from the violence of her climax.

Baran had one arm wrapped around her. Judging from its weight, he felt just as wrung out as she did. She sighed, aware of a niggle of uncertainty. "Where are we going to go from here?"

"Before I came down," he said softly, "I told Command I wouldn't be taking any more wet missions. General Jeffers offered me a command post."

She lifted her head to look up into his eyes. "That's wonderful!"

Baran shrugged. "He'd mentioned it before, but I'd always turned him down. I had too many monsters to kill."

Jane smiled and cuddled into him. "But all the monsters are dead now."

He closed his eyes. "Yes. We got 'em all."

They lay together another long moment, deliciously content. Finally she roused herself enough to ask, "What about Frieka?"

"He'll be my aide. We've been together too long to break up."

She took a deep breath and expressed the fear that had been lurking at the back of her mind. "And what about me? I don't know a damn thing about this time."

"You'll learn. You're up to the challenge."

"Hell, I know *that*. But what do I do with the rest of my life?" She grinned wickedly. "Other than have frequent, mind-blowing sex with you."

He grinned back. "Anything you want. I've just got to program that personal comp for you, and it'll teach you whatever you need to know."

Jane rested her chin on his chest as a thought occurred to her. "Do they still have writers? Storytellers?"

He looked down at her, lifting a dark eyebrow. "Well, of course."

"That's it then." She nodded in satisfaction and nestled into the curve of his shoulder. "Because I've got a hell of a story to tell."

Warfem

ACKNOWLEDGMENTS

Several good friends helped me with this story by diligently checking it for logic holes. Any I failed to plug are my sole responsibility.

My thanks to Martha Punches, Morgan Hawke, and Katherine Lazo, as well as my wonderful critique partner, Diane Whiteside.

And as always, thanks to my agent, Roberta Brown, and my wonderfully patient editor, Cindy Hwang.

One

The thugs followed Alina Kasi out of the bar. Three of them. Two were obviously muscle—a big, beefy blond and a wiry rodent of a man who looked like the kind who'd carry a blade. Then there was the one she figured for the brains of the trio, a thoroughly unremarkable brunet with a pleasant smile and cold, cold eyes.

Alina, planning her trap, was careful to give no indication she'd seen them. Instead she strolled down the pedwalk, tilting her head back like a woman enjoying the cool evening air. Zipcars ghosted overhead, sighing softly in the darkness. Across the river, Jarnalda's two moons rode high over the arches and spires of the city skyline. It was all pretty enough for a tourist trid, if not for the three men skulking along behind her like a trio of wolves.

Just out for a stroll, boys, she thought. *Come try your luck.*

Rajin would be outraged, of course. The Femmat aristocrat would expect Alina to tuck herself safely away in that miserable hotel Kasi House had booked for her. After all, Alina was only scheduled for a one-day layover on this planet, waiting for the jumpship that would take her on to Calista. She shouldn't be out looking for trouble.

All true. A responsible courier working for a responsible employer would never take this kind of chance with a file. But Alina wasn't working for a responsible employer, and she was just frustrated and pissed enough not to care. Besides, these three were no real danger to her.

They were, at best, entertainment.

The trio had been shadowing her since she'd arrived that morning, except they'd changed height, weight, and even species with every encounter. Alina figured they were using some kind of imagizer to project disguises over their true forms. Must be using high-end equipment, too. The illusions would have been good enough to fool her if her sensors hadn't told her the same three men had been tailing her all day.

All of which added up to data thieves. She wondered how they thought they could get the file out of her computer implant. The comp wouldn't give it up even if they killed her, so they must believe they could force her to upload it to whatever storage unit they had.

Idiots.

She did hope they didn't have a data stripper, though. In theory, one of those devices could bypass her comp's security and gut its files. Of course, to use the stripper, the thieves would first have to hack open her skull, since her comp wound through her brain in a mirror of her neural pathways.

That wouldn't exactly be easy, because Alina was a Samurai Class Warfem, genetically engineered for combat. Her bones and muscles were so heavily reinforced, she was stronger than all three of the men who stalked her. And given her battle computer and the sensors implanted throughout her body, she could also out-think and out-fight them.

As she would shortly demonstrate.

So what are they carrying? Alina thought to her comp.

The leader and the blond have stun batons, while the small dark one has a nano-knife, the computer replied in its soundless mental voice.

That all? Every other time data thieves had jumped her, they'd been armed like men going after a Soji Dragon. Alina had still protected her files, but she'd had to work at it.

There are stiff penalties against carrying beam weapons on this planet.

Which means nothing to data thieves. Any interesting talents? Cybernetics?

Standard human. No apparent implants beyond data jacks.

She frowned, wondering if they might be setting a trap of their own. What kind of fool would send three standard humans to take a Warfem?

Fools or not, though, they were getting ready to try for her. Alina could almost smell it in their sweat. *Go to full alert.*

Instantly, the implant began readying her body for the coming battle, preparing the chemical dump she'd need if she decided to go into the berserker state called *riaat*. She didn't think it would be necessary, but one never knew.

As the comp did its work, Alina took a moment to decide on her next move.

It was 2500 hours, almost midnight on this planet. Alien constellations spilled overhead, the star population thinner out here on the galactic rim than back home on Vardon. Stores and shops rose to either side of the pedwalk, utilitarian boxes built of ferocrete, square and unimaginative compared with the soaring, curved shapes back home.

Trid signs, some of them amazingly lewd, gave the scene what color it had. Women, strutting eternally in midair, wearing some designer's idea of the latest fashion; men posing in jump shoes and very little else; an alien doing . . . whatever that was. All of them cooing come-ons or chanting their respective stores' hours.

But the only sound that interested Alina was the scrape of her pursuers' boots on the dirty pedwalk behind her. There were no other footsteps. Despite the illusionary company of the signs, she was alone with them.

Which was exactly the way she wanted it. She needed room and privacy to break a few bones and get a few answers. Who were they, and who were they working for?

And in the process, they'd hopefully put up a good enough fight to let Alina blow off some steam. After years in the emotional cage Rajin had built for her, she needed it.

They were almost close enough. One . . . Two . . . Three . . .

"Kaaassssi!" Lifting her voice in the ringing battlecry of her House, Alina spun and charged.

She caught them completely by surprise. Somebody shouted as she slammed her fist into the big blond's jaw. He rolled with it at the last moment, so the punch didn't quite land as hard as it should have. Still, backed by her genetically engineered strength, it put him down.

In the same smooth motion, she grabbed the right wrist of the rodent-faced one as he went for his knife. Spinning him around, she seized his left shoulder and cranked his right arm up and back until the joint gave. He howled in agony, and she shoved him aside.

Pain sliced into her ribs, ripping her breath away. Instinctively, she whirled and rammed her fist into the cold-eyed leader's nose, winning a howl. His stun baton lost contact with her ribs, and she could breathe again.

Her computer snapped a mental warning, and she ducked the blond's roundhouse as he came at her again. Pivoting on one foot, she slammed a knee into his balls, then gave him an uppercut that clicked his teeth together. He hit the ground. He wouldn't be getting up anytime soon.

Her comp confirmed it. *Opponent unconscious.*

"Fuck this." The rodent man reeled off. Apparently the dislocated arm had discouraged him. She turned her full attention to the leader.

He bared his teeth at her, his nose streaming blood. "If you're smart, you'll give the file up now."

"Got a better idea, thief." She bounced on her toes, her blood singing with the raw enjoyment of a good, clean fight. Finally, something she could hit. "You tell me who sent you, and I won't break every bone you have."

The leader only smiled.

Alert! the computer howled. *Tevan combat cyborg, closing fast from the rooftop!*

"Told you," the thief mocked, evidently reading the instant alarm on her face.

Blazing hell, it *was* a trap. Alina snapped into a spinning kick that slammed into the side of his head. His jaw broke with a wet crack clearly audible to her enhanced hearing.

Then she whirled and ran. No way was she going to try to fight a Tevan cyborg. One of those bastards could take on a Warlord and win. He'd beat her into paste.

Worse, if the Tevan had a data stripper and got his hands on the file, Rajin would take out her anger on Galar.

Should have thought of that before you went after these fools, she thought, furious with herself.

The Tevan hit the ground behind her with a meaty thud. "Warlord's slut, get back here!" His rumbling roar made her blood chill. Big boots boomed on the pavement. She put her head down and ran faster.

What have we got?

Tevan cyborg, 2.3 meters tall, two hundred and ninety kilograms. Skeletal structure reinforced with titanium laminate. Nano-cybernetic muscle implants give him strength superior to a Warlord in riaat. And he's gaining on you. Eight meters . . . 7.9 . . . Seven meters . . . Those pounding footsteps grew louder.

Give me riaat. *I need to outrun him.* She certainly couldn't outfight him.

Fire flooded her consciousness, as the computer released a

wave of neurochemicals from reservoir implants throughout her body. In seconds, the chemicals did their work, quadrupling her strength and decreasing her ability to feel pain. Euphoria replaced her fear with a hot, feral joy she knew was an illusionary product of *riaat*.

Time to make things a little tougher on the Tevan. She lengthened her stride, bounding now, feeling as light as if somebody had suddenly cut gravity in half.

The Tevan is still closing. Four meters . . . 3.8 . . .

A low building stood off to her left, no more than three stories, its gray face gleaming ghostly in the light from the two moons. Alina veered toward it and leaped. Her feet hit the roof, knees bending to absorb the impact.

Something heavy slammed into the side of the building behind her with a crunch. Before she could jump clear, a massive seven-fingered hand clamped around her left ankle and spilled her to the roof. She rolled, trying to kick free. The reptilian bastard hung on the edge staring at her, his four yellow eyes glittering with battle madness. Before she could kick him in the head, he plucked her off the roof and slung her across the pedwalk.

Alina twisted in midair, tucking in her chin and saving herself from a headfirst collision with the building. The impact still knocked the breath out of her.

Stunned, she hit the walk with a teeth-rattling jolt. This time she did see stars.

Up! the computer demanded, its metal voice as strident as an enforcer's siren. *The Tevan is closing!*

Alina lifted her spinning head. Blood poured hot and wet from her nose, and her scraped face stung. She glimpsed the Tevan's armored boot drawing back, aimed right for her head. She flung herself clear as it flashed by.

Panting, bleeding, Alina reeled to her feet.

The Tevan stalked her, two meters plus of muscle, orange scales, flame-red armor, and cybernetic implants. He had a short, bearlike muzzle, with a crown of spines that protected his four small yellow eyes. His hands and feet were broad, with seven thin, agile digits on each. Peeling back his orange lips, he revealed a mouthful of razor teeth. "Surrender the file, and I won't kill you," he rumbled in Standard, his voice a chilling basso growl as inhuman as the rest of him.

"Blow that," Alina snarled, knowing if she lost this fight she was dead. And worse, so was Galar. "You want it, you're going to have to bleed for it."

"Warbitch, I'm not the one who's going to bleed." He lunged.

She ducked the huge fist flying at her face. Pain faded as her computer pumped endorphins into her bloodstream. Her concentration narrowed on the task of staying alive.

Alina shot a punch into his ribs hard enough to shatter ferocrete, but he just plowed another punch toward her gut. She twisted aside and pumped a kick into his thigh.

The Tevan growled and sprang. Alina leaped back to circle just out of reach, looking for an opening. With *riaat* jacking her strength to superhuman levels, she could stay out of his way, but that wasn't good enough. Her reserves would run out long before he tired.

Despite his vastly superior strength and reinforced bones, she had to put him down long enough to make good her escape.

Then it happened. Alina ducked one vicious fist—right into the path of the other. A sun went nova in her skull. The world spun as she slammed into a wall for the second time. Then the ground came up and hit her in the face. Her comp shrieking warnings, Alina tried to scramble to her feet.

She didn't make it. Her knees gave out, and her cheek collided painfully with the pedwalk.

The Tevan's massive boots rang on the rough surface as he stalked her. "Now, Warbitch, you're—"

A male bellow cut him off in mid-sentence. Something massive flew out of the darkness to barrel into his back. This time the Tevan was the one to hit the wall.

Dazed, Alina watched the flurry of movement—fists, feet, arms, big bodies surging and striking at one another. *Who the . . . ?*

Command beads glittered in her savior's long hair. *A Warlord.*

A Warlord had come to her rescue.

Two

Yes! They had him now! The thought banished Alina's pain, sent strength pouring through her. No matter how battered she felt, she damn well wouldn't just lie there while a Warlord fought for her. Reeling to her feet, she yelled her battle cry and charged.

The Tevan rolled one yellow eye toward her, but he didn't dare take his attention off the Warlord who was powering punches into his head and body. The air was full of meaty thuds and grunts, the smell of sweat, and the Tevan's lizard reek.

The Warlord has cracked the Tevan's armor, her computer said as she looked for an opening. *Right side, between the eighth and ninth rib.* A set of red crosshairs popped into her vision, pinpointing the weakness.

Alina rammed her fist dead in the center of those crosshairs. Something in her own side shrieked in agony with the force of the blow, but the cracks widened. The Tevan roared and twisted to strike out at her. She ducked his wild punch as the Warlord hit him squarely over his cracked armor. The acrid scent of alien blood rose.

With a bellow of frustrated rage, the Tevan broke and ran, lumbering like a galloping bull. Alina and the Warlord raced after him, tearing down the darkened pedwalk in the exaggerated strides of full *riaat*. A zipbike flashed low over their heads, probably a passerby wanting a closer look at the chase. The Warlord reached out a powerful arm for the Tevan's armored shoulder.

But the alien leaped straight up, grabbed the back of the zipbike, and heaved himself astride behind the driver. Before Alina and the Warlord could do more than curse, the bike arched skyward, its gravlevs glowing blue against the night.

She broke stride, panting as she stared after the Tevan in rage. "Well, that absolutely grinds." Shaking her head, Alina turned toward her Warlord savior. "Thanks for—" She broke off.

He was easily two meters tall, with the lean, powerful build of a Comanche class Warlord, built for agility and speed as much as strength. His hair was a rich dark sable, and a small, neat beard framed his sensual mouth. The intricate tattoo of Arvid House spilled down the left side of his handsome face in brilliant iridescent blue and scarlet.

Her attention narrowed into the small circle at the base of the tatt, right over the hollow of his strong cheekbone. The circle had not been filled in. Like her, he was still unmarried. After all these years.

The lust that was one of the side effects of *riaat* rolled through her in a hot and burning wave, blended with pure longing. It had been so damn long since she'd seen him, touched him. "Baird," she choked, her voice shaking. Sweet Goddess, she wanted him.

Too bad she could never have him.

Baird stood frozen, staring at her, taking in the blood smearing the side of her face, the loneliness and hunger in her eyes. His own blood burned with *riaat* lust and pain, and he took a step forward, tempted to push her to the pedwalk and take her right there.

Instead he stopped and clenched his fists, fighting himself. He didn't mind the desire—he understood that. The aftermath of *riaat* always engulfed his body in an erotic storm.

What bothered him was the pain. It felt as if someone had scooped a huge, aching hole out of the center of his chest, and the only thing that would fill it was her. Despite the investigation, despite duty and honor, despite the long, bitter years that had passed, he wanted her still.

He couldn't afford that. He had a job to do.

Comp, kill the riaat *lust,* Baird ordered. Instantly, the desire began to drain away, leaving his body feeling cold. Yet the pain remained, searing him like a beamer burn.

"Damn you, Alina," he gritted. She had no right to such power over him.

She opened her mouth as if to retort, but her face suddenly paled. Her eyes widened and rolled back in her head.

Baird jumped forward to catch her before she hit the ground. She felt lighter than he remembered as he lowered her to the pedwalk. *What are her injuries?*

Concussion, fractured cheekbone, two cracked ribs, and extensive bruising and lacerations, his internal computer replied. *Given the extent of her injuries, a medtech is advisable.*

And yet she'd waded back into the fight with the Tevan to back him up, then helped him chase the bastard down the alley. Some of that lunatic endurance had been *riaat,* but the rest had been pure, stubborn Alina.

Call a unit, he ordered. Aloud, he said, "Alina? Alina, talk to me."

She lifted her blond head, combat beaded braids clinking. "Baird. Goddess, Baird, been so long. Missed you . . ."

He had to control the impulse to tighten his grip on her. His comp was draining off the chemicals of *riaat,* but he was still more than strong enough to hurt her without meaning to. "I missed you, too, brat." He had to stop to clear his throat. He'd always hated seeing her hurt.

Her eyes rolled. "Galar. Where's Galar?"

"What?" He remembered his files. Galar was Rajin's ten-year-old son. Why was she asking about him? But before he could question her, her head dropped against his shoulder.

Maybe Rajin had her working as the boy's bodyguard when she wasn't using her for . . . other tasks.

The rising wail of a medunit's siren drew his eyes skyward. The big vehicle came in fast and low, riding on its intricate arrangement of gravlev fields. As it set down, Baird walked to meet it, cradling Alina gently in his arms.

A woman in the blue uniform of a medtech towed a gleaming transparent tube from the back of the unit. "Put her in here," she said as the tube's lid slid back.

Baird placed Alina in the tube and stepped back, watching anxiously as the curving lid sealed and a pink gas pumped to fill it.

A trid of Alina's body appeared over the tube, her injuries outlined in red. The tech studied them and murmured a few soft commands before turning toward him. Her skin was a metallic silver that contrasted vividly with the pale blue of her hair. She was as human as Baird was, which meant her coloring was either a product of genetic tinkering or cosmetics—it was tough to say which. Faint lines around her eyes suggested she was well into her eighties. "How about you? You've got some bruises, too," she said, stepping over to aim a handheld scanner at him. "What the hell happened, anyway? Did you do that to her?"

Outraged, he glared at the tech. "What, beat her like that? Don't be ridiculous. We're both Vardonese warriors."

The woman's gaze lifted, belatedly taking in his braids and command beads. "Oh, yeah, I've heard of you." Cynicism gleamed in her eyes. "You guys take some kind of vow. Vardon is one of those matriarchal planets, right? You've got that female aristocracy, the Femays or something."

"The *Femmats*."

Two hundred years before, a group of idealistic scientists had colonized Vardon, intent on creating a utopia. Since most violence was committed by young men, they decided to tinker with their own genetic code to eliminate male aggression. But they'd also realized they needed protection from all the aggressive colonies around them, so they created a defense force of super warriors—the Warlords and their female equivalent, Warfems.

Raised in Warlord Creches to learn loyalty and obedience, the Warriors were indentured to the companies that created them, then sent into military service. They all took a vow to protect those weaker than themselves, male or female, adult or child.

Now guilt pricked Baird's outrage. Alina had been his partner, his lover and his best friend for five years. For him, that had been a very strong bond, even if Alina had turned her back on it in the end.

Yet his actions today had put her in that regenerator.

Still, if what they suspected was true, her bond with him wasn't the only one Alina had violated. That was why Baird had volunteered for this mission. He had to find out if she was guilty, prove her innocence if she wasn't, and stop her if she was.

It was a matter of honor.

"So if you didn't do it to her, who did?" the tech asked.

"A Tevan cyborg."

Pale blue eyebrows flew upward. "A Tevan? Who did you two piss off, anyway?"

"I have no idea. The Tevan was beating her, so I stepped in." Which was the truth—more or less.

The tech snorted. "Good thing you did. The lizard probably would have killed her."

"It certainly looked that way." And when he got his hands on the bastard, Baird was going to kick his ass.

Alina woke as the regenator's pink mist drained away. Disoriented, she watched the transparent lid slide back, blinking hazily at the stars overhead.

"Alina? Are you all right?" The deep voice cut through her mental fog, snapping her instantly to attention.

"Baird?" Her heart leaped. He stood beside the tube, looking grim as a medtech trained a scanner on her. Alina started to roll off the tube stretcher. The world reeled around her, almost dumping her on her face.

Baird caught her. "Take it slow, Alina. You always get the spins after a session in regen."

She gave him a look as she steadied herself against his strong chest. "I'm touched you remember." She was surprised he'd even care, particularly after that last row they'd had over Rajin's ultimatum.

Twenty years ago.

A long time. No wonder he's changed.

Baird had been barely twenty the last time she'd seen him. He was taller now, harder, more muscular than the boy she'd fought beside for five years.

That was only to be expected, she supposed. They'd been half-starved little animals then, fighting the Xeran invaders with all the savagery of wolf-cats. Now the Xer were gone, and the great Femmat Houses of Vardon were richer and more powerful than ever. Which wasn't exactly a blessing, at least in Alina's case.

Baird frowned down at her, visibly worried. "How are you feeling?"

She straightened away from him, though she wanted nothing more than to rest against his strength.

Unfortunately, it was a luxury Alina couldn't afford. In all the ways that mattered, nothing had changed where she and Baird were concerned. "I'm fine." And she was, she realized, probing her face with cautious fingers.

"You weren't half an hour ago," the medtech told her. "Concussion, fractured cheekbone, cracked ribs. Stay out of fights with Tevans, okay?"

"I'll take that under advisement." Alina inhaled, pleased to note the lack of pain. Everything felt solid and sturdy again. The regenator had done its job with its usual efficiency.

"Good." Nodding, the tech turned to shepherd her machine back into the emergency unit.

As it lifted off, Alina couldn't resist another look at Baird. Examining the beads braided into his hair, she spotted a ruby that signified a captaincy in the Vardon Stellar Command, along with twenty years' worth of service and combat decorations. They made a glittering display against his sable mane.

He was wearing the uniform, too, a blue unisuit piped with command red, a captain's scarlet insignia decorating his high collar. The dark colors drew attention to his face, with its strong, angular bone structure that was, if anything, more handsome than she remembered.

Yet there was something in those golden eyes that was much older than she knew him to be. Warlords didn't live as long as Femmat aristocrats, but forty was still quite young.

So why did those eyes look so weary, so hard and disillusioned? What had happened to him on the way to all those combat decorations?

Still, Alina felt a twinge of envy for his military splendor. All she wore were the beads she'd won in the invasion. Rajin Kasi had refused to let her serve after that. *"Kasi House spent a great deal of money on your genetic engineering, your cybernetics, and your education,"* the Femmat aristocrat had told her. *"We mean to get a return on our investment."*

As a gesture of gratitude, most Houses had emancipated the genetically engineered warriors who'd fought to free Vardon from the Xer. The reasoning went that no matter what each company had spent creating their Warlords and Warfem, the fighters had more than paid it back during that five-year guerrilla war.

Rajin, as Kasi House president, hadn't agreed. At least not when it came to Alina. But when she'd forbidden further contact with

Baird, Alina had seriously considered suing for her freedom. Unfortunately she knew what price Rajin would exact.

She hadn't even dared tell Baird why she hadn't, which had resulted in that last bitter fight. He hadn't spoken to her since.

Until tonight.

"The Tevan hurt you," Baird said, jolting her out of her painful preoccupation. His golden eyes were fixed so hungrily on her face, she'd have thought he was still in the aftermath of *riaat* if her computer hadn't told her otherwise. Lifting a big hand, he brushed his knuckles across her healed cheekbone in a tender gesture at odds with his curled lip. "He's lucky he got away. I'd have killed him for that."

Alina inhaled sharply at his warm, calloused touch. She tried to cover her reaction with a smile. "You always were protective."

"I've missed you." His deep voice sounded a little hoarse.

"You're not . . . still angry?"

Those beautiful eyes flickered, and she knew he lied. "No. You were only doing your duty to your House."

Which wasn't what he'd said at the time. He'd called her a coward then, too gutless to stand up to Rajin's blatant abuse. And she hadn't been able to explain.

For ten years, Alina had wondered if he was right about her cowardice. Then Galar was born, and she'd known her sacrifice was worth it.

Too bad she still couldn't explain to Baird. She'd love to damn the consequences and spill the whole story, but she wouldn't be the only one to face Rajin's rage. She couldn't take the chance.

Instead she changed the subject, gently tugging one of the braids that swung by his temple. "Judging by the beads, you've done well for yourself."

His smile flashed white. "Judging by the murder attempt, you're still pissing people off. What was that all about, anyway?"

She stiffened with the automatic wariness of twenty years as a courier for Rajin Kasi. Then she forced a shrug and a grin. "As you said, I must have pissed someone off."

"Need a bodyguard?"

Goddess, yes. Data thieves might dare an attempt on her, but they'd steer well clear of a Warlord. And if they didn't, they'd regret it. But . . . Reluctantly, she shook her head. "Rajin would throw a rod. You know how she is about us."

He lifted a dark brow. "Is Rajin here?"

"Waiting for me on Calista."

"Calista is twenty-four light-years away. She doesn't have to know." Baird frowned. "Besides, hasn't Kasi House emancipated you by now? Even if you weren't a Xeran Invasion veteran, most Houses demand no more than ten years' service."

"Rajin says soon." She'd been saying "soon" for the past ten years. Alina knew "soon" would never arrive unless she found a way to force it.

"You could take Kasi to court, sue for emancipation."

Not a day went by that she didn't dream of doing just that. "It's complicated."

Perceptive golden eyes studied her face. "Why don't we go some-place a little more secure, and you can explain it to me?"

She wavered, tempted despite the risk. Goddess, she'd love to tell him the whole story, face his rage, and get it over with. Maybe he'd listen and forgive.

Maybe he'd even help her get Galar away from Rajin. She'd sacrifice anything for the boy's safety. Hell, she had already sacrificed her heart, her happiness and her honor. Nothing else was left.

Except the boy's life.

No, she couldn't risk that. But she could be with Baird, if only for tonight. Feed her hunger for him. Make love to him again. Store up memories. Surely she deserved that much? "Yes," Alina said, her voice hoarse with need. "I'd like to . . . catch up."

She wanted to do a great deal more than catch up. And judging from the bulge in those snug uniform trousers, so did Baird.

Three

Baird's smile flashed white against his darkly tanned face. He took Alina's hand. "My hotel?"

His hotel. His bed. "Sounds good." He probably rated better accommodations than she did. Kasi House always booked cheap lodgings for her, which usually meant a spacer's hostel in the worst section of whatever port city she landed in. The theory was that she could look out for herself. Which she could, but she'd frankly gotten very tired of sleeping in vermin-infested sackracks.

As Alina watched, Baird turned his gaze skyward, his handsome profile outlined against the stars, and sent out a call for a zipcab through his communications implant. Automatically, she looked up, too.

"Alina," he said suddenly.

She half-turned, and he stepped against her, all dark male strength, his hands big and warm as they came to rest on her waist. Then his mouth lowered to hers, and she forgot all her worry and bitterness. Hot, wet, flavored with some delicious alien spice, his lips moved over hers. They were much more skillful than they'd been when he was a pretty young warrior just coming to his power. This was the kiss of a man who knew exactly what he was doing and the best way to go about doing it. She found herself sinking against him with a low moan of need.

God, she wanted him. On her, in her, however she could get him. Now. She wasn't even all that sure she could wait for a bed.

A burst of musical notes played, jerking them from each other's arms as the zipcab descended. It came to a hovering halt, announcing its rates in a purring female voice. Shaped roughly like a curving wedge, it wore a brilliant paint-job advertising some local bar. Its forward passenger door slid open in invitation.

Baird looked down at Alina, a warm gleam of anticipation in his eyes. "Shall we?"

"Goddess, yes."

They scooted inside to sink into deep blue upholstery. Alina sat back with a sigh, her tired body enjoying the luxury. The seats adjusted as they settled in, cupping around backs and butts. In the event of a crash, they'd also surround the cab's occupants with soft, protective cocoons.

The cab had no driver, though it did have a triangular yoke that thrust from its dash—part of its manual emergency controls in case the navigation computer went down. Baird murmured the address of his hotel, and the cab took off, soaring straight up to merge with the traffic overhead.

Alina barely had time to glimpse the lights of the city receding below before he pulled her out of her seat and into his lap. His mouth claimed hers, demanding and hot. She moaned and kissed him back.

For long, sweet moments, she simply forgot herself in the kiss, in the heat of his mouth, so familiar and yet so different. She wrapped one arm around his shoulder and the other in his long hair as he cuddled her in his lap. It was a pose they'd assumed a thousand times all those years before, but it felt very different now. He was hard and strong and broad in a way he hadn't been then, making her feel almost delicate. She found the differences deliciously arousing.

And so were his big, clever hands.

He found his way beneath the hem of her tunic to the skin that lay beneath, stroking gently across her waist and belly, then up to the curves of her breasts. "You're bigger than you used to be," he said softly, cupping her in long, warm fingers.

Alina smiled against his mouth. "So are you."

"You have that effect on me." He rolled his hips against her backside. The bulge of his erection was thick and long, making her shudder in longing greed.

She drew back to bite tenderly at his lower lip. "Taller. I meant you've grown taller."

He looked into her eyes. There was regret in his. "I was a boy then."

"Well, you're definitely not anymore." Alina wrapped her fingers in the thick black silk of his hair. Lowering her head, she took his mouth in a slow, sliding kiss.

He groaned, the sound vibrating deep and rough, and kissed her back.

Fear and bitterness spun away.

Despite Baird's suspicions, despite everything he knew about her, the taste of Alina was magic. In her arms, he felt a boy again, trembling with need and hunger for his first lover. Finally he had to draw back, gasping, to look into her face. The regenator's mist had cleaned the blood away, and the bruises and swelling were gone. He could see her now.

Alina looked even lovelier than she had twenty years ago. She'd lost the haunted look of partial starvation, flesh filling in the stark hollows under her high cheekbones. Her body felt solid with healthy muscle, and her breasts filled his hands with their soft weight.

But her pretty mouth had the same sweet curve, and those eyes were just as big and violet as they'd always been. Even the beads in her blond hair were the same. That probably galled her; she should have a collection of promotion and campaign honors as impressive as his. That bitch Rajin had refused to let her serve.

She'd evidently had other plans for Alina.

Hate stirred in his heart, chill and bitter. If his lover had violated her oath, it was because of the Femmat.

Yet Alina could have walked away at any time. The girl he'd known would have, rather than be involved in Rajin's crimes. Why hadn't she? What hold did the Femmat have on her?

"Baird?" Alina lifted her head, frowning. "Is something wrong?"

He forced a smile and raked his thumb over a tight nipple. "Nothing, sweet. Nothing at all."

They were still caressing each other when the cab chimed, announcing their arrival at their destination. With a groan of frustrated reluctance, Alina drew back from Baird's deliciously tempting mouth.

Resting his forehead against hers, he said huskily, "Patience, love. I want to take you in a bed, not a zipcab." He drew back and rested his palm on the cab's payment screen, authorizing it to charge his credit account. The fare paid, the cab popped its door and let them out on the pedwalk.

Straightening the hem of her tunic with a jerk, Alina looked up at the hotel towering over their heads. She'd been right—this was no sackrack, though not an aristocrat's lodgings either. It was the sort of inexpensive, decent place that catered to travelers of Baird's rank and class. She should be able to get a good night's sleep here, uninterrupted by sexual groans penetrating inadequate soundproofing.

Though she strongly suspected she'd be too busy making pleasure noises of her own to notice anyone else's. She really didn't anticipate getting all that much sleep, not judging from the hot male hunger in Baird's eyes.

Though there'd been a moment when she'd seen something else, something that looked a lot like rage. Something fresher than two-decade-old anger over their breakup.

But when he reached for her hand, she gave it, threading her fingers gratefully between his long, strong ones. Even that chaste contact made her body hum.

They walked into the building together, past the trids advertising exotic liquors, restaurants, clothing, and sex entertainers. The lobby itself was bright and well lit, decorated in bright colors, with a soaring, transparent ceiling. A massive central mobile constructed of flowing shapes dominated the vast space, chiming softly.

Alina and Baird didn't linger to sightsee, instead heading straight for the glass-enclosed antigrav lift. It opened at their approach, and they stepped inside. The double doors closed with a musical trill, sealing them in the tube as it slid smoothly upward. Through the glass, she noticed a pair of grav-dancers soaring around one another in the center of the lobby, their bodies nude except for swirls of glittering paint. No sooner did they come together than one or the other swooped away, so that they dove and soared like birds. Watching them, Alina felt her heart ache.

"They're a pretty good metaphor for us, aren't they?" Baird asked softly, watching her face.

"You always were far too good at reading my mind." She turned away from the dancers and forced a smile. "I don't want to think about that now."

His face hardened. "No, I don't suppose you do." The doors opened. "And neither do I."

Before she could move, he bent and swept her up into his arms, startling a laugh out of her as he carried her out into the hall. Alina wasn't used to feeling delicate, yet cradled in those powerful arms, she did—and she loved it.

Baird strode down the corridor with her, surefooted and powerful. Alina stared up into his tight profile, wondering at the hint of danger she felt from him, the edge of anger.

Yes, this was more than the old grudge. But what?

His room responded to his biological signature at their approach, and its door slid open in welcome. He carried her inside without breaking step.

The room was a simple enough affair. Its only furniture was a small table in the corner flanked by a couple of chairs, and a huge oval bed covered in dark blue slick-sheets that matched the carpet.

Baird tossed her lightly on the bed. Alina landed with an unwarrior-like gasp and giggle.

"Strip," he growled.

She'd have told another man exactly what he could do with his commands, but this was Baird. Smiling wickedly, she rolled onto hands and knees and stared at him through the curtain of her blond braids. "Do I look like one of your recruits, Captain?"

"You look like a Warfem who's about to get fucked." He grabbed the seal of his unisuit and dragged it down in one ruthless motion. As she watched, breath caught, he stripped the suit off to stand boldly naked. His cock bobbed free, flushed and thick.

Alina swallowed, her hungry gaze fixed on his broad, sculpted chest. It was furred in a dark ruff of chest hair that narrowed to a trail leading straight to that impressive cock. His legs were long, the thighs and calves thick and round with brawn. As she stared at him, dry-mouthed with desire, he strode to the wall. A panel slid open at his approach, and he reached inside to pull out a length of flexible forcecable.

She raised a brow, interested but not shocked. Warlords tended to be fairly inventive when it came to sex. "We never did bondage before."

Baird shrugged, braids swinging beside one high cheekbone. "It seems to suit my mood. You're still not naked." His eyes were glowing red, a Warlord's indicator of stark lust. He was on the verge of losing control.

Heart pounding, Alina reached for the hem of her tunic and pulled it over her head. He went still, watching as she flicked open the closure of her breastband. The band fell away, freeing her breasts. His eyes widened and flared bright red.

Deliberately taunting, she rolled onto her back and slid her boots and trousers off, taking her time, letting him get a good look. Smoothly, easily, she lifted one leg and pointed the toes at the ceiling. He licked his lips and dropped his gaze between her thighs, and she hid a smile. "Is this naked enough for you, Captain?"

"Perhaps a little too naked," he said, his voice hoarse. "I think you need to accessorize."

Baird moved so fast even Alina was taken by surprise. One minute he was across the room, staring hot-eyed at her nudity. The next, he was on the bed and spinning her around so she was on her knees with her back to him. He pulled one of her wrists behind her back and wrapped it in the forcecable, then bound the other wrist, too.

Alina inhaled at the wild arousal that exploded low in her belly. She twisted around to grin at him. "You taking me captive, Baird?"

For just a moment, she thought she glimpsed bitterness in his golden eyes. "It seems to be the only way I can keep you."

Four

Before she could question that flash of dark anger, Baird caught her breasts in his warm, long-fingered hands, and she gasped. Skillfully, he rolled her tight nipples between thumbs and forefingers until pleasure furled through her like a red silk ribbon. "Believe me," she wheezed, "I have no desire to go anywhere."

"Are you sure?" He raked his teeth gently over the straining cords of her throat.

She shivered. "Ooohhhh, yes." His fingers tightened, pulled, pinched. Each tiny motion created glittering sensations that raced through her body in a river of fire headed straight between her thighs. "Especially when you do that."

"Then I'll do it some more. You have the most luscious nipples." He twisted the little tips until she squirmed her butt against the hard ridge of his cock.

"Glad you"—she had to stop to pant—"glad you approve."

"Oh, I definitely approve." Baird reached down between her thighs, finding the very spot that craved his touch. His fingers slipped easily in the slick cream that had risen as he'd played with her. "And I'm not the only one."

"That's putting it mildly." Alina let her head fall back against his shoulder as he strummed nipple and clit.

"Bed," he ordered the mattress, "I need a little hump. About fifty centimeters high and forty across." Obediently, the bed extruded a soft mound of mattress. Baird draped her belly-down across it, then moved in behind her.

Alina licked her lips in anticipation. With her wrists bound at the small of her back, she felt deliciously vulnerable and intensely aroused. She'd never played sexual games before—which probably wasn't surprising, given that her encounters had been rare and hurried, usually driven by *riaat* hunger more than true attraction. The only man she'd ever really wanted had been Baird.

And now, for tonight at least, she had him.

The bed shifted under her knees, and she tensed, swallowing. Shooting a quick look over her shoulder, she saw him kneel at the foot of the bed and lower his head to her backside. His fingers parted her labia for his tongue.

Alina groaned as he gave her sex a long, slow lick that ran right between the seam of her lips up to her clit. "Oh, sweet Goddess!" She stopped to pant. "You do realize I don't really need any more foreplay?"

"Perhaps not." He took one of her lips between his teeth and gave it a gentle, teasing tug. "But I've waited for this a very long time, and I'm going to make it last." He released her, then went for her clit, his tongue dancing over the hard little nub.

Pleasure jolted through her body like bolts of current. "In that case"—she had to stop to moan—"be my guest."

A long forefinger slid into her sex, slowly, as he angled his head and licked. Each flick of his tongue felt like a hot little flame, and Alina writhed, maddened. She could feel her climax heating, stoked by that working finger and his clever mouth.

Her sweet young lover had grown into a big, skilled, outrageously sexy stranger.

The orgasm built like a storm about to break, hot and fast and . . .

He stopped. "Not yet."

"*What?*" Outraged, she tried to grind down on the finger so temptingly deep inside her.

Baird snatched it away from her and slapped a hand down on her hip, stilling her. "Not yet."

"You can't . . ."

"I can." His tone was hard and inflexible, one she'd never heard from him before. "This time I set the course. Not you. And fucking well not Rajin Kasi." The tip of a calloused finger circled her clit. Sparks of heat and arousal danced at the contact.

"Yes, master." She'd intended the words as mocking, but they emerged too faint, straining under the weight of desire.

"That's better." The humor was back in his voice again, though it had that dark, bitter edge she kept glimpsing in him.

"You carrying a grudge, Baird?"

"Who, me?" His laughter was a sexual rumble that made tiny muscles ripple inside her. "What gives you that idea?"

And Baird drove his cock into her sex in one hard, long thrust that made her back arch. "Just wondering," she wheezed.

"You okay?" The question was abrupt, almost as if he didn't want to ask.

"Fine," she managed. He began to pull out, and the sliding pleasure made her moan. "Better than fine."

"Good." There was that dark satisfaction again. He was definitely working off a grudge. And he was entitled to one. Imagining his reaction if he knew her secret, she winced.

Then Baird was pushing inside, and she forgot everything else but how good it felt to be full of him again.

He thrust slowly, taking his time. Sometimes he added artistic little touches, working his way to the balls and then grinding his hips, raking both her clit and the walls of her sheath with merciless pleasure.

Alina hunched back at him, dying to come. But every time she was about to go over, he pulled away.

"You've got a mean streak," she managed, the third time he stalled her orgasm.

"Now that you mention it"—he drove in yet another hard thrust that tormented her sweetly—"I do. Maybe you should keep that in mind."

"Noted." He did that wicked little thing with his hips again. Unable to stand it any longer, she writhed, whimpering. "God, Baird, please . . ."

"Please, what?"

Her temper snapped. *"Let me come,* blaze you!"

He drew out, eased in. "You could always have your computer send you over."

"I don't want the flipping comp! *I want you!"*

Male satisfaction rang in his voice. "That's all I wanted to know." He started pumping, long and strong and hard, grinding just enough.

The climax he'd been holding off exploded through her body in a silent rain of sparks. She yowled, almost blinded by its savagery. It was so much fiercer than anything she'd ever felt, a feral erotic storm that made her convulse like a woman in a seizure.

Distantly, Alina heard Baird's triumphant roar as he began to shoot his seed deep inside her.

Limp and thoroughly sated, she scarcely noticed when Baird untied her wrists and told the bed to flatten out again. She roused only when he picked her up, flipped the covers back, and slipped between them with her. "That was . . . I can't think of a word to do it justice."

He curled muscled arms around her and pulled her back into the sweaty warmth of his big body. "I can safely say it was my pleasure."

Sweaty or not, he felt good. "Goddess, I wish I could stay with you."

Baird stiffened. It was slight, but she knew him well enough to notice. "Do you have to leave now?"

Alina sighed. "Not now. I'm supposed to ship out to Calista in the morning. Rajin's waiting for me there."

"As it happens, I'm headed for Calista, too." When she glanced up in surprise, he shrugged. "I'm joining my new ship there. We didn't have anything headed that way, so I'm taking a civilian transport. *The Antares Empress*."

"That's the same ship I'm booked for." Alina hesitated. Had he been a stranger, she'd have found that detail a little too coincidental. But this was Baird, and he would no more work for an enemy of Vardon than he could breathe hard vacuum. "We could spend more time together."

He lifted a dark brow. "Won't that torque Rajin?"

Alina grinned, feeling suddenly reckless. "I'll argue I need a bodyguard. After the business with the Tevan, she won't kick too hard."

Baird studied her face, his golden gaze perceptive. "Why do I get the impression you're not terribly happy with the old . . . Femmat?"

"I haven't been happy with Kasi's esteemed president in twenty years."

"Then sue. You know damn well you'd win."

Alina looked away. "I can't afford an attorney."

Baird frowned, visibly puzzled. "Aren't you a member of the Guild?"

"Of course." She'd joined the Vardonese Guild of Warriors decades ago.

"Then they'd provide you with an attorney, given the circumstances. That's what they're for—to intercede between warriors and the Femmatocracy."

He was right, of course, but there was a great deal he didn't know. "As I said before, it's complicated." She gave him a hot grin. "And I'd much rather make love than explain."

Baird looked at her for a long moment, his gaze wary. Then he smiled, though it looked a little tight. "You've got a very good point."

The night passed in a delicious blur of passion that ended in sated, exhausted sleep.

Baird woke the next morning as he'd woken so many times twenty years before—with Alina cuddled against his side, warm and trusting.

He lifted his head and looked down into her sleeping face. One of her blond braids lay across a high cheekbone, adorned in the campaign beads she'd won risking her life beside him. In the bright morning sunlight, he suddenly noticed faint shadows under her eyes, as if worry and guilt were constant companions.

And well they should be, if his suspicions were true.

Seeing her lids lift, he forced a smile. "Good morning, sweet. Hungry?"

Alina yawned hugely and gave him a grin that made his heart catch. "After all that *riaat*—and all that sex? I could eat a Soji Dragon. Raw."

His smile was more genuine this time. "I trust the hotel restaurant can produce something a little more tender than that."

"God, I hope so. Does this place have a real water shower?"

"I think so."

She rolled out of bed, long and lithe and breathtakingly naked. Her breasts were high and full, and she had a tight waist, a sweetly curving backside that felt perfect in his hands, and long, muscular legs. "Good. The sackracks Kasi likes to stick me in have nothing but sonics. I know they get you clean, but I never really feel like it."

His eyes followed her delectable backside as she made for the bathroom. He rose and strode after her. "Then by all means, let's get wet."

By the time they emerged from the shower, they were both prune-skinned and pleasantly sore from yet another dizzying sexual encounter. "Why don't you go down and order for us," he told her as they dressed, him in his captain's uniform, her in the violet tunic and black pants that made the most of her dramatic coloring. "I need to make a few calls."

She gave him another of those flashing, wicked grins. "Make it quick, or I'll eat your breakfast, too."

He forced a grin. "I'll risk it. Get me something with plenty of meat."

"Okay." She frowned, scratching her eyebrow. "We're going to need to catch a cab and swing by my hostel before we head to the shuttleport. We have to be aboard *The Antares Empress* by 1400 hours."

"I know. We've got plenty of time."

Alina nodded and sauntered out. Baird's gaze lingered on her swaying hips until the door closed behind her. He locked his sensors on her as she walked down the hall, scanning her progress through the walls.

It was only after he knew she was gone that he walked to the wall panel that hid his secure com unit. He could have used his internal communication system, of course, but there was a chance Alina would somehow manage to intercept it.

And considering the call he was about to make, that would be very bad.

Five

The panel sensed him and slid open. Baird pulled out the oblong bag that held his gear, opened the seal, and spilled the hand-sized unit into his palm. Popping open the small screen, he sat down on the bed and murmured the voice command. There was a long, annoying wait while the unit set up communications with his contact.

Then the Tevan's familiar face appeared on the screen. They'd been partners for five years, ever since Baird left ship service for the intelligence branch of the Vardonese military.

"I'm in," Baird told him. "We don't have to keep trying to convince her she needs my protection."

Four yellow eyes rolled. "Gods and goddesses, that's the best news I've had all day. You broke my ribs, you bastard."

"You deserved it. I told you not to hurt her, Ualtar. She had to go into regen."

"So did I." His partner's amber gaze searched his. "And may I remind you, if she's involved, a few bruises are the least she deserves."

Baird frowned. "I still can't believe she knows what's going on."

"You don't sound as convinced as you were last night."

He raked a hand through his long hair. "She seemed . . . unusually evasive."

"You mean guilty." Ualtar shook his spiked head. "I told you, Baird. She's in this up to her horns—if she had any."

"Ualtar, there's no way she's working for them. Not Alina."

"It's been twenty years, brother. You don't know what she's capable of." The Tevan leaned closer to the pickup, his expression grim. "And I don't want you finding out the hard way."

"I can handle her."

"Not if you keep thinking with your dick. You have to maintain your objectivity on this, or you're going to end up dead. These people do not play around."

"Believe me, Ualtar, I know exactly what they're capable of."

"Yeah, but they're not the real problem, are they? She is."

Baird killed the com link and clicked the unit closed. Brooding, he tossed the little device aside and leaned an elbow on his thigh.

He'd become an adept and skillful liar after joining Vardonese Intelligence, but lying to Alina had been surprisingly difficult. He ached to confront her with their suspicions and beg her to prove herself innocent, but he couldn't. There was too much at risk. If she was involved in treason and discovered he was on her trail, the enemy would slip through their fingers like smoke.

Still, he couldn't believe the laughing lover he'd known during the occupation could have become a traitor. She'd been too forthright, too loyal, too courageous.

Restlessly, he rose from the bed and began to pace in long strides. As much as he hated to admit it to himself, two decades had changed Alina. She'd become closed and wary. Too often last night, he'd seen fear in her eyes. But fear of what? Him? The thought made something clench tight in his chest.

Because she had reason to fear him. If she was a traitor, he'd destroy her. Considering the rage that boiled through him at the very idea, he didn't think he was even capable of showing her mercy.

He hated traitors. Over the past five years, he'd watched them work to destroy their own people for personal advancement. He'd do anything to stop them. Anything at all. Lie, kill, whore, or steal, it didn't matter. Nothing mattered except stopping them.

He'd loved Alina with everything in his soul, and she'd turned her back on him. But had she also turned her back on everything they'd once believed in? Everything he still believed in? Sweet Goddess, he hoped not.

Because when he'd lain with Alina in his arms last night, looking down into those brilliant eyes, he'd realized he loved her still. Despite everything she'd done to him, despite the decades of separation. None of it mattered. He loved her.

If she was a traitor, her destruction would be his own.

The *Antares Empress* catered to professional spacers and soldiers from a dozen different worlds. Its accommodations were not lush by any means, but they were relatively comfortable.

The ship itself was shaped roughly like a star, with a globular central body that housed passenger and command functions. Several long, spine-like pylons thrust out from the core, housing the generators that created the jumpspace bubble around the ship, permitting it to travel at supralight velocities.

Baird and Alina got settled into their respective quarters, then arranged to meet in the ship's workout deck. Building and maintaining muscle was almost a religion for Vardonese warriors. The trip time was an opportunity to get in a little training.

Among other things.

They could have ended up with worse facilities, Baird decided when he walked onto the exercise deck. It was completely open, wrapped around with a heavily shielded viewport that gave a stunning view of jumpspace. Stars streamed past, bleeding a kaleidoscope of hot colors—the radiation of this alien dimension, where the laws of physics no longer quite applied. If it hadn't been for the bubble of normal space that protected the ship, the bizarre forces around them would have torn the *Empress* apart.

The deck itself was equipped with benches and assorted equipment designed to work specific muscle groups. Baird preferred the simplicity of gravity bars. He picked up one of the featherweight rods from the rack that held them and chose a spot where he could keep an eye on the lift.

He was doing arm curls with the gravity bar when Alina walked in. The sight of her was incendiary, clad in that narrow breastband and hipsnugs that displayed every lush curve of her long body. Baird almost dropped the bar as his cock hardened with a rush of approval.

Evidently his body didn't share his doubts.

Alina grinned and returned his hungry gaze, violet eyes mischievous. Since he wore nothing more than a pair of snugs, there was a lot of him on display. He barely suppressed the urge to flex.

She strolled over to one of the racks that held the bars, chose one of medium length, and lifted it down. Steadying it with both hands, she murmured, "One hundred kilos." The wiry muscles in her arms leaped into relief as the bar immediately increased its weight to the setting she dictated.

Lazily, she began to rotate the rod like a quarterstaff as she strolled toward him, arms flexing as she worked to control the weight. "There's something about a man concentrating on working up a sweat that makes me want to . . . distract him." Looking at the rod he held, she lifted a blond brow. "But considering how much weight you've got on that bar, I'll refrain. Hate for you to put a hole in the deck."

Baird breathed deeply and did another slow, deliberate curl. His arms felt as if they were on fire, but his ego wouldn't even let him grunt. "I'll try not to drop it."

"You never used to lift that much." She grinned. "But then— you've grown."

"Like I said, so have you." His gaze lingered on the full mounds of her breasts, barely contained in that band. "I remember when you were a skinny little fifteen-year-old, all legs and bravado." The thought of her innocence then stabbed him in the heart. He had to look away.

Alina laughed and moved away until she had room to swing the rod without hitting him. Falling into a combat stance, she took a deep breath and leaped into the air, whirling her weapon in a mock attack on imaginary opponents. Unable to resist, he found himself watching her again, admiring the flex and play of her slender muscles.

"I was so damn green, I pissed chartreuse," she told him. "Which I did frequently, since I was terrified all the time." She stopped, one knee lifted high, the bar held in perfect balance. It was a breathtaking display of strength and athleticism even by Warlord standards.

Baird lowered his own bar to watch. "I thought you were very brave." And honest, and loyal. Had he been wrong?

"Had you fooled." She whipped around, slicing the bar in a hissing arc. "But the lieutenant saw through both of us."

He smiled slightly, remembering. "Lieutenant Grev and Sergeant Avo. I wouldn't be alive today if the sergeant hadn't saved my ass. Five or six times." Baird had been a half-grown kid fresh out of House Arvid Creche, pressed into duty only because the invading Xer would have shot him on sight simply for being a Warlord. Grev and Avo had taught him and Alina tactics, discipline, and the art of staying alive.

Pumping a kick at one imaginary opponent, Alina thrust the bar in a move Avo had taught them both. "God, those two loved one another. First time I'd seen married warriors."

Baird nodded. There had been six warriors in their guerilla unit to start out with, but two of them fell to the Xer early on. Over the next four years, Alina, the Warfem Grev, and her Warlord husband, Avo, had become the closest thing Bard had ever known to family.

The two adults had loved each other with such utter commitment, they'd inspired Baird and Alina to start playing at passion. In time, what had begun as imitation love grew into the real thing.

"There's a reason you don't see bonded warriors that much, though," he said, brooding. "His wife's death at the Xer's hands gutted Avo. He got reckless and sloppy. And it got him killed." Good thing Baird and Alina had been nineteen by then, seasoned by four years in combat, or they'd never have survived without him.

"Love always carries a cost." The long muscles in her arms were beginning to tremble slightly, but she didn't seem to notice. Her gaze had turned inward, brooding. Then she smiled, sudden and blinding. "But it's worth it."

No. No, it wasn't. There'd been a time after Alina had left Baird that he, too, had courted death. But he'd been in the stellar service by then, and too many other lives depended on him. He'd steadied down, done his job, earned his medals.

But he'd never fallen in love again.

"You remember the Ortaris?" Alina asked suddenly.

Brows lifting, he looked up at her. "Yeah." They'd encountered the little family right after Sergeant Avo was killed. Baird himself had been badly hurt in the failed attempt to rescue the sergeant. Since there had been no regenator available, he'd had to heal the hard way. For the month it had taken him to recover, Mr. and Mrs. Ortari had hidden Baird and Alina in their basement. "The Xer would have killed us if it hadn't been for them."

Alina nodded. "Big risk, particularly considering the three kids."

"Yeah, that's right," Baird said, remembering. "There was the little baby, the ten-year-old son, and that teenage daughter."

"The one with the crush on you."

He grinned. "Suyo." The girl's attention had been almost as flattering as Alina's incandescent jealousy.

Apparently catching sight of his smug expression, Alina turned and stuck out her tongue at him, a gesture she'd learned from Suyo herself. Baird roared with laughter, then had to throw up an arm to ward her off as she waved the gravity bar at him. "I should have known you'd remember her, rodent," Alina growled, thoroughly irritated.

"Rodent" had been her favorite insult before Avo taught her how to swear. Baird laughed even harder.

With a huff, she turned away and pretended to ignore him while he tried to get control of himself.

When his gasping laughter died, they settled into a companionable silence. Suddenly Alina asked, "Did you ever wonder what it would be like to have a mother?"

Baird frowned. Technically, neither had any mother beyond the genetic engineers who'd constructed their DNA. Both had been raised in their respective House Creches among several hundred other genetically engineered children. Their caretakers had been civilians and a few warrior instructors.

"I suppose," he admitted. "But I've always been a little skeptical about the whole mother concept. It seems a bit like one of those stories they tell little children, like the ones about fairies and talking wolves. It can't possibly be as good as they say."

Alina gave him a wicked little smile. "Actually, I've met a talking wolf or two."

Baird shot her an impatient look. "Cyborgs. You know what I mean."

"Yeah." She took up the combat pose again. "You were unconscious most of the time, but I got to watch Mrs. Ortari with her children. It was like Avo and Grev with us, except more so. Very warm and . . . nice." She swung the staff in a circle. "I envied those kids. She let me hold the baby sometimes."

"Oh?" Interested, he looked at her. Somehow he had the feeling this detail was more important than it sounded. "What was that like?"

"Frightening. And yet it was . . . there was this tiny person with these big eyes and miniature hands, and she looked at me the way nobody has ever looked at me before. Like I was . . . everything. At first it was uncomfortable, because I was so afraid I'd hurt her. But then"—she shrugged—"I liked it. I missed her when we left."

Baird frowned, realizing this had obviously been a major experience for her. "You never mentioned it."

"No. Thought about it a lot, though." Alina turned her attention to the bar. "Off," she told it, and went to put it away. "There's a zee-gee tank next door. Want to . . . practice?"

Something about the way she said the last word told him she had something more than martial arts in mind. "Sure. Why not?"

Already hardening in anticipation, he followed her across the corridor to the soaring, three-story, zero-gravity tank. Like most jumpships, *The Antares Empress* maintained simulated gravity, but the fields had been known to fail, especially during combat. Thus, anybody who ever served in space made it a point to practice zee-gee hand-to-hand techniques.

Besides, it was a hell of a lot of fun.

In zee-gee, Baird's size and weight advantage became mass he had to maneuver, which meant he and Alina could compete as physical equals. More or less.

Not that either of them had much competition in mind.

Six

As they entered the tank, Baird checked it out with the wariness of long habit. You could get seriously hurt in a poorly designed tank.

Luckily, this one was first-rate, with well-padded curving walls one could hit at speed without breaking anything. More important, the jutting handholds were of the breakaway type, rounded and flexible, so a fighter didn't have to worry about impaling himself or his opponent during a throw.

"Gravity off," Alina told the ship's computer.

For a moment, Baird had the sickening sensation they were plunging downward, as if the chamber had become a elevator in free-fall. But that was just an illusion created as the artificial gravity vanished, and in a moment, his battle computer compensated.

From the corner of his eye, he saw Alina flex her legs and launch herself at the opposite wall. She hit the thick padding, bounced, and shot straight back toward him like a deliciously curved cannon shell. Baird kicked off and twisted, grabbing for her as she shot by. He managed to snag her upper arm and got towed along for his trouble, but as they tumbled toward the wall, he started wrapping himself around her. He needed to get those long arms and legs under control.

Then he'd have her.

Yet Alina had no intention of allowing herself to be had, at least not yet. She twisted as they hit the wall, grabbed a handhold, and heaved him clear before he had time to get a good grip. While he flailed, she kicked lazily away.

By the time Baird got himself stopped, she was grinning at him from the other end of the tank. "Point for me," she said, gently mocking.

Baird bared his teeth at her as his competitive instincts awakened in a hot rush. "That's the last one you get."

"I don't think so." Alina sprang.

This time he was ready when she barreled into him. Allowing her momentum to carry them toward the wall, he snagged her right wrist and slung a leg over her hip. Zee-gee or not, he was still stronger than she was, and his arms and legs were longer. If he could get a good grip on her, he could do whatever he wanted.

And he wanted to do plenty, especially with that round little backside rubbing against his groin.

For whatever time they had together, he wanted all of her.

Unfortunately for his frustration level, Alina had learned her way around a tank sometime in the past twenty years, and she was flexible as an eelcat. She rammed an elbow into his sternum, squirmed loose when he gasped, and kicked away. He shot after her, his cock as hard as fero-crete behind the tough fabric of his snugs.

Alina hit the wall an instant before he did and caromed off like a billiard ball. He bounced after her, kicking hard enough to give himself the speed to catch her.

The trouble was, all that mass and momentum was hard to stop. As he overtook her, she twisted, grabbed him by the hand he reached with, and heaved. The physics of equal and opposite reactions sent him shooting in one direction while she shot in the other.

Laughing.

"That," he told her, "was a mistake."

She grinned. "Probably, but it was fun."

Baird peeled his lips back from his teeth. "We'll see."

There was something wickedly intoxicating about pushing her luck with Baird.

Probably because Alina could see the exact moment when it ran out. He looked at her across the width of the tank, his eyes flaring bright red with frustration and erotic hunger. His black hipsnugs barely contained his cock, which looked on the verge of escaping his waistband any minute. Hard muscle flexed all along his body as he gathered himself.

He wasn't playing anymore.

Her heart pounded hard, and her nipples were tight beneath the fabric of her breastband. She was already wet between the thighs.

Most men got sloppier when they were ticked off. Not Baird. Thanks to his training, he grew colder, more controlled. More dangerous. She deliberately gave him a goading grin and watched him explode.

He shot across the tank like a mortar shell. Alina launched herself off at an angle, determined to stay out of his grip as long as she could. She knew if he got his hands on her this time, she wouldn't be getting away until he was finished with her. And they'd both enjoy it more if she made him work for it.

Behind her, Baird's feet hit the tank wall with a meaty bang. She could almost feel him barreling after her, but she didn't look back as she bounced off one wall and shot toward another. A big hand swiped at her ankle and missed. She didn't stop to gloat, too intent on ricocheting off every flat surface she could find.

Chancing a quick look, she saw him at the other side of the tank, clinging to a handhold and watching her with predatory intensity. Her eyes widened as he launched, hard and fast. She tried to twist away, but she had too much momentum.

He hit her with a growl of male triumph, snapping one arm around her torso and knocking them both into a dizzy tumble. Blinded by her own whipping hair and flying beads, Alina tried to plant an elbow in his gut and kick free. He refused to let go. Instead he wrapped one long leg around her right hip and the other around her left calf. She drew a fist back for a quick punch, but he engulfed her wrist in one hand. Cursing, she tried for a left cross, but before the blow could land, he'd captured that hand, too.

Alina looked at him as they tumbled in midair. Her sense of humor pricked her instinctive competitive streak like a balloon, and she smiled. "Oops."

He grinned darkly at her from a tangle of free-floating hair and glittering beads. "Oops indeed. You seem to be caught."

"Maybe." She gave him a testing wiggle, but he tightened the grip of both legs, silently making it clear she wasn't going anywhere. If this had been a true fight, she'd have had to do some real damage if she wanted to break his hold.

Instead, Alina rolled her hips against the thick ridge of his erection. It felt so hard, she licked her lips in anticipation. "Well, now," she purred. "Apparently you've got me after all. What are you going to do now, Warlord?"

"What I'd do to any captured enemy." Baird's teeth flashed as he circled both her wrists with one big hand. "Search you for weapons." With his free hand, he pulled up the hem of her breastband. Freed, her breasts bounced, nipples tight and tingling. He grinned at them. "You do seem to be well-armed."

He swooped down to engulf one of the hard peaks with his mouth, gave it a slow, thorough suckling as he caressed the full mound with his free hand.

She inhaled sharply at the lazy rise of pleasure. "You've got a weapon or two of your own."

Baird looked up, gave her a slow, heart-stopping smile, and rolled his hips slowly against her belly. "And I know how to use them."

"That's putting it mildly." With a moan, Alina savored the teasing promise of that big shaft, imagining how it would feel thrusting deep inside her. She rocked against him sinuously. "Here's a thought. Why don't you let me show you what I can do with that particular blade?"

He lifted a brow, intrigued. "You've talked me into it."

When Baird released her wrists, she went for the waistband of his snugs and started pulling them off. It wasn't an easy maneuver in zero gravity. They found themselves tumbling slowly while she peeled and he tried to squirm free.

Baird started to laugh in a rich, almost tactile rumble that soon had Alina joining in. The laughter, and the clumsiness it engendered, only made them tumble faster.

Finally he snagged a handhold and steadied them long enough for them to strip, clinging together like giddy children.

"Damn, that felt good," Alina said, wrapping her arms around his waist as their clothing floated away. "It's been too damn long since I laughed like that."

The humor faded from his eyes as he studied her face. "I gather Rajin hasn't mellowed out of her bitch streak."

"No, not exactly." Alina looked into those golden eyes and thought about telling him everything. But secrets, after all, develop their own inertia, and she found she didn't know where to begin.

Instead she reached between his muscled thighs, cupped his full balls in one hand, and watched his gaze go vague as passion rose. He'd softened a little as they'd played, but at her touch he hardened again. She stroked up from his sac, exploring his warm silken length. He groaned, the sound full-throated and hot with pleasure.

Anchoring herself with a hand on his butt, she bent to take him in her mouth. His taste was instantly familiar, even after all these years—the clean male scent of his body, the tang of his arousal. Her eyes drifted closed.

Gods, she'd missed him. She'd been so lonely.

As she suckled him slowly, a big hand came to rest on her head, threading through her blond hair. "Let me taste you," he asked hoarsely.

Agile and eager, she drew back and twisted around in the air until she hung head-down relative to him. Strong, warm hands caught her hips and pulled her close. She spread her legs, giving him access to her sex even as she caught his shaft in her fingers and bent close to suckle. He tasted salty with pre-come as she took as much of his thickness as she could.

Baird spread her lips with two fingers. Alina felt the warmth of his breath an instant before his hot tongue claimed her in a long, delicious lick. She moaned around his cock and sucked harder. His tongue danced over her clit in answer, and an index finger slid deep in her core. He groaned approval.

So they licked and nibbled at one another, spinning slowly, bouncing gently off walls, but too lost in each other to care. The pleasure rose and fell in shimmering waves, each crest building on the next.

Until Baird tore his head away, only to pull her around in the air until they were face to face again. "I've got to have you," he gasped. "Now."

"Yes!" She spread her thighs for him, and he slid between them.

His thrust made them both moan. Desperately, she wrapped her arms and legs around him as he began to pump. The sensation of gliding thickness was hot and slick and wonderful, and it made every nerve in her body vibrate with arousal and delight.

"God, that's good!" Baird clamped a hand over her hip and one thigh, bracing her so he could ride faster, surging hard and deep. She writhed against him, loving the way he felt, relishing the steep build of climax.

It burst free with a soundless pop of glittering heat, ripping a startled cry from her throat as she arched, coming. Aware even as she lost herself of Baird's strong hands, his big body, his crooning words of praise and pleasure.

* * *

Alina looked so beautiful as she came, her face taking on a hot, lost glow as she threw her head back and cried out. The sight alone would have been enough to bring him.

Given how slick and tight she felt on top of it, he didn't have a prayer of holding off.

Baird climaxed with a wordless shout, clinging to her as they spun lazily in the air. Out of control, and not caring.

Long moments passed with his mind empty of anything but her lush curves.

"Forget her." The words burst from his mouth without any conscious thought on his part.

She opened those lovely violet eyes and blinked lazily, startled. "Who?"

"Rajin." This was insane, and he knew it. Yet he couldn't seem to keep the words from spilling out of his mouth. "Don't meet her on Calista. Come with me." His hands tightened, pulling her closer. "Bond with me. Marry me."

Seven

For just a heartbeat, joy blazed in her gaze. Then it guttered and went out. "Baird, I can't do that. I'm a courier. I've got to deliver a file she's expecting."

"You don't have to do a damn thing. She's kept you a virtual slave for twenty years. You owe her nothing."

Alina sighed. "Baird, Kasi House is a military contractor. If they're using me to carry this file, it's probably important."

"So why the hell are they sending it to Calista? That's not a Vardonese colony, and there are no Vardonese contractors there."

"It's not a courier's job to know what he's carrying. I just go where they tell me to go and protect my files until I get there. You *know* that. Why are you asking me these questions?"

Baird pushed away from her, the better to fight for control. He could almost hear Ualtar cursing him for his impulsiveness. He was on the verge of blowing the whole thing, yet he'd made the offer anyway. Goddess, he wanted to save her so badly.

But what if she didn't deserve saving?

He needed to shut his idiot mouth—and distract her until he

could figure out what the hell was going on and what he was going to do about it. "I'm pushing because I'm tired of missing you, Alina. Because I don't understand why you won't sue for emancipation, when you know perfectly well Kasi can't legally keep you. You've served your time. What hold has Rajin got on you?"

Baird turned back just in time to see the telltale guilty flicker in her eyes. "Nothing. Not a bloody thing. I'm just making a living and doing my job. The same as you. Kasi pays well enough."

"Not well enough to afford a lawyer, evidently."

"There are other benefits than money." Her jaw jutting stubbornly, she looked around for her clothes. He watched her kick after her floating breastband, collect it, and jerk it on over her head. "Look, this has been a delightful trip into nostalgia, but we're not kids anymore, Baird." Her breasts bounced as she went after her hipsnugs, but for once he was in no mood to appreciate the view. "The fact is, it's been twenty years. We don't really know each other now. You have no idea what my life is like, and no business pushing me into running off with you." She tried to wiggle back into the snugs, but between her anger and the lack of gravity, it was tough to do. Frustrated, she snapped, "Computer, gravity up."

Anger simmering, Baird sank toward the floor as his weight slowly increased. He watched her jerk on the snugs, roll to her feet, and stalk toward the door.

Just before she stepped outside, she turned to look back at him. For an instant, pain, longing, and fear filled her face before she wiped away all expression. "I don't think it's a good idea to see each other again, Baird."

"Dammit, Alina, let me help you!"

"I can't." She turned and walked out.

Alina spent the next two days in her cabin, brooding. About Baird, of course, wishing for the hundredth time she could explain without risking an implosion of everything she loved. She hated leaving it like this, but she couldn't risk it. At least when she'd lost him before, there hadn't been this anger and bitterness.

Then there was Galar. She missed him with an aching intensity, as she always did whenever Rajin sent her out on one of these interminable missions. She almost hoped the Femmat would bring him along, except Rajin only did that when she intended a little extortion.

It would be best if the boy stayed back on Vardon. Especially since Baird had a point—why had Rajin sent her to Calista with the file when Kasi House had no contractors there?

Alina frowned as a cold, creeping fear slid through her veins. Rajin loved pushing the bounds of common decency, true—but treason?

And if she had turned traitor, what the hell was Alina going to do about it?

Under normal circumstances, the answer was obvious—stop her cold. But there was Galar. Alina couldn't turn a blind eye to treason, but she couldn't allow Rajin to use the terminal command either.

Yet the fact that the Femmat would even implant such a command was a strong indication she'd gone beyond her former petty sins. Alina had been afraid of something like this ever since she'd learned what Rajin had done to Galar.

Softly, Alina cursed Rajin and herself with equal bitterness. She should have killed the bitch then, even if it meant being executed as a rogue. The trap had closed so slowly she hadn't seen it coming until it was too late.

Alina had unintentionally created the trap herself when she'd impulsively decided to have Baird's child after they'd learned the war was ending. It hadn't been difficult; her computer gave her perfect control over her own reproduction. She'd wanted a baby like Mrs. Ortari's, and she'd expected Kasi House to liberate her. She'd planned to ask Baird to bond with her.

They'd have been a family, raising Galar together.

But when she returned to Kasi House for what should have been the last time, the medtechs discovered she was pregnant. The House was losing all its warrior veterans to emancipation, so when Rajin spotted a way to keep one, she jumped at it. She'd refused to emancipate Alina and ordered the fetus removed and placed in cryostorage. Rajin told Alina she could have the baby back only if she agreed to serve Kasi House for another ten years. By then, the next crop of warriors would be mature and able to serve.

Rajin also forbade her from seeing Baird again, and warned her not to reveal their son's existence. Alina had considered flouting those orders, but soon realized she'd stepped into legal quicksand.

For one thing, half Galar's DNA had been created by Arvid House engineers. Even if she and Baird bonded and successfully sued Kasi House for custody of their son, Arvid House could also put in a claim. After all, a Warrior was an expensive piece of property. She and Baird might win a suit against one House, but two? The fetus could end up in legal limbo for years. In the end, she decided that the only way to keep her son was to play Rajin's game. It was infuriating and terrifying, but she'd felt she had no choice.

Rajin was good at taking away choices.

So Alina had served Kasi as a special courier for ten uneventful years, carrying files containing warship designs between the company, its contractors, and the Vardonese military. As they'd agreed, at the end of nine years, doctors reimplanted the fetus. Galar had been none the worse for his time in cryostorage, and Alina had carried him to term. Kasi House even implanted the computers, sensor, and Warlord neurochemical reservoirs the boy would one day use to go to *riaat*.

Then Rajin had sprung her next ugly surprise. Though Alina might have completed her service, the boy was the product of Kasi House engineering through his mother, and as such, was legally company property. He was to go to the Warlord Creche—unless Alina agreed to continue her service. If she agreed, Rajin would permit Alina to raise him. When Alina was off on missions, Rajin would see to his care.

She'd had no choice but to agree.

For the next nine years, Alina had no cause to regret the deal she'd made. Galar was a bright, intelligent boy, the image of his father, mischievous and handsome. They existed in a happy bubble of contentment. And they were able to spend a great deal of time together, since other warrior couriers had come into service and her missions were relatively infrequent.

Until the day last year when Rajin called her into her office and gave her a pouch of firegems she wanted delivered to a buyer on Calista. Kasi House didn't deal in gems, and they both knew it. *"Consider it a personal favor,"* Rajin said, with a sly smile.

Rajin was stealing from the company.

Alina had delivered the stones, found out who the buyers were and which Kasi House department the gems had disappeared from.

At last. Here was the evidence she needed to free her son. But before she could present it to the Kasi House Council of Femmats, Rajin called her into her office and told her she'd ordered a termination virus loaded into Galar's computer implant. It had programmed his computer to fill his *riatt* reservoirs with a neurotoxin. All she had to do was broadcast the code, and the boy's comp would flood his bloodstream with the poison. He'd die in agony, his body so damaged no regenator would be able to repair it.

Reading the death in Alina's eyes, Rajin said, *"Keep your mouth shut, give me one more year of service, and I'll erase the code and free you both. But if you touch me, he dies now."*

One year.

It was a devil's bargain, and Alina had known it. She would have killed Rajin on the spot, except she feared she wouldn't be able to do it before the Femmat transmitted the code.

It was tempting to try some surprise means of assassination, but she knew she'd be executed for murdering a Femmat, regardless of her reasons. Her son would be left an orphan, the child of a rogue.

So Alina had agreed, secretly planning to hack into the boy's implant and disable the code. Unfortunately, she'd quickly discovered that any attempt to destroy it would result in its activation. And she didn't dare go to the authorities for help, because Rajin would activate the code and kill her son. She'd had no choice but to abide by the agreement and hope Rajin kept her vow.

Rajin had taken full advantage of her blackmail. There had been other deliveries after that—not many, but a few. Mostly gems, some objets d'art. All were items that had mysteriously gone missing from Kasi's treasury.

But was Baird right? Had Rajin gone beyond petty theft to treason—and made Alina an accessory to the crime?

It was time to go to Baird and tell him all the painful truths Rajin had forbidden her to tell. If anybody could help, he could.

But what if something went wrong? What if he tried to move against Rajin and got Galar killed?

By the time the *Antares Empress* arrived at Calista, she'd decided it was time to take a chance. Back when they'd fought together, Baird had always found a way to turn defeat into victory. If anybody could help her get out of this mess, it was him. Besides, she was tired of shouldering the burden alone.

When she called his quarters, he'd already left, so Alina hurried to meet the next shuttle, hoping for a chance to talk to him before he caught transport elsewhere. But arriving at the shuttle deck, she found the line to board reached all the way down the corridor.

There was nothing for it but to wait and pray she got to him in time.

Alina descended the shuttle's ramp behind a lushly curved woman with a mass of bright green curls spilling down her back. Her boots clicked as she stepped onto the tarmac.

Warily, Alina scanned the port. All around, other shuttles stood— long, sleek shapes with aerodynamic lines designed for travel into planetary atmospheres. The beacons encircling one of them suddenly began flashing. With a blaring hoot of warning, the huge craft lifted off, floating slowly upward balanced on a delicate antigravity field. It drifted gently higher, lazy as a soap bubble, until its thruster fields abruptly cut in and shot it toward the horizon with a rumbling sonic boom. The field generators in its stubby wings glowed a shimmering blue as it zipped off over the obelisks and broad flat discs that made up the city's architecture.

Baird was somewhere out there. And she needed to find him quickly, if she was to have any hope of escaping the trap she was in.

Scan for him, Alina told her comp.

Pinpointed, it replied after a pause. She looked around to see a set of red crosshairs appear in her field of vision. Hefting her bag over her shoulder, Alina strode in that direction, ignoring the rest of the travelers headed for the sprawling terminal building.

At last she reached the edge of the buffer zone of vegetation that lay around the landing field. The local equivalent of trees were blue with alien chlorophyll, their leaves feathery, more like giant ferns than anything else. The "grass" that covered the ground beneath them was just as blue and equally feathery, leaves spreading out rather than up.

She'd just stepped out under the trees when her comp began howling. *Warning! Xer lifesign! Baird is under attack.*

What? Sweet gods. What the hell were Xer doing here? Their home world was fifty light years away. She slung her bag across her back by its strap and began to run through the trees. *How many of them?*

Six. The comp flashed her a mental image of what her sensors were picking up—seven figures, six of them attacking a lone man.

Where the hell did they come from?

Unknown. It appears to be an ambush.

Give me riaat. She clenched her teeth as the burning chemical storm began, swirling through her body like a wave of lava. In a moment, strength poured in after it, and she was bounding.

What kind of capabilities do they have?

Insufficient data at this distance.

Well, tell me when you figure it out! Alina put her head down and concentrated on running, darting around trees and leaping any shorter vegetation in her path.

She burst into a clearing and almost ran right into them. The six Xer wore civilian clothing: long tunics split for leg room, and one-piece pant-boot combinations, all in dark colors. Silver skull rings jutted from their shaved heads, implanted in patterns. Like the Vardonese, their ancestors had been human colonists, but a couple of hundred years of genetic engineering had left its mark in great strength and vicious intelligence.

Just the sight of them sent rage searing through Alina. Twenty years ago, their kind had invaded Vardon and laid the planet waste. They'd raped and murdered and stolen every bit of Femmat technology they could get their hands on. It had taken Vardon's warrior class five long years to drive them off, and countless good Warlords and Warfems had died in the process.

Alina didn't even break step before slamming into the first of them with a howl. The impact tumbled them both halfway across the clearing. When they rolled to a stop, Alina was straddling him, powering her fist again and again into his face. He was out before he could get in a punch.

Then she was on her feet again, leaping for the remaining five, who had Baird down on the ground and were struggling to hold him there. She grabbed one and spun him around into a punch.

As he fell, Alina danced back, more than ready to fight. To her relief, she saw Baird throw off one of those holding him pinned and hit another in the face. The Warlord surged to his feet, bleeding, his lower lip swollen, his eyes burning red with *riaat*.

"Change of heart, Alina?" he snarled, dancing backward, slamming punches into the three remaining Xer warriors who were attempting to close in on him again. "Or don't you have the stomach for treason?"

Eight

"I'm not a traitor!" she spat, and grunted as the Xer she was fighting rammed his baton into her side. The blaze of pain sent her to one knee, fighting to breathe.

"Lights out for you, bitch," the Xer snarled, stabbing his baton toward her unprotected neck. If it touched her spinal cord, she'd be out for hours. She threw up an arm in an instinctive block.

"Shit." Baird barreled into her opponent, taking him down hard. Alina gasped in relief and reeled to her feet. Despite the pain, she aimed a kick at the Xer's balls, as he struggled with Baird on the ground. She hit her target; he convulsed with a bellow. Baird threw him off and rolled upright as the remaining Xer closed in. For a moment, he and Alina exchanged a single, searing glance. "You can't believe I'm working for these monsters!" she spat.

She watched doubt war with their battle-tested bond. The bond won. "If I had, I'd have let him hit you." Baird and Alina moved into the fighting pose that had become habit twenty years ago—back-to-back.

Where the hell did these guys come from? Alina commed to him through her computer.

Don't know. One minute I was cutting through the park to meet somebody, then . . .

She caught movement coming through the trees and glanced in that direction. Rajin Kasi stepped into the clearing. The Femmat had forgone her usual aristocrat's robes for a civilian tunic and leggings. Her shimmering violet hair was piled on top of her head, held there with an intricate arrangements of combs.

But Alina's attention was focused on Galar. The boy's young face was cold with a terrible rage. Alina could almost feel the fear he was struggling to hide.

Rajin rested a hand on his shoulder in a gesture that might have been mistaken for motherly. Alina knew it for the threat it was and felt her heart catch in her chest.

The Femmat's chill silver eyes met hers across the clearing. *Stop at once.* The command rang through her comp's communication's unit on the private frequency Baird couldn't hear. As a Femmat, Rajin had a communication's implant, but no battle computer or cybernetics, and no more than human strength.

Sick fury rolled over Alina. *"You* are *working for the Xer! You traitorous bitch!"*

"Take him down."

Her gut turned to ice. *"Who?"*

"You know who." Rajin's commed voice was implacable. *"The Warlord. Your lover. Take him down now, or watch the boy die now. Choose, Warfem."* Something vicious rose in that metallic gaze, and Alina knew she'd do it.

But the idea of betraying Baird wrapped her in sick horror. He trusted her, had asked her to marry him.

Then an image flashed through her mind: Galar writhing in agony, his face blackening, his eyes begging her silently to save him.

"Now!" Rajin screamed. Her slender hand tightened on the boy's shoulder.

Galar's golden eyes blazed. *"Don't do it,"* he said through his own comp. *"Don't let her . . ."*

Rajin's lip curled. *"I will not tell you again. Now, or watch your precious boy shriek out his life."*

Galar half-turned toward Rajin, tensing. He was going to attack her, and she'd kill him.

With a howl of anguish, Alina pivoted with all the power of *ri-aat* and slammed her fist into the side of Baird's head. He stumbled and went down.

For just an instant, the golden gaze so like their son's met hers. *"Damn you, Alina,"* Baird said on their old battle frequency. *"Damn you to hell. I believed in you!"*

Before he could roll away, one of the Xer leaped forward and jammed his shock stick into the base of his skull, where spinal cord met brain. He went limp, instantly unconscious.

Sick, Alina looked away as another of the Xer stepped forward and snapped some kind of collar on him. Goddess only knew what it did.

She wanted to throw up. Then her gaze fell on Rajin. A cold, deadly rage replaced her guilt.

Galar saw his chance, and knew he'd better take it. The situation had reached critical mass, as he'd always known it would. Rajin had finally pushed his mother too far. People were going to start dying.

Galar was going to make flogging sure it wasn't him or his mother. Or the Warlord. He'd grown up hearing stories about Baird, his mother's heroic partner—and his father. He badly wanted to get to know the man who'd sired him.

Fortunately, a Xer sprawled unconscious barely a meter from his sneakbooted feet. The agent's stun baton lay forgotten by his head. Better yet, nobody was watching; the agents were too busy collecting the Warlord and dealing with their injured, while his mother and Rajin were focused on the hate swirling between them.

In one smooth motion, Galar stepped forward, scooped up the baton, collapsed it by pushing on either end, and slid it into a pocket. The baton was one of several weapons his mother had trained him to use. All he needed now was a chance.

His stomach knotted at the risk he was taking, but he ignored his fear. Kid or not, he was a warrior.

Pretending to need reassurance, he moved to his mother's side and leaned against her hip. Normally she'd rest a hand on his shoulder, but now she stood coiled, almost vibrating with rage. Yet her face was perfectly cool and expressionless. Oh, yeah. She was getting ready to kill somebody. She'd put up with a lot out of Rajin over the years because of him, but this had pushed her into a meltdown.

If she went rogue . . . Galar swallowed. He'd seen a rogue warrior shot down once when he was six. As he'd watched the man writhe and die, Rajin had leaned down and whispered, *"See what could happen to your mother . . ."*

He had to do something.

Silently, Galar told his comp to eavesdrop on the conversation. The adults had no idea he'd figured out their private frequency and codes. It was a good thing Rajin had never thought to keep him from using his computer to its full potential. But then, she wasn't a programmer, so there wasn't much she could do about it anyway. One of her flunkies had designed the virus that installed the terminal code and programmed his computer to manufacture the neurotoxin.

Besides, she persisted in thinking of him as a normal ten-year-old, and he was careful to maintain the illusion. She hadn't known enough warrior children to realize how computer implants stimulated brain growth and intelligence. And Galar was good at playing dumb.

"What's in the file, Rajin?" his mother asked in that cool mental voice of hers. Above the clearing, a white zip-truck swooped low and prepared to land.

"That's none of your concern."

"Given that you've made me an accessory to treason, I think it is."

Rajin folded her hands, her elegant face serene. *"It's nothing of great import. Not compared to the money they're paying me."*

"Been gambling on Wekita, again, I assume." As Rajin's eyes widened, she smiled coldly. *"Yes, I know about that. I've investigated you thoroughly."*

The Femmat shrugged with an elegant lift of one shoulder. *"The Wekita are not a forgiving people when it comes to so much money. They go to great lengths to ensure debts are paid."*

"Yet you keep gambling there."

"The risk is part of the attraction. And there was a very pretty little dragon flying in the Soji races. Quite fast. Just not as fast as I'd hoped."

"So you betray Vardon to pay for your vices."

"I do what I must. And so will you, unless you want me to transmit a certain word to the boy."

Gelar went sick and cold. If Rajin used the command, there was nothing he could do to save himself.

His mother reached out and put her arm protectively around his shoulders. *"I strongly suggest you think twice about that,"* she said. *"I may not be able to open your file, but I can delete it. And I doubt the Xer would be particularly understanding."*

The blood drained from Rajin's face. *"You wouldn't dare."*

"I once attacked a Xer tachyon cannon emplacement with no backup except Baird. There's very little I wouldn't dare."

"The Xer will kill us all!"

"So be it. This isn't petty theft anymore, Rajin. Vardonese Warriors will die if you hand over military secrets to the Xer."

"What of it? We'll just make more of them." Her lip lifted in a sneer. *"But can you make another Galar?"*

He felt her hand tighten on his shoulders. Daring a glance up at her face, he watched cold determination flare in her eyes. *"I'll make you a bargain, Rajin. I'll give the Xer the file if you erase the code and free us."*

Rajin stared at her a long moment. "Very well, then, damn you. You have your bargain."

His mother's grip eased, and Galar slumped in relief.

The truck landed, and the Xer got busy loading their men into the vehicle. He hoped none of them noticed the agent's missing stun baton.

A tall, muscular Xer approached, implants shining in the sunlight. He eyed Alina dubiously, then turned to Rajin. Beyond them, a long, black zipcar landed beside the truck. "If you will accompany us, Femmat Kasi, we will make the transfer."

Rajin nodded in an abbreviated Femmat bow. "It will be my pleasure, sir."

Galar followed the adults as they got into the car. As he prepared to slip inside, his mother's hand fell on his shoulder.

Coded transmission from your mother, his comp said.

"Nice work on stealing that baton," she said, her comp transmitting in the private code they'd created. *"I assume you remember how to use it."*

His palms were sweating. *"Jam it into the base of the skull. Knocks them right out."*

"Right. That's going to be a tricky spot to get to, since you're shorter than the Xer. But luckily, Rajin tells everyone you're her son, so they won't expect you to be as strong as you are. Pretend you need to go to the bathroom, then stun your guard and run. The Xer have a jamming field set up to prevent our calling out, but as soon as you're beyond it, contact the Calista authorities. Tell them the Xer have kidnapped a Vardonese agent and plan to kill him. The Calistans will set Baird free and clean up the mess."

What mess? *"What about the terminal code?"*

Something cold and dark flickered in his mother's violet eyes. *"You let me worry about that."*

Pain rolled in a searing wave from the base of Baird's spine, burning its way all the way into his skull. Despite his fight for control, it jerked all his muscles tight, arching him into a bow of agony in the chair. Somehow he kept the scream between his teeth.

One thought kept hammering in his brain, adding to his agony. *Alina betrayed me. I was wrong. She's working for the Xer after all.*

His beautiful Alina was a traitor. And if he escaped, he was bound by duty to kill her.

After a white-hot eternity that was probably a minute and a half, the pain faded, leaving him to slump, sweating and nauseated. But worse even than the pain was the black despair.

Alina.

"I can keep this up all night," the Xer torturer said, her voice light, almost pleasant. "And so can you. That's the wonderful thing about the collar. It doesn't break bones, it doesn't burn the skin off your body, it doesn't ram spikes into your eyeballs. It only feels like it."

Panting, Baird glared at his enemy as sweat rolled stinging into his eyes. The control collar they'd put on him felt as if it was slowly choking him, but unfortunately, it wasn't.

He wouldn't get off that easily.

They sat in what looked like a perfectly ordinary office of the kind found in private homes. Baird knew the Xer didn't have a military compound on Calista; it appeared they'd had to make do with renting a house. The carpet under his feet was thick and lush, and the walls were a soothing blue. The Xer was seated comfortably behind a faux wood control desk, while Baird sprawled in a blue, thickly upholstered armchair in front of it.

He wasn't even bound, though he might as well have been. The collar interrupted his brain's signals to his body, leaving him completely paralyzed, though his muscles responded well enough to whatever stimulation the torturer chose to inflict.

"Come on, Baird, don't do this to yourself," she said, her smile flirtatious. She could have passed for pretty with her platinum blond hair and perfect face, if it wasn't for the viciousness in her sky-blue eyes. "What do you boys know about the *Femmat*? We know you've been following her courier."

He licked his lips. "Look, Alina and I are old friends. We just got together for a little sex."

The torturer's perfect pink mouth drew into a bow. "Don't insult my intelligence. We know who you work for. We . . ."

"I want my daddy!" A child's voice rang clearly through the closed door. Apparently there was no soundproofing in here at all.

"Look, kid, your daddy's not here," the guard in the hallway said, sounding frustrated. "You go on back to the Femmat now."

"You're lying! I know you've got him in there!"

"Kid . . . Shit!"

Thud.

"Dadddyyyyy!" the boy yelled at the top of his lungs.

"Retar, you idiot!" With a huff of frustration, the torturer rose and stalked to the door. Baird rolled his eyes, trying to see what she was doing, but she passed out of his field of view. The door sighed open. "Retar, could you get that child under . . . AH!" Feet scuffled. Baird heard the distinctive buzz of a stun baton, then the thud of a body hitting the floor.

Somebody grunted with effort, followed by rustles and a series of thumps that sounded like a body being dragged across the floor. "Damn, lady, what have you been eating—ferocrete?" Baird's eyebrows rose. That sounded like the kid.

Another series of thumps, and the door closed.

Frustrated, paralyzed, Baird growled, "All right, somebody want to tell me what the hell is going on?"

To his astonishment, a ten-year-old boy walked into his field of view and sat down at the torturer's desk. The kid gave him a bright, white grin. "Hi, Dad."

Nine

Baird blinked in utter astonishment. He recognized the boy from a trid in his files. It was Rajin Kasi's son, Galar.

But though Baird had been paralyzed, his computer and sensors still worked. And both were telling him the boy was not the purely human child he should have been. "You're a warrior."

"Yep." The boy didn't look up, too busy peering intently at the desk's touch screen, evidently trying to puzzle out the controls.

"If you're trying to deactivate the collar, hit the red square." He'd gotten another agent out of a Xeran collar once before. "Why aren't you in a creche?"

"Because I'm a hostage." The boy touched the desk.

The collar opened and fell into Baird's lap. Cautiously, he stretched, making sure everything was working, but his attention was focused on Galar. "The Xer are holding you?"

"No, Rajin is. She's been using me to blackmail my mother."

Baird blinked, belatedly seeing the resemblance. "Alina."

The kid nodded, his blond hair the exact same shade as hers. His mouth was drawn into a familiar line Baird knew from a hundred combat missions. "And you're my father."

About to roll out of the chair to have a go at the computer desk, Baird gaped at the boy. He'd assumed Galar had been joking when he'd called him Daddy, but it sounded as if he actually believed it. "What leads you to that conclusion?"

Galar shrugged. "Mother says so." He frowned down at the desk console, frustrated. "I know all about you. She told me all kinds of stories about when you were her partner during the war."

The pain was stark and breathtaking. Alina had dared tell her son such a lie before betraying Baird and handing him over to the Xer. *I never knew her,* he thought in sick rage. *I never knew her at all.* He fought the anger down long enough to address his comp. *Does he actually think I'm his father?*

Sensors indicate he believes what he says.

Despite the fury sizzling through him, Baird rose and stalked to the desk. He had a job to do, which meant he needed to disable the Xerian's communication jammers so he could call the Vardonese embassy.

The child moved aside for him without being told. Baird glanced him and felt a stab of pity. None of this was his fault. "I don't know what they've told you, Galar, but your mother and I haven't been together for twenty years. I couldn't be your father."

Level, golden eyes met his. For a moment, it was like looking into a mirror, but he knew that was an illusion. "My mother loved you, Baird. That's why she had me."

He wanted to rage and swear, but forced himself to speak calmly instead. "She misled you. If you were my son, you'd be nineteen."

"My mother doesn't lie!" Temper flared in those too-familiar eyes. "Look, she thought Kasi House would emancipate her, but Rajin refused. Mom was still pregnant with me when the old bitch ordered my fetus surgically removed and put in cryostorage. She said Mother could have me back if she continued to work for Kasi. So she did. Eleven years ago, they thawed me out and let her have me. Rajin's been using me to manipulate Mom ever since."

Baird frowned, considering the idea. It sounded plausible. Goddess knew it sounded like the kind of thing Kasi would do.

Could this boy be his? Had Alina given birth to him as an expression of love for Baird? The thought was so staggering, so painful, he shoved it away. The little traitor had lied to her son, just as she'd lied to Baird. "Look, I don't have time to argue about this . . ."

"No, we don't," Galar said. Fear and impatience whitened his face, though to his credit, his voice remained controlled. "We've got to get to Mother before she tries to kill Rajin. Because if she's not fast enough, I'm dead, and even if she succeeds, the Xer will kill her."

"What are you talking about?"

As Galar explained the trap he was in, Baird used the desk unit to hack into the Xer's communications and security systems. By the time the child finished describing the death he faced if Rajin used her codes, a great deal was painfully clear. "So that's why Alina went along with Rajin's treason," Baird said. "It doesn't make it forgivable, but . . ."

"My mother is not a traitor!" The mouth so like Alina's drew into a mutinous line. "She didn't know Rajin was working for the Xer, and now that she does, she's going to kill her. And as many of the Xer as she can take with them!"

Baird frowned. "She'd put you in danger like that?"

"No, she told me to leave and call the authorities so they could rescue you, but I took the chance of turning you loose instead. You owe us, Warlord. And if you don't help us, we're both dead."

Lifting a brow, Baird studied the boy. Galar had taken a hell of a chance to free him—not only in tackling three full-grown Xer, but in braving Baird's own disbelief and anger by telling him his story.

And those golden eyes—it was like looking into a mirror. *Computer, give me a DNA scan of this child. Is he my son?*

The mental silence that followed was long and nerve-wracking.
Yes.

"Sweet Goddess," Baird whispered, stunned.

*S*ometime *in the past twenty years, the* Xer *had figured out how* to build neuroweb computers, probably with tech they'd stolen from the Vardonese during the invasion. According to Alina's sensors, the leader of the Xer agents had one, though her computer pronounced it inferior to Kasi House tech. Too, given Major Jenci Csaba's age, it must have been implanted in adulthood rather than infancy, so it wasn't as well integrated into his brain.

Inferior comp or not, Alina's instincts told her she'd better keep an eye on Csaba. The number of sensor scans he'd sent her way over dinner certainly indicated he was suspicious. That was no doubt why he hadn't requested she transfer the file to him. He was afraid of a virus.

As well he should be—she had one all loaded up and ready to send him. He'd be dead before he hit the ground when his comp stopped his heart. Of course, the Xer could restart it again with a regenator, but Alina figured dropping him would still cause some very satisfactory chaos. With luck, she could use the confusion to escape and free Baird.

Though if Galar had succeeded in getting away, the boy might even now be summoning the Calista authorities. The fact that the Xer hadn't raised the alarm over his escape was a very encouraging sign.

Alina leaned back in her seat, playing with her fork as their server brought in dessert—something showy and flaming. Her attention was focused across the elegant table, where Rajin flirted with the Xer major. Csaba probably wanted to enlist the Femmat as a long-term asset. And Rajin, the traitorous bitch, seemed interested.

Alina rolled her fork between her fingers and calculated the angle and force she'd need to bury it in Rajin's eye socket. It was a tricky shot, but doable.

But if she missed, was Galar far enough away to be beyond Rajin's code transmission? The boy had been gone half an hour. It was a good thing Rajin and Csaba were so wrapped up in their little waltz of treachery. Alina needed to move before either of them missed him.

And Goddess only knew what the Xer were doing to Baird in the meantime. The thought made her stomach twist, so she pushed it away.

She'd get to him in time. She had to.

Suddenly Rajin looked over at her as she and the Xer rose. "Alina, come. It's time to give Major Csaba what he's paid for."

Finally. Alina smiled easily, put her fork down, and stood. She considered telling her computer to prepare for *riaat*, but Csaba might notice. She'd have to do this at normal strength, but if she hit Rajin hard enough, fast enough, the woman should be unable to get the command out.

Hopefully. It was the only game in town, in any case.

She rounded the table, mentally cursing herself for not killing Rajin earlier. She'd delayed too long, hoping for a better chance, for a way to both save Galar and keep him.

Csaba and Rajin were moving ahead of her into the next room. She lengthened her stride to catch up. Her breathing slowed, calmed. Her mind went cold and still.

In one smooth, powerful motion, she scythed her leg up and across, aiming for the side of Rajin's head with her boot.

Csaba whirled in an blur of inhuman speed, throwing up a forearm to block the kick that would have shattered the Femmat's skull. Alina didn't hesitate, throwing herself at him, punching, kicking, trying to drive past his guard to get at Rajin. Her heart slammed in panic. *No! Galar!*

From behind the protection of the Xer's shoulder, Rajin stared at her with infuriated terror. "He's dead, bitch!" the Femmat screamed. "You just killed your son!"

Alina cried out in anguish as her comp picked up the stream of code pouring from Rajin's communication's implant.

If Galar wasn't out of range, he was dead.

Go to riatt! she ordered the computer, as she kept trying to beat her way through the Xer's guard. *Keep a lock on Rajin, I want to be able to find her when I'm finished with this bastard.*

The Xer's fist shot toward her head, and she jerked aside, backhanding him so hard he slammed into the wall behind him. But before she could close in to finish him, a dozen agents charged into the room. She spun to meet them, her teeth bared in despair and rage. She might be done, but she was going to take as many of them with her as she could.

Then a familiar war cry stopped her in her tracks. A big male body charged in behind the Xer, beads flashing in his braids.

"*Baird!*"

"*Yeah, it's me.*" Baird plowed into the agents like a tachyon shell, sending some of them reeling, as the others whirled to fight.

With a cry of joy, she ran to help.

"*You do realize,*" he said on their old battle frequency, "*I'm going to kick your ass when I get done with these idiots.*"

Alina plowed her fist into a Xeran's gut. "*I guess I've got it coming.*"

She only hoped she wouldn't have to tell him their son was dead.

Heart in her throat, Rajin slunk out of the room, praying neither of the warriors saw her go. She knew she had to catch a flight to whatever ship was in orbit, or she was dead. Alina wouldn't stop until she had revenge for her brat's death.

Sweet Goddess, but this situation had melted down with staggering speed. She'd be lucky if she . . .

A door hissed open behind her.

With a strangled shriek, Rajin whirled to see Galar step out of what looked like a closet. Something silver gleamed from around his throat. Shocked, Rajin gasped, "Why aren't you . . . ? And why are you wearing a Xer control collar?"

"To block your fuckin' signal, bitch," the brat said, and flicked his wrist, snapping the stun baton out to its full length.

Before she had time to jump back, he shoved it right into her belly. Rajin bent double with a howl of agony. She never felt him jam it against the base of her skull.

The boy watched her tumble to the ground at his feet, out cold. He bounced the baton in his palm and grinned. "Damn, that felt good."

T̲hey were fighting back-to-back again as the Xer circled, look-ing for an opening. Baird growled, *"These odds really grind."*

"We've faced worse." Alina was sweating, and her mouth tasted of blood from her cut lip.

He snorted. *"Not in the past two decades."*

Suddenly her computer began to howl. *Tevan lifesign approaching! What?*

Alina jerked her head around just in time to see the huge reptile step through the door, a tachyon rifle lifted and aimed in his seven- fingered hands. A number of other figures followed be-hind him, all armored and armed. Alina's heart sank. *"Oh, we're screwed."*

"Not exactly." Aloud, Baird added, "What the hell took you so long, you big lizard?"

"Traffic was a bitch," the Tevan growled, as his armored backup leveled their weapons at the Xer agents. "Hey, assholes—you gonna give us an excuse?"

Cursing, the Xer straightened and backed away, throwing their batons aside.

"Mother!" A small figure raced around them.

"Galar!" Alina caught him as he leaped for her. "Sweet Goddess, you're all right!"

"I knocked Rajin out!" he told her happily. "The Warlords took her away. Baird reprogrammed his control collar and put it on me so her signal couldn't get through, and then he told me to hide in the closet, but when I heard Rajin in the hall . . ."

"What—wait, slow down!" She put the boy on his feet, barely noticing as the Vardonese agents started forcecuffing their prisoners and hustling them off. "What are you talking about? Explain."

"Actually," Baird drawled from beside her, "he's not the only one with some explaining to do."

Alina paced at Baird's side, every muscle tense with a blend of fear and hope. They'd stepped outside the Xer's headquarters while he questioned her. Now they walked together under the alien trees, as zipcars sighed overhead and a warm wind blew in their faces.

He told her he worked for military intelligence, which in retrospect made a great deal of sense. It was obvious their encounter yesterday had not been chance.

It turned out an official at Kasi House had learned about Rajin's theft of those gems. Yet because she was the company's president, it was virtually impossible for the lower-ranking Femmat to confront her. Then Rajin began showing an unhealthy interest in a Vardonese warship the company was building, and the official reported her to military counterintelligence.

Baird was one of the agents assigned to the case. When he learned Alina was involved, he volunteered to make contact with her.

He explained all that with a cool dispassion that somehow hinted at boiling rage. Alina had tried to blunt his anger by holding nothing back, from the night she'd decided to get pregnant through Rajin's blackmailing her into carrying the gems. When she finally worked her way to the present, he said nothing for five steaming minutes.

When he finally spoke, it wasn't what she'd expected. "Obviously, I have a conflict of interest here. One of the other agents will have to question you further. You'll be required to undergo a deep scan of your comp's memories to verify your story. Assuming you've told me the truth, I doubt you'll be charged, though the ultimate decision will, of course, be up to the Femmat chief prosecutor."

Assuming you've told me the truth. She winced. "Baird, I'm sorry."

He shrugged, his broad shoulders stiff. "You did what you believed necessary to protect your son."

"Our son."

Baird's golden gaze flicked to hers. The rage she'd sensed blazed up in his eyes. "I do have one more question. Were you *ever* going to tell me?"

Her mouth went dry. "As soon as we were free, we were going to come to you. I wanted to be with you. That's why I got pregnant. I saw a baby as the physical embodiment of our bond. Then he was born, and I realized how much more he was. He was so precious, so fragile, and he depended so completely on me."

A fine muscle worked in Baird's jaw. "And you didn't trust me to protect him. That's what really galls me—not that you didn't tell me your plans, not even that you smuggled for that bitch. I *always* trusted you."

"Baird . . ."

He stopped and spun to face her, big hands fisted at his side. She forced herself to meet his angry gaze. "Deep down, I trusted you even when my superiors, logic, and simple common sense told me you had to be knowingly involved in treason. Part of me knew Alina Kasi would never stoop to treason. Period. Hell, when you coldcocked me and I woke up in a torture collar, the minute your son showed up with another explanation, I leaped at it. But you wouldn't trust me to do the one thing I was born to do—the one thing I took an oath to do: protect the innocent."

It was then she saw the pain. Deep beneath the incandescent anger was a stark hurt that she hadn't believed possible in him.

"And you did find a way to protect him," Alina said softly. "No-body but Baird Arvid would have thought to reprogram the same torture collar the Xer had used on him to save Galar. I kept trying to come up with ways to block Rajin's signal to the comp. It never even occurred to me to block the comp's signal to the reservoirs."

He said nothing, simply staring down at her from his great height, his eyes burning.

She gathered her courage. "You're right. I didn't trust you, and I should have." Reaching out, she took one of his hard, strong hands. "I'm trusting you now. I love you, Baird. I've loved you from the time I was fifteen years old. Forgive me. Bond with me. Give our son a father."

He blinked as if she'd said the one thing he hadn't expected. "Alina, I've never been a father. I've never even had a father. How do you know I won't get it wrong?"

Alina smiled, despite the hot prickle behind her eyelids. "I trust you."

His smile was so white and wide, it was blinding. Then she was in his arms, so strong and sure around her. "Thank you for our son, Alina," he said, the instant before his mouth covered hers, hot and joyous. They clung together in the kiss as the pain drained away.

Ten

Alina leaned her shoulder against the bulkhead, watching her son and Ualtar play some alien board game the Tevan had produced to kill time on their trip back to Vardon.

His little face lighting with triumph, Galar moved his stone piece and clicked it against the reptile's. "Hah! Got your *behrooz!*"

The big alien sat back with a grunt of disgust. "Kid, you're a menace. You sure you've never played this game?"

"I learn fast. Gimme."

Ualtar shook his horned head and reached into a pocket of his unisuit to pull out a credit chip. As he handed it over to her crowing offspring, he said, "You've raised a hustler, Alina."

Baird stepped up behind her and slid his arms around her waist. "It's like I keep telling you, partner—if they've got a battlecomp, don't play strategy games with 'em."

"That wasn't just computer. He's definitely your kid."

Baird grinned. "Thank you."

"It wasn't a compliment." To Galar he added, "Set the board up again, brat. I want my credits back."

Baird cleared his throat. "If you two are going to be busy for a while, we're going to go in the back and . . . check the prisoners."

The boy looked up at his new friend, his expression mischievous. "They want to get gooey again, don't they?"

Ualtar reached over and ruffled his hair. "Get used to it."

With a laugh, Baird tugged Alina back out of the wardroom and into the hall. "Man knows me too well."

She threaded an arm around his waist. "I can't believe you had me convinced that scaly teddy bear was a killer data thief."

Baird shrugged. "Ualtar's a good actor. We've been running scams like that for years." He slanted her a look. "Though that particular fight got a little rougher than I intended. I'm sorry about that, by the way."

"Considering you thought I was selling the plans for the next Vardonese warship to the Xer, I wouldn't have blamed you for shooting me on the spot."

"Well, we did need you to lead us to your contact." They started down the corridor of the little ship together. "And as I said, I couldn't believe you knew what was happening."

"I didn't, but I certainly should have. I did know Rajin had been stealing from Kasi House."

"It's quite a jump from there to treason."

"Maybe, but the Kasi board of executives will probably bring me up on charges anyway. I knew what I was doing when I transported those gems for Rajin."

Baird laid a comforting hand on her shoulder. "Given the threat to Galar, I doubt they'll charge you. Particularly when you've got excellent grounds for a lawsuit. According to the evidence we've collected, our source at Kasi House wasn't the only one who knew Rajin was dirty. The others cooperated because she paid them off in advancements and incentives. I wouldn't be surprised if some of them even knew about what she'd done to Galar. Somebody definitely helped her poison his implants. When we find out who they are, they'll be charged as an accessory to attempted murder."

"I only wish I could get to them first." Alina gave him a wicked grin. "Hey, there's an idea. How about looking the other way while I slip off to the brig and beat the bitch out of Rajin?"

Baird grinned back. "No. First, I need her in a large enough piece to stand trial, and two, you're about to be much too busy to worry about her." A corridor door slid open, and he waltzed her into his quarters, a room scarcely big enough for both of them and his bed.

"Does this mean we're about to get gooey?" She wrapped her arms around his neck.

"Oh, yeah." He leaned down to take her mouth with his.

His lips were just as warm and clever as she remembered, and she sighed in pleasure. "You know, you're very good with that mouth," she told him when he let her come up for air.

"Want to find out what else I'm good at?" He slid his hands under the hem of her tunic.

Alina smiled as his long fingers caressed and explored their way up her ribs. "I've already got a . . ." He reached a nipple, and she caught her breath. "Ah! . . . Pretty good idea."

Baird withdrew his hands and started to turn away. "Well, if you're not interested . . ."

"Wait one minute! Where do you think you're going?" She bent, caught him behind the thighs, and hefted him off his feet. He made an awkward armful even with her enhanced strength, so before she could lose her grip, she turned and tossed him lightly onto the bed.

Flat on his back, Baird smirked at her. "Now, is that any way to treat a Warlord?"

"Yep." She pulled her tunic off over her head and popped open her breastband. Her breasts bounced free and bare.

"Okay, you've got me there." He sat up to watch with lecherous interest as she bent and started wiggling her way out of her tight pants. "Why don't you bring those pretty little nipples over here, and I'll show you all my favorite tricks."

She propped her fists on her hips. "Take off your pants, and I'll show you mine."

Laughing, Baird started stripping off his uniform. Alina took advantage of his distraction to pounce just as he got his boots off, knocking him back so she could straddle his broad, brawny chest. "Got you."

"Possibly." He caught her thighs in his big, warm hands, high up, right at the groin. His thumbs stroked her labia. She gasped at the sweet rise of pleasure. His golden eyes glinted up at her. "Then again, maybe I've got you."

Alina settled back on his muscled belly, gazing down into his handsome, angular face. The joy that swelled in her heart was almost giddy. Finally, she was free to touch him, love him as she chose. "Or maybe we've got each other." She sobered and touched his tattooed cheek. "I'm sorry."

He lifted a dark brow. "Sorry you've got me?"

"Sorry I hurt you."

He gave her a tight smile. "I got you back. I sicced the three-hundred-kilo Tevan on you."

"Mmm." Alina bent low over him and licked one of his nipples, her gaze on his. "And yet, I feel the need to atone."

Baird drew in a breath as she gently nibbled. "Well, if you insist."

She smiled, spreading her hands over the warm, muscled ridges of his chest. Licking, suckling, she stroked her way gently downward, exploring the tight line of his abdominals. They flexed as he gasped. Tenderly, she raked her nails through the thick ruff of hair on his chest. She inhaled, drinking in his scent.

One of his hands slipped between their bodies to cup her breast. He squeezed gently, then rolled her nipple between his fingers, sending sweet pleasure radiating through the peak.

But this was for him, so Alina drew away and moved lower down his body. His cock curved over his belly, thick and silken, more of that thick hair covering his balls. She cupped him with one hand, and the big shaft leaped in anticipation. "Hi, there," she purred, bending over the silken head.

"Hi, yourself." His voice sounded hoarse with need. A bead of pre-come gathered on the tip of his cock, silent testimony to his hunger.

She flicked it off with her tongue, enjoying his moan, then circled the thick rod with her fingers. Angling him upward, she took him into her mouth, slowly, taking her time. His skin felt slightly nubby against her tongue as she swirled it back and forth. Tightening her lips, she began to suck in deep, slow pulls.

"Goddess, Alina!" Baird gasped. One hand came up catch the back of her head, fingers tunneling through her hair.

Smiling around his width, she slid him deeper, slowly, a centimeter at a time, spinning out the pleasure as long as she could. At the same time, she cupped him, stroking his heavy balls through the velvet skin of his sac.

He twisted under her. There was something so delicious in his arousal that she felt her own cream gathering. Baird wasn't a passive lover; she knew it wouldn't be long before his control snapped.

He lasted longer than she expected under her slow, delightful torment. But when he finally broke, there was no doubt about it.

"Enough!" Baird sat up, grabbed her around the hips, and rolled her under him. She spread her thighs eagerly as he settled between them, wrapping them around his backside as he lifted himself just enough to aim his cock for her slick core.

He entered in a single hard, deep thrust that took him all the way to the balls. "Goddess!" When he threw his head back, the cords stood high and stark on his powerful throat.

"Oh, more!" Alina writhed in mingled pleasure and joy as he began to shaft her in long, hard strokes. Each deep entry raked her clit with sweet friction, while every withdrawal pulled her inner flesh.

Her climax began to gather like a hot offshore storm, building every time his hips slapped hers. In the instant before they blew into pleasure, Baird's golden gaze met hers. "I love you."

"Yes! Goddess, Baird, I love you!"

The fire poured over them, blinding and hot, slinging them into sweet, dizzying heights. When the pleasure faded, he collapsed panting beside her, then promptly pulled her into his arms.

She lay across his hard chest, listening to his heart pound a fierce rhythm her own echoed. Her mouth drew into a sleepy curl. "It took me twenty years, but I'm back where I belong."

Baird's strong arms tightened, drawing her even closer. "We both are."

AUTHOR'S NOTE

Though previously unpublished, the next two shorts—"The Warlord and the Fem" and "Baby, You've Changed"—were actually my first stories set in the Warlord universe. I have a Yahoo! group at http://groups.yahoo.com/group/angelaknight/, and I penned the two stories as a gift for the fans there. Even though I was really just fooling around, I liked the universe I'd created, so when Cindy Hwang at Berkley asked me to submit a novel, I immediately thought of doing a Warlord novel. And so *Jane's Warlord* was born.

Be warned: "Baby, You've Changed" is really kinky compared to most of my Berkley fiction. I tend to go a little more hard-core for my Yahoo! group than for New York publication. You'll also notice both stories have a similar core idea. And yes, I know the hero in "The Warlord and the Fem" has the same name as the hero in "Warfem." Since I hadn't planned to publish "The Warlord and the Fem," I decided to reuse the name, which I really liked. There are also some background details that are a little different in the stories. Still, I hope you enjoy them!

Best,
Angela Knight

The Warlord and the Fern

I had no idea everything was about to change that day. We were all killing time in the ship's big recreation hall, some of us sprawled on the thickly upholstered couches and chairs, either drinking or watching simmies on VR glasses, while others played cards or simmie games at the scattered tables. Most everybody was waiting their turn to go on leave.

Planets usually don't like a big group of mercs hitting the bars at one time. Leads to public disorderly conduct and the occasional drunken homicide, so the captain liked to send us out in shifts to keep the trouble down.

Me, I'd already found trouble at the Dirtside Grill the day before, so I wasn't all that eager to go out again anyway. I suspected the War-lord would be looking for me, so I was just as happy to play poker with Lyonet and keep my ass safely aboard *Drunna's Victory*.

So when the Warlord walked in with Captain Drunna, I damn near swallowed my tongue. His narrow black eyes locked in on me, and my heart leaped into a hard, fast beat at the dark determination in his gaze.

Oh, Lady! He'd found me.

"This is Baird Airell," the captain announced, and the entire company looked up from whatever they were doing to study the Warlord with calculation. "He wants to join the unit. Says he's genetically engineered for combat." Drunna sounded justifiably skeptical, since every merc says he's genetically engineered for combat. In the Warlord's case it happened to be true, but I sure wasn't going to vouch for him.

"Looks to me like he's genetically engineered for sex," Lyonet whispered in my ear. "And a woman designed him."

Though he was all the way across the rec hall, Baird's gaze sharpened as he looked at us. He'd heard her low murmur, of course; a Warlord's hearing could put a ringbat's to shame. He smiled slightly, the barest curve of his hard, erotic mouth. I felt my face heat. Lyonet was right, damn it. He had been genetically engineered by a woman. And it showed.

He had the unearthly beauty of all the Warlords. Chiseled cheekbones and a broad, square jaw, a narrow nose that flared slightly across the nostrils, a wide mouth with full, sensuous lips framed by a short, dark goatee. On his right cheekbone glittered an iridescent blue tattoo—a sharp slash of color against his tanned skin. His hair fell around his shoulders in careless waves, one lock of it twisted into a thin braid that swung beside his cheek. He'd worked a red gemstone and silver beads into the braid, and they gleamed against the dark silk of his hair. In a fight, I knew, he'd club back that long mane and leave the gems at home.

Looking around at my fellow mercenaries, I saw the males looking skeptical, the women, sexually interested but doubtful. I knew what they were all thinking. On the one hand, he was just too damn pretty. On the other, that body was one you had to take seriously.

I was probably the only one who knew just how seriously you'd damn well better take it. The others had never even heard of Vardon and its Warlords, and had no idea what Baird was capable of.

He had the big, powerfully muscled build of a Warlord gene-gineered for hand-to-hand; he probably could have put his fist through a deck plate without so much as a scrape across the tough skin of his knuckles. But he was also lean, with long legs and long arms, so he also had speed and reach. Not a Pershing, then. Commanche Class, maybe. I couldn't be sure; I'd never seen anything but a Pershing, and that was long ago.

But the captain and the others didn't realize what they were dealing with. I did. I also knew something they didn't. Baird Airell didn't give a rat's ass about joining Drunna's Rangers.

He was after me.

Captain Drunna lifted one dark hand for silence, and the murmur of speculation flooding the ship's recreation hall cut off. Drunna was a big man, with a round, merry face and the coldest eyes I ever saw, and when he gave an order, you damn well obeyed. "Mr. Airell, here"—he nodded at the Warlord standing beside him—"has offered to give a demonstration of his skills with one of you. . . ."

"Me, me, me!" Lyonet whispered, grinning, and I kicked her under the table. Baird would probably be more than happy to give her the demonstration she meant, though. Unbonded Warlords were notorious womanizers, and Lyonet, with her curvy little body and wicked green eyes, attracted the attention of every man she met. Men looked at me, too, but it tended to be the kind of look that mixes intrigue and caution. They liked the breasts and the legs and the ass, but I looked too much like the fighter I was. Besides, I was taller than damn near every human male in the rec hall. Except for Baird Airell. Next to him, I'd look delicate.

Why did I find that thought intriguing?

Captain Drunna looked the length of the hall and said, "Mr. Jogox, would you mind giving Mr. Airell a hand here?"

"Or a fist," someone shouted. "Or maybe a kick . . ." Everyone laughed.

Baird smiled tightly, grabbed the hem of his black tunic, and pulled it off over his head. The sight of him cut off the laughter. His magnificent chest more than fulfilled the promise of those broad shoulders. Every inch of it was plated in thick muscle, beautifully defined, forming a lovely sculpted V covered with a pelt of chest hair that looked tempting and soft. He saw the eyes locked on him and shrugged. "Don't want to ruin the tunic." He folded it neatly, his biceps bunching and rippling with the movement, then placed it on the bar running the length of the room. Then he turned to stride toward Jogox, now rising endlessly from his table.

Like all Zurines, Jogox was well over two meters tall—he never met a doorway he didn't have to duck under. His skin was white as milk and tough as plate armor, and he was so broad, he looked like an animated wall. He had four sets of bright red eyes that glowed against his pale face, a mouth full of razored teeth and huge, seven-fingered hands. I'd seen drunken Marines run from him, but he was normally a very sweet man.

Normally. In a fight, he underwent a personality change. There weren't many men I'd hesitate to mix it up with, but big, sweet Jogox was one of them, because sometimes his instincts overcame his judgment. And then people tended to get hurt.

My shipmates had hastily cleared all the tables and chairs from the center of the room so the two would have a place to fight. A crowd already ringed the space, so I stood up on my chair to get a better view of the proceedings. My mouth was dry as sand, but I had to wipe my damp palms on my unisuit-covered thighs.

I wasn't sure even a Commanche Class Warlord had the strength to mix it up with Jogox. A Pershing, maybe, but the Commanche Class, though inhumanly strong, was designed for speed and agility. Baird could end up badly hurt. That would solve my problem, true, but I found I didn't want it solved like that.

"Hey," Lyonet said suddenly, looking at me as she stood on her own chair. "I just realized something. That tattoo on your cheek looks just like the one he's wearing. What's the deal?"

I ignored the question, too busy concentrating on Baird and Jogox as they stood on either side of the circle, sizing one another up. Captain Drunna stepped into the middle of the space, obviously ready to play referee. "Okay, gentlemen," he said. "I don't want anybody hurt badly enough to need an extended stay in Regeneration. Begin." He moved back.

And with a blur of movement, they did just that.

Jogox came in charging, probably figuring to knock the Warlord cold. Baird Airell just flowed away from his attack like liquid mercury, the long, powerful muscles in his bare torso shifting as he ducked and spun. He also gave Jogox something to remember him by as he danced away: a hard punch in the gut that tore a grunt from the big, pale alien.

Jogox eyed Baird a moment, and something malevolent slid through his four red eyes. His lips drew back from those razored teeth, and I swore under my breath.

"Ooooh!" Lyonet gasped. "He's pissed Jogox off! The shit's hit the turbos now!"

I chomped down on my lip. Jogox was going to rip off his head, and it would be all my fault. *Stubborn, stupid stallion, more balls than sense* . . .

The Zurine charged Baird again, swiping at him with one of those huge hands, and again the Warlord ducked. But this time Jogox was waiting for him; a backhanded blow caught him across the face and sent him flying like a spiked grav ball, slamming into the crowd behind him. People tumbled amid a chorus of yelps and curses, and chairs went flying at the impact. I caught my breath, hoping the Warlord wasn't hurt. . . .

Then he catapulted out of the mass of bodies in a low, hard rush, those dark eyes glittering, no expression at all on his bloodied face—not rage, not fear, just cold, inhuman determination. I was probably the only one in the room who knew what that look meant.

Baird had entered *riatt*. Like the Viking berserkers, a Warlord in *riatt* becomes insanely strong, but what's more, he feels no pain or pity. He will keep going, relentless and remorseless, until his enemy falls or he dies of injuries too severe for his supercharged body to survive.

The crowd he'd hit were still regaining their feet when Baird rammed into Jogox like a torpedo, one big fist scything out to hit the long white nose. A spray of lilac flew, Zurine blood. The big alien staggered, then regained his balance and struck out, rapping Baird hard in the jaw. The Warlord shook off the blow as if it were nothing.

The next few minutes were a blur as Baird and Jogox pounded at one another, flat footed, trading punches like boxers. I caught my breath. The Zurine was so much bigger than the human, yet Baird's ferocious blows staggered him, while the Warlord himself didn't seem to feel the impact of those huge white hands at all. In minutes, the watching crowd was spattered with red and lilac and sweat as they fought.

"Damn," said Lyonet, awed. "I've never seen a human hold his own with Jogox before. The big guy's actually looking worried."

Baird, on the other hand, simply looked feral, the gold striations in his brown eyes expanding as he went deeper into *riatt*, sweat and blood rolling down his magnificent torso. His powerful arms worked like pistons as he shot punches into Jogox's white hide, the thick muscle of his chest rippling with every blow.

I had never seen anything like it. I grew up hearing my mother's stories of the Warlords, been quietly envious as my sister boasted, but the reality was breathtaking. It was all the more unnerving when I knew what his real objective was.

Me.

Baird never looked at me, never took his eyes off Jogox; he was too utterly focused on his opponent. But I knew. In his mind, I was the prize he was fighting for.

I tried to reject the thought. No one would fight like that, suffer like that, just to clear the way to me. What was I, after all? He was doing this for his own pride, his own honor.

Yet deep in my mind, some illogical Fem part of me saw a

message beaten out in the rhythm of every punch and kick: *I'll have you, I'll have you, I'll have you.*

Suddenly he finished it. There was a blur of movement, as Baird swarmed up Jogox's massive back. He wrapped his powerful thighs around the Zurine's torso and both arms around the thick white neck, applying a vicious choke hold. Jogox fought it, clawing at Baird's arms so hard he left bloody furrows. Still the Warlord clung and choked him. I saw disbelief in all four red eyes as the Zurine realized he was losing to a human.

He slammed down on his back, trying to break Baird's hold, but the Warlord would not release him, though Jogox's weight was crushing. Somehow Baird managed to flip them both so he was on top, riding the Zurine like a horse.

And that treacherous Fem part of me showed me an image— myself, stretched out under Baird's masculine power. But in the dream, those big, hard hands were gentle and skilled on my skin.

I shook it off.

"Enough!" Captain Drunna called, throwing both arms up and stepping into the center of the ring of spectators. "Don't kill my Zurine, Baird."

It took the Warlord a moment to come out of *riatt* enough to obey, but finally he released Jogox and let him gasp in a hard breath. Baird rolled off the alien and shot to his feet, staggering a little.

Drunna put out a hand to brace him. "Easy there, Airell. Damn, I didn't think you could do it. Guess you really are gene-gineered." He clapped one thick, bloody shoulder. "You're in, boy. Welcome to Drunna's Rangers."

Baird's gold shot eyes went to me and narrowed. "Thank you, Captain."

The rest of the crowd pressed around him, slapping his back and congratulating him while medtechs raced to tend Jogox.

"What a fight!" Lyonet said breathlessly. "I've got to meet him. Come on, Kyna. Let's introduce ourselves."

She scrambled down off the table and I followed mechanically.

My first impulse was to run, but I'd never run from anyone in my life. I wasn't about to start with Baird Airell. So I stayed where I was, listening to the sounds of backslapping and congratulations as my comrades welcomed the Warlord into our midst.

I heard a shout of approval as Jogox made it to his feet. There was another surge of movement as folks started toward him to commiserate and compliment him on the fight.

Then Baird stepped out of the crowd and started toward me. Frozen with a kind of feminine panic I'd never known before, I watched him come.

He gleamed under the rec hall lights, his skin slick with sweat, muscles rippling as he stalked me. Blood marked him in red and lilac like alien camouflage, and the silken hair on his chest was slicked down and matted.

He kept coming until he loomed over me. Every muscle in my body tightened, including those down low in my belly.

Baird stared down at me. His brown eyes looked wide and wild still from *riatt*, and the gold striations snaking through them gave his gaze a manic glitter. I met his stare uneasily, taking in the tight triumph on his face, the hungry line of his sensuous mouth.

"You said you would not leave your crew," he rumbled in a dark, purring bass so much deeper than the voice he'd addressed the captain in. "So I have joined it."

I clenched my fists, feeling panic rise. I couldn't handle him, and I knew it. "Baird . . ."

"You wear the half circle," he interrupted, simply plowing over what I was going to say. "I mean to fill it."

I lifted a hand to touch the tattoo on my cheekbone. It was different from the one on his—except for one mark: a half circle that hung from the bottom point. When I became bonded, my mate would add the other half of the circle, showing my new status. And I'd do the same for the one he wore.

Baird lifted one hand and brushed his index finger across his blooded lip. Frozen, I watched his big hand approach my face, felt his fingertip press against the half circle. Covering it with a full circle of his blood.

I closed my eyes as the tips of my breasts began to tingle.

The hand brushed my lips, and my eyes flew wide as I tasted the smear of blood he left. Leaning forward, he took my mouth in a kiss.

It seared me as no touch ever has—the softness of his mouth, the feeling of his long, powerful body pressing against mine. I felt the sweat and the blood and the heat of his battle, and I gasped.

Jerking free, I did the only thing I could do.

I ran.

Fems are genetically engineered for speed, and there are few that can outrun me. But I'd barely hit my full stride in the corridor when Baird Airell's big hand closed on my arm and pulled me to a stop. I wheeled on him, snarling.

"Let me go, Baird!"

"Not until you do me the courtesy of telling me why you run!" A tendon ticked violently in his broad jaw, but every muscle in his powerful body was tight with self-control.

I opened my mouth to growl something insulting, but looking into those dark eyes, I saw confusion and hurt. Almost at once his face slid into expressionless lines, but I knew what I'd seen. And it surprised me. I hadn't realized my rejection would hurt Baird. I thought he viewed me as nothing but a broodmare, but now I saw I'd been wrong.

I groped to explain. "Baird, I wasn't raised on Vardon."

He frowned impatiently. "None of us were raised on Vardon, Kyna. They drove us from the planet thirty years ago."

"But you told me you grew up on one of the colonies. I didn't. We lived on mercenary vessels. My father was a Warlord, but he was killed when I was five. I have lived all my life in that culture. I don't know if I can submit to you."

The hard lines of his face softened into a smile. I thought again how breathtakingly handsome he was. "The submission is only in bed, Kyna. You are my equal otherwise."

I shook my head. "No, I'm not. And that's the point. I'm at least twice as strong as any man I've ever been with. But you . . . I've practiced with Jogox myself. I didn't last five minutes before he put me halfway through a bulkhead. You not only lasted with him, you put him down."

He lifted a dark brow, that beautiful mouth curling in a one-sided smile. "What I have in mind for you is not a contest of strength, Kyna." Suddenly the smile faded, and shock flooded his dark eyes. "You don't think I would hurt you?"

I made a dismissing gesture. "No, no." The Warlords might play hard in bed, but they're also strictly raised to honor. They're taught never to turn their formidable strength against anyone under their protection, particularly bond mates and children. To abuse one's own is a mark of great dishonor.

"If you don't fear my strength, I don't understand your objection," Baird said. "Aren't you tired of sleeping with civs?" He spread his beautifully muscled arms, and for a moment I was distracted by the play of shifting sinew. "It's like trying to make love to a soap bubble. I dare not release my passion lest I deal some injury. By Our Lady, I have had to confine my attentions to my own hand."

Hooo, boy. "How long have you been celibate?"

He shrugged, the play of contours in his torso a marvelous thing. "Five months, perhaps."

Which, for a man with a Warlord's appetite, is a very long time. Lust would be riding him hard. For a moment my treacherous imagination summoned an image of what it would be like to have all that ravenous hunger turned on me. I felt my nipples harden. What would it be like to share one night in a Warlord's bed? "Perhaps . . ."

His dark eyes sharped on mine, and I saw calculation flicker in their depths. Then, reluctantly, he said, "One coupling would not be enough for me, Kyna."

I lifted a brow at his honesty. "Another man might have taken me to bed, thinking to seduce me into yielding."

"Aye," he said steadily, and reached out a big hand to touch my cheek, his fingers leaving a wake of heat. "But another man would not be me."

And another man would be easier to resist, I thought. But I could not yield to him. I knew what it meant to be bonded to a Warlord, and I did not think I could submit so utterly.

"But perhaps," he said softly, "you'll allow me to court you as a civ male would. Give me a chance, Kyna."

I looked at him, at the warm, heated chocolate of his eyes. "Very well," I said, before I knew what I was about.

Then, silently, I cursed myself.

One month later

I *watched Baird's long fingers close gently over the black queen* and move her into position to threaten my king. "Check," he said, his deep voice amused.

Damn it. I scanned the board, realizing he'd beaten me yet again. He'd ruthlessly, systematically stripped me of my pieces, and I had nowhere left to go. True, I'd made inroads of my own; all he had left were his king, a knight, and the queen, but even so, he'd managed to trap me.

With a groan, I tipped over my own king in a gesture of defeat. "Damn, Baird, you got me again." Laughing, I looked up into his eyes—and froze.

His dark gaze was hungry and fixed on my mouth. "Ah, if only you meant that."

I felt heat roll from my belly all the way into my face. Disgruntled, I knew I was blushing. I never blushed. I looked away from his face and began putting captured pieces back on the board, concentrating hard on what I was doing. "Another game? You've won ten games to my eight, and I want revenge."

"I think not. I find I am too . . . restless." He stood. I didn't look at him, knowing the sight of that big, hard body clad in a snug black unisuit would do serious damage to my eroding self-control.

But as he strode away, I couldn't help stealing a look at his muscular butt. Oh, Lady.

Lyonet blocked my view of it as she stepped up to the table we'd occupied in the rec hall. "On behalf of women everywhere," she said, and swatted me across the side of the head.

I yelped in shock. "Hey, what was that for?"

She leaned across the table and glared into my eyes. "Every woman on this ship would give her left nipple to sleep with that man, but the only one he looks at is you. And all you do with him is play *chess*. He gets up from this table with a hard-on that I, personally, will dream about for weeks, and you just sit there playing with your pieces. Are you flatline?"

My fingers tightened around Baird's knight. "It's more complicated than you think."

"It must be complicated as all hell if you're playing board games when you could have both legs wrapped around that incredible ass. And don't tell me you're not tempted, because I saw you leering at it as he left."

"Yeah, I'm tempted, but he wants a lot more than one night of hot sex."

"Good. Give it to him." Lyonet dropped into his abandoned chair.

"You don't know what he wants." To give my hands something to do, I gathered up the remaining pieces and put them briskly on the board.

Lyonet leaned forward and looked hard into my face. Her jaw dropped. "You're scared of him. I didn't think you were scared of anything. What's going on?"

I didn't answer as I carefully lined up the pieces, concentrating on getting them in mathematically straight rows.

"Talk to me, Kyna," Lyonet said, one of her hands wrapping around one of mine. "I've seen you charge mercs twice your size with a grin on your face and mayhem in your heart. Why on earth would you be afraid of sleeping with the hottest thing either of us has seen in years?"

"He's a Warlord, Lyonet. Genetically engineered."

"Yeah, I figured that out when he kicked Jogox's ass. So? And what the hell's a Warlord?"

"It's a long story."

"I'm not going anywhere."

I sighed and picked up Baird's black knight again. Nervously, I began to turn it over and over in my hands, concentrating on its smooth contours. "About three hundred years ago, a group of colonists settled this planet called Vardon. It was back when all those weird little colonies sprang up, all those religious sects and lunatic groups. This one wanted to form a matriarchy—women running the show. They thought they could create a perfect world if they eliminated male aggression through genetic engineering, making their male citizens more like women."

"Sounds like a real good way to get a lot of lousy lovers," Lyonet said, rolling her eyes.

"Exactly. Anyway, it wasn't long before they started having trouble with a neighboring planet. Colonists there wanted Vardon's mineral reserves. The Vardoneese fought them off, but just barely. After it was over, they decided they needed a race of warriors to fall back on if they ever had a similar problem, so they created the Warlords. Stronger, faster, nastier than damn near anything human, and a lot of things that aren't."

She nodded. "Sounds like Baird, all right."

"Uh-huh. Thing is, turns out their perfect soldier came with a sex drive that was that much more powerful than an ordinary human's."

Lyonet's eyes lit wickedly. "This is sounding better and better all the time."

"Not to the Vardoneese. They'd been systematically eliminating their own sex drives, so the sudden presence of all these amorous males disconcerted them, to say the least. Plus, the men were so damn strong, sleeping with one could be hazardous to your health. They tried eliminating the sex drive, but what they got was even nastier—a warrior who was cold and vicious and basically uncontrollable. So they decided to go with the oversexed version, while adding loyalty and a highly affectionate nature. Then, to give their supersoldier something to sleep with, they created the Fem—female versions of the Warlords."

I saw her jaw drop. "That tattoo on your face—you're one of them. Why the hell didn't you tell me you were gene-gineered?"

"Because I'm not, technically. My parents were. Dad was a Warlord, Mother was a Fem. I just inherited their genetic characteristics."

"The strength and speed."

"Right. Anyway, about thirty years ago, the Vardoneese went through one of their periodic political convulsions. They decided the Warriors—that's us—were responsible for the wars they kept getting themselves in. If we didn't exist, they wouldn't be so quick to rely on violent solutions."

"Oh, bullshit," said Lyonet. "They'd just end up hiring merc units like everybody else."

"Probably, but they didn't see it that way. They deported the lot of us. Every last Warlord and Fem, to the far corners of the galaxy. They were afraid if they put us in one place, we'd come back and conquer them."

"Paranoid bunch of bitches."

"Got it in one. So anyway, Baird was raised on one of those colonies. But everybody in the colony had come from the same basic root stock. They didn't have enough genetic variation to sustain the population. The colonists decided to send their unbonded Warlords and Fems out to look for Warriors they could bring home as mates."

"And Baird found you."

"Looks that way."

"And he wants to make it permanent."

"Yep."

She leaned forward and glared into my eyes. "So what the hell's the problem?"

I clenched my fingers hard around the knight. "I don't want to become his slave."

Lyonet blinked, startled. "Come again?"

"The Warlords are very . . . dominant in bed. And Fems . . . we're designed to give them what they want. To submit."

She leaned back in her chair and lifted an eyebrow. "I have trouble imagining you as submissive."

"We're not. Ordinarily. In combat, we're designed to function as backup. Not as strong, but better at some things Warlords can't do because of their sheer size. Agility, speed, getting into tight places. We're cool and controlled when they're in *riatt*—the berserker frenzy Baird used to beat Jogox. We keep them from getting carried away and making mistakes."

"Sounds like equals more than master and slave."

"And equals are exactly what we are—outside the bedroom. Inside . . ."

"He wants to tie you up and screw your brains out. So? I don't see why you'd find a few sex games intimidating."

I shook my head. "What if it's more than games, Lyonet? I've never actually known any Warlords other than Baird, and I'm not sure what I'd be getting into. My father died when I was young, so I never really knew him." I swallowed and looked down at the knight, finding I could not quite meet Lyonet's perceptive green gaze. "My sister bonded with a Warlord she met off-planet when I was fifteen or so. She brought him to our home on Fairworld, but they stayed only a short time before they left for his colony."

Her eyes sharpened, and I knew she'd read the discomfort on my face. "Something happened during that visit, didn't it?"

I glanced up, then away. "I saw them together. One night. I heard her cry out in pain, and I went to help. They were out in the garden. She was tied, and he was . . ." I stopped and swallowed. "God, he was beautiful, but the look on his face was so feral. And my sister—she was in pain, and yet she loved it. I didn't interfere, but I didn't leave, either. I just stood there in the shadows, frozen. Watching."

"Yeah, I can see how something like that would spin out a fifteen-year-old virgin." Lyonet's expression was compassionate. "But just because your brother-in-law played rough, that doesn't mean Baird would."

"But that's how Warlords are, Lyonet. Erotic dominance is part of their nature. I researched it on our house comp, and I talked to my mother about it. She said I would understand once I was bonded."

Lyonet's eyes widened. "And that's what you're afraid of."

I nodded. "What I saw in that garden scared the hell out of me. But part of me was . . . excited. I don't want to lose myself that way, Lyonet. I'm a soldier. I don't want to be mastered by some genetic imperative a bunch of techies programmed into my ancestors."

She shook her head. "Damn, girl. I see your point. But here's another thing you need to keep in mind." Leaning forward, she met my eyes. "Baby, you're not fifteen anymore. And I think it's time you find out just what your nature is. Because it sure as shit isn't going away."

I knew Lyonet was right, of course. I just wasn't sure I had the guts to explore that particular dark corner of my psyche.

For one thing, I'd have to go to Baird to do it, and I wasn't sure he'd let me go.

A̶nother month went by as Baird continued to court me—with more restraint than a civ male would have shown, to tell the truth. We played chess and talked, me of my life as a mercenary, him of his as a Warlord. But no matter how carefully he hid it, I could sense his hunger, humming just under the surface like thousands of volts of electricity flowing through a power cable. When he'd touch me, I could almost feel the snap of it.

At such times, the part of me that feared him would babble a warning. I was testing his control to the breaking point, and I knew it. Yet I found I didn't want to back off. He was so damn charming, so intelligent, so rock-bottom decent that I couldn't bear to walk away.

And he wasn't the only one who hungered.

So often, some casual movement of that big body would send my desire leaping—the flex of a muscle, the curve of his chest, the hot, dark glitter of gold striations in his eyes.

What I didn't realize was that Baird knew it. And like the skilled warrior he was, one day he took advantage of my weakness.

He asked me to fight.

"It's been a long time since I've practiced with another warrior," he told me over lunch one day. "I'm afraid my dueling skills are getting rusty. The first time somebody challenges me to a formal duel, I'm going to get minced."

"I don't know how much competition I'd be," I told him, ignoring the flare of heat that rose low in my belly. "I haven't practiced with a sword and dagger since I left home. Mercs don't duel—it's either fists or straight to homicide."

As I watched, the gold striations in his eyes brightened. "Oh, I'm sure any contest with you would be well worth my time."

I knew what he was up to, of course. I suppose that's why I agreed. The part of me that hungered for him wanted to overcome the part of me that feared him.

He wasn't the only one who wanted an excuse to lose control.

We reserved one of the small practice courts during the late watch. When I arrived, he was positioning a padded exercise mat on the floor for us to fight on. I didn't comment, though our people have never been concerned with falls during practice. If you're so clumsy as to get hurt hitting the ground, you probably deserve it.

I knew Baird wasn't concerned about falls.

He rose from his task as I sauntered in. As he turned to look at me, his eyes widened. So did mine.

I wore a tight black breastband that left my arms and belly bare

and revealed a great deal of cleavage. A pair of skintight black huggers cupped my ass and hips, ending at midthigh.

He'd also dressed to tempt in the male equivalent—his own pair
of huggers and nothing else, so that his beautiful chest was bare.
His eyes were shot with gold striations of hunger like a night sky
cut with lightning bolts. He'd left that long, silken hair loose to tumble around his broad shoulders.

Baird, no fool, knew what my weaknesses were.

But neither of us commented on the other's dress—that would
have been an admission that we knew what we were really there
for. Instead his eyes flicked to the blunted practice sword and dagger
I held in either hand as he gathered up his own from a case on the
floor. "Nice weapons."

"Not as nice as yours. May I see?"

He moved over beside me. I was instantly aware of the heat of
his body as he handed me his sword and took my own. I made a
quick pass through the air with the blade, feeling the precise balance that made it seem almost weightless. "Beautiful." I held it at
full extension. "It's a little long for me, though."

I looked up to see him staring hungrily at my cleavage. "I think
you can manage," he murmured.

"I'll stick with my own for now." I hid a smile, feeling my excitement leap as I returned the sword. "Shall we begin?"

Baird smiled slowly. "Oh, yeah. I'm more than ready."

My heart pounding hard, I turned and moved to the other side
of the mat as he fell into guard on his side. Lifting my weapons, I
stared into his gold-shot eyes and waited for the signal to begin.

"Begin," he murmured, and we did, stalking each other slowly,
watching eyes and hands. Baird wore a hot and wicked smile, but
his eyes glittered with fierce determination. Two months before, I
would have viewed his intentions with misgivings, but now my nipples peaked at the thought of what he wanted to do to me. I realized at some point I had begun to trust him. Anything he did when
we made love would be something we both enjoyed.

He tested me with a flick of his blade. I parried neatly and riposted, driving in my own attack, which he scooped aside with his dagger. At the same time, his blunted rapier tested my defenses again, and again I parried it with my own dagger. We disengaged and danced apart again.

And so we toyed with each other. With his greater strength, he could have pounded my weapons aside and scored off me easily, but he fenced on my terms—his speed, agility, and skill against mine in a lovely dance of steel.

I found myself half-hypnotized by him, by the grace and quickness of his big body, by the flex and play of muscle as he moved. And I could feel his eyes on me, on my breasts and legs, lingering between my thighs as I lunged or retreated. The mood of sensuality growing between us intensified until I felt my breath come shorter, not with exertion, but with desire.

Suddenly the blunted tip of his blade flicked out and raked gently across one of my pointed rock-hard nipples. I gasped at the wave of heat that zinged through me at the contact.

Baird's gold-striated gaze met mine. "A touch," he purred.

I nodded, acknowledging the point as a hot blush of raw lust rolled up my face.

I attacked in a long, hard lunge that shot my body forward. Baird knocked my sword aside with his rapier, but at the same time his dagger dipped. The rounded blade stroked right between the lips of my sex in a bold, erotic caress I could feel even through the tight fabric of my huggers.

Stunned, I let my body collide with his. For a moment we were chest to chest, his hot, damp skin pressing against my breasts. Eyes widening, I stared incredulously at his face. He gave me a taunting grin.

"Point to me," he said, his breath puffing gently against my face, smelling ever so slightly of brandy and mint.

I leaped back. He laughed softly.

Lazily, he began to circle me, moving not in a swordsman's

crouch, but with shoulders back, his magnificent chest on display in all its heaving, sweat-streaked glory. Letting my gaze dip, I saw he had a massive erection.

"You may not know this," Baird said, his voice a dark rumble, "but back on Vardon these were called mating duels. Fems and Warlords would meet to test each other. If the Fem won, she'd usually seek another opponent. But if the Warlord won . . ." He grinned. "He didn't let her go for a very long time. Often she'd end up with her circle filled."

I remembered the touch of his fingertip on my tattoo a month before, filling the half circle with his blood.

"Sounds like a plan to me," he said softly.

My mouth went dry, but I made myself give him a taunting smile. "Only if you win."

"Oh," he drawled, his eyes darkening, "I will."

If Baird's arrogance was meant to tease me into a reckless attack, it worked—but not the way he intended. I launched another lunge in a burst of blurring speed. He retreated, flicking my sword aside with a bat of his rapier as he sought to parry my dagger with his own.

His eyes widened. I knew he'd felt the delicate, teasing stroke of my blunted knife's point along the steel-hard length of his erection. I smirked at him. "I think you missed that parry, Baird."

"So I gather," he said, sounding a little breathless.

In that moment, the contest changed. Suddenly we were no longer competing to hit one another, but to inflict teasing little touches. Our eyes met as we clashed, hot as the grins on our faces. My nipples were as hard as his erection, and I could feel the electric trickle of cream in my sex.

Suddenly he straightened again, dropping both his weapons out and to either side so he stood with his arms spread, the thick bulge of his cock an irresistible target. His gold-shot eyes dared me as one corner of his sensuous mouth kicked up.

I darted forward, wanting only to touch that brazen masculinity with my blades. In a move almost too fast to follow, he swept his weapons around and up, entangling mine. He rotated those strong wrists of his, and the skillful leverage he brought to bear sent my rapier and dagger spinning from my hands in opposite directions. At the same time, his pull brought me stumbling against his massive chest. He dropped his blades and grabbed my forearms as he hooked the back of my ankle with a foot and pivoted to one side.

With a yelp, I hit the thick, padded mat on my belly—and was suddenly covered in his powerful body as he gently twisted both arms behind my back, then trapped them there. "At this point," he said, his voice a seductive croon in my ear as his hard cock pressed against my bottom, "I think it's safe to say this fight is over."

Slowly, deliberately, Baird rolled his hips. I bit back a moan at the sensation of that rock-hard erection grinding against my sex.

He transferred both my wrists into the grip of one hand and kept them pressed to the small of my back. Wary, excited, I turned my head and watched as he delved into his pocket with his free hand. When I saw what he pulled out, I swallowed. Hard.

It was a length of cuffcable, padded so it wouldn't cut the skin. He meant to bind me.

He wrapped the strong, flexible cable around my wrists in a figure-eight pattern, then lifted himself. Bracing one booted foot beside my hips while kneeling across me, Baird flipped me over on my back. I stared up at his handsome face, stark and predatory with hunger, and felt my knees part of their own accord.

His big hands went to my breastband and pulled it up with one rough jerk, baring my tits. His eyes blazed at the sight, but he wasn't done. Next he slid off me and grabbed the tight fabric of my huggers, then stripped them down my legs with a single, ruthless yank. Tossing them across the room, he rocked back on his heels, taking in my bound, naked body with eyes so striated with gold they seemed molten.

He raked the length of me with his gaze, thoroughly, posses-sively. A dark smile kicked one corner of his mouth. "By Our Lady,

I've dreamed of this moment since the instant I looked across that bar and met your eyes. You've led me on such a dance, I wasn't sure I'd ever have you."

When he looked into my face again, his eyes were narrow and hard, and his mouth took on a cruel, determined slant. "You're going to pay the price for tormenting me, Kyna."

Oh, I certainly hoped so.

His big hands closed over my breasts, stroking, fondling, taking possession of them. Calloused thumbs stroked my hard nipples as he caressed the soft skin. The sensation made my breath catch in the back of my throat. I closed my eyes.

Only to snap them wide again as something hot and wet closed over one nipple as he twisted the other with delicate brutality. Gently, he licked and nibbled, his tongue, his lips, his teeth sending heat rolling through me in thick, honeyed waves. At the same time, his long fingers tormented the other pink tip, twisting and pulling and stroking until I writhed.

He came down over me completely, his body resting across my thighs, trapping and immobilizing me even more while he tormented my aching breasts. Feeling him pressing thick against the notch of my thighs, I whimpered in lust.

"Baird," I gasped, my pride melting in the heat he generated. "God, please, take me!"

"Not yet," he said, lifting his head from my breasts, his eyes dark and determined. "You haven't even started to pay."

Then he slid down my body and buried his face between my thighs. I sucked in a hard breath at the sensation of his mouth pressing against my most sensitive, desperate flesh. "Take all the revenge you want," I gasped.

He lifted his head, his eyes glinting up at me from over my cunt. "Oh, I will."

Then he began to lick, slowly, thoroughly, tasting my desperately creaming sex, licking the labia he spread wide with two fingers, circling my clit, thrusting his tongue deep up my snatch. I rolled my head against the mat and whined in mindless pleasure, loving it, loving everything he was doing to me, feeling my orgasm building, building. The pleasure grew with every hot pass of his tongue, heat and pressure building until I rolled my hips desperately against his face, grinding, striving for the peak that was so close, so close. . . .

Then he stopped.

"Baird!" I cried, desperate. "Don't stop!"

"Am I your master, Kyna?"

The question made me gape. I lifted my head and looked at him, looming over my sex, his muscled biceps bunching as he watched my face with a predator's hunger. "What?" I couldn't believe he'd asked the question.

He lowered his head and flicked my clit, punctuating each word with a skillful stroke of his tongue. "Am . . ." Lick. ". . . I . . ." Lick. ". . . your . . ." Lick. ". . . Master?"

My climax was so close I could only twist mindlessly. "Yes! Oh, yes, whatever you want!"

"Good." He sat back on his heels, leaving my stiff, desperate clit to cool without his mouth. "Then your master wants the satisfaction you have denied him."

He reached down and caught me by the shoulders, pulling me onto my knees facing him. Dazed, I could only watch as he rose easily to his feet and opened the fly of his huggers. His cock thrust out, so broad and thick I was momentarily startled. I had never seen an organ of such menacing size. "Take it down your throat," he ordered.

Wide-eyed, I lifted my gaze to his. Those gold-shot eyes were narrowed, fierce. Demanding.

"You've been torturing me for weeks, Kyna," he growled. "Now you're going to use that sweet mouth for something besides telling me no."

He reached out a big hand and wrapped it in my hair. Helplessly, I leaned forward, opened my mouth, and took that big, threatening cock inside.

"Yeessssssssss," he hissed. "That's it. Like that. Deeper." He rocked his hips, forcing the massive shaft more fully into my mouth. He tasted hot and salty, and the texture of his skin was slick as his cock slid past my lips. I felt hot cream flooding my cunt, shockingly aroused by his dominant pose. It should have offended and outraged me, but it didn't. Instead I saw it as a mark of his extreme arousal. And his lust sent mine spiraling even higher.

He wrapped both hands in my hair, holding me still as he rolled his hips, forcing more and more of his cock down my throat. I choked, and he backed off, but only slightly. I could sense his ruthless intent to come in my mouth. With my hands bound behind me and his hands controlling my head, he could use me as he pleased. And he did, fucking my mouth as I sucked him, rumbling blunt orders about how to use my tongue and lips. Orders I, helplessly aroused, could only obey.

Until he drove in a thrust that made me gasp around his shaft. The big, plum head jerked, and something hot and salty flooded my mouth as he groaned out a low, animal sound of pleasure.

"Very nice, my captive," he rumbled at last, releasing me. I collapsed gasping, my cunt burning in helpless lust. "Now I can tend to you properly."

He stepped around behind me. In an instant, my every erotic instinct went on alert. With a helpless moan, I drew my legs up under my body and lifted my hips to him, offering him my desperately needy cunt. He tapped my thighs with one foot. "Wider, captive."

Licking my lips, I obeyed. My face pressed to the cool mat, my ass in the air, I waited. It was a gallingly subservient pose, but I didn't care. Suddenly I understood why my sister had been so willing to play this game with her Warlord husband.

He stepped away from me for a moment, and I shut my eyes, fighting the need to beg.

Something cold touched my hot cunt, and my back arched in shock. "Baird!" I gasped.

I heard him laugh. "I thought you liked the touch of my blade?"

A long, cool object sought the opening of my cunt and pressed inside. I yelped and jerked my head around.

Baird was fucking me with the hilt of his rapier. He grinned at me wickedly as he pushed the thick, leather wrapped grip deeper into my creamy cunt. Until finally the long quillions of the guard pressed my sex and ass, cool steel grinding against my clit.

Helplessly I moaned. The lust I felt scalded me.

Eyes dark gold with raw lechery, Baird slowly began to fuck me with the hilt. Each time he drove it in up to the guard, he twisted it so the cold metal raked my clit. The sensation made me writhe.

But despite the wicked pleasure, what I really wanted was the feeling of that hot satin shaft of his, driven all the way to my core. "Baird, please," I whimpered. "Take me!"

"Baird?" He withdrew the hilt and drove it in hard. I yelped at the brutal pleasure.

"Master! I meant, Master! Please, give me your cock!"

"Do you really think you deserve it, after the way you've tormented and denied me?"

"Aaah!" I sucked in a breath as he twisted the hilt skillfully. "No, but . . . but you do. Oh, please, Baird. I'm so wet. . . ."

"Yes," he growled. "You are. I can scent you, hot and slick and wanting. But is your cunt all you want filled?"

"No," I groaned, knowing it was true. "I want you to fill the circle. Give me your mark, Baird. Please."

"Finally!" He jerked the hilt from my body and threw the sword across the room. No sooner did it bounce clattering off the bulkhead than he flipped me onto my back and covered my body with his. In an instant he was in me, driving to my heart with one hard thrust of his cock.

I screamed at the sensation of that broad shaft filling my cunt. But he gave me no quarter, no time to catch my breath. He simply started ramming me in long strokes that hit me deep and hard, just where I needed it.

I keened at his rough possession, staring up into those narrow, gold-shot eyes. His lips were pulled back from his teeth as he fucked me. Every stroke sent pleasure spiraling tighter, deeper. Until I could not take any more. I felt it rise in me like a molten wave, searing every last thought, every last feeling, out of me. Leaving only the mind-detonating sensation of his cock, shuttling inside my spread and helpless body.

I threw back my head and screamed. He roared in pleasure and drove to the hilt, freezing there, pumping out his come.

Finally the storm was over. He rolled off me to lay beside my sore, well-used body. I groaned softly as my strained muscles protested deliciously.

Suddenly one of Baird's long fingers slid into my cunt, making my back arch in shock. Before I could yelp a protest, he withdrew his hand. Something wet and white covered his fingertip—his come.

With a wicked grin, he pressed the finger against my cheekbone, filling the circle just as he had two months before with his blood. "Now," he said, grinning with smug male possessiveness, "you are mine."

I eyed him, then reached between my thighs and slipped my own finger deep. Then I pressed our mingled juices against his arrogant cheekbone, covering the half circle tattooed there. "As you're mine."

He smiled, the dark light lifting from his eyes. "I love you, Kyna."

I grinned back. "And I love you, too, Baird." Lifting my head, I kissed him, sliding my tongue deep in his mouth. I heard a startled growl of lust. . . .

And then it began all over again.

Baby, You've Changed

I'm told everybody squirms a little on seeing somebody they made love to years ago as a teenager. Maybe you gained weight. Maybe he picked up a few scars. Maybe, like me, you said something stupidly thoughtless when you broke it off that makes you wince as an adult.

But I suspect my reunion with Captain Gage Deauxville hit new depths of God-awful unplumbed in the history of romance.

To begin with, our little meeting didn't exactly take place at a Star Academy reunion. No, I and the rest of the crew of the *Xe'vit* had just been captured by Deauxville's *Intrepid* after running a four-hour space battle during the conquest of Arcana.

Not that we made it easy. After the *Xe'vit* was disabled by several well-placed *Intrepid* antimatter volleys, we fought like hell to repel the enemy's boarding parties, with me and my Arcanan Marines in the lead.

Didn't do much good. Deauxville's mercs were just too damned battle-hardened for a shipload of human draftees, no matter how desperate. Most of my mates were grass-green fresh recruits, no match for Deauxville's troops, fully half of whom were either vamp or genetically engineered anyway. I knew when the boarding started we were fucked, and I was right.

After the obligatory ass-kicking—and the post ass-kicking trip to the ship's medtechs for treatment of some ugly beamer burns—all us Marines were ordered to report to the *Xe'vit*'s quarterdeck. My boys and girls didn't like the sound of that much, and to tell the truth, neither did I. My old lover had built himself a very dark reputation, so dark I was still wondering whether it really was him.

Until they lined us up on the quarterdeck, us unarmed in our shipsuits, them in boarding armor. Deauxville came out to review us all, and my heart sank. It was him, all right.

Of course, he was a hell of a lot bigger than the half-grown seventeen-year-old I'd seduced as a bitchy little teenage Fem. Hard to tell how much of it was him and how much was that matte-black boarding armor, but he towered over every Marine in the line. Except maybe Tiny, who wasn't really human to begin with.

But that face—that face I knew. He'd been such a pretty kid all those years ago, with that beautifully sculptured bone structure that looked like something Michelangelo had chiseled, with big blue eyes and a sweet, kissable mouth. A young archangel I had thoroughly enjoyed corrupting with all the wicked experience that comes from being a whole year older.

The beauty was still there, but it was darker now, harder. A scar slashed from his forehead, across one eye, and down an elegant cheek, but it somehow set his looks off instead of ruining them. I imagined what the original wound must have been like and winced. It was a miracle he hadn't lost that eye.

I also wondered why he hadn't had the scar surgically removed. What kind of statement was he trying to make with that?

As he walked down the line of my Marines, I saw him study each of them in turn, meeting their eyes with an icy crystalline stare. If any of them had any thoughts of giving the *Intrepid*'s crew a hard time, they didn't by the time he went past.

Watching him terrorize my unit, I remembered the time I used my Fem strength to hold him down and suck his beautiful young cock into a gushing orgasm. I remembered the adoration in those blue eyes when he told me he loved me.

And I remembered telling him I could never fall for a mere human like him.

With the sort of thoughtless cruelty only a teenage girl can manage, I'd told him I was a Fem, genetically engineered for battle. I wanted a man of my own kind who could match me strength for strength, and more. Dominate me, even. Not a guy I could hold down and suck off without working up a sweat. I wanted a Warlord.

God, what a fucking idiot I'd been.

I don't know whether Deauxville read the wince of apology in my eyes when he reached me in that line. I do know he stared down into my face for a long, long time while I tried to decide what, if anything, I should say. Then, slowly, chillingly, he smiled, revealing half-inch fangs.

My beautiful Gage Deauxville wasn't a "mere" human anymore. He was a vampire. And one of the nastiest military commanders in this part of the galaxy.

Without saying a word, he pivoted on his heel and aimed an off-hand command at the *Intrepid* trooper behind him. "That one."

"Aye, sir." The trooper lifted his stun rifle and pointed into my face.

Shit.

Before I could react, the lights went out.

I came to lying in a puddle of drool on cold deck plate. Eeeeww. I lifted my head—which promptly began to pound so hard I dropped it again. Making a supreme effort, I managed to roll over and blink at the ceiling a long way over my head. It wasn't a familiar ceiling. I wasn't on board the *Xe'vit* anymore.

No sooner had the thought registered that I must be on the

Intrepid than I realized something else. My back, pressed against that cold deck, was completely bare. Lifting my head, I discovered that so was the rest of me.

I was naked.

To make matters worse, Gage Deauxville towered over me, his blue eyes locked on my face with a distinctly hostile gleam. And he was just as naked as I was, every last centimeter of tanned, gleaming muscle on breath-stealing display. Including his huge, rock-hard erection. As I watched, completely frozen with astonishment, he deliberately squirted a tube of something into one hand and slicked it over his shaft. He'd always been hung, but . . .

"Damn, you've grown." I wished I could recall the words the instant they were out of my mouth.

He gave me a slow, nasty smile, still slowly stroking that massive dick. "A lot of it in the last few minutes."

Lying on the deck was beginning to seem like an invitation. I scrambled to my feet, though my head throbbed in protest. Licking dry lips, I eyed the hand stroking that long, thick organ. "Is there a reason you're greasing your cock, Gage?"

"I'm planning to celebrate my conquest." The smile widened, making it uncomfortably obvious just where he intended to do his celebrating.

I swallowed and met his hot, threatening gaze. Even without the armor, he was a full head taller than I. As a merc, I was no stranger to beautifully sculpted male bodies, but Gage was as powerfully built as a Viking Class Warlord, from corded throat and massive chest all the way down to his big feet. He dwarfed me in every dimension. If he'd still been human, I could have kicked his ass anyway; my Fem strength would have been at least three times greater. But he was a vampire now, and that meant he was significantly stronger than even a Warlord. Which meant I didn't have a prayer.

I lifted my chin anyway. "The Gage I knew wasn't a rapist."

"You dumped the Gage you knew." He stepped closer to loom, a wall of male muscle and hostile sensuality. "At the time, you said you wanted someone who could . . . take you. Hand to hand."

"I said a lot of shit I didn't mean." *Including the part about not loving you.* "I was too young and dumb to know better."

"Don't try to play me, Tamir." There was genuine anger flaring in his eyes now. "You meant exactly what you said. I've researched Warlord culture—all those elaborate courtship and dominance games. You would never have treated a Warlord the way you treated me."

Because a Warlord would have seen my actions as the sexual challenge they'd been—an invitation to a dominance duel. And if I'd lost that fight, he'd have seen it as his right to indulge in what my people view as the ultimate act of conquest: a hard, deep ass-fucking. The kind Gage evidently had in mind now.

Something I'd still never experienced—though I wasn't about to admit that to my vampire captor.

My mouth was completely dry. Involuntarily, my eyes drifted down to his long, thick cock, imagining the way that broad shaft would feel forcing its way into my anus. Deep down, as humiliating as it was, some part of me was getting turned on. God help me, my sweet young lover had turned into the kind of hard, dominant male my darker fantasies had always revolved around.

So why did I feel . . . regret?

"I never meant to hurt you." The minute I said the words, I mentally cringed. Not a smart thing to say to a guy you've humiliated.

Sure enough, the nasty glint in his eyes brightened. "Don't worry, darling—I plan to get my revenge." His gaze flicked downward. I followed them automatically. And saw what I should have noticed immediately, had I not been so hypnotized by Gage's gorgeous cock.

On the deck at his feet lay a broadsword, with a lethal point and a visibly sharp edge. It definitely wasn't a practice weapon. I felt something cold coil in my belly.

When I looked up again, I found him watching me, cool and calculating. "Pick it up, Tamir."

I took a step back. "What?"

"We're going to fight my own variation of a dominance duel." He crouched and picked up the blade himself, giving it a few effortless practice swings. "If I win, you become my bloodslave, and I do my . . . celebrating in your tight little ass while I feed." His smile revealed fangs so long, sharp, and white, I instantly imagined how they'd feel sinking into my throat. With an offhand gesture, he tossed me the sword. I caught it automatically. "If you win, you avoid a permanent spot on my personal menu. Know how to kill a vampire?"

Of course I knew—I was a Space Marine. I'd even done it, when I'd had to. But the idea of beheading Gage Deauxville made my gut twist in such horror I almost dropped the sword. "Gage, I am not going to fight you."

"Good." He bared his fangs. "Bend over wide, Tamir."

I stared at him as he began to stalk me. He was fucking huge, in every sense of the word. It hit me again that this wasn't the Gage I'd known—this was a vampire. I didn't know what he was capable of, what had happened to him over the past fifteen years, what—or whom—he'd done. Though part of me found him deliciously arousing and part remembered the Gage of my girlhood, I was too much a hardened mercenary to turn myself over to a vampire without a fight.

I lifted the sword. "Kiss my ass."

"Actually, I'd rather fuck it." And he came for me.

I jumped back barely ahead of his lunge, my heart bounding in my chest. Automatically, I swung my sword at him, pulling it at the last minute. Not that the strike would have landed anyway, judging from the cat-quick way he twisted aside. Damn, the man was fast.

His chilly blue gaze flicked from my blade to my eyes. Slowly, he smiled in dark satisfaction. I knew he'd realized I had tried to avoid hitting him at the last second. And I knew he interpreted that to mean I wasn't nearly as opposed to being fang banged as I should have been. I snarled at him, my pride stung. Dammit, I would not be easy prey for him.

When he came at me again, I put my back into my swing—but I aimed at his leg. I still didn't want him dead, just stopped.

Not that it did me any good. He leaped over my swing and lunged for me. I barely eluded those big hands. I'd fought vampires before, but he was even faster and more powerful than my previous opponents.

Warily, I retreated as he stalked me, forcing me to dance aside to avoid his long, powerful reach. I knew if he got his hands on me, it was over.

I also knew I could finish it just as fast. I'm good with a sword—all my people are. If Gage had been any other vamp bent on anal rape and stupid enough to face me unarmed, I'd have taken his head in a blink. But every time I looked in those hot blue eyes, I couldn't bring myself to use any of the openings I saw.

But he did.

Curling his lip back from those razored fangs, he lunged at me, straight on and fearless, forcing me to shift my blade aside to avoid skewering him through the chest. As I gasped at the close call, one big hand engulfed my wrist as a foot swept my ankles. He slammed into me, and we both hit the ground. I managed to hold on to the blade, but before I could roll away, he was wrapped around me, a hot, muscled blanket, one hand holding my sword wrist pinned, his feet hooking my calves. I writhed, trying to jerk free, but he only laughed, a dark, masculine chuckle that reverberated in my ear.

"Dinnertime," he purred.

"Fuck you!" I heaved and struggled, desperately trying to work free of his hold. I got nowhere. Despite my resistance, he coiled around me like a human python until he had me stretched out and immobilized in a wrestling hold.

"Oh, baby," he whispered in my ear, his deep voice wicked and amused. "Looks like I'll be having my favorite dish—Fem kabob." I felt his cock jerk against my butt, long and hard and eager.

"Son of a bitch!" I gasped, straining against his powerful body—with absolutely no effect. He had me in a hammer lock, one massive arm curled around my shoulders, holding my left arm raised and trapped over my head even as he reached past my head to grip my sword wrist. No matter how I fought, I couldn't free myself. I was completely helpless against his overwhelming vampire strength.

And I'd never been so hot in my life.

"Speaking of someone who's grown," he said, reaching his free hand around to toy delicately with the peaks of my arched, heaving breasts. He palmed one quivering globe, weighing it in his hand. "These have definitely improved with age." Gently, he squeezed, then caught my nipple between his fingers and pinched with such wicked skill that a moan escaped before I could suppress it. I could feel my cunt flooding. "Sensitive, too." For several long moments, there was no sound but my rapid breathing as my captor milked pleasure from my desperately hard tips, first one, then the other. It was all I could do not to rub my ass against the forged-steel length of him. Until he said, his voice rough with lust, "You do realize I've got you exactly where I want you?" Delicately, he licked the taut cord in my neck and slid his feet higher up my calves, prying my thighs apart, forcing my butt back against him until his shaft pressed hard against the cleavage of my cheeks. "In this position, I can slide my cock right up your tight little asshole while I sink my fangs into your throat." He licked the thin skin again, then opened his mouth wider until he could scrape the points of his teeth across my pulse. Just hard enough to make me shiver. "Give you a deep, grinding fuck while I feed. Possess you more thoroughly than any of your precious Warlords ever could. And you'll love it, even when you feel like I'm splitting you wide. That's why every horny vamp dreams of capturing a Warfem. You've all got this delicious masochistic streak."

"Go to hell!" Not the most clever response in the world, but with my cunt going so wet, I was finding it hard to think. I jerked and writhed, but he held me easily.

"Oh, yeah!" he purred. "Rub that round little ass against my cock. God, I love this position." I quivered helplessly as he brushed his long, strong hand over my belly on the way to my pussy. When he got to it, he slid a big finger boldly between my lips. And laughed, darkly triumphant. "I think you like it, too, judging by all this slick cream. Too bad, babe." He rolled his hips, rubbing that long, thick shaft against my butt. "I'm afraid I've got another orifice in mind for this particular fuck. Speaking of which . . ." He pulled his finger from my hot cunt as I bit back a moan, reached deeper between my thighs with that long, muscled arm . . .

And found my anus.

I sucked in a hard breath as he slowly forced his forefinger into the tightly crimped little opening. The sensation of being penetrated there was so hot and just slightly painful that I gasped, jolting against him. "You a virgin, Tamir?" he rumbled into my ear.

I licked my lips, trying to decide whether to admit it. "Maybe I am. Maybe I'm not. What do you think?"

I could almost hear the wicked grin in his voice. "I think maybe I'll be merciful." A second finger forced its way deep, sliding alongside the first. I sucked in a breath. "Or maybe I won't." He pressed deeper, scissoring his fingers, forcing me to stretch. I couldn't quite suppress the whimper. "On second thought, forget mercy. Buttfucking Tamir Adair has been my favorite kinky fantasy far too long." He rolled with me, flattening me under his weight as he slowly hunched his powerful hips against my butt. "Virgin or not, darling, you're in for a very rough ride."

I went limp under him, abandoning even the pretense of resistance as excitement burned hot trails along my nerves. "Jesus, Gage," I moaned. "You're making me hot."

"That's it," he crooned. "Submit. Relax that tight little asshole for your new master's cock. God, I'm hard. I'm going to make you scream."

I moaned, my face pressed to the deck, staring sightlessly at the sword in my lax hand, totally absorbed in the sensations of his body lifting off mine, his hands catching my cheeks, preparing to spread me.

It was then that I realized my sword arm was free.

In that instinct, my mercenary's fighting instincts told me I had him. All I had to do was twist around, swing that sword and . . .

I'd win. I'd be free. I wouldn't even have to kill him, just wound him. Otherwise, I'd become his Bloodslave, prey to his fangs and cock, his to spread and fuck whenever he wanted. Mouth. Pussy. Ass. Blood. All his.

I looked at the sword in my hand, feeling my muscles coil, ready to spin around and . . .

Instead I opened my fingers and watched them slide away from the hilt. Leaving the sword where it lay, I braced my elbows on the floor and lifted my rump, offering myself to Gage Deauxville. The man I'd never stopped loving, despite my stupid teenage fantasies of dominant Warlords.

Gage laughed in my ear, softly triumphant. "That's my girl. Spread your cheeks for me, Tamir."

Startled, I looked over my shoulder at him, realizing suddenly he'd given me that opening deliberately. "What would you have done if I'd gone for the sword, Gage?"

He bared his teeth. "Slap it out of your hand, ream your ass, and let you go."

I eyed him. "And now?"

The bared teeth became a hot grin. "Well, I won't be letting you go."

I grinned back. "Good."

Then I caught my rear cheeks in both hands and spread myself for my new master's use.

He took that massive cock in hand and set the rounded tip against my sensitive virgin anus. I had to swallow a whimper as he began to force it inside, stretching the delicate tissue mercilessly.

Jesus, he was huge. That big shaft felt as if it was going to rip my ass wide open as he slowly, relentlessly worked more and more of it into the desperately tight opening. "Damn, Tamir," he rumbled, "you're so fucking luscious." I felt his big hands wrap around my hips, drag me closer, impaling me completely.

"God! It's . . ." I didn't even know a word intense enough for it. Taking Gage Deauxville's dick up my ass was overwhelming, painful—and darkly, powerfully erotic.

Finally, he had all of it inside, as far as he could reach. I was lying there, limp and dazed and skewered, when I felt him suddenly come down over me completely, wrapping his legs and arms around me in that immobilizing wrestler's hold again. He rolled with me so he was half under me, half on his side. Then, when he had me stretched helplessly over his big body, he slowly began to thrust.

It hurt. And yet—there was a luscious pleasure to it, too, a pleasure that intensified when he reached his free hand down between my thighs to stroke my hard clit. I jolted and quivered as the wicked delight grew with every buggering stroke of his cock. I went bonelessly limp in the face of the pleasure-pain, moaning helplessly. Barely aware when he lowered his head to the arch of my throat.

The sharp prick of his fangs sinking into my skin tore a groan from my mouth. "Jesus, Gage!"

He rumbled something feral against my throat and began to drink in long swallows as he slowly thrust his hips, using my ass, still stroking my clit.

The climax took me by surprise, tearing a scream from my throat as I arched my back to force his cock even deeper up my ravaged anus. Distantly I heard his triumphant growl, and then he was hunching hard, screwing me without mercy as he fed. I screamed in pleasure-pain, and the orgasm intensified, pounding through me in time to his ruthless anal strokes. Until, finally, I felt Gage come deep in my ass, shooting me full of hot sperm.

It was a long time before either of us moved. "Now that," he said in my ear, "was worth becoming a vampire for." He gave the small wound in my throat a tender lick.

My eyes widened as I twisted my head to look at him. "You be-came a vampire for me?"

He shrugged. "You wanted a master." He grinned, flashing his fangs at me. "Now you've got one."

"Yeah," I said. "Seems I do."

I turned in his arms and found his lips with mine. His kiss was hot and skillful, and his mouth tasted of my blood. My asshole burned; I could feel his cum inside it. I didn't care.

Despite my teenage stupidity, despite years of empty loneliness, I had Gage Deauxville back. And that was all I'd ever really wanted.